To Be Black and Poor and Beautiful and a Woman

"Richly woven, turbulent, bursting with horror and degradation, fire and color, shot through with vitality and nobility. . . . The heroine is Mariah Upshur, a creature from classical Greek tragedy: a Negro mother living on the Eastern shore of Maryland and fighting everything—starvation, her husband, her sons, herself . . . fighting for a chance for the unborn child she is determined to have."
—*Charlotte Observer*

"Excruciating beauty and terrible magnificence . . . takes us into a world where most of us have never trod . . . a world of sounds and smells and blood and sweat and hate and love. . . . But most of all the people, black and poor and beautiful." —JOHN O. KILLENS

"Sarah E. Wright is a woman who has been the full route and knows where she has been. Her narration is like the hand on the wedding guest, maintaining our knowledge of where we are and whom we are with—mankind . . . BEAUTIFUL, BEAUTIFUL, BEAUTIFUL!" —*Chicago Sun Times*

THIS CHILD'S GONNA LIVE

by SARAH E. WRIGHT

A DELL BOOK

No single individual deserves as much thanks for his incalculable concern and assistance as my husband, Joseph Kaye. To him a most sincere dedication.

To the children of my life—to all children— through whose eyes I saw all meaning for the future, love. But especially to my own Michael and Shelley and my grandchildren and hopefully more to come, my wishes for a pretty day.

Published by
DELL PUBLISHING CO., INC.
750 Third Avenue
New York, New York 10017

Dell ® TM 681510, Dell Publishing Co., Inc.
Reprinted by arrangement with
Delacorte Press/A Seymour Lawrence Book
New York, New York
Printed in the U.S.A.
First Dell printing—October 1970

1

Sometimes the sun will come in making a bright yellow day. But then again, sometimes it won't.

Mariah Upshur couldn't see herself waiting to know which way it was coming as she fretted to see through the sagging windows squeezed between her upstairs roofs. The bed with Jacob's legs sprawled all over her was a hard thing to stay put in.

Strain cut in her face in such a heavy way, she thought, "My skin must be sliced up with the wrinkles the same as an old black walnut." She touched it and found not a single line.

She had the same tight skin, the same turned-up nose that people used to say went with her "high-minded gallop" when she wasn't doing a thing but marking time on Tangierneck's slowing-up roads. Pyorrhea in the gums had taken all of her back teeth, but her jaws stayed firm and slanty—pretty as a picture of any white girl's she ever saw on those Christmas candy boxes that her mamma used to cut out and hang on the cedar tree and the walls. Little "star light, star bright" twinkling angels, that's what Mamma Effie always hung on that tree. And she told Mariah, "You got to be *that* good and pure before the Lord's gonna bless you with anything."

"But I got a different set of eyes in this night, Jesus. If you'll spare me, me and my children getting out of this Neck."

Such a chilliness crept over Mariah, and she cried all down in herself, for she couldn't wake her children. She'd been dosing them up all through the night with the paregoric so they could get some easement from their coughing.

"Done promised you me and the children getting out of

here so many times, Jesus, you must think I'm crazy. But you ain't sent many pretty days this way lately."

With a start Mariah caught herself criticizing the Lord and said, "Excuse me, Jesus. I'm willing to do my part. Just make this a pretty day so I can haul myself out of this house and make me some money. Jesus, I thanks you for whatever you do give to me. I ain't meant to say nothing harsh to you. Jesus, you know I thanks you. I thanks you. I thanks you."

Then it felt to Mariah as if the comforts of the Lord's blessing spread all over her.

Soft sleep rested so lightly on her eyes, and she was home safe in a harbor warm, just a-rocking in the arms of Jesus. And the spirit of the Lamb became a mighty fire prevailing in the woman's eyes sunk now to dreaming, and she could just about see how this new day's sun was gonna come in.

It was gonna sail up blazing and red and hoe a steady path on up to the middle parts of the sky. Clouds get in the way? It was just gonna bust on through them and keep on sailing until it rolled on up easy over the crest of those worrisome waves.

Then it was gonna rock awhile—all unsteady like—until it made up its mind that it was on high and it hadn't sailed through anything but some feathery nuisances. Rock awhile and then turn all yellow and golden as it smiled at the cloud waves turned to nothing but some washed-out soapsuds foaming on the treetops of what Mariah liked to call this Maryland side of the long-tailed Dismal Swamp.

It was gonna sit there a long time grinning and spilling those fields full of itself, making every potato digger—leastwise herself—feel good down to the quick same as if it was summer still.

And she could dig a-many a potato on a day like this. Just scramble down those rows and flip potato after potato into those four-eight baskets. Dirt flying in her face? Well, honies, she wasn't even gonna mind. She'd eat that dirt and hustle on. She wouldn't even mind how the dirt got packed under whatever fingernails she had left—not even mind when the hurting from the dirt pressure made her shoulder blades cleave all up to themselves. She was just gonna suck her fingers every now and then—dirt and all—and keep on tearing down those rows. And when Bannie Upshire Dudley's hired man wrinkled his old pokey face in consternation from handing her "that many!" tokens for all those solid loaded baskets she got such a shortness of the breath from lugging up to the field shanty, and when he snickered to her, "Mariah, ain't you done stole some baskets from Martha from on Back-of-the-Creek?" she was gonna sic her big bad word doggies on him. Gonna sound worse than a starved-out bloodhound baying at the teasing smell of fresh-killed meat, ten thousand times worse than the menfolks do when they're away from the white-man bosses—all except that no-talking Jacob she was stuck with.

"Jam your dick up your turd hole, cracker, and bust from the hot air you bloated with. You believe every colored person that's getting a-hold of something's stealing. I believes in working for my money. Give me my money, man. I ain't no thief like the woman you working for. *That's* the thief!"

If he said half a word back to her she was gonna grab his squelched-down, corn-colored head and twist it to the east and the west and the north and the south so he could get a good look at all the scores of acres that used to be in Jacob's papa's hands. Didn't care if she rang it off like she'd do a chicken. "See, see you ass-licking poor white. See how Miss Bannie done glutted up our land. Now you want to talk about a thief, you talk about her. She knowed most of the colored was renting land off of Pop Percy. She knowed it just as good as anything when she went and lent him all that money to get his affairs straightened out. Then she come charging him interest on top of interest with things as hard as they is. Knows we ain't able to pay it. And selling food for the hogs and things as high as mighty. She knows good and well we ain't got no way into Calvertown to buy it cheap since the steamboat stop running. I ain't like the rest of the niggers you and Miss Bannie got, saying your shit don't smell bad when you use them for a toilet. I ain't saying tiddely-toe and grinning when you fart in my face no more, when I know good and well that tiddely ain't got no toes and your fart don't smell like perfume."

Then she was gonna tell him where his old bleached-out papa come from and his weak-behinded mamma too, if she could stomach herself getting down that low. She was gonna stomp his ass good, buddies. Set it on fire. Gonna

send him popping across those fields the same as if he
was a never-ending firecracker. Wishing she had a razor on
her like most white people thought colored carried, so she
could catch up with him and cut his old woman-beating
fists off and then slice out his dick so he wouldn't plug up
that simple-minded Anna of his anymore with his corn-
colored bastards to tease her little Skeeter and Rabbit
about the way they looked. But she wasn't gonna waste
any time dwelling on that, for the old fart-bloated cracker
wasn't worth her getting a murder charge laid against her
name. She was just gonna be glad she sent him running.

And then in the plain light of day—yes, yes, my God, on
that pretty day! She was gonna reach up to that culling
board where he had a habit of spreading out a pile of tokens to glisten in the sun so as to entice the colored people's eyes as they scrambled up those potato rows. Gonna
scoop herself up a handful of tokens, just a-singing to the
world. "No more short change for me, my Lordy. No more
shitting on me and then telling me I smell bad 'cause you
won't let me wash it off. No more! No more mocking my
children when they come down to this field to help me out,
calling the little naps on their heads 'gun bullets' and making them feel bad. No more!"

And all around here there was gonna be such a commotion. With people running up from the rows to the field
shanty, crying, "Glory Hallelujah, Mariah done chased
the money changers out of the temple." And black working
hands looking so pretty next to those gold-colored tokens
were just gonna be scooping them up. But most and especially there was gonna be little old hickory-nutty Aunt
Saro Jane with all those little winning airs she put on even
though she must be going on a hundred, saying, "Mariah,
now you know you ought not to have done that white
man that way. We colored in Tangierneck have to depend
on those people!"

"Look like they the ones been depending on us, Aunt
Saro Jane. We built up this Tangierneck and now they taking it away from us."

"Can't help that, Mariah. They got the money. They got
the banks."

"But we doing the work for to make that money, Aunt
Saro Jane."

That's the way Mariah was gonna talk back to her. Then

she was gonna stroll on off. No, she was gonna stomp on off, and run. Head thrown back the same as if she were a wild mare filly. If anybody stopped her to ask where she was going, she was gonna just holler back, "I'm on my way to the North. Going to the city where me and my children can act in some kind of a dignified way."

As she ran she wasn't gonna worry about a thing except maybe whether or not she'd scooped up enough tokens to pay for Skeeter and them to get some good clothes instead of having to wear those tow sacks she sewed into garments for them, and some medicine for the colds in their chests and things like that.

She might give a thought or two to giving Jacob a little piece of the money she'd have, for after all it was Jacob that put in all of that time last year pulling out the crabgrass and the jimson weeds from around those potato plants. He tended that field so good when those potatoes weren't anything but some little old twigs and promises. My, how he sprinkled that nitrate of soda over that low ground so as to give those little brown potato babies something worth eating for to suck on. Spent a whole heap of time plowing that ground so it would be soft and tender for those things to nestle down in and nurse until they got good and fat and ready for the harvesttime. And now Miss Bannie done claimed that field for herself, too.

She wasn't gonna take up too much time with Jacob though, for he wasn't going one step to save his own life. And when she grabbed her children and headed for the road going North, she wasn't even gonna look back at Jacob standing in the yard telling her that her talk about the children needing this and that for to grow on was nothing but a whole lot of "horse manure."

Even in that last minute, I mean buddies, in that very last minute, he woudn't have the spine to grow an inch taller on. He never could so much as say the word "shit" when he meant it. He was just weak, weak, weak, that's all there was to it—and always hiding behind the Lord. If the crops failed, it was the Lord's will. If the children stayed sick with the colds, it was the Lord's will. And she never was able to tell him anything, honies, about those little corn-colored children of Bannie's field man calling Skeeter and them out of their names when they came down

to the fields to help her out. All of that was the "Lord's
will."

She used to say to him, "Jacob, everything ain't the
Lord's will. Some of these things happening is these Maryland type of white people's will. I don't care how much they
go to the church, they ain't living by the word of the Lord.
They living by their greedy pocketbooks. They got a different set of white people in them cities up North. Your
brothers done gone, Jacob. You the only one sticking to
this land."

In spite of the devil, Jacob would answer her with something like, "But they'll be back, Mariah. They ain't doing
nothing up there in them cities but getting pushed around.
Trying to do some fancy singing they got on them radios
up there, but there ain't nothing to it. They don't own
nothing, Mariah. Ain't a cent they got they can call their
own. Paying off furniture on some time plans and all of
that kind of foolishness. A man is his land. In other words,
what he owns that he paid for outright. A man is his
land."

Then he'd quote from some old simple-assed poem he
learned from his father:

> I am master over all I survey
> My rights there are none to dispute
> From the land all around to the sea
> I am Lord o'er fowl and brute

Said to him a-many a time, "My children ain't no fowl
and brute. I wants my children to live. They human beings
just like anybody else." But if he thought she was gonna
stop and whine those words to him now, he had another
thought coming, for she was running, honies, running.
And it wouldn't be worthwhile for her to turn around and
say one thing at all, for all he was gonna do was call her a
nag.

Nag, shit, the woman panted in the dreams of morning.
All I ever been trying to do was tell him something in an
easy way of speaking, so as not to hurt his feelings. Just
run now, that's all she was gonna do.

Littlest one of her children, Gezee, weighed heavy in her
arms, and her stomach was so swolled up with the gas, his
sleepy weight just caused her to ache so much.

"Skeeter, Rabbit, you all come along here! Skeeter, what you doing letting Rabbit drag you along? You the oldest. Don't be trying to hang back with your daddy. Skeeter, stop that coughing, child. We can't slow down for you to catch your breath. I got a heavy enough aching on me as it is."

She couldn't let Skeeter's lagging and waving his arms back for his daddy hold her up one bit as she went sailing over those sand dunes going down the hill past blabbermouth Tillie's house, past those distant-acting in-laws of her's high-and-mighty-looking house.

It's a long stretch of road when you're running with such a weight bearing down on you. Renting-people's little shanty houses stretch a good ten-minute run along that sandy road when you're in good shape. But Lord help you when you're heavy. Children linking themselves around Mariah's arms and legs felt just like chains in the running. They weighed heavy on her when she tried to run past her own mamma and papa's house. Slowed her down to a standstill, and she couldn't fight her way past her papa standing there in the road.

Papa was something to fight. The only man in Tangierneck who ever paid off his land entirely to Percy Upshur. He liked to broke his back doing it, but then Pop Harmon was a mighty man. If you measured him by inches he wasn't so tall. She'd give him five feet and seven inches, but she couldn't measure Pop Harmon by the inches. She had to measure him by the squall in his face and his shoulders all flung back. He was a deep mustard kind of yellow, but he called himself black. It wouldn't do for anything frail to be getting in his path. He'd just mow it down.

"You too high-minded, woman, too busy gazing for the stars to see the storm clouds right around us. Folks have to navigate their ways through the rough seas of life before they can set back and feast their eyes on the stars. You think you seeing some stars now that you're running up to them cities? Well, honies, I'm here to tell you you can't see no stars anywhere at any time with your naked eye in the time of a storm. It's the time of a storm all over for the colored man. They lynching colored men every day by the wholesale lot just south of this swamp, and up there in them cities, too. But in a different sort of way."

"But what about the colored *woman?*" Mariah tried to

answer him back. "All I keep hearing is you all talking about the hard time a colored *man's* got."

"See my scars! See my scars! Colored woman's always been more privileged than the man. You ain't got no hard time in this community." He roared against her terrible screaming of "Papa, let me go!"

But his powerful shoulders pushed her back, flail out against them all she pleased. He almost knocked her down in the shifting sand. She came back at him like a foaming-mouthed terrier. But nothing came out of her mouth except a moan.

"Don't talk to me about the colored woman, gal, until you see my scars." In a split second he was naked, standing in a blazing sun. Bleeding all over his back. "See my scars, woman, see my scars!"

And all Mariah could see to him was his scars. Even as naked as he was, she couldn't make out a thing else about him except his scars.

"White men up there to Baltimore Harbor liked to beat my ass off when I landed in this 'land of the free.' They said to me, 'Horace, you come here all the way from Barbados hid down in the hold of our ship. You ain't paid a cent for the passage. You ain't worked for us, you ain't done nothing. Now what you gonna do, you little monkey?' I says to 'em, 'Monkey your Goddamned self. Let me go!' Now heifer, I want you to know they let me go 'cause I went into them for the kill. See my scars. . . ."

Last shades of night hung on for Mariah, and deeper into sleep she sank. The dream kept coming: her papa pushing her down in the sand, in the choking sand while he called up to that little squeezy house she was born and reared in for her mamma, Effie, to come to the road.

"Effie, Effie, this gal of yours is getting out of control. Bring your switch out here and beat this gal, Effie. Whip her ass good!"

Mamma Effie always was a good beating-stick for Papa. He did the talking but Mamma did the beating. Her whole body was like a whipping switch, thin and lean and crackling. Her great dark eyes were always filled with lightning, and most of the time she never said a word to her children except something like, "I'll beat the living daylights out of you if you don't listen to your papa."

There was but one of those children left now, and that was Mariah. Mariah tossing under the quilts Mamma Effie made for the times of her giving birth. Mariah heavy with a sleep that wouldn't let her go. Mariah groaning in her sleep from the beating. A switch can draw blood, but getting beat up with a stovelid lifter can make a person cry for her own death. Those things are made of iron. A beating on your back and legs with one will make a person's soul cave in.

As her mamma beat her, her papa talked on.

"Stop that running, gal. You ain't getting past me. You can't run your way through the brambles and the bushes of life. You got to chop down those vines and creepers first before you go headlong through them. Old rattlers are coiled up in them. Pretty flowers on them vines is just there to entice you out of your senses. Rattler's going to sink his fangs in you on this road.

"All of this talk about you going away to the cities to make something of yourself don't mean a thing 'cause you still don't see nothing but the flowers on the bushes. Ain't a decent woman *enough* for you to be? You'd better pray for God to send us a pretty day tomorrow so we can get out of here and pull some holly out of this swamp. We got to pay off this land."

Mariah couldn't wiggle out of her papa's hands. He had some big, strong hands. Just holding her. "Effie, beat her, beat her. Beat her ass good. Make her work. A child is the servant of the parent."

A violent wrenching of herself got Mariah free to hobble, broken, on up that road. Saying to her papa, "I ain't no more child, Papa. What you all holding me up for? You ain't suppose to be talking to me like when I was a child. I got my own children." Moaning, "Come on, Rabbit. Come on, Skeeter. Help me to carry Gezee. . . ."

Mamma Effie tore after her, hollering, "Come back here, slut! Look a-here, here comes Jacob bringing that little near-white affliction you done bore to him. If you gonna leave, take 'em all. The thing ain't Jacob's. Why you leave that burden on him?"

"I ain't got no other child, Mamma! Why you always trying to accuse me of something!"

With a jolting start Mariah sat up in the bed. She cried, "Jesus!"

Her eyes groped in the darkness for something to hold on to. A bit of light from the kerosene lamp she kept in the hallway helped her out some. The woman prayed, "Jesus, it ain't dawn yet."

The little attic type of a room took shape. Little by little the chest of drawers with the blue paint peeling off it, and the wallpaper gone limp and nipplely from the damp and the winds easing their ways in between the boards of her upstairs roof sank into her head. She thought she heard Jacob mumbling from under the quilts, "Woman, go on back to sleep." And maybe she did, but she couldn't be quite for sure, for his legs were such heavy weights on her. He must be sound asleep.

She inched herself toward the edge of the bed as much as Jacob's warmed-up, pinning-down feet would let her. A fearful sickness rolled through every inch of her lumpish body. She tried to get free, but every time she tried to move, the way Jacob had of throwing himself any which a-way in the bed so he got the quilt tangled up and locking her in wouldn't let her.

Teeth wiggled in her gums so bad they hurt. Gritting her teeth too much. Gums hurt her. Head was just a-pounding, but she couldn't feel a thing else. Just her gums aching and the pounding in her head.

She hissed into the night that looked like it was never gonna go away, "Move!"

But Jacob did not move.

Outside in the nearly-about-morning world, the wind growled and hawked and spit the same as if it had a throat. Wind wasn't doing a thing except messing up everything in God's creation, spitting in the face of hopes for a pretty day, moaning nothing but more of what Tangierneck mostly was these days—a place of standing still and death.

"Death!" Mariah could hardly say the word, for it seemed the thing was creeping its way into her soul-case. She had seen a naked man in her dream!

"No, he wasn't naked! He wasn't naked, God Jesus! I ain't seen it, have I?"

A stillness came over her. Jaws became solid frozen. Her elbows cracked as she let her hands go trembling over the mound rising up from her middle parts. She could hardly ease her body down to wait for the coming of dawn. A shudder started in her shoulders—locked her neck to the pillow.

"Why, the child hadn't moved in a good while! Dreams are a sign. . . . Oh my God, my God, I done killed it! It can't be dead!" She drummed on the skin stretched tight on her belly. Tried to sound out life, but no matter which combination of taps she drummed, life wouldn't sound back. "Must be lazy this morning. Bet you's a girl. Girls is lazy." Terror scalded her eyes. The dream flooded over her—the running into her papa naked, and Mamma Effie's accusation.

"Jacob's your daddy, honey. I talked it over with Jesus. Know he wouldn't lead me wrong." She pleaded softly to the unborn child, but the child didn't make a single move.

A loathsome sickness wormed in her throat. Shame for everything washed all over her. The cussing and the anger of her dream. Maybe if she prayed to God to wash her sinful dream away the child would move!

She opened her mouth to scream, but no sound came. A whisper jerked its way out. "My child's all right, ain't it, Lord?"

"Woman, what in the name of God you doing, pulling all the covers off of me?" Jacob's voice came over the thundering in her skull.

Mariah let go of the covers. Didn't realize she was pulling them. There was nothing eviler and more contrary than Jacob if the cold air got to him when he was sleeping.

"Woman, lay on back down will you, or stay still or something unless there's something the matter with you?"

Mariah froze. Couldn't answer Jacob to save her life. The man said no more.

Humble yourself to the Lord, Mariah. Apologize one more time. If she could only speak. If she could only run. Get on that speeding-up Route 391 and run. Wished she'd kept on running when she went to see that Dr. Grene. Run right past him. Gone on to the Calvertown Hospital clinic.

"Didn't believe they'd treat me right though, Lord. Thought it'd be easier to talk to that new colored doctor about my headache—tell him about the screaming that backed up in my head when Mary died . . . Jesus!" The woman cringed in startled panic.

"Jesus!" Her lips moved without a sound. She fixed her eyes on the little white lambs flocking around the white-robed figure on the Jamison Funeral Home calendar.

"You know that's over with, Jesus. You ain't gonna punish me no more. You ain't let me kill this young'un, has you?

"I know I ain't nothing but a woman filled with sins. But I cares for my children. Remember, you said to me, 'Now Mariah, you're on the side of life. You're a mother. Two sins don't make a right.' I know you had to talk to me right smart, Jesus, because I was scared. But you know how people do when they get scared. Do anything. But you snatched that other bottle of Febrilline out of my hands before I had a chance to pour it down my throat when my head was wobbling from that first bottle of quinine mess like it was fit to roll off in one of those oyster buckets. . . ."

Her head filled now, tighter than a skin drum full of water. "Let the child kick. Let the day come in nice. Spare the child, Lord, and I promise you, if I use every last bit of strength I got, we getting out of this place."

She closed her eyes, for a little voice far back in her head said, "Jesus is just testing you out, Mariah, Jesus just testing you out." And right along with the voice came a movement around her navel, soft as a little spring breeze.

She smiled to the Lord. "Gonna stop thinking about death. Ain't gonna cry no more."

Later in the dawn she cracked her eyes again, and a little light did come in. October sun comes so late. She dug her chapped knuckles into the deep, warm places her eyes made, and lifted her heavy lids.

She wondered sometimes how the sun ever made it at all coming from the easternmost part of God-knows-where down to low-laying Tangierneck. Lowest place on the whole Eastern Shore of Maryland, she did believe. Wonder was that it hadn't been washed away, the way that big, wide, bossy, ocean-going Nighaskin River keeps pouring water down into the mouth of the Neck until Deep Gut swallows all it can hold and backs the rest of it out for the ocean. Orange ball bouncing on the Nighaskin Sound, heaving and setting and hardly climbing up at all. Oyster boats tossing helplessly.

She balled her hands up until they hurt. "Jacob, I swamp

it, Deep Gut's filled up with wind again. Spewing out ponds all over the fields. There's not gonna be a cent made today."

Every muscle swoll in her craning neck. She swallowed hard. Last night's terror left a nasty morning taste. "Nothing here, Jacob, but death. Nothing down here but nothing."

Jacob stirred. "Death coming sooner or later, woman. What you all the time harping on it for?"

"Children ain't had no milk in the longest kind of time. I ain't neither. I was thinking to myself I'd send Skeeter down to Bannie's to get us some. . . ."

Jacob flew right into her. "Don't send Skeeter nor nobody else down to Bannie's for nothing. I done told you once. I ain't gonna tell you no more. And another thing, woman, I don't want to catch you digging no more potatoes for Bannie."

"Tell me the Welfare people's giving out cans of Pet milk by the case full. . . ."

"Shut up, woman. I done told you now. I provides for my family."

Silence hung between them like the deep maroon drapes in Jimmy Jamison's funeral home parlor. She might have known he'd act like that. But there used to be a different kind of time, the woman thought. There used to be a time when she could really tackle Jacob. She'd tell him in a minute about picking up his own trash behind himself, or about throwing his money down on the table for her to keep them and the children halfway going like he was throwing a bone to a worrisome pet dog. He'd throw the money down and stroll on out of the house, not even saying as much as "Dog"—that was the least he could call her—"here's the money for this or that."

In one day and time she'd go in to Jacob like lightning with, "Man, why don't you change your drawers a little more often and wipe yourself good? Any dog gets tired sometimes of scrubbing out somebody else's shit from their drawers."

That kind of thing would set him on fire, but she'd go on. "Sparrow, they tell me that Uncle Marsh Harper's about the cleanest man on the oyster rocks. Tell me when he gets through doing his business, he wipes himself good with his glove, then leans over in the Gut and washes himself off and his glove."

"He's about the purest fool we got on the boats, woman!" Jacob would thunder back. "Fool's gonna catch the pneumonia first and last splashing that cold water on himself."

And Mariah, she used to play a little bit, too. "Did you say first in the ass, Jacob?"

Then he'd have to break down and laugh himself. But then he'd go on and give her a lecture about cussing and how sinful it was in the eyes of the Lord. But those times were all over with now. . . .

There was no sense in her mentioning the Welfare to him anymore, because he wasn't gonna answer. But somehow she couldn't help herself from wishing that they had some milk. How many times had she wished the milk in her breasts could flow by the gallon—enough for all of them to drink. She could almost see herself pulling Jacob's bony, hurtful-looking face to her breasts. . . . But she was leaving Tangierneck. Talked it over with God. Taking her children and leaving death. And she wanted to take Jacob, too.

"Death's so close to you now, Jacob, you can reach out and touch it."

But Jacob did not answer, nor move his reddish, tight-faced head one single inch. He just rubbed his teeth together over and over again, making a terrible grating sound.

"It's been a bad October, Rah. November's almost here. There's a time in the land."

Sounded almost like a cry. Mariah moved closer to him. Tears worked around in her eyes. "Stop gritting your teeth, Jacob. Stop it. You hear me. Don't, I'm gonna give you a dose of Bumpstead's Worm Syrup to work those worms out of you."

"Cut out the foolishness, Rah. Getting too near your time for you to be carrying on like that." Covers fell away from his bony shoulders and he sat bolt upright in the bed.

"My time, Jacob?" If she could only get the sight of him out of her eyes. "My time! And what you done about it?"

"Rah, I done told you. . . ."

"Don't want no Lettie Cartwright, nor no other midwife killing another child of mine. Mary would've been here today if she'd been born in the hospital. . . ."

Jacob didn't take his red, wind-eaten eyes off of her. Tired, beaten-looking eyes with a little bit of stubble for eyelashes jiggling on his sunken cheeks.

"May as well cut out the foolishness, Rah. We ain't got no hospital money, and we ain't getting on no Welfare."

He turned his back to her, mumbling from under the quilts where he buried his head, "You done took all the teas in the world, and some of that Dr. Grene's medicine, too. How come you always harping on death? You need to pray, Mariah. Have a good talk with God."

"You must think you the holiest thing out, Mr. Jacob. Let me tell you how I talked things over with God!"

But the man didn't move. "Rah, I'm going to want my breakfast now and in a few minutes" was all he raised the quilt to say.

"That's all you got to say. That's all you got to say?" Her heart pounded. She was gonna break down and holler at him in a minute.

But he didn't answer.

"Well, let me tell you something, Mr. Jacob. I got something to say."

And all the horror of the night just gone flooded out of her.

"Me and my children getting out of this death trap, Tangierneck, and you can stay here, buddies, 'cause we don't want you with us."

He threw back the quilts. Mariah tried to catch something that happened in her husband's face. It wasn't tight anymore. It fell all to pieces. And though her hands wanted to reach for him, she couldn't bring herself to touch him.

His lips hardly moved. "Cut out the foolishness, Rah."

She wanted to gather up the pieces. If only she could do something nice for him. Get up and fry some oyster fritters, open a can of corn—if she could put her hands on one— set his breakfast on the table, snappy and hot, with some milk to go along with it. Fool ought to know he needed milk. It would clear up the rattling in his chest, make him feel like singing. And she could call him Sparrow once more, for he really was a regular song sparrow before his mouth got clamped down with hunger and worriation. But there were no oysters, for wind had bossed the rocks for two whole days, and there was no corn—just a single can left for Sunday—and there was no milk.

The salt of tears burned through the chapped crust on her lips, and she turned her eyes from Jacob's twitching face. "Ain't nothing down here but nothing."

"Yes, it is too, Rah."

Looked as if his bony hand was going to make it across the quilt hills to touch her. "Why don't you tell it like it is, Mr. Jacob?"

She couldn't bear to look at his torn-up face. "Let go my legs, man!" She jerked herself free. "You'd stay down here until the year 2000 if you could live for seventy more. You gonna pay off the land, huh, Mr. Jacob? Gonna collect all the money that's due on your pappy's land. Pay off Miss Bannie. Gonna make the County give a schoolhouse to your children."

"Woman!"

But she couldn't stop. "And if this child dies, gonna be your fault! So sorry you were when the last one died, you gonna see to it this one comes here in the hospital. . . ."

"Woman!" He shoved a swollen-jointed finger up to her eyes. "Just lift one finger to take either one of my children out of Tangierneck, and I s'pect that'll be the last finger you'll ever lift. . . . And another thing, woman. Child dies, gonna be your fault for lifting and lugging them potato baskets. Told you to stay out of them fields. Never thought you wanted this young'un no way. Sometimes I get the feeling that if you had your way you'd a-killed it."

All over her it was cold. Nothing in her moved. But she stepped out of bed, snatched her hair free of its pins. "I'm going, Jacob." And the trembling-faced man said no more.

Her head was nothing but a throbbing hunk of mostly hair with a little bitty brown face screwed down under it. *Heavy head to tote in the morning, Lord. Heaviest head I ever had.* Almost had a mind to go downstairs and run a straightening comb through that mess of hair so it would flow long and wavy like Jacob used to say he liked it. "But I'm going, Lord."

For a moment she stared at the wall of her husband's back. Wanted to tell him so badly how sluggish the child was acting. *But it ain't his,* evil mind wanted to tell her. Nerves felt like they were about to give out on her.

Jacob's back was a hunk of stone. She twisted her hair tightly into a bun again, pulling her face and mind and everything in her tight. "Done talked it over with the Lord," she muttered, and straightened herself on up.

She bounded down the steps, pulling the big, second-hand robe over her stiffened shoulders. Worried to craziness by the stillness, sniffling angrily at the morning mustiness of her body and the thought of the man. Hitting her soles on the bottom steps to stir up warmth, she announced to the early morning darkness of the kitchen, and the wind that crept in between the baseboards, and the wallboards and the places she'd chinked and chinked until she wasn't gonna chink no more, and the sounds of rats and mice gnawing in the molding: "I'm gonna make me a fire. Ought to burn down this place. . . ."

She rubbed her bare feet, one on top of the other, screwed them around on the cold linoleum. Kindling wood bent in her toughened hands, some so damp it would hardly splinter. She took the front lids off the big, black kitchen stove and filled it with wood. The oil that was left in the coal oil can wasn't enough, so she went back up the stairs and got the night lamp burning in the hallway. Blew the flame out and dumped all the kerosene in the oil chamber on to the soggy pinewood.

"Gonna make me a good fire!" And she struck a match. In the gray morning a flame shot up. Up the chimney roaring, out of the sides of the stove, through the cracks between the other stove lids, out of the bottom grating, shooting last night's ashes all over her feet.

There was an orange pain in her eyes and her arm was on fire and she almost cried "Jacob" but she didn't. She smothered her burning arm in the cavity between her breast and her belly, and with her free hand she crushed the last embers in the smoldering sleeve.

Such a kicking went on inside of her!

She stood still while her hands burnt and the lashes of her eyes fell down over her half-fried cheeks. She grinned real wide in the smoked-up morning light. Grinned real wide at the sounds of rats and mice a-gnawing in the molding.

"That's right, baby, kick. Kick all you want to." The bony ribs under her heart hurt. Hurt all the way through her heart and . . . "Kick, you contrary thing. Don't care if you kick my guts out. . . ."

She cried as she greased her face down with Vaseline. "That's right, baby, kick . . . thank the Lord, thank the Lord, thank the Lord." And the grease wouldn't stay around her smarting eyes, she cried so hard. "Jesus, God, and all your little angels, thank you, Lord." She choked up and swore in the light of the quieting-down flame. "Ain't gonna say no more to Jacob about it. Just make this a pretty day, Jesus, and I'll go out of this house and make the hospital money my ownself. Gonna get my children out of this Tangierneck."

Her greasy lips pursed in determination as she went out to the cornhouse to slice off the last slab of fatback, not even wrapping herself up good from the wind.

2

Morning of that day with the dreams still tugging at
Mariah set in with a weak yellow light—sand color was all
caught up in it. Wind smelling of a sea squall pushed the
clouds down low and rustled the skimpy leaves of the old
chinaberry tree in her yard. Thing was no use to anybody.
Just some kind of a decoration and a pain to keep up. Still,
still a decoration is a pleasure sometime. Even when it's
going bald in the autumn of the year, it's a comfort to
lean against. So Mariah leaned and searched the sky for a
sign from her God.

Clouds hung mighty low—huffed themselves up like dirty
white leghorn roosters ready to fly into each other over a
hen. And the new day's light moved in slow gray splotches
all over the pinched-up rooftops of Tangierneck's mostly
two-rooms-up and two-rooms-down whitewashed houses.
Brightest sun rays leaked through just over Cleveland's
Field—nestled in the marshy earth east of that stern-look-
ing clapboard church—hung around the feet-ends of the
newest graves in the field, so the souls bound for heaven
could walk a shining path, she guessed. And that was all—
all there was to the bright light. Pretty morning hadn't
come in yet. Hungry pain gnawed behind her eyeballs.

Gray light crept all over the land—misted around the
dormered roof of her in-laws' house just down the road
from her. House used to be no bigger than anybody else's,
just four little rooms, but now it was seven, with dormers
and everything so it looked right bossified—a regular
plantation-style house. The thing loomed big. And Mariah
tightened all over remembering how the smell of fresh
paint on those new boards floated in the air all the way up
to her house in that spring three years gone now. Three
years gone since Pop Percy got all of that money from
Bannie Upshire Dudley to do such things with as build

onto his house and clear virgin land so he could go into farming in a big way. He even went up to Calvertown and bought himself what must have been the first car thrown on the trash heap, to hitch a cart to and haul his produce to the auction block. Car was some old Cadillac limousine, looking for all the world like a hearse car.

She couldn't tolerate the sight of that house! *Have to find a way out.* But when she turned she couldn't see the bigger houses resting on the shoulders of the Neck, way up on that Haimawalkin Road, with the potato fields sprawled out all around them.

Houses had the meanest set of white people in them. Pretty in their living but nasty in their ways. She never could figure out how the Lord prospered them to have so much of the good things of life and all the say-so they wanted over other people's lives. Banks wouldn't lend a colored family a cent unless big red Haim Crawford or his family said so, and he was a nasty thing to come up against. Holler and cuss at you the same time as he'd be trying to deceive you about how he was looking after you. Treat you the same as if you were nothing but a senseless spittoon, some kind of receiver for his spew.

How you gonna get out, Mariah? You can't run your way through the brambles and bushes of life. Voices of her dream came back to her and she wrenched herself from the tree, trembling.

Ain't no point in stopping stone still in the morning, especially when you're out of doors and didn't even get your work clothes on yet, especially with a sweet little baby laying in your belly.

She tried to fling her whole self into the chores of morning. Had to wash up, put on her everyday clothes. Had to mix a pan of bread, sift a-many a maggot out of the flour first. Had to find an onion and sprinkle some sugar over it, set it out in the yard in good hopes the sun would come up strong and draw the syrup out of it to ease up Skeeter's chest. Had to get those washtubs down from the house. It was gonna take her a good half hour to pump enough water for that bunch of dirty clothes. Family looked like they were ragged until it came time to wash. Then it was "My God have mercy" as she went up and down, up and down, up and down, over that scrubbing board. Her back might as well go on and break into pieces, she wouldn't feel any different—just numb somehow—after the scrubbing. Had to feed those two or three Bantam hens she was saving for a Sunday dinner in some good day and time when company decided to come. Wasn't hardly anybody gonna stop by and see her though since she stopped going to the Church, except maybe Vyella. Bighearted, blooming-faced Vyella. Wish I could see her now. She got a mind—got brains enough. Had to look over Skeeter and Rabbit's homework before she got them up so she'd be prepared to give credit where credit was due. Had to figure out what in the name of God she was gonna feed that bunch for supper —rummage through somebody's wintercrease patch she guessed. Had to pack some molasses sandwiches for the children to eat for their dinner. Her hands faltered on the King-Po-T-Rik molasses can. Done told Jacob a million times the children's gagging off these sandwiches. Had to fry some meat to pack up for them today. Using the last slab of fatback or no, it didn't make any difference. Children were going to have some meat sandwiches today. She was sick and tired of hearing about them gagging in school. Sick and tired! Sick and tired! That's all there was to it. The feeling of the knife slicing through the salty white meat brought a little easement to her shoulders, and the baby nudging gently now under her heart, a little comfort. So she thanked the Lord.

She had to keep the fire going. Started to bring in a few chunks of wood, but she remembered that was one good thing about Jacob. He'd always bring in wood the night before if he didn't do anything else. Wasn't gonna do anything else either for the house, for the children, for her. He'd just sit with his feet propped up by that stove and see her fall right over on her face with the work in a way of speaking and not do another thing else. She was sick and tired.

Day coming in set up a storm in her heart, and she went back outside to meet it in a proper way—have her morning prayer in the sun.

"I'm going to Miss Bannie and get me some help. You can like it or lump it, Jacob. You ain't gonna know nothing about it until I've done it." She spoke to herself. "This child'll not die by Lettie Cartwright's carelessness."

The sun on her face felt as strong as prayer. She moved from the cornhouse steps. "Got to get on the move!" She hustled on back in the house. At the stair steps she stopped, for no, she wouldn't be getting everybody on the move. Deep Gut itself would be a death trap on a day like this. She wouldn't get Jacob on the move. "Fool, fool!" Tears tried to get a-loose from her eye sockets but she blinked them back, looking over the shed kitchen that the fool built onto the house when he married her. Hear him telling her now how it was just temporary at the time. He was going to build a regular house, make her a queen on the hill.

But that's all over with! She got herself together and went up on the steps, calling to her children about the chamber pot left open in the hallway, shaking Skeeter and calling him by his proper name, William, as she did when she was dead serious about a thing. Told him that if she'd covered him up once in the night she covered him twenty times, and how he was the worst off of all three, coughing all night. And he'd better keep something wrapped around his shoulders and get on downstairs and get dressed by the fire and make it to school if he could. "Get something in your head, boy, if it ain't nothing but this community history mess Frannie Jefferson keeps digging up or making up. I don't know which one she's doing. Ain't no history to this Eastern Shore worth telling that I can see. All the history ever made left here when that Harriet Tubman left. History of this place ain't nothing but work, work, work."

She pulled a piece of dirty clothing from the five-eight basket she kept in their room for a hamper and handed it to Horace, the one she'd named after that papa of hers, because he'd lay up and sniff and snot until doomsday. Didn't even have any cold though. Lazy about everything but playing and grinning. Guess he wouldn't grin and cut up so much if people didn't make him feel funny by calling him Rabbit on account of his harelip. And a poem writer, too. Now ain't that something! Going around telling people that. Heard him no longer than yesterday telling Skeeter he could make up a poem a minute. Biggest liar you ever heard. Wouldn't blow his nose unless she pushed his head in.

"Little Gee, if you don't stop flooding this bed and keeping Skeeter filled up with the cold, you gonna have to come back in the room with me and your daddy. You almost four years old now. Big enough to know better."

She shoved the bureau close to the window, trying to stop a draft. Draft came right on in. It skirted all around the thing layered with coat after coat of different shades of brown paint. Didn't stop the draft but it closed out the sight of Frannie Jefferson's tacked-onto house. Woman teaching history, getting people all wound up in money-saving schemes that never came to a thing, building onto her two rooms herself while that tongue-wagging Ol she got for a husband walks around selling anything the sea'll give up to his nets, and telling people that Frannie was the best educated woman on earth—only woman in the community who had sense enough not to wash that poontang off herself.

"Skeeter, get on up like I told you and get ready for that mess of a school. But I'm telling you this one thing, we ain't gonna stay. . . ." No, she wasn't gonna say it just yet. Didn't know how she was ever going to explain to them so they'd understand it. Skeeter wouldn't know how to make two steps without his daddy.

"You all pick these clothes up off the floor. You all acts right scornful. Guess you ain't pleased with them 'cause they stitched out of feed sacks." But she picked them up herself, the better to hide her tears. Clean clothes she'd laid out on the foot of the bed the night before, all kicked off, getting dirty. "Get up now. Breakfast be ready now in a few minutes."

"Skeeter, don't forgit to ask Mamma. . . ."

"Ask me what?" She cut right in on Rabbit. Peppy talking's the best way to keep from crying. She could see the movement under the quilts. Rabbit trying to poke Skeeter's ribs in.

"Go on boy, you the biggest. You in the second grade. I'm not in nothing but the first!" Rabbit's little black brows screwed up angrily at his shaking brother.

"Nothing, Mamma." Wheezing in Skeeter's chest would hardly let him speak a clear word.

"Is so something. You said you was gonna ask last night."

"Boy, I told you Mamma ain't gonna let me go nowhere."

"Go where?" Children is a mess. "Lord have mercy."

"Miss Jefferson said for all of us to bring in our 'What Does School Mean to Me?' poems, and two cents apiece to get red coal oil so the lamps'll look pretty out to the Hall tomorrow night because Halloween promenade suppose to be a cheerful thing . . . and some man coming over here from Countess Ann to give us a new school if the people . . ."

"Hold up a minute, boy. Just hold on." Her big boy was nervous all over.

"Boy, you don't know how to ask no questions, and you the biggest one, too." Rabbit jumped out of bed just as mad as you please.

"Hush your mouth, Horace, before I ram my fist down your throat. You too, William. Boy! Ain't I just got through telling you that you coughed all night? What you want me to let you do—go out there and catch TB for sure?"

"Mrs. Jefferson says if you wrap me up good from the wind, I can come out. Says the poem I'm making up gonna be good. . . ."

"What Mrs. Jefferson know about you? She ain't raised you up from nothing but a twiddly switch. Truth is you ain't nothing but a stick now." Child's face was too peaked looking. Seemed like the taller he got, the littler he looked. Eyes growing more than his head. Circles under them just like real sick people had. Kind that made up poems just before they died. Could never figure why Rabbit was the poet and not him. But he'd be something important, too. All my children, all you-all gonna live and be something besides ignorant country scrubs like me.

"You ain't going nowhere, boy . . . less'n . . ." And she couldn't stand the way he looked at her all hurt about the mouth. So she turned to the one she'd named after her Lord and Master, Jesus. He was just a-sucking on his thumb. "Ain't you weaned yet, Gezee?" She snatched the finger from his mouth. Turned to Skeeter with his big eyes calling her back to him again. "Less'n . . . less'n . . . less'n you git up out of this bed this minute, help your brothers get downstairs and get their clothes on, and bake that cold out of yourself. I got a good fire going and you better keep your coat buttoned up when you go out in this wind, and don't take your sweater off in that drafty-assed lodge-hall schoolhouse, and you better bring me home some A's." That boy's face lit up and she turned to Rabbit. "As for you, Mr. Scoundrel, you ain't going one step 'til you learn to speak for yourself. . . . And don't answer me back because I know you fixing to."

Skeeter got a fit of sneezing.

"Boy, ain't two years long enough for you to've had that cold?" She braced the boy's head in the crook of her arm and held a rag up to his nose. "Blow!" He blew so hard he had to steady himself with one hand on her breast. "You ain't weaned yet, either." She hugged him to her breast, and noticing the way Horace acted like he didn't know the right side of that grass sack outfit he'd been wearing pretty nearly every day, she let go of William's little feverish head and tried to give Horace a little bit of love, too. Took the grass sack shirt out of his hands and turned it to the right side for him. "Boy, what you acting so spoiled for?" And she rubbed his puffed-out cheeks, letting her work-coarsened fingers touch his little misshapen mouth. Be so glad to get him to the city where people didn't waste time making people feel bad over things like that. "You ain't nothing but a baby." Would have kissed his old shining eyes that minute, but you have to be careful with children. Let them know what they mean to you and they walk all over you. They walked all over her anyhow. Seemed like the harder she tried not to give in to them and their sly, cuddling ways, the more she'd give in to them. But not their daddy. Now he could handle that bunch. Didn't hardly say two words to them either, but let evening fall and him not be up from the rocks and she couldn't to save her natural life unglue their faces from the kitchen window, announcing every lantern light they saw coming up the road. But their daddy's lantern, they all knew. Even Gezee was trying to walk with a beaten-down wobble like his daddy. Skeeter and Rabbit already copied it to the minute. . . . *But you ain't gonna be copying it no more.* . . .

"Get on downstairs and get dressed by the fire." And the woman screamed at the sneezing, shaking, snotty-nosed bunch. "Gonna get your daddy out of that bed, now."

Shaking all over and she didn't halfway know why, she was going across the hall and into the room and calling a wind-beaten, life-beaten going-nowhere man. But before she could catch herself she hollered, "Jacob, get up." But he was already up, shaking the crusty sand from his socks onto the linoleum she just got through scrubbing yesterday.

"What you trying to do, woman, alarm a whole nation of people? Ain't you raised enough cain this morning? Here it is just a little after six o'clock in the morning and you hollering loud enough for people all over Tangierneck to hear you."

"Don't care if I do alarm the whole nation. Time for people to wake up. It's morning, Jacob." She pulled the string on the tattered green window shade, and it flew up with a bang.

He fell down. The whole bony mess of him fell down on his knees in prayer. First thing he asked the Lord for was to calm the wind on the rock. Next thing he asked was for the Lord to steady Mariah-the-Second on the waves if the Lord couldn't see his way clear to calming the wind because he had to make it out in the Gut and get a-hold of some oysters and some money.

"Don't listen to him, Lord." Mariah prayed in the midst of her husband's prayer. "It ain't fit for a dog on that rock today. He ain't going nowhere."

She folded her arms over her breasts. Jacob's prayer was always long. She couldn't keep her eyes down long. She kept staring out at the mounds of sand piling higher and higher on the graves in Cleveland's Field. Her ears did not follow her husband's prayer for the wind kept singing through the marsh bullgrass on the western edge of Cleveland's Field the song people claimed little Cleveland sang just before he died. People been chanting it for three or four generations:

> Carry me way from Tangierneck, Daddy,
> Daddy, Daddy,
> Don't want no buzzard picking at my neck,
> Paddy, pick, paddy pick, paddy.

But this morning it sounded like a girl baby—her own Mary singing in Cleveland's Field. . . . Just fourteen months she'd been laying in that ground. Germy navel bandage laid on her belly by that Lettie Cartwright, calling herself a midwife.

People said Mariah had her children too close together. People said she never should have had William in the first place until Jacob came home from the Western Shore in '23 and married her. But they didn't talk about that anymore. Instead they just remarked about Horace popping up like a rabbit just fourteen months behind William, and then

Gesus. But they stopped talking for a few days when Mary came. Just came over to the house to say how sorry they were that the child couldn't open its mouth to suck. Offering this kind of remedy and that to unlock its jaws. And the baby couldn't even cry. That's what hurt Mariah so and she cried because she knew it was hurting and rubbed its jaws down with some kind of Watkins oil and some salves that Bertha Ann mixed up. And on the fourth day, when the baby lay limp and starving, Mariah tried to pry its jaws open—squeezed some milk down into the tiny slit of a mouth from which death sounds came. But the milk ran all back up out of the baby's mouth and out of its nose and Mariah said to it, "Oh baby, blow your nose. Baby, baby, blow your little nose." And the child went limp in Mariah's arms and she buried its face in her long bush of sweaty hair and sucked its nose. Sucked the last shuddering breath and the milk ran all down Mariah's chin and out of her own mouth and she hollered up to the Lord, "Had to be anybody, Jesus, Jesus, why'n't you let it be me?" Shaking the baby and crying. Thing was dead to the world, but "Mary child, baby, blow your little nose." Shaking the baby and hollering, "Jacob, Jacob, come here. See what God done done." But Jacob was away on the rocks.

She didn't stay upstairs now watching Jacob taking the bed apart to bring down into the parlor so it would be ready ahead of time.

When the first piece hit the bottom steps, she looked at him once. "May as well take it back, Jacob." After that she closed her mouth.

He didn't say a word to her either, no more than to ask her if the place he was planning to put the bed was all right.

"All right?" she exploded. "Show me a place in this drafty-assed shanty that'ud be all right." She buttoned her lips to keep from crying right there in front of her children. "It ain't all right, Jacob. It ain't, Lord knows."

He didn't answer her. Just got a few potatoes off the stove for himself and gulped them down behind some molasses. Sat all off to himself, staying out of the way of the children. Gezee knocked the molasses can over. Think Jacob'ud pick it up? Starving! Bony shitty-assed man! If

she propped his meatless frame in a cornfield crows
wouldn't come near it. Acting like he was sacrificing himself for something! For this land, this Church! Said to him
a-many a time, "Jacob, the Lord don't call for you to make
all of that much sacrifice, even if you is a colored man.
You supposed to eat regular, your children supposed to
eat regular." But Jacob, he'd just back on away from her
wrath, looking off like his head was up in the stars some-
place.

He walked out of that house this morning, too, as if his
eyes were never gonna make contact with earthly things
again. Cornhouse was the best place for him, looking like
a scarecrow and that's exactly where he went, pulling in
boat equipment and making a whole lot of noise. *Minute I
leave Tangierneck they'll be sending for me to come back
for his funeral. He won't half eat.* "But I'm getting out,
Lord, Getting out of this place."

"What you say, Mamma? You leaving us, Mamma?"
Rabbit always kept a close watch on her mouth, even
when she wasn't doing a thing but talking to herself.

"I ain't said nothing to you, boy. Stop looking down my
gullet." And she scooped up a spoonful of potatoes from the
iron frying pan sizzling on the stove and slammed them
on Rabbit's plate. "Eat, eat, eat! Get this shit down your
gut. I'm giving you some meat sandwiches for your dinner.
Stop paying so much attention to me when I'm talking
things over with the Lord."

She meant to push the plate up closer to that seeing-too-
much, talking-too-much, hearing-too-much Rabbit's reach.
"Stop looking at me, boy!" And the plate went splintering
to the floor. "Stop it, you hear me? You ain't got to look at
me like that when I'm talking to you. What you fixing to
cry over, boy? I ain't hit you. I'm giving you another plate
of potatoes!"

Rabbit's big eyes welled up. Maybe it was her he was
about to bawl his guts out over. *Little-son-of-a-bitch don't
be crying over me, a no-good whore!* Thought flew
through her head the same time as her hands went a-flying,
and Skeeter jumped up from the table hollering at Rabbit,
"Boy, you done broke my plate. You ain't had no business
taking my pretty plate," and Gezee bawled at the top of his
lungs, scurrying across the floor to get out of her way. Her
hands flew before she got a chance to hold them back, into

Rabbit's little face and his head and his little body cringing on that Goddamned floor. *Meant to hold her hands back, but Jesus, Jesus. My hands is killing him.... . Cut off my hands, Jesus.* The woman wept. *I ain't meant to hurt up his face like I did. I ain't meant to do it.*

She grabbed that little old body quivering the same as it did when he was first born. "Rabbit, Rabbit, is you all right? Rabbit, don't be looking down my gullet no more. If I go anywhere, I'm gonna take you, Rabbit." And she sucked her knuckles where she cut them on Rabbit's teeth. Licked the slobber and the snot and the blood from his face. "Go anywhere, Rabbit, I'm gonna take you."

Silence reigned over the chilly air, and the cleaning up of the mess from the floor. Children didn't say another word. Skeeter kept his eyes glued to his plate, mashing his potatoes over and over again. Gezee sucked on that empty bottle she hadn't broke him from yet, with his little old shoulders heaving up and down, making some big hard sniffles to comfort himself. And her old scoundrel, Rabbit, with a bump from the hit she gave him rising around his lip, kept tracing patterns with the dirty sweat leaking from his fingers onto that oilcloth she tried to keep white and sanitary so the family could sit down to the table and "make eating a joy" like that Homemakers Club up there Countess Ann sent around a woman to tell you about. Ain't nothing but a few scraps of potatoes on these plates and the rest can wait!

Didn't mean to hit that boy like that. His mouth's already messed up enough without me lamming my fist into it. . . . *Jesus, Jesus, help me to save my soul.*

"Get up from there, Rabbit, and wash your dirty hands."

Got to get out of this place. Sound of little Rabbit's teeth cutting into her knuckles grated on her eardrums. And the sight of him, Lord, sitting up there just as stiff-shouldered as you please, tracing those nonsense ducks and things onto the oilcloth when she already done told him to get up and wash his hands was enough to make anybody walk. Just walk on away. Somewhere, anywhere.

But she didn't go any further than the pump bench, and sucked her knuckles a time or two. Tried to stop herself from tasting that blood. Must taste like the blood curdled in the bruise she laid on that boy's lip. Salty. Salt. And *Jesus, Jesus, I ain't no good. Cut my hands off.*

Mariah spit to clean her mouth of the salt and the tears and the slobber. Had a hard time seeing what she had next to do. But she wiped those tears before they even got a chance to roll down.

Wished there was somebody I could talk to, Jesus. Somebody with some sense.

She poured a tin can full of water down the throat of the pump. Rust flakes on the handle crumbled in her hands gone wild. She smothered the mouth of the cold iron and made it gasp and choke.

The water flowed. It flowed all over her feet and she didn't even care. Got sucked down as fast as she pumped it, in the sand bogging her feet down. Had to get a tub up there now to catch that water! She pulled the washtubs down from the house. And she wished there was somebody she could talk to. Somebody with some sense. Please, Jesus, please.

She talked to the clothes, a whole funky-smelling heap of them piled by the pump bench. "May as well put a few dirty pieces in soak before I head for the fields. . . . Miss Bannie's . . . Mamma Bertha's . . . Miss Bannie's!" Thoughts swung like a loose door on hinges with a powerful wind knocking it back and forth. Her gaze tried to fix itself somewhere, but it flew all over the scraggly paths of Tangierneck, running like the gray husk of scratches on an arm afflicted with the itch. It followed the smoke struggling from the chimneys of the little squinchy houses. People in them loaded down with debt and worriation. And besides that, a meanness and spitefulness that even now made Mariah cringe, remembering how spite-work once started against her never let up. She felt right cold. Water flew from the pump. *Somebody to talk to, Jesus!*

As if thinking could make it real, Irena flowered into sight, away down the road. Coming up the road with her little titties-forward-first self. Well, that's the way girls acted when they weren't anything but seventeen. Going off to the city soon if Mamma Bertha has her way. A girl as pretty and sensitive-faced as Irena ought to be going off to the cities. Tangierneck wasn't going to do anything but drag her down.

And right behind Irena, arms flaying the morning air and waving, was coming that powerful-bodied Vyella. Always did bloom big. A hardy sunflower if Mariah ever saw one. Boss late summer, boss fall, shine all through the winter if it came in green. She had a bossified look on her that just wouldn't wait . . . that was Vyella. Big, toothy-mouthed grin smiling the blessing of the Lord all over the place. Could see her even if she was at least a eighth of a mile off. Hollering for Irena to slack up. But both of them were just a-coming! *Coming my way in the morning!*

Caught up with each other. What a sight to see! Hugging each other up the same as if they were real sisters. Didn't matter if Irena was the only sister to Jacob and them and Vyella just the adopted. Didn't matter one bit. Girls hugged each other on that sandy road.

Water just dribbled from the pump, and Mariah swallowed, forgot the water. *Wished somebody'd come and hug me like that.* Felt the juices flowing every which way all through her. Could let herself go in a minute if she wanted to. A heat that felt good to her thighs crept up and nudged her in the belly. . . . But the sisters went off the road into Tillie Ried's house. Sight liked to have made her heart give out!

She said to herself after that, "I ain't gonna pay nobody no mind. Gonna go to Miss Bannie's and get me some help." Baby nudged her a little bit and she lifted her gaze from the over-flowing tub.

"Hey, Jacob. Hey, Jacob, come here and help me get this tub of water on the stove." She hollered at the noise coming from the cornhouse.

"Mariah, ain't you got no sense? I done told you a-many a time to set these tubs on the stove and then you tote in the water, in a bucket."

"How many steps you want me to make, Jacob, 'fore I topple over and die? How many steps? It takes a-many a trip to fill this tub, bucket by bucket, when I set the thing on the stove first. I do it that way when you ain't home, but how come you want me to do it when I ain't able? How come you want me to do it when you're right around here doing nothing?"

"Woman!"

Let the stiff-shouldered son-of-a-bitch turn purple as a beet.

"Woman!" And Jacob flew from the cornhouse steps and poured out most of the water she'd pumped.

"That's how you're supposed to handle water, woman.

Whether I'm home or not. How you get the clothes washed when I'm not here? I'm fixing to go to the rocks and you acting like a fool, pumping this tub full. . . ."

"I got more to do than make all them trips to the kitchen." She almost went into Jacob. Almost hit him. Could've killed him right there on the spot. But the Lord rooted her feet in that yellow sand by the pump bench. Listening to the hassling amongst her children almost made her fly into everything, but she turned her back and pumped the water—watched the long stream of it flowing from the pump, flowing from the muscles tight in her arms, slicing the water in the tub half in two. Closing up on itself and swelling high. Water is a bossy thing. Fit anywhere it wants to. Sometimes it goes quiet. Sometimes it goes noisy. But any way it goes, it'll take over.

It was water that cut Tangierneck off, left it all to itself. She pumped the water and wished she had its power. It don't need nobody. Don't need a single soul.

Vapors rose higher out of the dank, green swamp. Turkey buzzards sailed up. No matter if sand's all mixed up in the air, they'll be the first ones up. Right behind the vapors, they come sailing down the Neck in slow, belly swoops. A-spitting and a-flapping their black selves in the first light turning yellow. Always hanging over Tangierneck. Always picking at something's dead neck.

The muscles in her neck screwed up in balls and her ears drew tight as she saw Ol Jefferson coming up the back road, stopping at Aunt Saro Jane's little gray house, hollering, "Fresh fish!" But Aunt Saro Jane wasn't gonna open the door for nobody this early. Here he is coming on down the road hollering to her, "Got good wild ducks this morning, Mariah. Ain't a turkey buzzard in the bunch." Legs bowing fore and aft under his stumpy self. You couldn't beat that Ol for coming by to see *his* Jacob. Been crazy about those Upshur boys ever since he first moved from Kyle's Island to "join up with his proper family" as he put it, when Jacob and his brothers were just little old boys. Supposed to be some kind of a cousin to Jacob's mamma. Mariah didn't believe he was cousin to anybody in particular but the devil. Dirty bugger used to go around patting on little girls, too. Mariah shuddered. Always spinning yarns about the community and its history. Worse than his wife about that. All anybody had to do to get cheap rent off of Pop Percy was to "take pride in the community."

She pumped quicker because she didn't want to hear his snaggle-toothed telling of the same old buzzard tale, with his gamish eyes dancing about like he was laughing at something—stinking like a fish. Wasn't nothing but that poontang.

Didn't want to hear about time was and time when and time telling that once there were no turkey buzzards here, but dead Indians laid out so thick when they had no place to go but the marsh brought the buzzards here a-flying. "After they ate up all the dead Indians, they never went away. Fed on stray slaves after that, the ones that broke a-loose from the Haimawalkin farm. Got as far north as the marsh on Back-of-the-Creek. Some ran right into the Creek. Didn't have no ferryboat then to pull them across. Didn't have no ferryboat until Bard Tom Upshur came along and married Jacob's grandmamma, Margaret. Well, he was what you call a building man. And a sailing man, too. Built that church. Built this Neck up to something. Laid out Cleveland's Field for the decent burying of the dead. Now, ain't that something. And the buzzards got him after all. Picked his skin clean off his bones. Wasn't nothing for Mom Margaret to go and fetch but the neck bone hanging from the Royal Oak tree. Rest of the bones in chains on the ground. And she picked up all of them bones and buried them in Cleveland's Field. Laid little Cleveland in that field, right behind his daddy. Tell me Cleveland's soul went up singing, 'Carry me way from Tangierneck. Don't want no buzzard picking at my neck.' God's truth, Mariah. Ask Brother Percy if you don't believe me. Cleveland'ud been his oldest brother. We got to build this Neck up again. Now you take Mrs. Jefferson and what she says, smart woman, yes my God. . . ."

Mariah shoved the second tub down to the ground even though it wasn't full. Started to run in the house. Ol Jefferson was upon her. Couldn't stand to hear him tax her ears with the tale this morning.

A shadow floated slowly across the yard. Two shadows. A bunch of them. Buzzards swooped low. She lifted her head and smelled Ol Jefferson. He just about got up to the pump bench. Panting. Exhausted from his walk up the sandy hill. Right up on her with his mouth open ready to sell her a bird and a whole lot of talk about community history and building up the place. He might even pat her again like he did when she was a little girl, bringing disgrace on her.

She stopped him. "Don't want no duck. Ain't got no money." And she didn't care if he did stagger back at the sound of her voice. She was glad to see him turn and head for the cornhouse.

Ol hollered at the noise coming from the cornhouse. "How you, Brother Jacob? Meet me piece-ways down the road. Got something to talk over with you. Important!"

Jacob popped into the doorway of the cornhouse holding an old gray tong upright on the woodblock steps. "What's all the evilness you got into you this morning, woman? You wilder than the wind. Why you drive Ol off from here like that? Don't be careful, you gonna bring the baby here this very day."

Mariah squeezed her eyes tight, shutting out Jacob, and Ol Jefferson's back as he went hunching down the road, and the turkey buzzards. She turned around fast, kicked her toes against the crumbling block holding up an end of the house, letting the Tangierneck sand run out of the cracks of her shoes. Kicked until she stumped her toe. "Death, you gonna get out of my sight . . . I done spoke to the Lord. . . ."

Jacob's fingers hurt her arms. She didn't know how he got across the yard so fast.

His eyes were hard on her face. And mad and pleading all at the same time. "I'm gonna do something, Rah."

"Said that before, Jacob. But what you ever done?"

"Told you what I had to tell you." His fingers went through her arm.

"Let go of me, Jacob! Think you gonna beat and bang on me like that white mess does to their women up on Nighaskin road?"

"Shut up, woman! I ain't never hit a woman in my life and I ain't gonna start now."

"You ain't gonna start to do nothing now neither, Jacob. You might start but you ain't gonna get no further than start."

Fingers left her throbbing arms. Torn-up face turned from her sight. He got his long tongs out of the cornhouse. Started fixing something on them by the woodpile.

"Where you going with them long tongs, Jacob? You ain't going out in no Sound. First thing I know they'll be bringing your body up three days later." Kicking in her middle part cut the wind out of her chest.

"You hemming and hawing in potatoes, ain't you, instead of staying home and acting decent like a woman in your condition is supposed to do?"

"Don't be no fool, Jacob. What you fixing to do?"

"Just you wait and see, woman. Just you wait and see."

"You said that before, Jacob. All you gonna do with them long tongs is lean on them in the sand."

"What's it to you, woman?"

"I ain't waiting no more. I'm gonna sign up for the Welfare just like Vyella told Emma and them to do when she stopped off in the fields, yesterday."

"Woman, don't you be putting no Welfare food on my table! You hear how them Democrats over there to the Welfare talked to Uncle Isaiah? Asked him if they didn't catch him with a chicken and a few rows of strawberries last spring when he said he didn't have nothing. Embarrassed him right there in front of everybody, and then didn't give him a thing. . . ."

"Well Jacob, he didn't have no business going up before those people with a shoe and a boot on. You know he is got shoes to match, because you all took up a collection for his shoes at the Church. Vyella told me. . . ."

"And don't say that Vyella's name to me no more. Going around rousing up people. A man can make it in this Neck if he tries. All he's got to do is work. . . ."

"Vyella ain't rousing up nobody, Jacob. Starvation's doing it!"

"Don't say that woman's name to me no more, Mariah. I got something to do besides hang around here and try to talk reason to you. That woman don't know no Bible and trying to take to the pulpit. . . ."

Well, Vyella boss-walked up just in time to cut in on the argument. Jacob flew into that cornhouse.

"Ain't I seen you with Irena piece-ways down the road?" Words rushed from Mariah. Had to blink a few times to get Vyella situated in her mind. Smell of Apple Blossom cologne oozing from that tight-waisted green coat, and the sashaying way Vyella strutted around the yard overpowered Mariah for a minute. Must be on her way to Calvertown to work for her white people.

"Oh, Irena was just on her way over here to borrow a little piece of strick o'lean-strick o'fat for Mamma. But she got that off of Tillie. We stopped in there to talk over a new school proposition with Tillie. Ain't you heard nothing 'bout it?"

Mariah stared right vacant at Vyella, not answering her question. "I was wondering what happened to you all. I was good hoping you were heading this way." *Calm down, Mariah. Calm down.* Heart felt like it was ready to explode. "Mighty glad to see you!"

"Sis, what's the matter with you? What's the matter with you, hon?" Vyella's voice seemed to come from far away, even though she was right up on Mariah, pushing in on her with a right scary kind of urgency.

"Ain't nothing the matter with me. . . ."

"What you talking so low for, Sis? Is so something the matter with you. Is so!"

"I don't see nothing wrong with me, Vy."

"It's right nippy out here, hon, and you just as wet as you can be with the sweat. Has that brother of mine took a good look at you this morning? Go on in the house, gal. I'll finish pumping this water for you. . . . Let go this pump handle, gal."

But Mariah would not let go. *Had to keep on going. Had to get on going. Rabbit's alive if the next one ain't.*

"I'm gonna get that Jacob. . . ."

"Don't do it, Vy. I don't want him near me. Don't do it! He ain't deserving to be called no father. He ain't. . . ."

"You don't want him near you?" Questioning way Vyella answered worked on Mariah, and she thought, *Lord Christ Jesus, what did I say?* Mariah's hands ate rust from the pump handle. *Can't be putting my business out in the roads for everybody to chew over.*

"He's the papa of this young one, ain't he? Supposed to take some kind of interest!"

"He ain't . . . he ain't nothing!"

"What you mean he ain't nothing, hon? Well I do know what you mean in a way of speaking. Ain't none of our men worth enough to worry yourself over. Wasn't for my Ned getting himself a job driving that fertilizer truck up there to . . . What's the matter with you, Sis?" And Vyella threw her great arms around Mariah.

"I ain't gonna be here long, Vy, less'n I get out of Tangierneck. Death's coming to the land . . . coming to me."

"Girl, hush your mouth." And Vyella led Mariah to the bench under the chinaberry tree. "Don't take on that way, Rah. Things is going to get better around home here. Anything I can do for you, you know I'll do it. I'd stay with you now, but I'm due up in Calvertown today to work for my white people. I was just by Mamma's to leave Little Ned and Poonky so I can get on up the road, but I'll go by and get your mamma for you and—"

"Don't get no mamma, Vy. I ain't sick. Besides she's probably already out in the swamp pulling holly and ferns for the Christmas funeral wreaths. Ain't nothing the matter with me. I'm just trying to get myself together to go according to the Lord's will."

"Go where, hon? Now Rah, I know good and well you ain't gonna leave us here in Tangierneck. You got a lot to contribute to the community if you only would come back to the Church. You used to be so handy about decorating the churchyard and making everything look graceful and pretty for the Lord. You could be right smart help to us in getting these rallies for the school going."

"I ain't got no choice but to go, Vy. Lord sent me a message in my dream last night. Sent a naked man before me just as plain as day. And I was trying to get out of Tangierneck. Naked man held me up on the road. Before I ran into that naked man, I believe I slew another!"

"Means death of a female, Rah. Oh my good Lord! Means death of a female!" Vyella's voice faltered. Then she gave some little old halfhearted laugh. "Well Rah, you know we don't believe in those things anymore. We Christian women . . ."

"Saw it with my naked eye, Vy. Either me or this new one coming in, if it's a female, is going."

"Now girl, you know better than to be thinking things like that. You ain't praying enough, Rah. Ain't nobody can see the future but our good Lord. And he don't bless us with his vision of things to come. I want you to stay out of them fields, honey." Vyella's frightened voice fell like a tired leaf from the chinaberry tree. With a sudden start she let go of Mariah's shoulder and hauled herself across the yard. She cried, "Jacob, Jacob! Come out here a minute. What you doing messing around in that cornhouse all this time? I don't want Rah going out to those fields anymore. Why don't you with your old evil self let her go on up to get the Welfare? Practically everybody else is doing it."

But Jacob didn't pay Vyella any mind. He just strutted out of that cornhouse and went on off down the road. Took a minute before he left to say to Mariah, "Stay out of them fields, woman. You got enough to keep you busy right around this house here. Stay out of them fields!"

And he didn't even give Vyella so much as a goodbye look.

"Jacob, that ain't no way to be acting toward your own dear sister!" Mariah rose from the bench. She never did like the way Jacob acted lately toward his sister, adopted though she may be. That was no way to be treating her just because people tried to put out some lies about him and her. Saying that Little Ned she had right after they all came back from the Western Shore was Jacob's and not Big Ned's. Almost seven years gone now since that child came along right behind Skeeter and you wouldn't want a child to look more like his father than Little Ned looked like Big Ned.

"I'm gonna have to get that brother of mine straightened out," Vyella said. And she tore down that road after Jacob, hollering, "It's no need for you to be acting contrary to me, Jacob, when I mention the Welfare for your wife and your children. You ain't doing nothing for them. Why don't you all go on and cross that Virginia line? Big deal Upshur men can't do nothing but sing. They got plenty oysters over there in those so-called Virginia waters. You all always complaining that the line was never drawn fair. Always complaining that the whites got most of the water rented out on this Maryland side. . . ."

"We ain't no pirates, woman. We got some respect for the law! We ain't bound to get away from it," Jacob threw back at her.

"Can't get away from the judgment of your children though, Mr. Jacob! Can't get away from that." Vyella liked to have taken Jacob's head off hollering. "Your children's gonna sit on the judgment seat with the Lord Jesus and tell God how you denied them!"

But Jacob did not turn back.

No need for you either, Mariah, to be trying to get away from Jacob and his judgment. Seemed to Mariah something chilly came to the deserted yard. Thing hovered all around her. Even when she got herself up from the bench and went in the house to get her children on the move for the day, the presence followed her.

She shook her shoulders to get that cold touch off, but it closed her throat clean up. "I'm going, Lord," she managed to whisper when there wasn't anybody looking down her gullet.

You ain't going nowhere, Mariah. Ain't Jacob done told you?

"Gonna send for Pop Clem to come on and take me up the road. Gonna get the Welfare and see if he won't take me a little piece further up the road to sign up at that Calvertown Hospital. I don't believe in no dreams, Lord. That's some Tangierneck way of thinking. Gonna be just like Vyella. Gonna be free!"

The woman muttered in a mess of tears she just swallowed on down so she wouldn't give herself in to the panic. "Gonna go to Miss Bannie."

3

Jacob kept moving in a great big hurry, stumpy legs mashing down fresh sand mounds, making a new path crisscross the old road going down to Deep Gut.

Getting away from that prickly-pear Vyella. He used to think she was pretty. Used to think the sun rose and set in her cutting-up tigerish face.

But that was when she wasn't nothing to me but my sister. Ain't nothing to me now but just that!

He plowed on down that road, stomping down the memory of his sin. "My God, have mercy. Her children ain't mine!" He spoke out loud so he could hear himself tell himself out loud. And once and for all. Rather listen to himself than hear Vyella's voice grating on his brains.

"I ain't sinned no worser than nobody else! Ain't sinned as bad as most. Whole lot of men just go on and get themselves next to a nice hot piece every now and then, whether the one they got has turned cold or not. . . . I ain't been with Vyella but two . . . or three times at the most," he mumbled.

And Jacob could count that thing out on his fingers. He had some presence of mind. Even though he was clutching his tongs and wishing he could slide like Easy-Greasy on down to the Gut without having to put up with a consciousness of things that he wasn't even mixed up with anymore.

"Twice," he spit on the path. "That's all I seen her, when I was on the Western Shore . . . and just once or twice, two winters ago. But that was right after that baby died and Mariah commenced to nagging me . . . and even to looking right naggified and hurt-eyed. Just grieving and trying to get me all grieved up about how little Mary went away from here."

He couldn't even count the times she accused him of that baby's death! And even of this one's coming up! Shivering like to have tore him up. Wind went right through his clothes; thought he had on enough. The cold crept into his bones.

God, you ain't gonna let it come here dead? Is you? Is you?

Realized I promised Mariah a few things so we wouldn't end up in this condition, but you ain't gonna let it come here dead. I'm gonna cross that Virginia line. I mean, I would go across it if the law allowed. I done promised Mariah.

"Shut up, Vyella!" He hollered back to her voice just a steady calling without so much as turning around to see her. "I ain't studying after you."

If I cross that line, I'm gonna do it for Mariah. Not for you!

Nothing made him madder than for somebody to keep hollering at him to make a promise or do something he wasn't even quite sure about himself, especially after he already told them what he had to tell them.

"Go on about your business, Vyella. You better get your tail on up that road to your white folks, 'steada messing in my family's business."

And Vyella went on and took the shortcut leading past Aunt Saro Jane's house and out of Tangierneck.

But the warm woman smells of Vyella pursued Jacob, and that way she had of getting whatever she wanted done, done. "That's all in the past though, Lord." He spat on the path. But the smells and the tickling way Vyella had of getting next to him—all in the past! But all of it piled down on him, right now, this minute. "My God have mercy," he sent up a plea. "God Jesus have mercy."

And the niceness of her was something to dwell on. Warm and blankety as a mother's milk. A soft warm titty sweetness. Fold you all up in her no matter what the trouble, just like a mamma supposed to be when trouble gets a person all worn out. Like a sweet, pretty mamma. "Lord, Lord have mercy!" He shook his head.

Got to get something done. Got to cross that Virginia line.

And he huffed himself up to clear his mind of that nuisance by the name of Vyella. Settled on Mariah after that. And the day roaring in on his chest. Prayer can turn the day around. Heart liked to busted out of his chest. Had to stand still a minute and pray . . . but then he had to keep on going. Mashing down the confounded sand that piled up all under his feet over and over again, saying to himself, "If it's the last thing I do, I gonna get something for my family."

He hadn't gone any ways to speak of when something zinged through his head, saying, *Go on back home you blasted fool! Go on back home and reason things out with Mariah!*

He thought for a minute that it must be the Lord sending such a powerful urge through him. But then, he reasoned, the Lord don't speak to people thataway. Must be the devil got a-hold of my little mind. Telling me to turn around.

"Turn around I will, but turn around she won't," he snapped at his little mind. . . .

Still, still in all, Jacob, you ain't never seen nothing like the way she crumbled up lately. Wind on the oyster rock ain't gonna let you do nothing no way.

Devil messes with you when there's a time in the land. So Jacob threw his eyes up to heaven, opened his insides to God and sucked in wind. Raw, pine, marsh-scented wind fanned the fire in his belly, flamed all through him, and his eyes blazed all over his God's mighty world. Pines separating the hamlet of Nighaskin from his side of Deep Gut, bent their stiff necks down. Spruce trees tried to overtake them. "They'll never make it. Nothing bosses God, not even you, Mariah. Not even you, you devilish devil."

And not even you, Jacob. Little mind nagged him so.

Confounded woman didn't have sense enough to see that he'd stayed up to the house longer than he should have. All on account of her tossing and turning in the night.

Don't make no excuses for yourself, Jacob. You knew right good and well this wind wasn't gonna let you do nothing on the rocks today.

People would make him out to be a trifling man, just now heading for the Gut! Sun rolled a little piece higher in the sky. Nigh onto seven o'clock in the morning!

"Ho there, Ol Jefferson!" he called to the figure way down the road. Wind turned Jacob's voice around. Man didn't hear him anyhow. Too far down the road. Heading straight to find somebody else to tell his *private* talk to.

Going headlong to Tillie Ried's tacked-onto house. Now, she'd listen to anything, and talk, too!

Ol looked worse than some of those heathens living across the seas, or those migrant workers coming up from Virginia or Alabama and places like that. Wasn't any need for a soul in Tangierneck to go around looking like that. Jacob lied to himself, and somehow knew it. People were poor. Just plain out and out poor.

"Jesus!"

Nothing but a mess of sand piled under Jacob's feet. Stumbling got in his way. He almost swore but he caught himself just in time.

"Confounded women!"

Mariah and the rest of them just alike. Get independent minds when they're filled up with a baby. Always wanting to go off like a dog and lay boxed in a corner where nobody who cares anything about them can get next to them. Going to the cities! Humph! She ain't going nowhere. His feet ground deeper in the sand. She's lief to make me cross that line. Bulldozer motor's growling like to have busted his eardrums. Miss Bannie was at it again. Rooting up his family's trees.

I am master over all I survey

What kind of lying poem was that his father taught him to say? Ain't master over nothing! And he wouldn't look to the right of him where a great hunk of virgin land that used to be forested as pretty as you please to keep the mean winds of the Sound off a man when he came home to sleep had fallen into Bannie Dudley's hands. Now she's bulldozing up the trees. Even got the mail carrier job! Ain't she got enough money?

For a minute he had a vision of himself squeezing the wind out of Bannie's soft, pink throat, closing those impatient, hazel eyes. She had such a young person's eyes! Must be going on sixty, but if eyes could speak for a person, all hers would say is, "I'm entitled to whatever I want. And in a hurry."

Don't see how Papa got himself all mixed up with Bannie in the first place. But I'm gonna find out. Gonna find out how Miss-white-money-grabbing Bannie got her hands stuck down in my pockets squeezing my manhood. . . .

"Strumpet and a half. . . ." Jacob spat on the path.

Ought to haul himself off this road this minute and go on over to *Miss* Bannie's spanking brand-new house. Say to her, "Woman, give Papa back his land. Give me the papers he done signed over to you for the land. Where's the papers at, woman? Every time I ask Papa about those papers he claims he done hid them away, but I knows he ain't done no such thing. You got them. Or either the Nelsons you all tied up with up there to the Calvertown National Bank. Papa's paying this mortgage money directly to you so you must be able to produce the papers. Woman!"

Evil thoughts of doing something to get the whole mess over with wouldn't haul themselves off to save his life. They bossed him the same as if he were some kind of fool. Better to kill the enemies of God in the first place. But can a man kill and live with himself? Can't live, Jesus!

Tong slipped down in Jacob's hand. He didn't even realize he was squeezing the thing so tight . . . the throat . . . the soft, pink throat. Killing Bannie. Wasn't gonna lord it over him anymore! Killing every last one of her kind! Tong fell to the ground. A warning from the Lord! And Jacob trembled.

Anger is a sinful disease. "It ain't the way of the Upshurs to give themselves into the anger. I ain't a-going to do it. Not even for you, Mariah. Not even for you. It ain't the way of the family. God show me the way."

And Jacob slung the tong back over his shoulder and moved on down the road to the Gut. "I ain't a-gonna do it. Gonna get my brothers and bring them on back home here so they can help pay off this land. Don't care if Papa did write to them after Bannie lent him the money telling them he didn't need them, didn't want them. . . ."

A hot tear crept down his face. There was nobody looking at him close up anyway. Strong remembrance of his three brothers all gone off now to that city of Baltimore to try and make something out of themselves singing and slaving in the worse kind of paying jobs washed over Jacob. Little runty Levi who could still to this day call the birds with his voice tugged the hardest at Jacob's heart. But he did, too, worry about big, tall Tom who Jacob knew good and well would be trying to act like some big city hustling man with his hair all slicked back with piles of grease on it while he was just a-going for girls like he didn't have no control. Wasn't so much worried about Emerson. He was the steadiest one of all. Had the most sense. For after all, his Mamma Bertha had seen to it he got a little education up there to the high school. But still in all, Jacob did— couldn't help but want 'em home. Needed them so bad.

"Gonna get my brothers! Gonna bring them on home!" Jacob tore up some road.

"Yet and still," he argued with the thoughts the Lord gave him, "they is some singing boys. Can't never tell what might happen if they stayed away. Hear tell that Levi done hooked up with that Major Bowes up there on those city radios." Pride sent warm tingles all through him. "Ought to leave my brothers alone. Let 'em make a name for themselves. . . . Gonna leave them alone!"

Gust of wind hit Jacob and sent him over in the fields. For a minute he was glad the Lord snatched him out of the past. But then some brown, dead raspberry vines grabbed a-hold of his pants leg. "Did all I could do, Lord, to hold this place together." He unloosened himself from vines but the itching in his palms took him back.

Back to picking worms off of those raspberry vines this summer past. Dirty tough-hided buggers! Stamp them down in the hottest kind of sand, but the things would creep on up, laying fat and green and horny—cool to the blistered fingers. Give them four inches if he'd give them one. Never saw worms grow that big in his whole lifetime. Mashed them until he was sick of the green ooze squinching itself in between his finger cracks. Every fool knows worms ain't supposed to grow that big!

It was the hottest summer anybody in the nation could remember and everything else dried up. But not the worms. Kill a bunch of them one day and the next morning see a whole army, hard and damp and bloated with the dew, sucking the sweetness out of the land that Miss Bannie hadn't got a-hold of—destroying a whole winter's savings from off the oyster rock.

"Got to hold on to my land, good Jesus! Help me to hold on to my land, goody Jesus, Jesus!" he blustered. Shook himself up so much he had to turn in every old kind of direction to see who was looking out. Didn't want no folks talking about him wrong.

Well, this summer past, he'd asked the children in a nicē way one day. Got Mariah to break off a few switches the next day and tanned their stubborn hides. While he hollered at them, "Come on, boys, we got to beat the worms. Ain't no need of talking about you don't want to pick in the dark. You all ain't no girls. It ain't dark. It's just before day in the morning. Mariah, Skeeter, all of you-all, come on. We got to beat the worms to the berries!"

He could hear Mariah balking now, "I ain't no horse to be drove, Jacob."

Didn't know she was in a family way at the time. Hadn't had that much to do with her since she accused me of killing Mary. But with all of my driving, the worms won anyhow.

"But they ain't gonna win next year!" Such a desperate feeling rose up in him. Death . . . unless he got some help. Death . . . unless he brought Levi and them home to help him get back the rich, moist earth. Death on this sandy fit-for-growing-nothing strip Bannie done left. Death!

"God, Jesus! What's got a-hold of me? Mariah . . . woman would make anybody dwell on death. Death!" He spat on the dry field and the dead vines.

Something said to him again, Go on back home, Jacob. But he tramped all over that field.

"Sin!" Water groped for a path in his armpits. "Trouble with you and your no hopes, Mariah, is you done shut God out."

Sand, sand, everlasting no-good sand! But the wind kept whipping up more sand. Hold still, land! His throat was on fire.

Better go on back up to the house, Jacob. Land left to you ain't nothing but sand. Can't grow nothing worthwhile. Ain't no money on the rock today, either. Levi and them ain't gonna make no good out in the world. They ought to be brought right back home here.

"Devil, let go of me!" But Jacob stood rooted in the barren field.

Mariah's leaving you behind. Better turn around Jacob.

"My God, my God," the bare-skinned man cried. And the devil put in, *He done forsook you, Jacob.*

Wind busted his guts. Wind split the sands of his earth apart. Wind gulped the earth's top crust.

Tremble, Jacob. Poor sinner stands a-trembling. Put your lunch pail down, and your tongs.

A trumpet sounded within his soul.

Go down on your knees. Tabernacle of God is all about you. Make a joyful noise unto the Lord. For has it not been written that it will be easier for a camel to pass through the eye of a needle than for a rich man to enter into the kingdom of God. Thank God for your trials and a way will be opened unto you.

Every blade of grass seemed to tremble. Dead growth shook loose from the earth. The man clawed sand. But underneath, there was hope. The rye seeds Mamma Bertha told him to plant to sweeten up the land held tight.

The rye held tight! Jesus, Jesus. Wait 'til Mamma hears the news.

Sand under his sou'wester crept into his ears, making him sneeze. Sneezing took charge of his body. But maybe it was the tears. He backed out of the fields and glued his eyes to the path. Smiling unlocked his jaws.

"Thank you, God Almighty, and yes, God Almighty! Bannie'll not move me nor mine from this land." He wiped the bloody phlegm from his face.

Wind gushed from his chest box and wiped his throat clean dry! Drink of water sure would come in handy. Poplar-tree-tasting water from the low part of the land. From his old snapping-eyed Mamma Bertha Ann's pump.

Got to see that old Bertha Ann now! Talk about what else she learned over to that Countess Ann 4-H Club about how to turn sand into growing earth. Tell her how he just about made up his mind to go get Levi and Tom and Emerson. But he wasn't gonna tell her that to start out with because she'd get mad as the dickens. First off, he was gonna say, "Mamma Bertha, how you?" And while she was taking her own good time about answering, in that way she had of acting mad when she was glad, he was going to let his eyes rest on her warm, understanding face. Face with hopes in it. Face that led him to plant the rye!

Led you to plant it last year, too, Jacob. But the worms won, anyhow! Led you to plant it last year, but the worms won, anyhow. And the spring before, the worms . . . THE WORMS! GET YOUR GOOD GROWING LAND BACK FROM BANNIE! LED YOU TO PLANT . . . GET BANNIE LIKE YOU STARTED TO. GET HER!

Thing took charge of his feet and his mind and his soul just a-throbbing. Gonna get that Miss Bannie. He turned from the Deep Gut road, taking the shortcut to the witch's house. Fighting the brambles and the wind and the weakness in him that said, "Turn around."

Gonna get her!

But he hadn't gone any distance before a mishy-mish sound fell on his ears. He didn't even have to turn around to see what was taking place. Children were following after him.

He spun around, hollering, "Skeeter, you all go on right back up to that house and feed that hog!"

"What are you doing going through the woods for, Daddy?" Rabbit panted.

"Ain't none of your business what I was doing going through the woods." His shoulders fell down.

Children beat all, following after you. That's what he'd tried to tell Mariah. She'd cuss and they'd cuss. She talked about forsaking the land and the next thing you know they'd grow up and take a notion to do the same! He could hardly think for the steady hammering in his head, in his chest and all over him. *And on the path to murder they follow you too, Jacob.* He was wet all over. "I was just going into the woods to do my business, boys." Couldn't even talk. And yet it was his own tongue clacking against the dry roof of his mouth making sounds. Couldn't walk. And yet his feet moved from the spot where his soul stood naked before his sons. He followed them back to the main road, trying not to just break down and . . . and . . . he sniffled hard.

"Mamma says we ain't left nothing on the plates for her to scrape up for the hog. Sent you this cough syrup. . . ." Skeeter said.

"What's your mamma doing now? How's she feeling?" Jacob couldn't wait for the answer.

"She ain't doing nothing but looking for some pretty curtains to put up in the room the new baby's gonna get born in." Skeeter's voice was the prettiest tune he ever heard.

She ain't leaving, Jacob. She ain't leaving.

"And Daddy, I don't want my meat sandwich. You can have it in your lunch box." Skeeter squeaked through his hoarseness, singing the prettiest tune.

"Boy, boy!" Jacob hollered, but he couldn't sound mad

to save his life. Joy tremors ran all through him. He was back on the main road. Jesus!

"Boy, if you don't stop trying to get out of eating, I'll bust you wide open."

The sandwich in the skinny brown hand, and his own spitting image standing there all little and watery-eyed, and Rabbit halfway grinning and saying, "Daddy, I was thinking you went in the woods to pee and hockey. You ain't never done it. You gonna hold your water until you get to the Gut?" and Mariah sending him the medicine—all of it— every bit of it, and what could he say?

"Go on back home like I told you all now and feed that hog!" He couldn't even raise his voice at them. Confounded things!

"Grandmamma promised to help us out with our prayer poems 'cause Mrs. Jefferson said for us to bring them in today else we gonna get straight E's in everything." Rabbit kicked up little ruffles in the sand.

"Boy, you know right good and well your mamma can help you out with them poems."

"Mamma said she done got through praying."

Rabbit was the talking-backest thing. So Jacob drew himself up to his full stretching height, which was never tall enough to do all the things he had in mind. Hurting in his stomach sent a growling out of him.

"Boy!" he roared. *Mariah, Mariah, have you lost your natural mind?*

"She ain't said that neither, Daddy." Skeeter tried to stop him from going for the switch.

"She did too." Rabbit backed away, wrinkling his forehead worse than those sincere-acting confidence men in the cities. "You know Mamma say a whole lot of things around us that she don't say to Daddy."

"Ever hear you say a thing about your mamma like that again, I'm lief to kill you."

Skeeter panted on in Rabbit's defense. "Mamma just told Rabbit she give up praying for *Santa Claus* 'cause we bad. Said Santa Claus wasn't gonna bring us nothing but ashes in our stockings and Rabbit, he wants a train. And Mamma says trains are a waste of money. . . ."

"Git!" Jacob yanked a little switching branch from a loblolly pine decorating the side of the road. And the scoundrels flew with the wind helping them right smart.

Skeeter snapping at Rabbit, "Let go my coat, boy! You know Daddy ain't gonna hit nobody."

Rabbit snapping at Skeeter, "Boy, you wants that train as bad as I do."

Skeeter hollering back to him, "Daddy, Mamma said don't you go out on no rock. Wind ain't in your favor!"

My God, my God. Children liked to have torn him up. *Scoundrels ought to have that train. Mariah ought to have . . .*

He tried to cough the tangles out of his stomach. *Ought to go back home.* But he hitched himself up quickly, beat his own legs with the switch in rhythm with his walking. Heat soared up his legs. *Gonna keep going forward. Gonna make it on down to the Gut.*

4

"Hey, Jacob." Ol Jefferson ran out of Tillie's house and stopped him. What a queer sight that Ol was, blowing in the wind. No point in a man going around looking like that. A woman's shoes on. A prisoner's blue raincoat tied around him with a rope! Woman he had wasn't worth hardly nothing insofar as being a woman goes. Wouldn't sew a button on her husband's coat. Calling herself some kind of a schoolteacher!

Ol jarred Jacob so, he found himself speaking out of the ordinary. "You and Sandy Fitzhugh sure make a pair. Him walking around in the dead of winter with not a shoe on, and you . . . Ol, tell me the truth. What in the name of God is that you got on your feet?"

"Oh, they do for getting around here in this sand, Jacob. Who you gonna whip with that switch?"

"Never mind who I'm gonna whip, Ol. Just might be you." Nervousness made Jacob sound silly to himself. "What you want to talk over with me, Ol? Ain't you got your payment for Papa?" He squeezed Ol's shoulder to steady himself.

"Aw no, Jacob." Ol pulled away.

Tillie stood in her doorway grinning and abusing the door frame with her hulk. Just a-laughing at him. Yet she wasn't even laughing out loud. Her face was just a big round bubbling bubble, ready to bust wide open, quivering with knowing something, something all secret about him, turning him into some kind of a joke . . . in a messing-up wind. A confounded joke standing still in the morning, going nowhere. *Go on back home, you blasted fool!* Churning all inside of him. *Go on back home!* A landless joke who didn't even have the guts to take back what belonged to him!

"I got to hurry on, Ol." If he had wings he'd fly away

from Tillie. Busy mouth ready to start flapping, riding his back with a whole lot of rigmarole about the land. He knew it!

"I got to hurry on, Ol. What's on your mind?"

Wind beat the two men back. Ol more than Jacob, plowing on. Had to make it over the hill, get out of the sight of Tillie.

"Tillie and I was just saying, give the children an education and you don't have to whip them. Saw them young 'uns of yours back there on that road with you, just begging for a Halloween outfit of stripes and welts. What was they doing, Captain?"

Stop calling me captain, Ol! I ain't no captain. Can't guide no ship out of troubled waters. Ain't got no land.

"What was they doing, Captain, following after you on that path? You was on your way to see Bannie 'bout the land, wasn't you, Captain? Tillie said, 'I hope my die, I do believe that cousin of mine's heading for Miss Bannie's'. . . . Ain't never seen nobody go off that way just to take a shit. Woods is thin right in through there, Jacob. Anybody could see you squatting down. You was on your way to see Miss Bannie, wasn't you, Captain?"

"Got to hurry on, Ol. Wasn't gonna see no Miss Bannie, you hear me, Ol? I wasn't going to see no Bannie, nor none of her kind. Ain't got nothing to see her over!"

"You got plenty to see her for, Captain."

"Leave go of me, Ol. Got something on your mind just go on and say it. Just go on. Go on and say it!" *Say land, Ol. Say land.*

"Well, you must've been on your way to let out a load, Captain, 'cause you ain't emptied your britches yet. They sagging right underneath of you. I can see clean through your coat, Captain."

Laughter rolling out of Ol just got Jacob all stopped still and burning. *I'll kill myself a man this morning. Kill myself a man!* Jesus! Jesus! Crest of the hill coming up, Jesus, just let me make it over. And Jacob hugged his tongs to silence the growling in his belly. Wind broke out of him, in such a noisy way. He grabbed his stomach.

"What Mariah give him for to eat last night, Ol? My sweet cousin got the sick stomach, squeezing hisself up like that," Tillie panted, catching up with them. "Hold up, Jacob. Hold up. I'll run back to the house and get you some nutmeg for to suck on. It'll keep your bowels tight 'til you get to the Gut. . . ." Steadily signifying. Steadily coming. "He wasn't on his way to see no Miss Bannie, was he, Ol? He was just on his way into the woods to do his business. Wasn't he, Ol?"

Wind ate right through him. Woman's talk whipped him. Whipped him in his back. Trying to get away. But Ol held him there on the top of that hill.

"Let's wait up for Sister Tillie, Captain. She'll be right smart interested in speaking to you on the same topic I wants to deal with. . . ."

"I don't want to hear nothing out of Tillie, Ol. . . ."

"It's about the children, Captain! A good wind blowing for the children, if we just only help them out!"

"I'm doing all I can for my children, Ol!"

"Ain't doing all you going to be able to do though, Captain. God sent us a blessing over there to Countess Ann day 'fore yestiddy. All we got to do is seize upon the opportunity."

"What in the name of God!"

"Now you know Mrs. Jefferson, she's a right smart woman." Ol's eyes were wells of pride whenever he spoke of his wife.

"Yep, that she is."

"Well, she was over to Countess Ann day 'fore yestiddy. That was Tuesday, wasn't it?"

"Yep."

"That's the day the County Clubs meets. And Frannie, I mean Mrs. Jefferson, she always do turn the school over to Aunt Saro Jane or somebody so she can make them meetings."

"Yep."

"And at the meeting she brought up the subject of our children and their education. Well, I mean she didn't exactly bring it up by herself. Vyella was there. Your mamma was there, too, Captain. Ain't she spoke to you about it?"

"Nope, I ain't seen her."

"Said she was gonna see you, see you about going to see Bannie or getting your papa to do it, one or the other. . . ."

Jacob's temples throbbed. His head was caving in from the hammering.

"You all slack up!" And the mouthbox was upon them.

"Here's your nutmeg, Jacob. You all know my legs ain't so good, but I got to go out here and find me a way to make it over to Triville though. Get me some welfare. Upshurs ain't doing nothing but letting this Neck go down. Person can't even get enough out of this place for to keep mind and body together, anymore. Upshurs ain't gonna do nothing about it, neither. Ain't gonna do nothing about nothing but just knuckle down to Miss Bannie and let her have her way. Biggest mistake Margaret Upshur ever made when her old daddy pitched her down here in Tangierneck was not to change her name altogether. Going a little piece of the ways ain't done nothing but got her people confused. They still think they related to them white dogs. Just handing this land over to them. That's all they doing, Ol. Like one big happy family. Ain't no need of talking to them about the land, the children, nothing!"

"Looks like them 'white dogs' is giving you too much welfare food over there to Triville, Tillie. I wouldn't have a piece of it on my table, but I see you getting so fat off it you gonna turn into a greaseball first and last." Jacob struck out. Wind spun the water in his eyes into little needle pricks all across his eyeballs.

"You ain't the onliest one can increase your family!" The greaseball assailed him. Sizzled and popped in his face.

"Confound you, Tillie, I ain't knowed you was in a family way."

"Lots of things you don't know, Captain Jacob. Hear tell you don't know Mariah's with a baby either 'til she owns up to it." Laughter big and swollen busted out of the greaseball. Exploding. Burning him.

Jacob was hot and cold and the wind wouldn't even let up enough so he could rightfully know just what he was. Little bitty voice chimed in his head just a-ringing through Tillie's wangatanging. *Why don't you go back home, you old fool, you? Talk to Mariah. Wind on the rock ain't gonna let you do nothing but kill yourself. For what? For what?*

And all of a sudden, Jacob didn't seem to know for what. In the awful laughter coming out of Tillie and the way Ol wouldn't look up to meet the consternation Jacob felt tearing his face apart. *For what?*

Ought to turn around. Ought to go on back home. But

no, no, Jesus, he wasn't gonna say that to himself.

"I got to get on down to the Gut!" Want somebody to wear out with your yakkety yakking, go find that old no-account man of yours. Where's he at, anyhow? I bet he ain't heading to hit a lick of work today."

"You don't want to know where he's at, Captain Jacob. But I'll tell you, anyhow. My old no-'count man got his head stuck under your mamma's skirts. She sent for him, said she had something special to put on his head. Like I don't know how to take care of him. You might not like him, but your mamma sure do!"

"I don't appreciate you putting feelings in my words that I ain't put in them. Ain't I the one went up to Calvertown after him? Hadn't been for me and Rogie Harmon going up there to stand up for him, that cop Adolph'ud still be using his head for a punching bag. And the next time Adolph catches Willie Ried drunk and ranting and railing on them corners against white people, he's going to maul his brains for sure."

Jacob didn't believe in no whole lot of talking, but the only way to handle Tillie was to talk back.

"And who went and got him out, Tillie? Who went and got him? Me! We ain't never had nothing around here like that drinking mess 'til them migrant workers come along. Place had a respectable name. Can't even borrow money from the bank. First thing the bank man'll tell you is colored's too trifling."

"They ought to lend you the whole damn bank, Mr. Captain Jacob. The way you act, they probably don't even think your shit's got a smell to it. But you all got Miss Bannie so you don't need the bank. Humph! And furthermore, Mr. Jacob, if that cop Adolph ever lays a stick up beside my Willie's head again he'll never live to see the day he beats another nigger!"

"Don't pay Sister Tillie no mind!" Ol was everywhere. All going downhill. Wringing and twisting himself about.

"I ain't got no time for this kind of foolishness, woman!" Bullyfaced woman grew puffier. Getting bigger all the time. Ought to put her in a ring with a prizefighter.

"Told you I done heard two or three head say you ain't doing a thing but letting this Neck go down to nothing. Can't even keep a preacher out there to the Church. . . . Ain't even no preacher gonna find himself stuck in Sodom and Gomorrah. That's a fitting name for this place, Jacob. People wallowing in sin and contented with it. Wallowing in white shit!"

"Knowed you wanted to start a fight, Tillie, we'd a-never slacked up for you." Ol slammed his fishbag against his legs in a way that would've been comical if Jacob could only laugh. But what Tillie said, so said the community. So said all the people in the raggedy little whitewashed shanties tucked in the scraggly woods, all the way. All the way down to the Gut.

God help me to get to the Gut!

But the wind prevailed. And Tillie acted like she was never gonna let Ol have a clear word. But Ol kept trying. "I had something important to go over with Brother Jacob. Thought you did, too!"

"See how important the Upshurs thinks it is. Ain't none of them worth nothing but their mamma. 'Course she comes from over there on Kyle's Island just like you and me, Ol. Don't come from this white-behind-licking place."

"Papa ever ask you to pay a cent more'n what's fair, dirty mouth?" Jacob fixed his eyes on a busted pine twisting itself over the road. Few more steps and he was gonna cross that first marsh marking the beginning of Cleveland's Field. Walk over the graves and he was sure that Tillie wouldn't follow him. Sure as he was born to die, he was going to get rid of that nasty-mouthed thing. If she waited for him by the churchyard, he'd go through the woods to the Gut. "Come on, Ol."

Ol shook his head at Tillie. "You ought not to talk to Brother Jacob like that."

"Talk to him any way I please. He's my cousin once removed ain't he? Own flesh and blood though he don't seem to act like it."

"Well, you ought to act like the family. Ain't heard a one of you say a thing about doing one thing extra to help Brother Percy pay off the land. Most of us don't even bring in our payments on time."

"Do extra, Ol? Is you crazy? The way Percy Upshur done went up in our rents! Whoever told him to git in debt to that Bannie Dudley? And what he got out of it? That blue-streaked hearse limousine looking like a sick hog done spewed all over it. And he ain't even got control over that. Miss Bannie, mailwoman, got to use it to bring our letters to us. Hear her now, calling from the road, sweet voice running like molasses downhill on a hot day. 'Tillie, got a lot of mail for you, today.' Strumpet calling me out there to pick up all them threatening letters from the bill people. Why she got to borrow Uncle Percy's car anyhow? Ain't her kind got no cars up to Haimawalkin she can borrow?"

Jacob gritted his teeth and flew into the graveyard.

"Tillie's right smart upset with Willie's head messed up the way it is." Ol kept trying to smooth things over, following Jacob across the yellow grave mounds. "Ought not to talk to your family thataway," he hollered back to Tillie.

But still her voice wangatanged on. "Turn your back all you want to. I ain't studying after you. Got my own business to take care of."

Jacob anchored himself to a giant oak rising from an early grave. "Done told you once, Ol. I got to get to the Gut. Now what you want?"

Ol would pick himself out a slender willow to lean on, swaying and a-dripping any way the wind said it ought to.

"I ain't gonna take up much of your time, Brother Jacob. 'Cause I know you wants to get on down to the Gut. You ain't going out in no water though, is you? Mean wind's blowing." The little gray man scanned the pressing-down sky.

Coughing stripped the lining from Jacob's chest. Too much heat in the house. Fancy tin stove Mariah talked him into letting her buy wasn't doing a thing but burning too much wood. Dry heat like that busted his blood vessels. Bulldozers in the morning, still ripping on. And what a headache! Lord, what a winter's setting in. "What you all want, Ol?"

There was steadiness all over Ol. No more swaying. All of his grayness seemed to settle in his beady eyes, in a funny way now gone hot as coals.

"It's land, ain't it, Ol? That's all, all of you want!" *Dat-blamed-blasted greedy bugger*. Lump rose in Jacob's throat so big he couldn't swallow. *Greedy - stinking - bugger - hanging - round - home - here - just - so - you - can - live - easy - off - of - Mamma's - a - wiggling - and - twisting - to - get - something - out - of - Papa.* "It's land!" Jacob exploded. Graves turned right red as he stumbled on. Feeling low-down common for the swearing ripping through his head, discoloring his sight. And the Lord knew right good and well he didn't cuss!

"Land?" Ol said.

"You heard what I said!" *Fool, fool.* And Jacob turned on him. But he couldn't lift a hand to punch him. So he turned again, heading for the church.

"Well, yeah, Captain." Ol hesitated, and when Jacob didn't answer, he gathered himself and chased on behind him. "All we want is the land cheap as we used to rent it off of your papa before he got hisself all tied up in the debts to Bannie. We gonna need a heap more than we got for the spring planting when time for that rolls around, but right now what we want is school land for the children . . ."

"School land for the children?"

"Yep, and we ain't able to pay no kind of high price for it. Speak to your papa, Jacob. Tell him like I'm telling you. Rosenwald man, the one that owns the Sears Roebuck catalog, sent a representative to talk to the people down to the Countess Ann meeting. They's giving free schools to the colored all over the South. All we got to do is put up the land."

"Free schools?"

"That's right, Jacob. Free schools."

"Can't be nothing but some kind of foolishness."

"Truth, Jacob. God's truth."

"Rosenwald people Republicans or Democrats?"

"I don't know what kind of 'crats they is. But ain't that nice, Jacob? We can build this Neck up to something yet. Education is all Frannie, I mean Mrs. Jefferson, says we need."

"Can't be nothing but some trick, Ol."

"Ain't no trick, Jacob. Man'll be down to the Hall tomorrow night and speak before the Halloween Jamboree. All we got to do is put up the land!"

"We ain't got no land to put up, Ol. I ain't got none to spare. . . ."

"Your papa got land, Jacob. Land we always been using up to the time he borrowed that money off of Bannie. . . ."

"We can't get none of it back right in through now, Ol."

"Yes you can too, Jacob. What you all need is a lawyer. Mrs. Jefferson says you can get a-hold of one over there to Countess Ann if you all only would. I think the community would be more than happy to take up a collection to help you all sic Bannie out of these parts. . . ."

"Papa ain't gonna go along with nothing like that."

"How come, Jacob? How come?"

"You know good and well why not, Ol. We ain't never took nothing for free."

"Your papa's flirting with misfortune, Jacob."

Over the cushiony grave mounds Jacob plowed on to the church. Wouldn't look back at Ol. *No more. No more. My good God, show me the way. You ain't meant for me to kill, has you, Jesus?*

"Tell your papa like I'm telling you. He ought to get a lawyer. The community needs land. Needs school land right away. Folks around here's tired of begging the County for a school. And Mrs. Jefferson, she's long been saying it ain't fitting to squeeze every age of child in the Neck into this little hall. Drafts in it 'nough to kill a mule. Your Skeeter, he keeps a cold. Frannie worries a whole lot about the children, even though we ain't got a one to our name, and the County don't half pay her. . . ."

"Church takes up a collection. . . ." Throat was so dry, Jacob could hardly whisper.

And Ol drove on. "She ain't complaining about that part of it, Jacob."

God, send the green winter, he almost prayed. Almost prayed for the days of teetotal destruction.

"Papa ain't got charge of the land no more, Ol! You know just as well as I do, he's just renting it in a way of speaking off of Bannie 'til we get the loan paid off."

Wind and a headache and Mariah pulling on him. *Go on back home, fool. The Lord ain't leading you along this path. Gather up Mariah and the children and leave this land!* Wind! And Ol loading his shoulders down. Hurting, Jesus, hurting all through his chest. Ought to go in the church and sit for a spell. Pray off the burning eating into his windpipe.

He tried to plead with his God, somewhere, up there, stern and troubled. But his God had a face with the countenance of the clouds bearing down low over the giant poplars. Troubled clouds, filled with wind. Great tree heads moaned some kind of spiritless song. Dead winter setting in. *Must be another way besides all of this messing and messing around!*

And Jacob scratched blisters of whitewash from those heavy boards making the church into a building. Waiting for Ol to get through messing with him. Waiting.

Showers of brown leaves with orange flaming all through them swished around the two men. Settled themselves in a thick carpet on the yard surrounding the little clapboard buildings, the church and the hall. Hall leaned just like an old gray sailor on one leg and a crutch. Falling apart at the seams. Crouching for comfort and protection beside the thick sides of the Good Harbor ME Church of Tangierneck. Church built by his grandfather Bard Tom, going down. *Going down, Jacob.*

"People figure they done paid enough," Ol sighed and went on. "You don't have to tell your papa straight as I'm telling you. You can soften it up when you talk to him. But I s'pect you better let him know that folks ain't after paying all of this extra interest, or whatever else they call our hard work by, for him to turn over to Bannie. We got to live, too. Ain't many folks around here likes having to go up and get on that Welfare. When it was just lease arrangements between your papa and us, we got along fine. But you ain't telling folks nothing no more. Them trees on the land we was helping to clear off is just being stacked up for some new creosote mill, just like the one they got up in the Calvertown outskirts. Your papa ain't had no business letting this land get out of his hands. . . . And they ain't never hired a colored man around this county in one of them mills yet."

"I know that, Ol, but . . ."

"Tangierneck people ain't no wage workers no way, so they ain't particular about getting on up there when they do start another one up. But people wants some say-so about how this land's gonna be used. Judging from the few I talked to out to the store last night, they wants some school land right away. . . ."

"Done told you once, Ol, we ain't got no land." Big gulps of wind didn't ease Jacob's chest a bit.

Church that Bard Tom built wasn't even a comfort to lean on.

"You gonna ask your papa, Jacob. You gonna do it! Let's set down here. Keep the wind off of us." Ol plunked himself down on the mossy earth between the church and the hall.

"Gonna catch cold in your behind," Jacob started to warn him. Didn't even feel like warning his ownself and he sank down too. "What this free disease everybody's getting, Ol? You all talking like Democrats."

"Ain't no free disease, Jacob. It ain't like that. People's done worked for what they asking for."

Tillie moved along the mourner's path, trying to act like she wasn't studying after them. When she couldn't help herself, she hollered, "Is you done told him, Ol?"

And when Ol didn't answer her, she did carry on, way out of reason, until she spied a horse cart coming up the road.

"Ain't that Pop Clem? Well, I hope my die. Emma and them on the cart with him?"

Jacob tried to study reason. Man can't study reason in a minute. "Got to talk it over with Mamma, Ol."

The wind prevailed and the mouthbox on the road shrieked, "They going to Triville. I swamp it. And they ain't even let me know. Bet they wasn't even going to stop by my house. Let me get out here on this road. . . . Pop Clem! Emma!" Tillie hoed out a fresh path around the little gray church. Shaking her fist in the air and screeching, "They got that bugger Willie Ried on the cart! They got a nerve. Guess they was leaving me out here to catch a ride in your papa's Cadillac limousine."

Over her railing rose the tinny iron scraping of a car motor being cranked. And Jacob sweated for reason.

"That's twice our Miss Mailwoman, Bannie, done tried to start that car. Maybe she's just waiting for Uncle Percy to come up from the Gut and help her. White women's bad drivers anyway. . . ."

And in the midst of Tillie's shouting, a bunch of teenagers came sashaying along the road, clanking shiny Karo syrup cans full of molasses and syrup sandwiches and a few fried hog meat scraps, quarreling over whose turn it was to hitch a ride with Miss Bannie and who all had to walk them seven miles to Mantipico to hook up with the bus heading for Calvertown Colored High School. One thing was sure, she couldn't take all eleven of them, or maybe it was twelve or thirteen—children grow so fast. And on top of all that, the bulldozer plowed on, ripping up everything.

"Time in the land, Ol. It's a time in the land."

Ol crossed his legs as if he could wait forever.

Horses' hooves thudded in the dusty road. Pop Clem almost snapped his head off to keep from running over Tillie. His thin, clayworked-looking head reared back like a fine black steed. Gold earrings glistening in his ears just like a regular pirate. Women did get taken up with such foolishness. They all sugared Pop Clem up. Water crept down Jacob's nostrils and onto his lips. Had to cut his eyes hard to see the cart without turning his back. Didn't have enough patience with that bunch of Welfare gluttons to even look at them.

"Folks don't have no pride," he muttered. "Always want something give to them."

"Hey Jacob, tell Mariah to stop over to my house this evening. I'm gonna bake a couple of raisin pies with the Welfare raisins. One for us and one for you," Tillie hollered.

Women's laughter ran all through the trees as the cart turned to cut across a thicket. But as quickly as it started, the laughter stopped. One sure, strong voice called out, "Where's he at?"

Nobody in the world had a voice like that but his mamma.

Before he could crawl out from between the church and the hall, Bertha Ann Upshur was down from the cart, frame a solid ball of heavy motion waddling across the churchyard.

"What's the matter with you, boy? You got the devil in you this morning? Can't you speak?"

Wind quieted down for his mamma. Women snickered. Bertha Ann looked back and all the funny noises stopped.

"I . . . I was just coming to see you, Mamma. Deed I was. Said to Ol, no longer a few minutes ago, I had to talk all these things he's brought before me over with you. I ain't knowed you was on the cart, Mamma." What a face, what a face! Softest, toughest brown face in the world. But something hurried-up about her made him ask, "Mamma, you ain't going to Triville is you?"

"What's the difference if you knowed whether I was on the cart or not? You speak to everybody. They our people, ain't they? And furthermore, what's it to you where I'm going? You ain't been by the house since Sunday last to find out whether I'm still heaven-bound or got my feet sunk in the miry clay. And you know I been home. When you all caught any oysters for us to shuck? I ain't up to hustling no potatoes. You know I been home! And your Aunt Cora Lou home and you ain't even come by once. . . ."

"I told you, Mamma, I said to Ol, no longer than a few minutes ago I was going to have to stop and see you."

His mamma's huge breasts heaved under her faded brown coat. Didn't care how mad she was, he had to move closer to her.

"I was thinking about taking a trip over to Baltimore and see if I couldn't find Levi and them and bring them on home. Mamma, I wanted to tell you how the rye is holding tight in the land. . . ."

"Don't say another word, Jacob. Them boys ain't coming home. What you counting on doing, sharing your rich harvest with them?"

"But Mamma, I planted the rye like you told me. And it's coming up, Mamma. By spring, Bannie's bill'll be paid down to the point where we can take back at least twenty or thirty acres. We'll need Levi and them home right along in then. And that's the other point, Mamma—'bout this school land. Then'll be the time. . . ."

"Time's now, Jacob. Speak to your papa." Something was so hurt in that big soft voice.

"Mamma!"

"Time's now, Jacob."

"How you know the time's now?" But Mamma Bertha Ann moved on. Only the excited whirring of the blue-streaked hearse car, mixed in with the loneliest wind song, took Jacob's mind off her for the minute.

Everybody on the cart said, "How you?" when a little old firm-faced, red-haired white woman brought the hearse-looking car to a stop.

"Anybody want me to bring them anything from Haima-walkin Post Office except bills?" Miss Bannie said. She had a right pretty-sounding voice. Placed her words nicely. Had them confident eyes, though.

The only thing she got from the cart was a few "No Ma'am's, I thank you's." But Uncle Isaiah Hampton swung his lanky frame out of the hall-schoolhouse hut and said, "Bring me God's blessings." Just as the cart took off.

He turned to Jacob. "I got a right good fire going for the children. Just said to myself, 'It's a powerful long time Jacob's taking to come down that road.' Thought you'd sit with me a spell by the fire. But I guess you got to get on down to the Gut. So much time's gone by."

"Hold up a minute, Uncle Isaiah. I got to catch the cart. Ain't through talking with Mamma."

"I got a right good fire going."

"Knows you have. One of these days you gonna build too big a fire and burn the whole place down. Smoke's rising out of that chimney now same as if you sending up the school as an offering to the Lord." And Jacob started to edge off.

"Children's got to have some heat for to study, Captain. I sleeps all night up there in that loft over the classroom just as cold as I can be, waiting for the daybreak and a chance to build the fire." Uncle Isaiah tried to hold on to him but Jacob took off, Ol right behind him.

Old beaten-up agate saucepan in Uncle Isaiah's hand hadn't missed Jacob's eye. Man was always begging flour. He ought to have saved up something by now, been collecting community alms ever since they turned him a-loose from Haimawalkin Farms.

"Hold up a minute," the old withered oak of a man called up the road to Jacob. "I just want a little flour for to make my bread."

"Go on up to the house and get it! Rah's gonna be there all day!" Jacob managed to holler.

Singing on the cart rose almost as high as heaven!

> I'm on my way, and I won't turn back.
> I'm on my way, and I won't turn back.

Thought hit Jacob just as he hailed that cart. Mamma Bertha Ann really *is* going to Triville. Whole bunch of people going to Triville! With that Willie Ried leading the song. Migrant worker knows more trifling songs than a little. Never see him in church singing hymns. Head bandaged up and he's still singing:

> If my brother won't go, I'm gonna go anyhow
> If my brother won't go, I'm gonna go anyhow.

Jacob grabbed a-hold of the cart. Hollered, "Mamma!" Cart stopped.

He had to catch his breath. Shaking all insides, he said, "Mamma, you is going to Triville, ain't you?"

"What's it to you, Jacob? What you so worried about where I'm going for? What you worried about where anybody's going for except yourself?"

"Mariah ain't in no shape for to make that trip."

"Who said anything about Mariah? Go anywhere, she'll go by herself. What kind of a shape the gal in, Jacob? You ain't let nobody know she was ailing!"

"It ain't so much that she's sick. She just can't make that trip. Bouncing'll be too much on her." *Why don't you say what you mean, you trembling-brain fool!*

"Boy, what's worrying your mind this morning? You better stop chasing after horse carts. Gonna give yourself the heart trouble sure 'nough."

Pop Clem held his whip ready to slap the horses' rumps.

Jacob couldn't reach his mamma in any kind of way. Looking at her pleading didn't do any good. *Mamma, how you changed! You gonna try to get the Welfare just to spite Papa?*

Willie Ried snapped up the singing:

I'm-a onna my way, and I won't turn back!

Fool ought to be heading for the rocks with the rest of the men! Jacob railed again his own insides. But we don't want him there. Every time that fool sees a boatload of white people he gets the diarrhea and has to prop his ass over the stern of the boat and take a long shit in their faces. No matter what the weather. Fool don't even care if he's freezing his ass off! We don't want him. Let him go. Let Mamma and Emma and all of them go. Jacob sniffed dust as the cart pulled off.

"Go on up and get that Welfare!" The lonely man sniffled and stomped on down the path to somewheres. Almost disremembered that he was on his way to the Gut. Almost wished he could find his way back to the path heading toward Bannie Dudley's. Almost disremembered that Bannie just went by. Just zoomed on by! He felt right weak. *He hadn't killed her. Hadn't killed her!*

Singing on the cart kept right up—a-way down the road:

I'm onna my way

"You on your way to the rock, Jacob?" Mamma Bertha Ann was a mess hollering over the sound of the singing. "Your papa's waiting for you, and you walking backwards."

Laughter on the cart got all mixed in with the singing, pulling steadily up the road.

And when Jacob took notice of his situation so as to get himself together, he was facing home. Ol was right beside him. *Go on up the road! Get out of my sight!*

" 'Course, Jacob, I realize that things like the school you would want to take time and think over," Ol pounced on him.

Didn't care if Ol was staring at him, he was clean turned around, looking to his house, to his Mariah. She wasn't gonna desert him, wasn't gonna go against his way of doing things. Might argue with him right smart, but she was gonna keep her hand on the plow!

Cart stopped at his house. Well, that was no more than a person could expect. People have to stop and say "How you?" Cart waited a spell. Jacob didn't need to see the rest. And yet he stood and looked.

Mariah was making preparations to get on that cart!

He headed for the Gut. Never mind about Ol nudging him. Never mind!

He plunged a tong handle into the marshy earth. Didn't care whether Ol heard him or not. And he couldn't even seem to make the right connection with the Lord. He swore out loud like he never did before. "Well I'll be a son-of-a-bitch. Ought to kill myself a woman!"

"What you say there, Captain? I ain't heard you good."

"I ain't said nothing, Ol, excepting I'm gonna talk with Papa."

5

"It's time I got through, time I got through." Mariah talked to the housework. "Time I got through with this hemming and hawing. . . . Done made up my mind, Jesus. Gonna do just what Vyella said. Don't pay Jacob no mind. Take the plow in my own hands." Mariah lifted her chest, but she didn't lift it much. Fears of the night still nagged her.

"Skeeter, you back yet?"

"Yes 'um."

"Give your daddy his medicine?"

"Yes 'um."

"Want you to run over to Aunt Saro Jane's and tell her to get word down the road to Pop Clem that I want a way up the road with him when he goes. Gonna get us some Welfare over there to Triville, and then after I get through signing up, I want him to take me on up to Calvertown so I can make arrangements for the hospital. Won't take him long. It ain't that far away. I'll pay him something when I cash in my tokens on Saturday. Gonna get you all something to eat."

"That's right, Mamma, we tired of eating this old grease and molasses every morning." Rabbit answered before Skeeter even got a chance.

No you ain't, Mariah. You going to the fields. Jacob's against the Welfare worse than he's against the fields.

"Heavy load to heave around in the morning. Heaviest load I ever had." Talk out loud if she wanted to. Children weren't paying her any mind, anyhow.

Go on to the fields, Mariah. Race on to the fields. If I don't catch a-hold of you here, I'm gonna get you there.

Funniest thing the way that voice kept talking to her. Mariah tried to stare him in the face. Shades of a new morning standing still are worse than the shades of night. At least a person can understand the dark of night. It's not fickle like the day.

Prettified voice just droned on. Right restful sounding.

People said a change took place in your eyes and your soul so you could see him with your naked eye when he meant business. Heard him in her soul, Lord, Lord. Saying to her, *Give up, give up.* "But I can't see him with my naked eye."

Thing said to her, *Who you looking for, Mariah? What you scrounging around here looking for? I'm right here.*

Thing just kept advancing on her. "Must be a shortness of breath I got." In the leather chair she sank down. Close to the fire, but shivering and seeing only a violent whiteness, a comforting blackness, see. . . .

"Lord, let me get up from here and get my work done. . . . No, I'll just set still a minute." Mariah gasped, seeing. "Let me get up, Lord. Get back to work!"

But she sat. Didn't mind sitting, but it was the seeing still coming. The woman shuddered. People said your whole life flashed before you in those few minutes before the Messenger laid claim to you. And there was nothing a person could do about the seeing but just let it wash all over you.

So Mariah gave herself into seeing the days before her guilt was established before the throne of God. . . .

Seeing her best friend, Rosey, who always could outdo anybody doing anything, such as picking more beans than anybody, and catching more boys' eyes than anybody, and bragging more than anybody about how she was gonna get herself out of Tangierneck. . . .

But Rosey never got out.

Ended up just like you gonna do. You ain't getting out either.

Seeing that little old cute brown thing twisting in the last grips of death in the churchyard.

And hearing, too. Funny thing how clear the voices of the past came back along with the seeing.

Hear Rosey now just as plain as day, crying to Mamma Bertha Ann and Mamma Effie and her own mamma—long gone by that time to glory—and Miss Naomi, string-bean looking follower of the heavy-breasted mammas who came all the way over to shout with the prayer-meeting band from on Back-of-the-Creek. Folks acted like they made up some kind of a committee, standing there judging Rosey!

But Rosey hollered on. Sound of her crying stoned "The

Committee" into silence. Alarmed the whole camp-meet-
ing ground into some kind of an old hustling-back-and-
forth-doing-this-and-that moaning silence.

Crying even stopped the raging song of the prayer-meeting brothers. Stopped them from jumping up and down in
jubilation and pounding out victory over the forces of the
devil's evil on last winter's cold oyster rocks around the
old tires going down in the bonfires to ashes.

And they all came to stare at little Rosey, gone out of
her mind with pain, pulling at the great strips of muslin
she'd tied all around her stomach to hide her secret. And
to bless her as she finally looked beyond the "Jesus-have-
mercys" and the "Save-the-poor-childs" and the voices full
of tears, dripping condemnation, hushed in the summer
heat, crying, "Shame, shame and scandal on Tangierneck.
. . . Now ain't this a sight for our guests to see. . . ."
And to turn away all stunned-eyed from the twisted gray
infant, still connected to Rosey's body with the cord of its
mother's life knotted around its throat.

Rosey smiled the hurtest death smile a person ever saw,
with her eyes, dead now, and all walled back, full of terror.
Must have caught a glimpse of that lean tall girl-chaser,
Georgie Long, just before she gave up the ghost.

Cocky-headed, thundering-voiced, lead singer, *Deacon*
Georgie Long dripped sweat by the gallon from prancing
around the fire and the righteous shouting and praying. He
mumbled with his eyes cast down, but slipping and sliding
from *his* dead infant to his wife. Mumbled, "These young
gals is just living too fast, that's all," as he stumbled into
the prayer the people called on him to lead. "Must've been
that hot dog she ate. . . . God!" He looked from person
to person. "Dear Jesus! Thing must have given her the in-
digestion."

Seemed like he went into the stiffest kind of trance, locking his sights on the nubble of a hot dog Rosey had flung
into the darkening sand. Prayer lost all connection as he
kept repeating, "God, forgive them for they know not
what they do."

He cried on while the Committee, the heavy-breasted
mammas headed by Mamma Bertha Ann, mourned sorrow, cried shame, blessed the sweat-matted head of the
sweet child Rosey, argued with each other over who was

the father of the child, and wished the man's soul to the bitterest judgment of God Almighty.

They prayed in the heat of the stifling church air where they carried the dead girl's body with the infant hanging on. Prayed in the dimness, in the smoldering heat of the little church smelling of moss and Sunday perfume and dried-out pages of old, old hymn books, and the sweaty fire of Pentecost, and the fires of pinewood Uncle Isaiah Hampton made in this winter past and for many a winter gone. They railed at the "fresh-tailed" young girls scattered in the half-empty pews, scared as trapped rabbits on a bald island in the swamp.

Most especially did Mamma Bertha Ann rail. She had all boys except for Irena and her niece Vyella, who she had to take in on account of her sister passing away over there on Kyle's Island. Word was out that they would've all been boys if Bertha Ann Upshur had anything to do with the choices that God makes. For it was well known to everybody that Bertha Ann thought boys could control themselves a little bit better than girls. So Mamma Bertha took charge of the girls in church.

"Don't bring no disgrace on your home, girls. Learn your lesson by this sinful child's disgrace. We had a lot of white people on this campground today, and some very important colored from the cities. And wasn't this a sight for them to see! People like that we got to depend on to get our school funds and job opportunities for our young folks in the cities. Want you girls to make something of yourselves." Mamma Bertha Ann's big, white-clad body shook with the tremor in her voice as she whipped the heat from her face with a Jamison Funeral Home fan. "Guests is gone now, girls. Sarah, take the little children over to the hall. Don't want them in here right now. . . . Come back here, Lydy and Ann. I ain't said a word about you all leaving. You ain't no children no more. You young gals gonna sit still and listen! First time we ever recollect having so many white people from Haimawalkin come to look over our camp meeting.

"Most of the money in this county is right up there in Haimawalkin . . . come back here, Joseph. . . . Don't neither mother's boy old enough to hitch a ride up to that Calvertown Colored High School walk out of this church. I got something to say to you all, too. I done seen to it that my boys got off from here to the city to do something with themselves. But that don't mean I'm through talking to boys. Sit down!"

Mamma Bertha Ann's fine hair flew loose and agitated as she paced up and down before the mourner's bench.

"Now, if you knows anything about your community history, your hearts would be mighty proud that the Haimawalkin white people came down here today. That only means one thing and that's that we pulled this community up so they have to respect us.

"Plenty other places along these shores allow drinking and gambling and card playing and dancing. But you all got something to be proud of. Tangierneck don't allow it. Don't allow no fornication either, but some of you children, especially the girls, is going astray.

"If any of you girls is in a family way, we want you to step forward so the church can help you find your way back to the Grace of God."

Fans beat the air.

"These white peoples come a long way since slavery times." A squall of tears stormed down Mamma Bertha's face. Old prayer meeting follower, Miss Naomi, jumped up to help Mamma Bertha Ann.

"You wasn't in these parts during slavery time, now, Bertha Ann. You wasn't even born then. But I can tell the children about that. I can tell them about the time Old Haim the Second used to send his little grandchild down here to this Tangierneck Church to see if we were acting respectable enough. They made it so hard on us we had to go off and pray in secret a lot of times. Couldn't even pray together, for that child, whenever he wanted us'n to stop praying, would ring the bell. Didn't matter what we were talking over with God, he'd just ring that bell whenever he got good and ready for us to get on the move. Sometimes we wouldn't be in this building no more than five minutes and he'd strut in and ring that bell! Children is impatient anyway.

"Well, Bard Tom, he got tired of that. Made a trip up there to Haimawalkin to see about putting a stop to it. And that was the last trip he ever made. Wasn't too long after that when Margaret found his bones.

"Poor thing must've tried to talk reason to them. He wasn't used to no slavery way of talking low. He was one of those what you call Blackamoors. Came here a free sailor on a ship when us'n was still bounded out for back debts up there to Haimawalkin. And he was a proud thing to behold. And a workingman! He pitched in with Margaret when this land wasn't nothing but swamp and sand and old cast-off residue and turned this place into something. Both of them worked right side by side, just as loving. Worked like dogs. Give a-many of us looking for freedom just that very thing. Hadn't been for them preparing a place for folks like me and Saro Jane, I s'pect we never would have been able to leave Haimawalkin farms. Them white folks still kept us in slavery way after Mr. Lincoln signed that Emancipation Proclamation. 'Course I don't live here no more. You all knows I got a place over to Back-of-the-Creek. But I got my start right here in Tangierneck. . . ."

"Hush, Miss Naomi, that ain't nothing to talk about now. There's a time of death in the land," Mamma Bertha Ann moaned.

"Is so something to talk about, Bertha. Children need to know how they did us. Need to know about them Paddy Rollers ripping through this very church. Need to know 'bout how us'n fought to hold on to this land for Percy and Johnathon, after poor Bard Tom and Margaret was done away with. Need to know how us'n prayed and tried to live a good and decent life in the eyes of the Lord so he'd bless us to prosper and overcome, and change the hearts of our white brethren.

"You gotta live clean, children. Got to live clean!" Miss Naomi wailed.

Church said, "Amen."

"It don't pay to be going against the will of God, children. It don't pay to be acting willful and common. . . ."

Church rocked, "Amen. Amen. Amen."

"Especially when there's white people around to see you doing it. They use any kind of an ol' excuse to take away from us what God done give us. And they act commoner than us a heap of times. Some of you children don't know what God done done for us! Don't know what your parents is been through to give you what you got. Don't even care!" Scream from Miss Naomi sent the church to rising fits of "Amens."

"Look at this little child Rosey. In what a condition!

Lord, Lord. Dead. Realize her mamma's gone, but we tried to raise her! Ain't we done right by her, Church? Ain't we tried to tell her right from wrong?"

Yes, and a yeah and amen, amen, amen, amen! Resounding amens tore through Mariah. Crying amens scalded her soul. Drenched her down in the smothering memory. Church school smothering, "Honor thy father and thy mother that thy days may be long upon the land which the Lord thy God giveth thee." And she gasped, reaching in her thoughts for Jacob, straining to feel him kissing her all over, straining to get a-loose from the wrath of a "just God" boiling up all around her. With tears rolling down her face and shaking all over in the presence of death she recalled Jacob saying in the spring just gone, "I'm just going over to the Western Shore to see about getting myself situated in the world like Mamma said and getting us a place for to move to, Rah."

Ain't never heard from him since that time! Roots of her nerves hurt. Jesus!

"Children, obey your parents else you gonna be dead way ahead of your time!" Mamma Bertha Ann rumbled in the air oozing doom.

Church was just a-rocking. A frail ship at sea in a bitter storm. Moaning Amen! Looking to Christ, tender Saviour. Singing all out of tune and in tune and every kind of way, mostly moaning:

> *Lead kindly light amid the encircling gloom*
> *Lead thou me on, for I am far from home.*

"Come forward. Come forward. All who have sinned and are heavy laden, come forward." Mamma Bertha Ann's great arms stretched out in the church night. "Come to the bench. Some among you have sinned. I wouldn't put it past my very own boys to have sinned up with you, flirting in their faces the way some of you fresh-tailed girls do." Looking dead at Mariah in the heat. Waves of black heat going red and pressing a soul down to hell. "Come forward!"

Walk to the bench, Mariah. Mourn on the bench beside your best friend, Rosey. Stretched out there now with her arms flung back like broken swords from under the white service uniform somebody done flung over her. Stiff. Dead.

With the statue of the Saviour and his little lambs on her chest.

"Come-a-umm, a-umm before death brings you to this altar. A-Lordy, ayah, come forward! Before the Reaper grabs a-hold of you. See him now. Seeee him now. Wading about on the banks of the River Jordan. River of Jordan's right here before me. And Death's robe is white, a-hah, a-hah. And his face is death white. Ain't wholesome looking like the Lord's. Gonna pull you down in the undertowing tide. . . . But God can save you. Call on Jesus, children, aaaaah-hah, a-come forward. Jesus'll take you out of the darkness of fleshy sin, bring the light of the world in to you.

"Yes, yes! Before the ignorant darkness grabs a-hold of your own throat like this stray child, Rosey's. A-hah-yah! And twist your own sweet mother cords around your own baby's throats in the darkness of your sinful wombs. Tell God! Tell God! Might spank you a little bit. A-um, but come forwaaard! Wake up in this night's morning. Life comes to you when you wake up. Tell God all about it, a-uh-hummmmmmmm!"

And the great church rocked in the puzzlingest kind of moan. Stomping the old New Year's song out heavy in the deadest kind of heat.

> Before this time another year
> I may be gone
> In some lonesome graveyard
> Oh Lord . . . How long!

Great white-robed woman, Mamma Bertha Ann, stood as stiff as God, over the corpse of Rosey, in the flickering yellow lamplight. Reaching out for Mariah with the Committee all around her, reaching. "A-come a-forward. Let us help you. Let God in on the secret."

And Mariah moved forward. Dashing away from the Grim Reaper. Swishing on up from the treacherous banks of the River Jordan. Saying, "No, Mrs. Bertha!" under her breath. Looking to the right of her and looking to the left. *Ain't you coming, too, Lydy? Ain't you coming, too, Ann Long?* But she was out there by herself. And Mariah pleaded with her eyes to Lydy and Ann. *You all were out there, too, in the spring, in the clearing in the woods in the spring! Spring got a-hold of you all, too!*

"A-come a-forward!"

But she was in the church aisle by herself. Moving forward. *Nobody but you, Mariah, moving to the mourner's bench. Go back! Go back!*

But the church had its eyes on her. Wide open eyes and moaning!

> Before this time another year
> I may be gone
> In some lonesome graveyard
> Oh Lord, how long!

Well, I'll go by myself! Going to Jesus, Jesus!

A stiffness grabbed her in the neck, but she didn't stop moving. Went all the way forward!

"A-come a-forward. Let he who has sinned with this child come a-forwaaard! God understands the passions of old men. And Jesus'll speak to him for you. Talk to Jesus!"

Who you pulling forward, Mrs. Bertha? Mariah's heart stopped beating on the banks of the river. By the mourner's bench she sank down as she beheld Ol Jefferson rising up from his pew, coming forward. "Go back, go back!" Her jaws just clattered like dumb loose things, and her voice was nothing but a whisper locked in her throat. "Go back. Oh my good Jesus!" But the little man moved forward, sweat pouring down his face. She threw her arms up to heaven and screamed, "It ain't his, it ain't his. It's Jacob's. Church, help me, God, it's Jacob's!"

"Don't lie before the throne of God, child. You've come this far. Now let the man who's sinned with you come to the bench and be cleansed by the blood of the Lamb same as you. Same as you, child." Miss Naomi caroled in comfort.

"I ain't accusing the child of nothing." Ol trembled by the mourner's bench. "I'm just accusing myself of patting her on the head, because God don't like ugly. I don't think Jacob's had nothing to do with her either. . . ."

"Dunce, dunce!" Mariah screamed. "Get that dunce out of my sight." She rolled down to the mourner's bench. Hugged the clammy form waiting for Jimmy Jamison Funeral Home people to take it away. "Rosey! Rosey knows it's Jacob's. His mother done sent him to the Western Shore so he won't be here to own up to it. That you know, Rosey. That you know!"

"Don't lie on Mrs. Bertha!" Miss Naomi hit her on the shoulder with a funeral fan. "Don't you believe in telling the truth?"

Ol skittered away.

Statue of Christ fell to the floor and broke. Church trumpeted alarm. Chorus of tramping feet and shrill feverish voices moved forward.

"Don't believe in nothing except getting a bellyful." Mariah heard her mamma just a-rending the air. "We sent her off to Back-of-the-Creek to work out in service so she could learn some sense. Service wasn't that hard. Wanted her to go on from there and make something of herself in the city. Wouldn't have brought her back home except she got such a cold in her chest."

"It was the TB I got, Mamma, and you know it!" Mariah couldn't stop herself from saying it, nor from the quaking.

"Hush your mouth, gal. Don't talk back to me now. I said you had the cold. Church, help me to raise her. Help me to raise her. Gal's so pretty. . . ." Mamma Effie broke down and cried, broke down and beat her all about the head. Mamma Effie flew all to pieces. Never saw stiff Mamma Effie break down before. Never knew a beating could hurt this much. "Help me to raise her, Jesus! Jesus! Don't want her to end up here in Tangierneck scrounging around for whatever the devil gives up to her . . . working her ass-behind off for nothing. She ain't but fifteen. Church, help me to raise her. . . . Child, don't lie to this church. Is you with a baby by that Jacob?"

"Yes'um."

"Don't 'yes'um' me." Slaps on Mariah's face were the startlingest things. Woke her wide awake to the clamor all around her. "Don't you know your papa come here hid in the hold on a ship? Starving hisself for days and nights. . . ."

"Jacob's been gone from here since . . ." Mamma Bertha stomped the boards, but Mamma Effie cut her off.

"Starving hisself for days and nights just to get here so he could start a little business to take care of you. Wasn't for paying off the Upshurs for this land he'd a been done got ahead. . . ."

"Mamma, I wasn't even born then. . . ." *Don't talk back to your mamma like that, Mariah. Don't do it!*

"But you was thought about, whore!"

"Shut up, Effie! Shut up!" A great man voice roared by Mariah's side.

Papa ain't that big, but his eyebrows move like the thunder of God on a mean, hot summer day, hotter than you can bear, clapping up a storm in front of Mamma, making her little and shut up.

"You ain't raised that gal right," the thunder boomed. "Fault's on you! You, Effie, you! Child said it was Jacob's. Now what you gonna do about it, Percy Upshur?" And Mariah's papa turned to the tall, fierce-eyed man with a beard as important-looking as Jesus'.

Reverend Michaels, the one that dropped in to pastor sometimes from on Back-of-the-Creek parsonage, threw his little bones in between them. "This is the house of God, brothers!"

"Upshurs built it!" Percy Upshur pushed the preacher aside.

"Landlords don't build everything. All the colored down here worked for the building. Talk to you in the yard, Percy Upshur!" Horace Harmon answered.

And the men talked so loud in the yard nobody understood each other.

"Lord, I got my killing lashes now," wailed Mamma Effie, as she beat and hammered Mariah down in the cooling-off sand of the churchyard. Found her as Mariah scurried in the evening's first shade, jumping over the grave mounds of Cleveland's Field, running away from the beating, and somebody yelling, "That's right, Effie. Lay it on her behind hot and heavy. Little hot-behinded girls disgracing the church and the community." And the single, solitary Aunt Saro Jane, hollering, "Effie, calm down! Child's got a right to a boyfriend," and "Lord what a sight in the presence of the dead. Done forgot about poor little Rosey," and the old Firestone and Goodrich tire bonfires dying out when nothing but some Cracker Jack boxes the children kept tossing on them to keep them going, spitting feeble little sparks up to the night and the tall-headed oaks.

"Tell me the truth, gal, is you with a baby by that Bertha's boy? Or do you even know who you is with a baby by? Gal, talk to me. Got so many dreams in your old eyes. Do you even know who you is with a baby by? I'll beat the living shit out of you on this road. Don't think I can catch up with you, do you? Slow down, gal. Slow down. You can run faster than me but you ain't got nowhere to go but home. I'll catch you there. . . . Gal, talk to me, before your papa gets here. Talk to me, gal, else I'm gonna shut your ass up so tight in that room, won't a living soul see you 'til I get ready for them to. Gal, talk to me. . . ."

"There was a time in the spring, Mamma. . . ." Mariah kept trying to talk to her. Tried to talk to her all through the beatings and the beatings on her head and on her shoulders, everywhere but on her belly. Tried to tell her, "Mamma, there was a time in the spring. . . ."

In the little room where Mariah's mother put her for months to keep her out of the sight of people most of the time, Mariah kept rehearsing the things she'd tell her if Mamma Effie would only break down. She would say to her, Mamma, there was a time in the spring when anybody could make a mistake. There was new green grass in that place in the woods where you cut across to go to Haima-walkin. Jacob was there. I didn't go there looking for him. I just went there to lay down awhile and let the sun bake my chest . . . and to remember a spring a long time ago when all us children used to go there to play, especially Jacob and Levi.

Jacob was such a boastful thing then when we were little children. Any old time he'd go running through those bushes, shouting things like, "Catch me, Indian killer! Catch me, Negro killer! I'm hid in the swamp and I can shoot you down with my magic slingshot!" How he used to go swaggering through the bushes with his brave-acting self. And Levi was always right with him, singing.

I did so much like to go there to remember, Mamma. We used to have the prettiest kinds of times together. Like the time I hollered out from behind a tree, "I can shoot them down, too, Jacob and Levi! Let me go hunting with you."

"Girls can't shoot down nothing," Jacob said. And he was rough, pulling my plaits and making me stand up to get judged in the clearing. "What you doing down in these woods, girl? Girls can't shoot!"

"Yes they can, too!" Levi tried to take up for me.

"You can't even shoot good yet, yourself." Jacob false-bassed and almost made little hunched-back Levi shrivel clean up.

"But I can sing! That's more than you can do. People call you Song Sparrow, but they call me a Lark!"

"You can't bass, though!" Jacob hollered.

"But you can't sing! You ain't nothing but song-sparrow. I can call the birds."

"You can't none neither, Levi, call the birds."

"I can so too!" Levi stomped in the green place. "I can call the rabbits and the fish from the Nighaskin River and the snakes too if I put my mind to it. But most especially, I can call the birds right down here with us. And everybody can fly away on their wings."

"That's all you can do, too, Levi. You can't bass." Jacob made his voice real big. "You can't help Papa out of his debts yet. You can't bass, Levi. Can't do nothing. Run down a row of strawberries quicker than anybody can do anything, including count to the number one. Leave me with the work, 'cause you ain't picked no berries to amount to anything. I'm the one picked most of those berries on Haim Crawford's truck. You can't bass, Levi."

But Levi called the birds to that place in the swamp, Mamma. Never saw so many birds before in my whole life. And I went back there a lot of times when spring rolled around to remember.

So Jacob found me there in this spring just past, laying down for a minute in that secret place, sweating in the sun to get those TB germs out of my chest. Letting go of winter and thinking about Levi and how he called all those birds to that time and place. That secret place in my soul, in the green grass woods, where the air is green and cool and the ground is warm. There was dogwoods all over that place last spring, Mamma Effie, smelling just like when Levi was here. And that's the truth. Smelling just like me when Jacob came into that clearing and started in teasing me about being a little brown fairy.

"I'm alive, I'm alive." That's what I said and threw my arms up to the sky, and wrapped them all around Jacob's head.

Jacob commenced to squeezing me and he wouldn't let go. All I said was, "Jacob, Jacob" over and over again. Don't know how anything after that took place but there was Jacob hard and liquid and melting over and over again inside me. Sweet in my nostrils and in my tears. "Can't help it, Jacob," flowing out of my eyes. "The birds don't lie, Jacob. Ain't it a beautiful spring?

"Juices running in my mouth and my legs. My nose feels funny. Gonna break myself all to pieces and laugh in a minute, Jacob."

"Don't see nothing to laugh about, Mariah." And Jacob kissed me with his eyes closed. "You the prettiest girl in this whole land."

"In this whole land, Jacob?"

"In this whole earth, Rah." And he cleared his throat in my ears.

"Gonna jump out of myself, Jacob."

"Like to see the day, Rah."

"I'm jumping out of myself, Jacob." I dared him with my eyes. In the green swamp swimming up to the sky. Soft and spilling and drenching us in the light of the yellow kissing day.

"You hurting me, Jacob."

But the pain went on over and over again. Jacob told me then, "Rah, it's gonna be better." Gave me all of his tenderest life. Gave it all to me all in my thighs and my back and my heart. Said to me, "Rah, I'm gonna take you out of Tangierneck so you can get them germs out of your chest. Gonna make you a queen on the highest hill in the land. . . . Don't cry now, baby. I done told you them doctors up there to Calvertown with their X-ray machines don't know nothing. You ain't gonna die. I'm gonna take care of you. I wants you to live. Rah, little baby, I wants you to live! Therefore that means"—and Jacob stood up big and proud—"that I'm coming back home to get you. But first I got to go and see about doing some things for Mamma's sake. . . ."

"But you done *done* it to me, Jacob. You done done it to me! Mamma!" I started in crying.

And just then Levi came a-running into the clearing looking all hurt and out of breath. Looked like to me he was even straightening out his broken shoulder so he could stand up as tall as Jacob and holler. "What you done to her, Jacob? What you done?"

Jacob looked like he was ready to take off and run. But he did break down and make himself stand still. And he bellowed at Levi first of all, saying, "I ain't done nothing to her." Then he turned to me and said, "Us boys is going off to the cities for to sing and get on the radio, but I'll be back home after you." Stood in front of me so Levi wouldn't see my clothes all wrinkled up. Steadily talking, he threw out first this hand and then the next, saying, "I'll be back home after you, Rah. Mamma do think right smart of us getting ahead in the world singing. You know, Rah, it ain't nothing down here in Tangierneck but a whole lot of worriation for Mamma and the family. Papa says if we don't stay close to home we won't hold on to the land, but Mamma says for us to get up and go."

Mamma, Mamma, Mamma. The sound of Jacob's voice in that time long ago—eight long years ago—cut through Mariah's heart as she sat now recalling—begging her Jesus to help her bury the dead, crowding in on her—half seeing Rabbit squirming in the doorway between *the* room and the kitchen with that bump on his lip rising, *God cut off my hands,* itching to ask her something.

"Go way from me, boy!" And she turned around to get her face out of his sight.

"Mamma, is you crying?"

"Ain't none of your business what I'm doing. What you all the time trying to get into grown-up people's business for? You ain't nothing but a child. . . ."

"Ain't got no business to go about right now."

"You is so got some business to go about. Wipe Gezee's nose. Don't you see him there on that floor sniffling and a-snotting? You is so got some business!"

"But Mamma, you crying!"

"Ain't none no crying. Get out of my sight!"

"Thought you was gonna get dressed up in your Sunday dress and go up to Triville. White people thinks nice of you up there to Triville if you dressed up nice and clean. Give us something else for to eat. . . ."

"Get going, boy."

"Ain't you gonna get ready, Mamma?"

"Get ready when I feel like it. Go on and wash them dishes."

"Can't get that hot water off the stove."

"Shut up, boy. Shut up and do what I told you. You ain't nothing but a shitting-assed tribulation to me!"

And the boy slunk out of the door, leaving her to recalling. Couldn't even half recollect what she had to recall, heart hurt her so. "Rabbit, leave that water on the stove. I'll get to it now in a few minutes. I just have to sit a minute and rest."

And Mariah rested, fidgeted, rested—had to get on up and wake that child laying in her belly. Thing wasn't moving one bit. Had to get up, but she felt such a need for resting. Person's arms do give out sometimes. Person just has to sit still and go back over things. Lord, how'd things come to such a pass?

Mamma, Mamma, Mamma. Jacob's voice filled her with doubt in those days of waiting and not hearing from him. Filled her so she even got right numb to the beatings and the beatings and the son-of-a-bitch-Mamma-don't-beat-me-anymore-beatings. Got right numb to everything but the coming of little Skeeter in a dim month of a winter that headed in green but turned out white. Glory Hallelujah! Baby came in alive in spite of the beatings. And a person could stand the waiting through the long January and the day that came in bright so the groundhog didn't even see his own shadow. Spring was on its way! My goodness, how the days picked up speed. By March of that year a person could feel the coming of spring clean down to the bones.

The smells of the wet ground under the room where Mariah was confined changed to a musty, throat-filling yeast. Voices of the people dropping in to see how Effie was making out with the affliction God placed on her shoulders, and those of the people passing on by rose high in the air. High and in a hurry like they woke up too late and full of throat clearing to get rid of the fogs of winter. Voices full of salt and twang, talking about sweet strawberries and raspberries they were going to raise, if they could only beat the worms. Talking up now recipes of phosphate and nitrate of soda and hog and horse hockey they could mix themselves because Hillman's Feed Store is too expensive for all except the white farmers up on the road. She heard a whole lot of talk about the biggedy Upshurs going down by letting all of the boys go so they didn't have enough hands left to keep up their place. And talk, too, about who went astray and who had a baby by who. Mostly that, over and over again—who had a baby by who. Crying disgrace, crying sorrow, crying shame on the community and the church. Bossing, "You ought to whip her ass good, Effie. Whip the devil out of her." Crying consternation, particularly "when we trying to get ahead and be some kind of a community in the world." Wailing death in the rising of the sap. Wailing death on the tail end of winter that went out white.

But Jacob came home and married Mariah. Promised her no more death. Promised to get her out of Tangier-neck.

"And here I still am, Jesus! Here I still am! Got to get going. Ain't gonna sit still listening after death no more!"

Mariah rose from the chair. Hollered to Skeeter, "Is you back yet? What did Aunt Saro Jane say?"

"Said, yes indeedy, she'd get word down the road to Pop Clem."

"Well, go on and help Rabbit with them dishes. You know he ain't able to handle no dishes in water as hot as you. . . ."

Mumbled to that thing advancing on her, "Death, get away from me. Hear me when I'm talking to you!"

And she tore on through that parlor, picking up first this thing and then the next, grabbing the dust rag from under her armpit every two or three seconds, inching the scrubbing bucket about with her feet, and leaving some things just where they were, trying to get everything straightened up, and it's a mess in the morning. Nobody believes in picking up behind themselves. Weak sun was pitched high enough for her to have got on her way somewhere!

But just about time she was getting through with the straightening up and comforting herself about how Jacob brought that bed down into the parlor and how the baby was gonna come here alive and bless God it was gonna be Jacob's, the thing crowded up in her soul. *Mariah, they gonna make you kill this child yet, or yourself, one.*

Chill of the Messenger's breath worked on up her arms. Stopped them for a minute. But she shoved that woodbox to a neater position behind the stove and got over that. No sense in dwelling on death for these things!

Things kicks you in the heart so bad when they're on

their way out into the world. Bruise your heart so bad it'll never stop bleeding. Skeeter and Gezee were the same way. Kicking and bruising just like this one. Bruise it worse after they get here with their snotty noses running from one year to the next. *Only thing is this one ain't kicking, Mariah!* "Death, get out of my sight." But Rabbit, he was different. Lazy as he could be. But he came here the fightingest one of all. Most to him was his mouth. Guess he got tired of her nursing over him. Got so lately he wouldn't keep a cough. Skeeter would cough in his face all night and he'd just act as if he didn't pay those germs any mind. Sassiest thing you ever saw. That dead young'un kicked her right smart, too. No, that wasn't exactly right. Last one acted just like this one. No! This one acted worse. It ain't even moving, Mariah! Dead, dead, near dead to the world. Her tongue played around on her dry bottom lip. Jaws just hung and trembled. Wind and the shadows from the chinaberry tree scraped against the house. Shadows drooped all over Tangierneck. Bullgrass wheat fields just stretched and crept around the trees. Yellow stubble wheat left from days gone by. Dead. Growing up barren, except for its seeds that produced more barren bull wheat. Looked like it was gonna be here forever growing up through the foundations of Tangierneck's little houses and choking them off. Everything dead.

She grabbed her guts for the kicking. "Jesus! Jesus! Time to come just like now. Not many days off or minutes either."

Baby's just as good as dead now, Mariah. That's not any kicking you feel under your heart. It's gas from the poison that sets in on you when something's dying inside of you!

Tried to push that gas out of herself, but her stomach just rolled and grumbled. She reached for something, but there was nothing to grab. Her arm fell down.

"Skeeter, bring me a piece of your notebook paper and a pencil, too." Sounds just scraped over her roughed throat. She leaned on the sideboard, and turned her back to the boy. Plunked her elbows down so hard she hurt the crazy bone. Giggling feeling gave way to tears, again and again. Gonna write to Levi.

Her face got lost in the sun rays glancing off the mirror on the sideboard. She shivered in the cold sun's stare. Got to get out! Pencil went by itself, tracing designs on the paper, trying to find somebody, far, far from Tangierneck. Got to get a-hold of Levi. *Time to come just like now!* She found herself seeing into that time to come, saying, writing, even if she wasn't making no headway with the writing now. She'd be writing then:

"Levi, hon, baby I was with when last you were home is dead. Died inside of me. Tangierneck'll kill anything that wants to live. Can't stay here no longer, Levi. Send for me, hon. I'll pay you back. Look out for a job for me. Tangierneck said I ain't got no right to feel nothing in my belly. Made me kill my child. Committee of my Judgment fixing to meet. It's a cross they're gonna nail me to. See it now as plain as day, Levi. See it now. Cross in the bullgrass. Cross in the yellow morning sun. Green trees to hide me far away. Just me and the blistering yellow sun. Or maybe they're gonna hang me in the orange sun on a day like this. Wind messing up everything and the sun red enough to drip for the crucifixion. They're gonna hang me to a cross, bleeding, with my legs stretched open. Nothing clinging to my skin but the spit they hawk on me. And my bare behind rubbing on the raw pine wood. With nothing but whore rags covering my private parts. Saying over and over again that I killed it because it was Dr. Grene's.

"Rabbit just as much as did it in front of his daddy night before the child died. Said right out as plain as day, 'Every baby coming in the Neck right now is more than likely Dr. Grene's.' Child heard that mess in that field one day when he came to pick me up. . . ."

Mariah looked up from the notebook paper. *Ain't gonna do you no good to write no time.* She prayed, "God Jesus, save me!" And her heart filled her chest with such a pain. "Gonna go to Calvertown if they come after me! Wonder what time they gonna get here?"

Air, air, if she could only get some air! She crumbled the paper.

No, you ain't going to Calvertown, Mariah. You going to the fields. . . ."

She threw her chest out and gulped in air like they taught her to do when she was in that time long ago before Skeeter was born, to get those TB germs out of her chest. Baby was gonna kick! Jesus please!

Children were getting too quiet for her. You be sad quiet

and they'll be dead quiet. You be noisy and they'll raise the roof. Had to get away from the past. Lord was gonna take care of everything!

With a terrible slam she threw a chunk of wood in the stove and threw the paper in behind it. Rabbit started right in, keeping up a racket.

> Wormy, wormy in his gut
> Wormy, wormy makes him glut. . . .

"Hush up, hush up you all. What kind of a mess is that for you to be making up for your school poem? It ain't nothing fitting to talk about in front of people."

"Gezee is got a worm."

"He ain't got no worm no more. I done give him enough of that Bumpsteads Worm Syrup to clean him out."

"Yes he is, too, Mamma! Long one in his diaper Skeeter just took off of him. Big white head on him. Tail part didn't come out. Inside of Gezee making more worms."

"Shut up, shut up, shut up!" Her scream ripped all over Tangierneck. "And go on and do what I told you."

"You ain't told me to do nothing, Mamma."

Mariah turned from the boy. Sobbing almost broke a-loose in her. "Go and bore a hole clean through to China! Help Skeeter out with them dishes."

She stood still for a minute in that room with the bed in the middle of the floor. Work wasn't all done. . . .

Ought to be an east window in this room where the sun could come in good and strong on a chilly morning. . . . People used to tell her when she was a child how she could bore a hole clean through to China. Starting out from Tangierneck! First you get about midways through the ground and you'll hear the devil and his wife fighting. Then if you get past them you can burst the rock and get to China. Told her they got more people there than a little. People don't mind having babies there. Sunshiny-faced people. Whole nation full of sunshiny-faced people. Don't mind having babies and letting them live. . . . Sun'll warm you up there and make you feel like you're somebody and everybody else is, too. . . .

Mariah felt the skin under her eyes twitch a time or two. Knew she was tired. Strength running clean out of her. About ready to break down again. But Gezee was looking up at her in a stranglehold of coughing . . . and she grabbed him up from the floor and just hugged him close to her breast. Rubbed his little snotty face all up in her breast where everything hurt to pop out. . . . But wasn't any tears gonna pop out of her in front of her children anymore. And she set him up in the big chair next to the stove . . . smoothing a blanket out around him so the cracks in the leather wouldn't pinch his little legs.

She didn't have time to be getting tired or upset with herself anymore because time was flying by. Looked like it had the devil's wings the way it kept rushing and flying hot and heavy in her face.

"Skeeter, keep a lookout for Pop Clem and them."

"They down to the church now, Mamma, talking to Daddy." Time hung still.

"They ain't coming this way, Mamma. Pop Clem turned off and went into the woods. . . ."

"Hush your mouth, boy. They is so coming!"

They ain't going your way, Mariah. Thing howled in her soul. *They ain't gonna take you with them. You ain't going their way. You going to the field.*

"They is so coming. Got to get this place straightened up. Skeeter, let me know in good time when they coming up this road so I can get myself fixed up. Ought to pull a hot comb through my hair, so I can look just as decent as them white people up there to that Calvertown hospital.

"Got to get this place straightened up. . . ." She kept on going.

Never can tell who's gonna stop by in the middle of the day soon coming up and roam through every room you got. Never can tell. It might be her that people were coming to look after without her even having everything decent for them to fix their eyes on when she lay up there after she came home from the hospital. Got to talk to Mamma Effie about getting that quilt she was fixing for her—prettiest quilt she ever saw with star patterns in it. She'd seen lots of quilts but nothing so fitting as this one to lay down under.

Never can tell who's gonna be on that cart, either, Mariah, if they do come after you in the first place. Lydy, Tillie, Mamma Bertha, Miss Naomi, Lettie Cartwright— Committee of your Judgment. Shouted you out of the church. Little mind worked in her same as a busy needle puncturing cloth. *Ought to have done it to you. You ain't nothing but a whore! Ought to have done it to you! Maybe you wasn't no whore then, but see what you done turned out to be.*

"I is so something else. I is so!" Mariah gritted her teeth and sped through the rinsing of the few clothes left in the tub. "I is so something else!"

Outdoor sun was a nice thing to be in, weak though it was, with the wind whipping steadily across her face and wet clothes flapping and sprinkling her face and arms. Had to hurry. Had to hustle. "I is so something else!"

She spied a horse cart coming up the road. Pop Clem for sure. Whipping those two brown horses like they didn't know the way! Cart loaded down. Wheels chewing up some sand! Coming my way head on. People singing up a storm. Let me get myself in this house and fix myself up decent. And she pulled at her clothes soaked from the washing she'd done, clinging to her belly like the skin on a polished Christmas apple. Clothespins she'd tried to force over Jacob's heavy overall legs snapped right in two in her hand, and the pants she'd scrubbed through three washings with the strongest kind of lye soap fell to the ground. But she couldn't bend her head to pick them up, for the whole morning busted open with sounds. Busiest kind of singing sounds a person ever heard.

"They come after me. They come after me." Rejoicing in her heart went right on singing as she went inside to change to her Sunday dress.

Singing on the cart gave way to talking. Loud, hurried-up talking when the cart pulled up.

"What's taking your mamma so long?" Mamma Bertha said.

"She's getting dressed up pretty. Gonna go up to Calvertown." Mariah could just see Rabbit grinning. He was so proud when she got dressed up nice.

"We ain't going no further than here to Triville. She got money to spend in Calvertown? Where she get it from?"

"Now Tillie," Pop Clem answered, "it ain't gonna take me that long to run her on up to Calvertown."

"Let her make some special 'rangements for to go up to Calvertown. People got to get on back home in a hurry and do something," Miss Naomi answered. "She's too high-minded for me."

"That's the way I feel about it, too," Lydy replied.

"Child, you all don't know that baby she's fixing to have gonna be something special. Woman was in the field yesterday talking about going to the hospital to have it. . . ."

"Ain't no specialer than nobody else's young'un," Lydy answered. "Ain't nobody else's young'un around here getting borned in the hospital. Mrs. Lettie can bring 'em just as good as that hospital."

"Children, children! When you all gonna stop fighting amongst yourselves?" Aunt Saro Jane's protest got lost in the chatter.

"Ain't fighting amongst nothing. Just telling it like we knows it. She gonna have herself something real *special.*"

"You all just jealous because she's pretty. And holds her head up so high." Aunt Saro Jane tried to take up for Mariah.

Tillie wrangled on. "Ain't jealous of nothing. I know one thing. If Pop Clem don't act like he's got some sense and come on back here straight from Triville, I ain't getting a way up the road with him no more."

"Me neither, me neither. I know good and well I ain't."

Vote's going against me, Lord. Mariah grabbed her work coat and wheeled out of the house.

Going out of the door and wind took charge of her stomach. Everything in her went bouncy bounce. Wind grabbed a-hold of her coat with its strong front teeth as she headed for the cart going north to Triville. Button popped off. She knew that button was hanging loose for weeks now. *Never do get time to sew for myself*—and people saw her Sunday dress!

Most of the eyes made war. Her heart ran backwards but her feet kept moving toward them.

"How far you going, Sister 'Rah?" Pop Clem didn't even look at her.

"I ain't going no further than here to Jerry Larmer's field. Can you give me a lift that far, Pop Clem?"

Voices urging her to come and go as far as Triville anyhow stayed with her even as she stood gathering the baskets Jerry Larmer had stacked against the store. She headed for the field, alone, except for Jacob's Aunt Cora Lou who wasn't eligible for the county's Welfare. Pepsi Cola sign on

Jerry Larmer's store was swinging in the wind, jutting way out from the store.

"This sure is a lonesome place. . . ."

It took Aunt Cora Lou to take her mind off the hurting, the lonesome hurting. Aunt Cora Lou was a lively high-stepper, anyhow. Only thing wrong with her according to Mariah's taste was that she wore powder and lipstick. Didn't even need that junk because she was so good looking in spite of her forty-some odd years. Had as good a heart as you'd want to find anywhere. It was just bruised a little and made her talk coarse sometimes.

Most of Tangierneck found a whole lot wrong with her. Married a migrant worker, or at least she said she did, but since she wasn't married in that Tangierneck Church and went off so funny without even saying goodbye to anybody, who can tell what kind of sinful life she's been leading. And she had two little babies that late in life. Her running off to the city that way wouldn't have been so bad if she hadn't deserted Pop Percy and her own dear sister, Bertha Ann, when they needed her so bad on the land. Wouldn't be so bad now except for her dropping those two little children on Bertha Ann. Couldn't say too much about her on that score though because she did send money down the road faithful to her sister. Man done left her. But she'd come on down the road, too, any old time to see after her children.

"Mariah, don't let this place get the best of you, honey! You ought to walk alone like me. I walked all the way out here by myself this morning. People around here just jealous of you because you so pretty and in spite of all they did to you, you go on living. Mostly they after you because you don't be with them."

"They put me out of the church, Aunt Cora Lou."

"They ain't exactly put you out of that church, honey, but they did do you bad. I was there and I saw. You and that poor little Rosey, Lord, Lord. . . . No, Mariah, you left that church because you couldn't stand their narrow-mindedness about life. Tangierneck'll kill anything that wants to live outside the shadows of their white man God. . . . Thinks they gonna get ahead that way. . . ."

"Aunt Cora Lou, you talking against God!"

"Child, hush, you know I ain't talking against no God."

"Who you gonna go to for help sometimes, Aunt Cora

Lou? You got to go somewhere. A lot of times to white people. I'm just waiting for Miss Bannie to come down the road. Gonna hail her and ask her to take me on up to Calvertown."

"Mariah, I wasn't gonna leave Tangierneck 'til tomorrow, but I swamp it, I'll go today and make arrangements for you myself rather than to see you turn to that woman for help!"

"She ain't done nothing to me, Aunt Cora Lou." A dull aching went all through Mariah.

"Might not've done nothing to you, but she done aplenty to my sister."

"That ain't none of my business, Aunt Cora Lou. I don't be listening to no gossip about people."

"You better start in listening to something, gal. I ain't in favor of you going to that Calvertown hospital neither. I works in one of those places in Philadelphia and they treats colored like dogs. . . . Tell you what I'm gonna do. Get me a ride up to Calvertown this afternoon and stop in and see that Dr. Grene about coming down here and looking after you. . . ."

"Don't want no Dr. Grene waiting on me. . . ."

"How come, gal? He's right good they tell me. Best colored doctor anywheres around."

"Ain't got no money for to pay him."

"Well, how you gonna pay the Calvertown Hospital?"

"Jacob'll. . . ."

"Jacob ain't gonna do nothing neither, gal. Even if he wanted to. Don't you feel this wind? I'll pay that doctor my ownself."

"No!"

"What you getting so upset about, Mariah? Ain't you just got through telling me about how you so worried with the condition of your children? Ain't you just got through saying how you want this child to live?"

"Yes 'um."

"Well, what's wrong with me making arrangements with that Dr. Grene?"

"It ain't nothing wrong with it, I don't expect, Aunt Cora Lou. Ain't nothing wrong with it, excepting . . ."

"Excepting what?"

"Excepting nothing."

6

Sand in the high part of the land shifts. Sandy ground along the swamp's edge is a slick muddy-looking sucker. Road changes so much. Yellow-gray going into oyster-shell mud. Getting low as it nears Deep Gut. Water of the steely cold Nighaskin River slurped out to meet Jacob. Crawled a considerable distance up his boots before he even got ready to deal with it. His shoulders almost fell down. But he traveled on. Couldn't even deal with a thing in a right way of thinking since Mariah took off on that cart.

"Now ain't that a heifer-and-a-half for you!" Must be the water flowing up from the Gut blurring his eyesights. Wind wouldn't even let up. Ought to talk to his God. . . . Never felt so disconnected from the Good Lord and Saviour before in his whole lifetime. But he couldn't even stop to take stock of himself. Just went a-slouching on to the Gut, thinking again how anger is a sinful disease. And how he was getting out from underneath all of these burdens. Getting his family out from underneath of them. Gonna have it out with his papa soon as ever he got to the Gut. Gonna tell his papa, I'm leaving! I'm leaving less'n you speak to Bannie about the land! And that was that. For he knew one thing for sure—he wasn't gonna be no murderer for Mariah, for those scoundrels chasing after him down the path from the house, for his mamma, for Ol jabbing him clean up to the hilt of the knife about the school for all these young'uns on his hands, for those dat-blamed-blasted rye seed, for nothing!

"I ain't a-gonna do it." He watched his spit sail away on the crest of the muddiest-looking water a person ever saw. . . . Getting down to the Gut. Papa'll have to get rid of the burdens Bannie saddled us with his own self. I ain't a-gonna do it! Gonna go right 'long with Mariah. Getting out.

Confounded headache of a woman ain't had no business getting on Pop Clem's cart!

Weak feeling washed all over him. Had to fight that thing off. Got to get to the Gut.

Water swung around trees, over the dead bullgrass lining the marshy road edge. Over the best strawberry-growing ground in Tangierneck. Over the black ripe-smelling earth steadily getting gutted of its pines and cypresses by some no-good-meaning body's bulldozer. And still the chugging growl of the bulldozer bossed his Tangierneck air.

Pain sliced his stomach half in two. He sank down on a damp tree stump, in a silent rage, a head-hammering rage, arguing with that Welfare glutton, Mariah.

"Queen of the hill, that's what I made you. Everybody talking, even though you'd done had a baby, about how good you looked when I come home and married you. . . . Still look good. Ain't a prettier woman in Mantipico county. But I married you, didn't I? . . . Still, still in all, Skeeter was mine. . . . And still, still in all, woman, I'm first responsible for any debts made in my family." And Jacob breathed deep and cleared his throat, where a mean song hurt to get out:

> Pull off them shoes I bought you
> Pull off them socks I bought you
> Pull off that hat I bought you
> You know you mistreated me
>
> Pull off that wig I bought you
> Let your devilish head go bald.

Woman mess with you enough make you want to sing anything before you catch yourself. Bitch! Bitch!

Such a sickness of his going-nowhere self came over him that he got up and moved on off. Held his lips tight for he really didn't believe in devilish songs like that boy, Willie Ried. That man believed in singing the first thing worrying his lips.

Besides, besides, his pretty-headed, mean-headed woman —soft-headed—my Lord, yes. Had hair enough to share with two or three women. Besides, besides, the few pairs of shoes she ever got she bought herself. But he was going to get the money together for them, if she'd a-waited. He was gonna get up money for shoes and everything else. And a hospital, too, if you please, Mam, for this new young'un. For he didn't have to have meat sandwiches stuck in his lunch pail. Some men complained about gas on the stomach from eating dried bean soup when there wasn't anything else. Some men just weren't gonna do right. Mariah ought to realize that thing. Bunch of them believed in talking that blackguard talk about women and things like that. But he didn't believe in that kind of foolishness. Mariah ought to realize that thing! Ought to realize there was nothing in the world meant as much to him as her and her wants. . . .

A voice setting up a regular cackle sprang out from a bunch of poplars just before he got to the Gut. "Jacob Upshur, ain't that you?"

"I reckon it is, Miss Louisa. How you?" He was in a hurry to keep on going but he stopped for a minute, giving the sharp little-eyed, chalky-colored white woman a chance to answer. After all, you have to be considerate of people even if you don't take to them much.

She never said how she was or anything like that. She just crept up along beside him, getting down that road. Clumping and sloshing that gnarled walking stick she was famous for carrying on and off the road. Must be going blind. Asking about the baby due in a whining high voice. Transparent veins ran all blue crisscross her brow and her hands. She whined to him, "Jacob, your last baby died a funny kind of death. Think this one'll make it?"

"God's willing, I pray," he barked at her. But to himself he said, "What you know about death, woman? You ain't never gonna die!"

"Cold's setting in, Jacob. Looks like it might be a stiff hard cold. But for all you know it might be a green winter after all. . . . I'm going to the swamp to get me some holly out. 'Spect I better get some fern, too. You can sell more funeral wreaths now it looks like than ever before. Good thing Mariah's daddy made the connections up there to Baltimore for to sell our wreaths. Don't know how I'd make it through the winter. . . ."

"You'll make it. I got to hurry on, Miss Louisa." Felt to himself like he did the double-splits getting away from that obstruction, smelling like mothballs and the old kerosene stove she used to cook on, and looking like starvation in person! Funniest thing to him was how Miss Bannie didn't look out for her own dear aunt. White people were the funniest set of people to him. Any way you look at it they didn't have no common and ordinary understanding. Desert their old when their old got down and out.

"Child died according to God's will," he flung back to Miss Louisa. And he kept straight on going.

That's the same excuse you gave Mariah, too, Jacob, when little Mary passed. Little mind sicced him on down that road.

And he almost said it to Mariah again this morning. For enough of her hangdog-faced mourning was enough! But if he had said that thing, she would have made him live it all over again. Made him see that little child laying up there on the bed with her fists all balled up. Give a woman a hint of what's on your mind and they'll tell you all you're thinking and then some. Make you see every detail of something. Something past ain't at all worthwhile dealing with.

Still, Jacob dealt with it now. Couldn't help himself. And the memory of that little Mary's death walked with him all the way to the Gut.

Face on that little one was nothing but hungry-looking lips. Blue and cracked. He would've tried to straighten out its little face. Didn't want to put it in the ground with such a look of discontentment on its mouth. But when he reached out to touch it, Mariah took his head off. "Tell your dead young'un it was God's will!"

"Calm down, Mariah. Calm down."

" 'Course, I guess God looks down in mercy on us simple-minded folks. What we offering the children but catch-as-catch-can?"

"Calm down, woman!" He almost hit her. Hadn't been for Willie Ried being over to the house at the time, guess he would've.

"I hear tell us niggers die a whole lot sooner than the white. Census people got it all wrote down." Willie Ried looked up from the little coffin he was helping to build.

"Tell him like it is, Willie Ried!" Mariah hollered so.

"Go on back to heathen country where you come from. Get out of my family's business!"

He could hear himself now trying to tell Willie Ried and Mariah, too, how God was in charge of things. But he

couldn't get a word in edgewise with Mariah's carrying on.
And he had walked off, down this same road, in search of
peace and a time alone with his God. But Skeeter hadn't
let him go off by himself. Followed him down this road,
clutching a-hold of his coattail, trying to help him sing:

> Why should I feel discouraged,
> Why should the shadows fall,
> Why should my heart feel lonely
> And long for heaven and home.

And busting in on his private thoughts: "Daddy, how come
God made us niggers?"

"I don't know, boy. Boy! Boy! How come you calling us
by that word?"

"Uncle Willie Ried just called us by that. Daddy, what's
a nigger?"

"Ain't no such a thing."

"Everybody calls us that. Ain't we nothing? Ain't I something, Daddy?"

"Sure you something. You my boy, ain't you?" And
Jacob kept right on singing:

> When Jesus is my portion,
> My constant friend is he,
> For his eye is on the sparrow
> And I know he watches me.

But Skeeter wouldn't let up on him. "Daddy, what's a
nigger?"

"Nigger ain't nothing but somebody who can't do no
better. But you can do better."

"Better'n who?"

"Better'n all who's gone before you. You can help build
this Neck up to something. You's an Upshur. Upshur built
this Neck up to what it is now. Built that church. . . ."

"Can I do better'n you right now?"

"Boy, what you trying to do, sass me? You ain't even
big as a wart on a fly's nose yet. You can't even think about
doing better'n me till you learn all what I did and what I'm
gonna yet do. Can you oyster? Can you pull up a whole
boatload of oysters from the bottom in a day's time? Can
you pick up a raspberry worm and mash him in your fin-

gers? Can you do without eating when other people's around you hungry?"

"No sir. But, yes sir . . . I was hungry for that piece of horehound candy I give to Rabbit yestiddy."

"Which part of you was hungry? Your stomach or your mouth or your eyes?"

"I don't know."

"Reckon if you hadn't eaten that whole pound bag down to a few stray pieces before Rabbit fastened his eyes on you, you'd a-knowed? Whole lot of things you don't know. Whole lot of things you got yet to learn."

"I knowed Mary was hungry." And still that boy wouldn't let go of him. "And I give her a piece of my candy when Mamma went running to get somebody to help unlock Mary's jaws."

"And what she do, boy?"

"Just hunched up her shoulders and backed off of it."

"Boy! Boy!" And it was nothing else for Jacob to do except sing:

> When Jesus is my portion,
> My constant friend is he,
> For his eye is on the Sparrow,
> And I know he watches me."

Child didn't know pure nothing.

"Boy, don't you know what rigor mortis is when it sets in? You got to learn a few things. . . . Build this Neck up to something."

"White man down to Jerry Larmer's says this Neck ain't never gonna be nothing. Says it's a lonesome place and people don't want to be in no lonesome place. Nothing but niggers. Daddy, is we part Indian? Indians ain't niggers. . . ."

"Don't say that word to me no more. Hear me when I'm talking to you."

> For Jesus is my portion. . . .

"Daddy, how come you ain't never done better till yet? How come you let Mary die?"

"White man ain't been inclined to let me do no better, boy!"

And Jacob looked down at his son in his grass sack outfit, and turned away in a hurry. Boy had too much questions in his big old eyes.

"Jesus a white man?"

"He ain't no such a thing. He ain't no kind of color. People who painted his pictures just put him out to look like that, I 'spect. . . ."

"Is the white man in charge, or God?"

"Let go me, boy. Can't you see I'm on my way to do something. . . ." *Can't you see? Can't you see?* He felt like crying out to the boy, "I ain't no nigger. I can do better!"

But instead of saying that he just sent that Skeeter chasing. Thoughts of that boy and his future pursued Jacob all the way to the Gut. And he tried to make haste to *do* something then. . . .

Just like now, he thought. And such a terrible beating of his heart took place. On this day which was well over a year—Lord have mercy, it must be going on two—since little Mary passed, he was still on the same path to *do* something. With a new young'un coming up, he still had got nothing done.

He picked up his feet and made it on down to the Gut. Gonna get something straightened out with his papa today!

Wind from the water is the coldest thing. Day on the land can be the least little bit cold, but the same day on the banks of the Gut with a ripping wind blowing is more than a notion to take.

Jacob thought these things soon as he hit the beginning of the long stretch of sand and mud all packed down with oyster shells right off the water.

In such a wind a man can't even breathe right, ordinarily, let alone if he takes up time talking with people and gulping down a whole lot of cold air. For the wind'll freeze every bone a person's got. It'll turn his lungs into a hunk of burning ice, if he's the kind that faces winter with one of those summer colds that lasts until it gets good and ready to go. And Jacob was such a kind.

Therefore he tried to speed on past that sandy-colored, poetry-reciting, self-appointed preacher, dunce, Sandy Fitzhugh. Aunt Saro Jane's boy, trying to hold him up with a reading from the Book of Revelations about how the world was gonna end in fire. That was the only way that Sandy could see in his misreadings of the Scriptures that the colored man was ever gonna get rid of wars and the "evil" white man.

"God's gonna send down the fire and burn them all up!" Sandy was a regular disgrace to the community. He dressed worse than some of those migrant workers since he came back home from the war the whole world got mixed up in. He was the only one of the nine men Tangierneck contributed that even got back home alive. And he came back crazy in the head from the poison gas. He didn't even have enough sense left to wear shoes in the dead of winter when there was snow on the ground. But he wouldn't catch a cold to save his life.

Jacob gave him a nickel and passed on. Thinking how you have to look out for your own when the whole world turns its back on them. You have to find some way somehow to keep your own alive. And his own was the whole Tangierneck, but most especially it was his young'uns and Mariah. Forever Mariah. And he was sick to his stomach from the needs and wants of his Mariah. And from the wind that wouldn't turn around no way, nohow. And the task before him—to speak to his papa about Bannie and the land.

His whole heart and brains felt tongue-tied as he hustled on down that shoreline toward Mariah-the-Second. Without a word, he sped past a heap of young men caulking a boat and whiling away time with a whole lot of bragging about women and complaints about Tangierneck not offering them a thing. And with hardly a mumble he greeted and passed by the grimfaced clusters of old gray fathers lacing fishing nets and consulting worn pages of the '29 almanac. Two or three head of them tried to get him to tarry and talk about Mariah and the new baby due in, and the wind— the "infernal wind," the "confounded wind," the "wind sent by a just and wrathful God to remind man who was boss. . . ." But Jacob wasn't gonna tarry no more!

Jacob's uncle Johnathon, hobbling about on one leg and a crutch, greeted him soon as he set foot on Mariah-the-Second with a "What you looking so mad about, Jake?"

"What you mean mad?" Jacob glared at his sunken-faced Uncle Johnathon who was always just as near drunk as he could be. Stayed that way ever since he got his leg broke off piloting some rich white people's pleasure boat up there to Atlantic City, New Jersey, in a storm. "I'm not mad, I'm just gonna get something settled with Papa 'bout Bannie and this land. Gonna get it settled this morning. Where's Papa at, anyhow?" Jacob started pacing.

"Went down the far shore few minutes ago. Said he'd be right back. If I was you, boy, I wouldn't bring nothing like that up to him. . . ."

"Well, what's this Bannie mess, anyhow, Uncle Johnathon?" Jacob exploded. A man can't turn in this community without somebody signifying some shi-shit! "I got a right to know. I got a new young'un coming up. I got children growing up. Don't want me to ask Papa? Who else I'm supposed to ask?"

"You could ask me." The gray-bearded man breathed heavily. Breath short from wind and that bootleg junk he kept sipping. Face all splotchy. Tongue slippery. He stared at Jacob steadily, repeating very slowly his offer.

"Well, tell me then!" Jacob got all squint-eyed. Jaws hardening to rocks.

"See, boy, Bannie is the issue of your grandmother's cousin by the name of Ella. Your grandmother and Ella grew up together up there on the plantation where Haim-the-First came a-walking and shooting and killing every Nanticoke Indian in sight. And they was just as crazy about each other as you please. Nothing could kill the love them two had for each other. Even when your grandmother got pitched down into this here Tangierneck by her old daddy, the second Haim, all because she was born to him by a mulatto slave and had started in showing her true colors by associating with the blacks, Ella used to sneak down to see her.

"I mean to tell you, boy, Ella was faithful to Mamma. She didn't even stop coming after Mamma married your granddaddy, Bard Tom. Didn't care if he was black. She'd come right on. She had a long trip to make, too. 'Specially after she married Jim Dudley over there to Countess Ann. And after she had Bannie and the child grew up to be some size, she would bring her right along to play with me and your papa. . . ."

"Yep," Jacob said. Looking away from the old man with his back stiffened now against the cabin, staring out into the troubled waters the same as if he was possessed by something. Breath getting shorter and shorter.

"Anyway, that connection was all cut off for a while when two of Ella's brothers and a half brother of Mamma's came down here before day broke a-loose on a Monday morning in September of the year 1875 and did away with Mamma. Rode with sheets over their heads to hide themselves, but all the colored knew it must've been them for they never did like Mamma's marrying Papa and turning this land into something. Those fellows had already done away with Papa—never would own up to it though. Told people they'd seen Bard Tom sail away from here on an ocean-going boat. But they hadn't seen nothing of the kind. Blood was all over their clothes when your Aunt Saro Jane went up to do their washing. Mamma Margaret learned from that. So she followed the sky trail of the buzzards up to the Royal Oaks tree and found the bones and things. Went a-traipsing over to Countess Ann to see the Law about investigating. It didn't do her no good.

"Wasn't two months after Papa's death that they came and got Mamma, too. They wanted this land back and wasn't gonna be satisfied until they got it.

"Dragged her down this Deep Gut road. Tore her dress clean off, dragging her over these sands." Johnathon's voice was getting huskier all the time. Jacob cleared his own throat hard. Picked mud from a stack of baskets and threw it into the water. The muddy, swollen waters of a troubled day.

"Had her all tied up into a two-mule-team horse cart, but she wiggled a-loose part of the ways and jumped from that cart. Couldn't get free altogether, though, and they just dragged her on. Over those sand burrs and briars and things like that. Me and your father saw the whole thing. We ran after that cart, crying and trying to raise a commotion to get the people up, but the people lived a considerable distance from each other in that day and time. We even saw Mamma go down in this Gut when the horses hove onto the ferry. Heard her hollering, 'Hold on to the land. . . . Keep up the Church your Daddy left you. . . .' and so on and so forth until the water closed her mouth clean up. . . ."

"Why you telling me all this, Uncle Johnathon? Ain't

many head that don't already know it. Ain't this all the more reason we ain't got no kind of business mixed up with Bannie?"

"I'm getting to the point of what you wants to know, son. See, in the years that followed, Ella kept up an interest in us, taking us over to her place sometimes to help out on her farm. . . . And your papa and Bannie grew closer and closer together until Bannie's papa, Jim Dudley, got scared of what might happen and chunked her on up in the cities. In fact, your father and Bannie . . . well, I don't know exactly how to tell you. . . ."

Anger took over Jacob's heart. Smote the part of his soul where the news crackled and smoldered, ready to break out in a fire he wasn't even gonna know what to do with.

"Why'd she have to come back to this section after all these years?" Jacob clawed mud furiously from the stack of baskets.

"That's just it! Her cousin, Haim Crawford, could have sold her a big hunk of land up there in Haimawalkin and not even missed it. But no, she had to come on down here and buy a piece of your father's land—and throw her ass at him again, too!" Seemed to Jacob the very temples in his uncle's head was just about to bust.

"I don't want to hear neither 'nother word about it!" Jacob cut him off.

"Well, I was just gonna tell you . . ."

"I said shut up about it!" Jacob kicked over the whole stack of baskets.

His uncle just backed back. Kept his mouth shut for the longest few minutes Jacob ever felt. And Jacob wished that the water lashing the sides of the boats would just swallow them all up. The whole knee-bending, broken-assed family—him, his father. And his uncle, too! 'Specially with him sitting now on the stool by the cabin door looking at Jacob with his eyes all full of pity, switching the subject, saying to him, "Jacob, this kind of weather don't make no kind of sense."

"No, it don't." Jacob answered all calm. Couldn't stand for nobody to pity him!

And from his calm, Jacob guessed, his uncle took heart and commenced in loading him down with talk like, "Jake, boy, if we could only make it over to the Virginia side of the water tomorrow, we'd be able to get us enough oysters to pay down on the hospital bill for your woman. Virginia side's got plenty of water that ain't even rented out. . . . Water was never divided fair in the first place. . . ."

"We ain't no pirates," Jacob kept telling his uncle. "God's gonna send a change." But his uncle didn't seem to hear him. He just kept right on saying the same advice over and over again until Jacob's father set foot on Mariah-the-Second with a raging against the wind and Mariah and the world in general. The giant-faced, bushy-bearded man stormed up and down the boat. His tallness bent to a stiff arc against the wind.

"Boy, what you been dillydallying up on the land so long for? You could have been down here an hour or more ago helping me and your Uncle Johnathon. You know your uncle ain't able to do but so much, but you got to waste working time on dry land, all hugged up to that no-account whore of yours!"

"You . . . you . . . devil . . . devil!" Jacob said it before he knew it. And his father staggered against the culling board. And it seemed to Jacob for a minute that the old man's very eyes bled blood. And Jacob almost reached for him to hug him, to hit him, to knock him out of his sight, but he ended up standing all clench-fisted and saying, "Don't you call Mariah no whore no more, Papa. The whore, if there is one, is *your* Miss Bannie. My children is half starved, same as everybody else's in the Neck on account of *your* Miss Bannie. You don't think I know what's been going on. But I know! And Papa, less'n you get yourself disentangled from that woman, I'm leaving. Taking my family and leaving!"

"Get your ass off this land!" The old man stood, unsteady and wheezing. "Never thought you'd get around to lying on me, too!"

He put Jacob in mind of a tall young sapling struck by lightning and killed, but still holding on all pitiful-like to the ground, thinking it could live. And for this Jacob lashed out at him again.

"You ain't no young man, Papa. Ain't no fool like an old fool! You act right feebleminded, Papa. You ought to go on up to the house and pick holly and make wreaths. . . ."

"Jacob, Jake boy. . . ." His father's voice faltered.

And before Jacob could say two more words, the old

man jumped into the water, kicking through the breakers on up to the shore. Head just a-shaking same as if he had the apoplexy or something. Announcing to the men gathering around him at the shore, "I ain't got neither son left."

Men on the shore flocked all around him, hollering, "Calm down, Percy," and the like of that.

A tall scary boy from another boat jumped into the water to head for the shore to get in on the commotion. Fool forgot he couldn't swim. And he foundered all about in the wind-filled water, crying, "Somebody save me! Save me!"

Somebody on the shore hollered, "Fool, get up and walk. You ain't in nothing but two feet of water!" And the youngster made his way on up to the shore.

"I ain't goin' nowhere!" Jacob raged in his guts. A hotter-than-hell kind of rage burned from his neck clean up to his eyeballs—stifled his holler. Felt like a fool! A standing-stone-still-kind-a fool. And a listening fool, too: "You ought not to have spoke to your father that-a-way. . . ." Uncle Johnathon advised until he gave up to Jacob's silence. A hard never-giving-in silence.

So Jacob got down to fixing the carburetor that didn't need fixing, and the fuel pump and the plugs, and just whatsoever he could unscrew, take apart, and put together again, but mostly he sank down to a cripple-hearted grieving for the day going nowhere. And finally, for the day clean gone and his empty hands. Empty for Mariah. . . .

In the rising boat, on the coming-in tide, he watched the sun ship west and the Nighaskin chop it into a million orange slices. It was night. He wanted to go home. But more than that, he wanted to stop by the old home place and tell his papa that he wasn't gonna leave. So Jacob raced ahead of every living soul on up the Deep Gut road, going home. Had to stop his papa's feelings from being so hurt! Felt like he wanted to tell how pictures of his childhood rose up in him in the waning day: A little plow that his father made for him out of tin cans and a branch from a hickory nut tree, the way Jacob used to get up earlier than his father in the morning and chase downstairs so he could be ready and waiting to follow his papa down to the Gut, and, more than anything, the sure-handed manner of his papa, taking him up on his lap when Jacob got too sleepy to chase and run, saying to him, "Boy, one day you gonna grow up to be master over all you survey. . . ." All of those things came to him in the late day, and took charge of him now as he hurried to get to his papa. And he made up his mind: "First thing I'm going to tell Papa when I get there is I ain't leaving him. No siree!"

There wasn't but one thing that got in Jacob's way and that was Rabbit and Skeeter waylaying him on the road and asking a whole heap of questions about what he did all day. Children brought him good news, too. Mariah didn't go to get the Welfare—and a new puzzlement: Aunt Cora Lou making some kind of arrangements with Dr. Grene.

That confounded Mariah wouldn't ease up on him. First one demand after the other! And any way Jacob spelled them out they all added up to money. But he wasn't gonna desert the land to get more money, to get nothing! Wasn't gonna leave! God have mercy. His face swoll up so that the path to his papa's house almost got blotted out, but he made it on up the road.

Jacob tried to tell his papa he wasn't going away. Tried to catch a-hold of his eye as soon as he walked in the kitchen of that big white house. His sassy-mouthed sister, Irena, managed to come out of her world of high school dreams to have a few nice words for him. Those two little girls his Aunt Cora Lou left in Mamma Bertha's charge, Lil Bits and Mamie, looking for all the world like little Concord grapes, had some hugs and kisses for him. Mamma Bertha stopped her eternal cleaning up of one thing after the other to ask him to sit with them a spell and have something to eat—but his papa sat silent, staring out into the night, not even so much as turning around when Jacob said to him a couple of times, "How you doing there, Pop?"

Pop Percy just sat for an eternity with his shoulders all hunched up like a bunch of tall rocks—like a mountain a man couldn't climb. A mean cold mountain. All he was doing was dipping a hunk of yellow cheese in a bowl of hot coffee and sucking on that cheese when it got soft. Man had never even taken his coat off since he came up from the Gut.

Finally, he broke down and said to Mamma Bertha without so much as turning around, "Take a good look at your son, Mr. Jacob, woman. You ain't gonna be able to feast your eyes on him much longer. He's deserting us. Just like you drove his brothers to do. That's what that heifer he's got stuck up on that hill is driving him to do!"

"Percy, don't talk like that in front of these children." Mamma Bertha's whole body tightened up.

Lil Bits and Mamie cringed under the table, and Jacob's mamma lumbered all nervous and heavy across the big steamy kitchen wiping off this and wiping off that. Always wiping off something! Hands were nothing but rough bark now. And her eyes were weary and tired and all filled up with aggravation. She could handle everybody in the world but not her own husband.

Jacob's stomach curled up in a gripping ball.

"Get the young'uns out of this room if you don't want them to hear the truth," Pop Percy rumbled. "Cora Lou ain't had no business leaving them here on us. Got time to tend to everybody else's troubles but her own." And he turned to Jacob. "Guess you know that strumpet Cora Lou took off from here today to go make arrangements for that high-minded thing you got stuck up on the hill there, boy. . . ." Louder and louder the old man roared. Shoulders rising higher and higher. "Lil Bits and Mamie, you all get out from under that table and go on up to bed!"

Room of people seemed to hang still, waiting.

"Children's got to do their homework, Percy!" Tired, tired to the bone, Mamma Bertha grabbed Mamie and Lil Bits, rushing them off to the parlor—throwing a look back at Papa like she hated him. And Jacob guessed she did. And he was tired. Tired of their wars and their hatred, and the way they just kept on clinging together and hating mostly. But it was *him* hating, he thought for a minute. And he wanted them to let go of him, to stop needing him! He started in coughing and swallowing hard to keep from vomiting. And he choked up so, he couldn't say a word. River of sweat poured down his face, and all he could do was swallow.

"Don't be lighting no lamp in that parlor, woman! I ain't got no children left here to study but this straying cat, Irena. All she's getting educated for is to desert the land. You send Cora Lou's children on up to bed. They done burned enough of my coal oil studying! I got to hold on to every cent. Hear me, woman! Every cent!" The big man rose from the chair, knocking over the bowl of coffee.

Cheese drippings quivered on his beard. His face was all a-quiver. Jacob didn't know what to say. He just stared at him. He tried to say "Papa" something, "Papa" anything, but the tortured man roared on louder and louder, stomping off toward the parlor, catching Mamma Bertha in the doorway as she was heading back for the kitchen. Bellowing over her as she sank down in a chair. "I got to hold on to every cent, woman. Got to pay off Bannie. I got to see her tonight, ain't I? Neither Cora Lou nor you and neither child I got cares whether I can meet the bill!"

"Percy, Cora Lou divided up the last cent she had with me before she went up that road." And Mamma Bertha pulled out the change bag she kept tucked in her titty strap. "How much you short in your payment to Bannie?"

"Git on in that parlor and blow out the lamps like I told you!"

And Jacob never saw anything like the way Pop Percy knocked the moneybag from Mamma Bertha's hand.

Never imagined anything like himself grabbing his papa and holding him, wrestling to keep him from messing with his mamma anymore. "You ain't gonna hit my mother. . . ."

"I ain't hit her, boy! Take your dumb-headed self and get out of my house."

But Jacob didn't, couldn't hear him.

"Not with me sitting here looking at you, you ain't gonna hurt her. Not for Bannie, not for nobody, you ain't a-gonna do it!"

The tired and mad-all-day man just spewed. He tried to draw in a good cleansing breath but he was too full to suck it down and the rotten mess just ran all over the floor, and every gut he had, it looked like, poured out of him, sour and fouling up the air, and all over his papa and over his mamma trying to get him off of Papa.

"Jacob, be yourself, boy! Be yourself!" Mamma Bertha smothered him into her bosom all hot and heavy, heavy and crying with those old deep chest-wracking spasms he hadn't heard since he left home a long time ago.

"Jacob, I ain't never thought you'd desert me. Ain't never thought it." The old man rose up. "Jake, I ain't never thought it."

Papa, don't cry that-a-way. Don't need you to walk with me to the door.

"Go on away from here, boy. I ain't nothing but some shit."

"Don't talk that way, Papa!" *Don't break down that way. Don't be leaning on me going to the door.* And he shook his papa from his shoulders. He'd had enough of weeping and moaning for a whole lifetime.

"Don't be throwing me off, boy, like that." The old man got his bossing voice back. "Don't be acting all hinckty to me when I done held up under more loads than you can ever carry. You ain't nothing! And I want you to take that no good whore of yours and get her off my land. That thing of yours'll give her cunt to any man she thinks is going to do her any good."

"She ain't never gave it to you, has she, Papa? She ain't never gave it to you!" And Jacob, he was all the way back in the house before he could even get himself started on the way home.

Cried to God. Cried to Jesus all inside of himself. "Don't you be talking about Mariah that-a-way, Papa. Now I want you to cut out your carrying on!"

Irena wasn't nothing but a teetotal mess, tearing herself away from those dishes she'd been slopping over, flinging herself into the middle of everything. Mamma Bertha stopped her grim-faced wiping up of Jacob's spew from the floor and hollered to Irena, "Get your stinking ass from between those two men. . . ."

"I ain't got no stinking ass! I ain't got no stinking ass! I wash up every morning when it's fitting to do so. Tired of you saying things to me like that. Be so glad to get out of here. . . ."

"Children, family, all you all quiet down!" Mamma Bertha shook her head and moaned, "Jesus, help me, help me." 'Til there wasn't anybody making any noise but Mamma Bertha wailing, "Come to Jesus. Family ought to kneel down and pray together."

And Irena whispering all across her, "Jake, Jake, I'm getting out of here. Mariah ain't wrong about this place. You going too? Jake, ain't you going too?"

"Children, stop, stop it, you hear? Family fight can't bring nothing but destruction! Children, let us kneel and seek for the ways of God," Mamma pleaded.

When Jacob flew out of that house there was nobody kneeling but Mamma Bertha and those two little Concord grapes, hugging up to his mamma and wiping her nose, dripping little drops of blood. Praying, "Jesus, save my family. . . . For we know not the hour or the day. . . ."

Jacob stood by the pump bench shivering. Well, that was nothing but the cold setting in hard, he tried to reason. Nothing but the cold. Green winter wasn't coming in this year. That's what the Lord was trying to tell by sending such cold before October was even out.

But he had the hardest time choking up that pump to get some water to wash the vomit off his coat. He was plain cold and tired.

But harder was the time of stomping on off home. Trying not to deal with the notion that Mamma's peculiar kind of nosebleed meant exactly what it always meant—death in the family.

Wasn't gonna be no death! Gonna tell Mariah that in a convincing way of speaking, soon as ever he got to that house. And he tried to still the raging torments flooding his soul. Feet just about ready to give out. Do him good to sit by the fire and soak his feet in a tub of hot water for a while. Do him good to be still.

But he couldn't stop himself from pacing up and down the floor of that squeezy kitchen once he did get in his own house.

Mariah did try to get him to have something to eat. She'd cooked up a nice mess of greens. He didn't know whose field she'd scrounged them out of, considering how rare greens were right in through this time of year. She kept saying to him, in that nice way she had of inching into somebody's feelings at the close of a weary day, "Jacob, now you know right good and well you ought to sit down and have something to eat."

But his feet wouldn't let him be still. And his soul wouldn't either. And to save his soul he couldn't even pray. Didn't know what to say to his God, what with Mariah sitting so drawn-faced up there by that stove in the midst of a stack of muslin and a whole bunch of old newspapers Vyella brought down the road for her to make bed pads out of for the time of birth. Looked to him like she was just about ready to break down and cry every two seconds. If he could only swallow the sickness in his throat, he'd say to her, 'Rah, ain't no sense in grieving for a death that

ain't even promised! But sorrow liked to have overcome
him. And Lord have mercy, those children kept coughing
and whining for this and that. He broke out in a fit of
coughing his ownself.

"You can't keep no cold out of your chest less'n you eat,
Jacob. A person just has to eat to stay alive and you ain't
been eating nothing now and lately, Jacob. . . ."

Call my name one more time, woman. Call my name
one more time and I'm just as lief to light up and wring
your neck, Jacob thought.

Call my name or my attention to one more idle-minded
thing. Just one more nagging thing, and I'm lief to do anything wrong and out of the ordinary! Just because your
hands is so tired, and your feet look like clay clods from
dragging yourself through that potato field this day. And
just because you keep humming that old nonsense kind of
tune. You ain't doing nothing but pushing air out from
your nose. You can't sing!

And just because something ought to be done. Especially
about that Bannie messing with his children's growth and
his Mariah and his papa and God have mercy! But most and
especially just because when a man gets good and tired
enough to do something there's nothing left but for him to
do something.

"Where you going to, Jacob?" Mariah said just when he
lit for the door.

"My bowels don't feel so good, 'Rah. I'm going out in
the field," was all he said before he took off into the night
to get himself together to do something.

7

"It's cold . . . it's cold . . . turning to a stiff hard cold, I hope, so it won't be no green winter. . . . Wonder the wind don't unhinge this house and sweep it over this shifting-assed hill. . . . Sand ain't no rock to build on."

Shudders ran all through Mariah's shoulders, ran in trembling, curdling liquid around the baby anchored in her belly—fidgeting. She laid her sewing aside and rose from the wobbly chair. "Jacob, why you gone so long?"

Wind'll make you talk to yourself. It makes an awesome company—growling and snorting worse than a dog gone mad. "Gonna lick and lap these clapboards clean off the house! Jesus!"

She added another chunk of pine to the charred stumps in the little tin stove. Thick, nose-biting smoke wrapped around her throat. Its sharp piny sweetness cut painful paths in her nostrils. She slapped the damper in the chimney too much to the side, trying to get the flames to draw, and she backed away, sucking her singed fingers as her free hand banged the damper up a little straighter. Long funnels of smoke were belched from the fire as it struggled to rise. Wind snatched the black breath and swirled it out of the room and into the kitchen and out of the busting-apart seams of the old slave house—out into the darkness, hanging as thick as those old drapes from the rich people she once cleaned house for.

"Jesus!" Wind'll take over. Snake into your senses if you don't shake yourself loose from it. Bash every sun-filled thought you ever had. Bash them to a boiling, popping pulp. "Jesus!" She reared back from the flame, blinked and closed her eyes—whimpered, "Jesus."

She thought for a minute: Life ain't never been nothing for me but wind. Wind in the night. She trembled. And the day just closed wasn't a thing but dreaming. Dreaming?

But it wasn't no dream! She picked up her sewing and laid it down. Death ain't catching hold of me. . . . Aunt Cora Lou's making the arrangements with Albert Grene. This baby's gonna come here alive! By a doctor's hands.

Wildness sets in when the house can't stand up against the wind. It'll make your heart thump, and thump, and bruise and bump! "Don't care if it is that sickening man doing the job. I don't have to lift my eyes up to him . . . don't even have to see him good." Her mind became a tunnel of wind, sweeping his good, white-people's kind of hair out of her mind's face . . . and his probing, sure-of-himself hands.

Hammering of the knotty chinaberry tree limbs against the outside of the house left her mind blank and fastened on the yellow-flowered curtains, flapping in a pretty, girlish way in the doorway between the room and the shed kitchen and at the three little windows rattling in the outside walls of the room.

Fear locked her limbs so that nothing in her moved. She tried to bend her knees and break away from the window facing Cleveland's Field. Tried to lift her arms to ward off the shadow moving up to the window—rapping on the window. Bones of her joints locked. "Jesus!" She moved, heard her elbows crack.

Shadow by the window was a man! Man talked to her. "Mariah? Mariah! Cora Lou's gone!"

"What you say?" Must be going out of her mind, talking to the wind. Better move away from the window, pile up some coats and things on the bed . . . make the fire burn hot for Jacob. But that won't be enough heat. He'll be cold all through. Nothing to him but bones. . . .

"I say Cora Lou's gone!"

It surely was a man talking. "Gone where?"

A river of blood flashed across Mariah's eyes. Couldn't let go of the curtain to save her life. *I ain't talking to no wind! That's Pop Percy out there!*

"Pop Percy!" Her breath came in short, jerking gulps. "Why don't you come in?"

"Where's Jacob at? I ain't got no time to be coming in!" The man's forehead twitched in a terrible way. His eyes were as stormy as whirlpools, shimmering through the pane.

"Out in the field to do his business. . . ."

"Tell him word just come down the road that his Aunt Cora Lou got run down by a carload of white young'uns up there by the Calvertown cutoff."

"Aunt Cora Lou gone?" Mariah's voice was something high and far away from her.

"She ain't had a bit of business going up that road this day. Hear me, she ain't had a bit of business. Wasn't for your fancymindedness she never would've gone. Guess you see now it ain't right for everything to be your way! God's gonna teach you a lesson!"

"Don't say that, Pop Percy!"

"Tell Jacob the body's already been picked up by Jimmy Jamison. Now I got that bill to pay. Onliest boy I got left home is leaving on account of you." His head just shook like he couldn't control himself. "She ain't had no business going off from here like that. . . . Tell Jacob!"

"Sure, sure!" That's all Mariah could say. "Sure, sure. . . ." Backed away from the window. *Got to tell Jacob. Aunt Cora Lou's gone. Got run down.*

And the stormy-eyed man moved away from the window. A way out in the night the man's voice broke in, growling with the wind, crying, snapping at whole creation.

Pop Percy, that was you, wasn't it? Pop Percy? And Mariah sank down on the floor, gazing at the daisy patches on the cold linoleum, crooking her neck so she could look up. Had to get up, but she lay, fixing her eyes on the cracks in the off-white plaster of the ceiling. Cracks got larger and larger. Everything was falling to pieces. Her hands moved out from her body, grasping and clenching as she fumbled to hold things together. She couldn't get a hold of a thing. Her hands jumped to her face, then plunked like dumb, no-good-to-her things on the floor. "Jesus." She shoved her knuckles into her mouth and gnawed at them. "I'm sorry, I'm sorry." Pushed on her front teeth so hard her senses tingled and hurt, and jelled into a stiff, cold order. "Must be the truth, Jesus."

And she rose from the cold floor, paced back and forth. "I'm sorry, I'm sorry. I'm sorry. Aunt Cora Lou, how'd you die . . . just like that? How'd you just go off from here and die? Die easy? Oh Aunt Cora Lou! Told you it was no sense in you leaving here like that. Why don't you listen to somebody sometimes? Oh Aunt Cora Lou. Whyn't you let me talk to Bannie today? She'd a-took me up to Calvertown. Now who's gonna look after them poor little things you done left behind . . . Mamma Bertha? Know she's broke up now . . . Aunt Cora Lou . . . my baby, my baby! What about my baby?"

Mariah sat on the jagged-edge wood box. Her whole body flopped, heaving against the chimney. Heat from the chimney, that's what she needed. Bearing down cold was setting in all over! Got to tell Jacob. How you gonna tell Jacob? After all, she was his own dear aunt on his mother's side. Looked after him and all the rest when they were coming up. Changed their diapers just as good as Bertha Ann did. 'Deed she did. Wiped their tears, too, they tell me.

"My baby, Jesus, my baby!"

Even though none of them were any too proud of her in these last years, hooking up with that migrant worker the way she did, leaving the land and going citified. Still, still in all, your flesh and blood is your flesh and blood. How you gonna tell him, Mariah?

"My baby! Jesus. Got to see Miss Bannie."

Catch her tonight! Don't wait for the day . . . How you gonna tell him, Mariah? Easiest way is the best way. Break it to him easy . . . break it to him easy . . . break it to him . . . don't even look at his sad old eyes. . . .

And she clung to the fire. Stayed close to the stove. Minutes moved by like hours.

And she broke it to Jacob in the easiest way her trembling thoughts would let her. Had a pot of hot sassafras tea ready when the wind shoved him in the door. She fussed about him in an extraordinary way. "Why you stay out in the cold so long, Jacob?" Ran her hands over his chilly head. "Been waiting for you over an hour or more." And finally, she stiffened her throat. "Jacob. God done called your Aunt Cora Lou home for her rest. . . . You know she was mighty tired when I saw her today. Acted spry and all that. . . ."

"Rah!" Jacob's eyelids quivered in such a way Mariah almost snapped. But she kept on, letting her words fall easy. "Pop Percy was by here almost soon as you went out. Brought you the news. . . ."

Jacob's face went tight, as it always did when he was getting so you couldn't talk to him anymore. "I'm going to Mamma."

Mariah's tongue flew loose. "But the baby, Jacob. Aunt Cora Lou was seeing after the baby."

"Baby?" He paused at the door like he was startled or something. "Baby'll be all right. Pray, Rah, hon. . . . Got to see Mamma."

"I knowed it, I knowed it." Her voice flung itself at the slowly closing door. "Last chance I'll get to talk with him 'til the funeral's over. Jesus!" And her anger crumbled. Nothing left nowhere but wind! "I got to go."

Mariah hit that road. Felt like she was going fifty. Feet dragged a bit, but her heart was racing. Wind didn't hold her back one bit. Fact is, it helped her out right smart. Nothing like meeting the wind head on. Sharp tongues of wind'll lick your mind clean. Make you see yourself as you really are—alone! Except for God. And who knows better than the mother. Who knows, Jesus, but you?

She switched from the Deep Gut Road and cut across the marsh swamp patch leading down to Bannie's house the back way. On the main road you're likely to run into people and have to talk about your business. Folks'll mess your business clean up. Won't tell it like it is to save your life. Folks'll be going around saying how it's a scandal and a shame she wasn't over to Bertha Ann's house. Hear them now saying if she was well enough to tramp the road to Bannie's house this time of night and leaving her children all alone and crying, she was in good enough shape to go over to Bertha Ann's in the time of death, and give comfort to the hurt ones. Children weren't even crying. She'd seen to that. Wouldn't have left Skeeter by himself with them this time of night if he hadn't woke up and leaned on her and rubbed against her titty and listened to her carefully when she told him he was in charge. As for the hurt one—well, Jesus, who knows better than the mother?

Pine trees stood out like stiff-necked hinckty-minded things, bunched together in clumps and sheltering each other from the prison farm bulldozers. But the wind worked through them, taking all the perfume and the sweet sighs out of them, flinging it out to the world.

Scrub in the bush by the pond running in from the Gut where the boys played pirate before Bannie took over the land was still as scraggly as ever. Now ain't that something. Children done made that clearing out to be a forest and it wasn't nothing but a few stray weeds. Thicket never will grow up. Sounds inched and jumped and fluttered up from the ground. Muskrats slushed through the weed-covered pond waters. A couple of jackrabbits broke out in a run. Something slid through the bullgrass. Bet it was a snake! Them things supposed to be going on to sleep by September. But a snake's a sly thing about hanging around, especially a copperhead, especially when the winter sets in green. Hard times when the seasons turn around! Death settles down on the land. Moss was like suckers to the bottom of her feet. Holly branches scratched her forehead. For the first time she stopped stone still and knew a fullness of death. "Aunt Cora Lou's death is just the beginning." No, God. No! It seemed that the very woods sang the messages of death. She tried to keep moving. "Aunt Cora Lou just the first to go . . . Aunt Cora Lou's gone." In a lonely, damp place Mariah quivered. Moonlight filtered through the dry, wailing pines. Moon was big and cold.

Grim reaper seemed to say to her:

Well, what you doing here, Mariah? On this path. In this swamp. Whyn't you follow Jacob to his mamma's house? You just like people say—ain't got no respect for the sacraments. . . . Well, how come you rooted in this moss, Mariah? Death watch over to Bertha Ann's house. This swamp ain't no place for you to be. After all, Aunt Cora Lou put herself out for you and the baby. Hadn't been for you maybe she wouldn't a-left Tangierneck in time to have her bones mauled and smashed under that car.

"Ain't none of my fault!" Mariah's feet moved faster than her mind told her they were going. "I ain't sent her. She the one asked to go!" Her arms thrust the clawing, scratching branches aside. "I ain't sent her. Told her Miss Bannie could be a right nice white woman sometimes. She'd a-taken me up to Calvertown. Told her, told her. Told her! Didn't I, Jesus?"

Felt to her like Jesus said, "Yes."

Every living thing Mariah came across was running. Some of them screeched. Everything was scared and running! "Got to save my baby!" Neither her feet, nor her heart, nor her mind would slow up. She got through the thicket so fast she had to hold still a minute when she got to the wide path where you go straight down to Deep Gut. Stood still and rubbed the lively little bundle in her belly. "Jesus." Wished for a minute for something warm to wrap herself in.

She looked over the marshy fields at the poor white's lamplighted window. No comfort there. She darted across the road into the woods. She could hear bruise-headed Anna crying now. Them Europeans sure did believe in beating their women, she'd heard. Made her feel sometimes like laying a stick up beside that burly no-English-talking man's head for busting that woman up with his fists, sometimes with his feet, too, they tell me. But long as Anna acts like she's better than anybody else, just because she's white, ain't nobody gonna take up for her.

The path drew Mariah onward. Spruce grows thick after you pass Anna's plot. Cypresses' knees are more than a notion to lift your legs over. It's a wet stretch of swamp from the thicket road to Bannie's house and the Gut. Don't be careful you'll step over to the side in a sinkhole. "Jesus!" You'd think God had gone to sleep and left the world all to itself and nobody to look out for it and the life twisting across it. "Jesus!" Nobody to look out for the searching things on it, but Jesus. He's a little closer to the ground than God is. He's right here by my side. *It'll be a pretty day tomorrow, Mariah.* Must be him talking to her right now. *It'll be a pretty day tomorrow.*

"I knowed you was with me, Jesus . . . I ain't scared."

Everything was as dark as you'd want it. Crying sounds sneaked up on her. Even the crying was dark. "Have mercy, Jesus!" She held onto her belly. Stopped. You is so scared, Mariah! . . . Whomsoever's crying can't even get they breath good.

A terrible hammering of her heart walloped her neck. Knocked the juice out of her throat. Her eyes flew wide. Her mind jumped out of the darkness and crouched again in the shaking pulp of her brain. "Jesus!" But she couldn't make a sound.

Something's in my path. Something . . . it's a woman. Must be a vision! Felt her senses reeling. She held on to her belly. Backing away. Aunt Cora Lou! Can't be . . . Jesus . . . Aunt Cora Lou! She clamped her hand over her mouth to still the scream rushing up in her.

But she had to look! If it was a vision, she had to look. Had to listen. Lord was sending it.

"Wah-dah. . . ." It was a woman weeping.

Mariah's eyes flew wide open. A plump woman's body was curled close to a tree. It was no vision. Words coming out of it were all twisted up. "Cat'h 'im." What in the name of God! Mariah moved toward it.

"Miss Bannie, ain't that you? Miss Bannie!" Legs folded under Mariah, and she found herself kneeling. Trying to get a-hold of the hurt woman's head and lay it in a restful spot.

"Oh my God. My goody, goody Jesus." Poor soul's head kept jerking around. Mariah's fingers flew through the woman's matted hair, tugging it back from her face. Jesus, have mercy! "Miss Bannie?"

You ought to get out of this swamp, Mariah. Leave this woman go! Ain't nothing but the devil talking to me. . . . I ain't got no right to run from nobody in this condition. Help me, Lord, Jesus. Help me.

"This is you, Miss Bannie! This is you." And she heard her voice hard and stuck all in her throat. "I was just on my way to see you, Miss Bannie . . . just on my way. . . . What's the matter with your tongue?" *Woman's sick, Mariah. Serves her right to be so. She ain't nothing but a land thief. Run!*

And Mariah prayed for the devil to let go of her, and her Jesus saw to it that he did. Her Jesus saw to it that she settled herself a bit and said, "You feeling poorly, Miss Bannie? Where you feel bad at? Miss Bannie . . . Jesus, have mercy." And her Jesus directed her to wash away her own sins by helping the fallen. "Jesus, thank you tender Saviour."

"Wah-dah."

"You want some water, Miss Bannie? What you saying?"

All Mariah got back was a sluggish, gurgling sound rolling in the sick woman's throat. "Cat'h him."

Mariah said, "Jesus, looks like her tongue done swoll clean out of her throat. Now if you'll help me, Lord, to get her up from here. . . ." And Mariah tried to lift her, but the weight gave her such a pain. She let go and set in to wiping off Miss Bannie's face and saying over and over again, "Miss Bannie, I ain't knowed you was prone to fits."

Baby socked her in the groin. Her thoughts bumped—all of them together against each other. And she said to the knocking in her belly, *Behave yourself young'un in the time of somebody else's troubles. I knows you there!*

Shudders from Miss Bannie shook Mariah's hand. Hard to keep a mudpack on her face. "Hold still, Miss Bannie, I'm trying to bring you to."

"Wah-dah . . . wah-dah . . . wah. . . ."   And   the plump body stiffened.

"Lordy, Lordy, she's fixing to have another fit. . . . I'll take you to git your water, Miss Bannie. I can't hurt my baby by lifting you though. Gonna get you on home. . . ."

A clammy hand pinched the muscles in Mariah's arm. It fell, clawing in the wet leaves. "You coming to, now. Now, now, Miss Bannie. Just set up easy. I'm gonna get you to some water." A million bugs and worms seemed to be in the handful of mud Mariah held on Bannie's head.

Bannie shook her head. Words started coming clearer and clearer: "Nig-ag beat me . . . tried to kill me, Ann. He always been trying to get me to give him some of my pussy. Ain't never been fair to me. You catch him if you go that way."

And it was like daylight to Mariah all of a sudden. In the moonlight filtering through the trees, she watched the puffy, bruised eyelids in the white face try to open. A ringing zinged and zinged through Mariah's head. She almost said: "I ain't no Anna," but instead she said, "What nigger, Miss Bannie? Who'm I supposed to catch?"

"Perthy."

Thunder, sudden and deep, rolled in Mariah's eardrums, and it was her own voice barking, "Percy, Miss Bannie? Did you say Percy?"

The woman's head snuggled on Mariah's arm gone lax.

"Who you say, Miss Bannie?" Mariah squeezed the mud and the black water flowed in sudden spurts all over the twitching face.

"Went tha' way. . . ." And Bannie's eyes crawled open for a second and closed. "Let go me! Let go me! T'ought you was . . ."

"Who you thought I was, Miss Bannie?" Mariah let go of the light-colored head. Let it fall. Let it roll any which way that woman saw fit to toss it.

And Mariah couldn't do anything else to save her life, but murmur to the romping all around and under and into her heart. "Baby, take it easy. Little baby, take it easy," and stare into the swimming darkness. Had to get a-hold of herself! Ought to run!

"Ah, ah . . . ah thought you was . . ."

Kicked dog wouldn't have yelped like that woman. Heart liked to have busted through Mariah's chest bones. *You son of a bitch!* She got herself up from there.

"Who you took me to be, Miss Bannie? Anna? Well, she ain't got sense enough left in her head to come out of her house even in the daytime . . . the way your hired man beats her." Every pore of Mariah's skin seemed to empty itself. "I ain't a-gonna hurt you even though I ain't no Anna. I ain't a-gonna hurt you!"

The eyes of the woman by Mariah's feet struggled to open wide but stayed closed down to slits. Woman's chest heaved in a terrible pumping up and down, up and down.

Wasn't nothing left for Mariah to do but to do away with her.

Mariah tried to call Jesus, but his name wouldn't cross her lips.

Jesus ain't got a thing to do with what I have in mind, now. Jesus don't have nothing to do with this sickening time in my soul.

"Percy ought to be strung up for hurting you like this, Miss Bannie!" Mariah was surprised at how softly she spoke. "I'm gonna see to it that he gets his pay! You poor thing, Miss Bannie." And she knelt to lift the woman.

Her breath came in short painful spasms. Thought to herself for a minute that she was laughing, but the salt water on her lips told her she was crying. And she said to the softheartedness in herself, *What you crying for, nigger? What in the name of God for? Stop your crying!* And she got all quieted down.

Said to Bannie, "That father-in-law of mine's one nigger that ain't worth nothing. Not even the tree we gonna pick out to hang him on." With the saying of those words, lightning fire burnt all in Mariah's eyeballs and in back of her head. And all up and down her belly the fire raged and the baby kicked and kicked, fanning the fire, burning her down to ashes. Felt to her that she was standing in the middle of time, all burnt down to ashes like a new child

that nobody ever said do this or do that to. Just ashes—
and new. Clear on what to do now for it didn't matter to
nobody, nohow. She could even sin at this time if she
wanted to and she wanted to! Had to save Jacob and the
children and Pop Percy. . . .

Cold hands found Mariah's ankles.

"I'm gonna take you to get your water, Miss Bannie.
Now you just catch a-hold of that tree. Pull up easy. Easy
now. I'm holding my hand out to you. That's it, hon. Don't
throw yourself against my baby. . . ."

"Mariah? Mariah, ain't that you, Mariah?" The tottering
body of the white woman swayed against the tree . . .
arms all flung out.

"Yes'm, Miss Bannie. But you needn't fear a thing. I'm
gonna look after you, poor thing! Come on." She
smoothed the woman's crumpled coat. Patted her shoulder.

"Always did say you was a nice girl."

White woman's words sputtered in the blue darkness, but
they were coming through clearer and clearer to Mariah.
Plain as day, in fact. *Pop Percy ain't done all that much to
her. She can walk as good as me!*

"You saying your words much better now, Miss Bannie!
Mud pack must've done you good."

Bannie's cold hands fumbled around Mariah's neck,
found her shoulders. Night eyes were working good for
Mariah. Said to herself, *She ain't in as bad a condition as
she's trying to make out. Most of her trouble is around the
eyes. Her eyes surely is messed up!*

"Lean easy on me, Miss Bannie. Get you to your water.
Then I'm gonna see that dirty bugger Percy gets tended
to. . . . Come on, hon. I'm going over to Mr. Larmer's
store this very night and see that he gets turned in to the
law." *Baby, hold on to the plow, hold on.*

Kicking hurt Mariah's very bowels. Swamp path's bad
enough to make it through in the dark, and a lynch-bait
woman leaning on you makes it something else. Can't
hardly make it.

"Lean more 'gainst my shoulder, Miss Bannie. Give the
young'un room enough to kick. . . . Step high right here
. . . that's it." Water don't never dry up in the swamp.

"Head hurts me so bad, Mariah. Can't hardly see nothing. . . ."

"You gonna see, Miss Bannie, poor soul. Hold still a

minute. Let me get a stick for you to lean on. Don't want you to mash my baby hard as you doing. I know you don't mean no harm, though, hon. . . ."

The path was as cushiony as tucked satin, lining a casket. And cold! When Mariah picked up that stick for Miss Bannie she felt like she was picking up a snake. *Never thought death would be this full of doing something.* "We almost there, Miss Bannie."

"My eyes is a-smarting," the clinging woman whimpered.

"Why you take on so, Miss Bannie? I done found you. Doing the best I can by you."

"Splinter's sticking in my hand. My feet's wet. You taking me home the long way, Mariah. Thinks I hear the Nighaskin."

"Head's just hurting you, Miss Bannie. Don't try to talk so much. Know your throat's a mess."

"Funny, how I thinks I smell the river. . . ."

"It's your head, hon."

"I'm just about give out. . . . You Mariah, ain't you?"

"Bannie, now you know I'm Mariah. Any other nigger be done left you right there on the road for some animals to feed off you."

"Taking us so long . . . wish I had some water. . . ."

"Can't do no better, Miss Bannie. Don't hit up 'gainst my stomach, hon! Got to give my baby room. It's about to kick my ribs out."

"That's right . . . can't hurt the baby." Bannie sagged against Mariah's stiff arm. "Baby's nicest thing in the world. Got such a headache. Babies only things count. . . ."

What does she know about how much a baby counts?

"You Mariah, ain't you?"

"Yes, I'm her. Why you keeps asking? Yes, I'm Mariah!" she said again. Silliest feeling came to her to holler it. Wanted to hear her voice tearing through the swamp. Ought to get back to her senses! Run!

But she neither ran nor hollered. Her mind was locked in a stiff march forward. A march she somehow felt she'd never get off of.

She did try to call Jesus a time or two, but her mouth wouldn't help her out. It was so dry. Only thing wet was her face. Sweat crawled over it same as if she was in an airtight room filled with sluggish flies dying from fly spray. *Dirty dog Pop Percy. Dirty dog!*

Tried to tell herself, Mariah, you the mother of Skeeter and Rabbit and Gezee. . . . New one in your belly kicking now to live! Get your children out of this Neck. You done promised the Lord. . . . Get off this path!

But she marched on toward the Gut. I ain't gonna be able to get them out of nowhere now. All of us'll be killed if this woman talks to Anna and them. Such a bitterness, a slimy hate wetted her throat.

"Feels like it gonna be rain tomorrow, Miss Bannie." Had to say something out loud. Make sure, perfectly sure, she was herself. Herself coming into the clearing. Out of the swamp. Leading a woman beaten blind to the water. Woman faltering on her. Giving way every few steps, mumbling, "Water."

Cold air from the Gut blew like death over the marshy path. Biting her lips, Mariah led the woman on, on. On down to the sandy stretch—down to the hungry tide. Seeing the white angel of death unloosening itself from the big moon wallowing over the black waters of the Gut, Mariah swayed. *Got to face the Lord when he opens up my grave on the Judgment morning. . . . I ain't nothing nohow. Ain't never been nothing.*

She stiffened. "Gimme your stick, Miss Bannie."

"What for, hon? I'll be heavy on your baby. Don't want to lean on you." And then her voice cracked in a high-keyed whisper. "Mariah, ain't we to the river?"

"You surely is sick, Miss Bannie. Let me get a good hold of you." And Mariah squeezed that woman's shoulder like she meant something to her.

"Don't want to lean on you!" Woman's legs almost gave out. "You one of the nicest niggers 'round here. . . ."

"Don't say that word no more, Miss Bannie."

"What's gitting into you, Mariah?" Her breath was warm and sweetish-sour. Mouth almost touching Mariah's cheek.

Mariah looked out over the flickering black waters. It was a mad river, bumping and tugging and belching. Nighaskin had choked Deep Gut full to the overflowing point.

"Gimme your stick, Miss Bannie!"

"Mariah!" The thin-mouthed woman straightened as stiff as a board. Tattered clothes ballooned in a gust of wind. Her hands flapped, but Mariah moved away.

"Your leaning days is over, Miss Bannie. You don't have to lean on me no more. I done brought you to your water.

Now all you got to do is walk a little bit to the head of me and bend over and drink all you want to. And don't try to run past me, else you'll ram your gut with this stick. There's water any way you turn, and you ain't getting past me." Stick flew from Mariah's hands—so easy it flew, the same as if it wasn't a thing but a feather, when Bannie stumbled toward her screaming, crying. Clawing all over Mariah's face, raking her chest, breaking every button from her coat.

"Leave go me, Miss Bannie! Leave go me! If you don't leave go me, I'm lief to. . . ." Mariah grabbed her head, her belly. *My baby, my baby.* Trembled and almost went down. Almost went down in the slushy sands where the woman collapsed, clinging to Mariah's legs, slobbering hot all up against her legs. Feeble hands stroked Mariah's ankles. "Take me home, hon. I can't see. Take me home."

"I ain't a-gonna do it. . . . You ain't gonna take advantage of no more people. . . ." Sobs broke a-loose from her. "You ain't getting no Pop Percy lynched. . . . Skeeter and them ain't got nothing but toe sacks for to wear right now on account of you. . . . White people ain't no good, nohow."

All around Mariah were the voices of the Neck, swelling in her ears, skeeing in and away. Roaring in the waters swirling up to the shore. Gulping waters. Coughing voices. Consumption hoarse voices. Especially Skeeter's . . . been coughing for going on two years now. . . .

Who'll be my witness, Lord? Who'll stand with me when they haul me up there to the County Court House? Who'll tend my children?

"Lordy, Jesus, help me." She heard herself praying, crying. They ain't heading for nothing but Cleveland's Field no way, and the worms, till you take them up to heaven. Worms gonna eat my children up!

She tried to unloosen her feet from the whimpering woman's hold. Felt like she was sinking. Sinking down into the grave and time's long judgment.

Ought to work my foot around on her hand. Break every bone in it. Like they did to Bard Tom's neck. . . . Might have broke a-many a-more bone before they strung him up. . . . Neck bone hanging from the Royal Oaks tree. Rest of the bones in chains on the ground. Ought to take one—just one white person with me when I go.

Ought to take a million. Clear the earth up of them. Ought to. . . . "Woman, let go my legs, else I'll bash your head in." She swayed. Tried to keep talking. *Let go my legs, woman. Don't pull and tug on me like that. Lord have mercy, where's my senses at? Help me, Jesus, to get her to the water. Won't nobody find her if the tides washes her on out to the ocean by morning. Won't a living soul ever see her again!*

Such a fulsomeness rose up in Mariah's stomach. She started in belching but the hiccoughs took over. The kind that hurts every time you try to draw a good breath. Make you double over trying to stand up.

And she couldn't stand up to save her life. *No more, Lord, no more.* So she just kept on a-going down, crying, "Jesus, little baby, Jesus, help me."

And that big load she was carrying in her gut kicked her. Maybe it was even whining. She tried to tell it to hush up. "Hush, hush!"

But the young'un wouldn't stop its kicking, its dat-blamed blasted infernal kicking. And it was hurting her, too! "Baby, hush. . . ."

"Let go me . . . let go me . . . I got something to do."

"Rah, please missy, take me home. Take me home. Don't shove me in the water. That ain't no way to treat nobody. . . ."

In the cooling water at the edge of the beach Mariah sank down. Sand and the oyster shells felt right rough to her legs. Water washed all up under her coattail . . . and in between her legs. And when it flowed out from her, it was warm. Warm!

"My water done broke." She tried to tell the Lord.

But you can't tell the Lord nothing with a mess of water flowing in your throat . . . a mess of sand in your teeth. Can't even breathe.

Mariah chomped on that sand. Chewed it. Tried to swallow it. "Jesus, let me get my breath." And she spit that sand out. Crawled to dry land. And God! Jesus! She got to her feet. Turned her back on that woman and stumbled toward the marsh path. "Ain't got no business mixed up in no shit like this. Got to save my baby." Feet couldn't seem to locate the path. Tried to run. Legs felt right heavy to her. "Jesus!"

Strong wind whipped her. Almost stopped her. Dried her out considerably. Legs felt right rough, rubbing one against the other. "My water ain't broke yet! Thank you, Jesus!"

Mariah inched on up that path. Feet hurt her so bad, she couldn't seem to move except by inches. Kept saying to herself, "If I could only rest my feet a minute," and things like that.

Woman behind her just kept up the crying, hitting and missing the trail as she stumbled after Mariah, slopping over her words a mile a minute. Wished God would reach out his hand and clamp it over that woman's mouth. Half blind as she is she's gonna fall over in one of those sink-holes first and last!

"I'm a woman just like you, Mariah! You don't know what's been going on 'twixt Percy and me. Help me to pray, Rah. . . ."

Wasn't no mistaking what she was saying! Saying wild things. Silly things. White people don't even know how to pray! What she doing asking me to help her pray?

Must be your spirit, Jesus, helping me to stop like this.

And Mariah found herself turning around, just a-listening and stumbling back to help Miss Bannie up the path.

"Help me to pray, Rah. I promise the Lord, if you'll just only take me home . . . promise to give you back your land. . . . I ain't gonna tell on no Percy! Promise the Good Lord, if you only will take me home. . . .

"Percy said I had the onliest thing he ever would love. Promised me everything . . . the land . . . said that to me way long before he ever met Bertha Ann. Give me a baby. I'm the onliest thing keeping that baby going."

"He ain't give you no baby, Miss Bannie. What kind of a baby? You don't know nothing about having no baby. You ain't never seen a baby live nor die. . . ."

"No I ain't never seen no baby die. But I seen to it one lived. Ain't never gonna see him die of want. Ain't gonna see it long as I can get a-hold of the money for to keep him going. He's gonna be the biggest doctor in these parts one day! Gonna be able to cure the whole creation. . . ."

"Who you talking about?"

"Albert."

"Albert? Ain't no doctors up there in Calvertown by the name of Albert excepting . . . Grene. . . . He ain't yours is he, Miss Bannie? He ain't yours!"

"He is so mine. . . ."

"How come . . . how come you don't own him?" Mariah just stuttered, "When . . . when you had him . . . how come you all don't own each other . . . how come?"

White woman clung to her and cried. "Help me to pray, Mariah. Help me to face my Maker. Colored blood was gonna show up in him. That's how come I left him in somebody else's charge till he growed up. But it ain't showed up yet! I could a-kept him! Could a-told people I got married when they sent me away, and had a baby, and then got divorced. None of the family would've knowed the difference. . . . But they would've killed me if I'd a-brought him back home and he turned colored. I supported him though. Hear me, Mariah, every last cent I could get out of anybody, I gave to him. Them houses on Webster Street in Calvertown that he owns I bought for him. Wanted to give him the whole Mantipico County."

Must have been God. No, it was the good Lord Jesus that sent Mariah speeding on up that path to home after she got through praying things over with Bannie and leading her on home and sticking her in the bed, and giving her the medicine and water she asked for. Gave her a whole shoe box full of medicines and pills to choose from. All kinds of colored pills that woman had in that box.

And the last words that poor woman said to Mariah kept ringing in her head, all the way up the Deep Gut Road: "I'll divide up whatever I has with you, Mariah, only don't tell on me. Send Rabbit down here tomorrow. I'll give you all, all the milk you want. When I go to pick up the mail tomorrow, I'll pick you up. . . ."

Don't think you gonna see no tomorrow, Miss Bannie, less I go up and wake Mr. Larmer for to call up the doctor. But I ain't gonna do it! Lord, everything is in your hands. Got to get home! Some voice tried to steady Mariah on that lonesome path.

And the Lord, must have been the good Lord Jesus, who took Mariah's hands, took control over her feet so they wouldn't stray.

She had the urge two or three times to go off somewhere. Thought she ought to stop by Jacob's papa's house and holler. Tell on everybody, tell on herself. Thought she really ought to go up and wake up Mr. Larmer. So as to use his telephone to call for Dr. Grene to come and help his mother. But the baby was a fitful mess inside of her. Thing needed to go to sleep! Said to the Lord, "I ain't in no mess like this, am I? Lord get me out of this mess!"

When she hit the road that leads out to Route 291, she commenced to throw out her arm. Might be able to hail one of those big GMC trucks hauling loads up north. The Lord snatched her hand back and she got across that road.

After all, she couldn't leave Rabbit in that house by himself. Couldn't leave Gezee! Skeeter could make out all right with his daddy. Couldn't unglue those two if you tried to pry them apart with an iron wrench. And besides, and moreover, "Jesus Christ, Little Lordy, I'm getting sick to my stomach. Got to lay my baby down some place."

She could hardly make another step. "That's the truth, Lord! Take my feet out of this miry clay."

But she made a-many a step in the panic that kept pulling at her when she finally did get home.

Children weren't half sleeping when she busted through that door. Skeeter was coughing the worst. She got the onion syrup off the kitchen workbench, took herself upstairs and chunked some of it down their throats. Laid down beside Rabbit. Had to keep him warm. Fool Rabbit didn't have sense enough to keep the covers over him. Gonna end up with the consumption first and last! Got to get him out of this place!

His head kept bruising her titty. Had to draw her belly back so he wouldn't hurt the new one. Children don't know no better than to toss and turn when they sleeping in a cold house.

Mariah got up two or three times to put some wood in that little tin stove. Even went outdoors and scrummaged in that creepy woodpile to get some more wood. Jacob hadn't filled up the woodbox!

Cried to herself. "What's taking Jacob so long to come home? People gets sleepy even if they is at a watch for the dead. . . . Everybody don't have to stay all night. . . . Got something I want to talk over with Jacob. . . ." Two or three drops of water crept down her face.

Said to Jesus, "I ain't meaning to cry." But she just couldn't help it. "Jesus, Jesus, Jesus! Why don't you send Jacob on home?"

But Jesus hadn't sent him when some wee little bits of

morning tried to come on in. And she was still laying down beside Rabbit.

She said to Rabbit, "I'm gonna get us out of this place. Now you just go on back to sleep. Stop your fidgeting. I'm tired. Got to get a little bit of sleep myself. Got to get some money tomorrow."

8

"First thing in the morning? Just what time is it?" So Mariah roused herself with the slamming of the downstairs door. Must be Jacob coming in!

She let go of Rabbit's head. Almost tumbled headfirst down those stair steps. Caught herself just before she tripped in the landing. Said, "Jesus, guide my tongue that I may serve you. Jesus, guide my feet."

She didn't know what was shaking the worse—hands or feet—when she did make it into that kitchen.

Jacob was nothing but a haggard-looking mess, and contrary, too, when she laid eyes on him by that feeble lamplight. Said to him before she even thought twice, "What time of the morning is it, Jacob? You just getting in here?"

And he said to her, "Woman, ain't you got sense enough to look at the clock?"

Clock hands were stopped going on nine.

Must have been just about that time last night when Pop Percy came and told me about Aunt Cora Lou.

"You ain't got sense enough to wind the thing up." And Jacob took the clock from the mantelpiece and set it at a few minutes before four.

"Ain't had no time nor thought for to wind it up, Jacob. It's been a bad night. . . ."

"I knows it's been that, Mariah. Ain't no two ways about it, it's been a night. It's been a night. But you ain't even been out in it. Least you could have done was to wind up this clock. You ain't had nothing else for to do."

But Mariah wasn't going to pay any mind to his nasty-acting scolding. Wasn't gonna do it!

Lord guide my tongue.

She blinked through a veil of tears. But the Lord didn't

seem to hear her. Something mad just rose up in her. Her tongue just went astray.

"Don't you talk to me that way! I is so had something else to do. Had to look out for the baby." She threw a bunch of kindling in the stove. Flames roared up, and she slung that pot of leftover greens on the stove. "Don't care how much death it is in the land, I got to make preparations for my baby to live!"

"You ain't had nothing for to do but stitch them bed pads, Rah. You ain't never even come over to the house to sit for the waking up of the dead. It was you that sent Aunt Cora Lou up the road yesterday afternoon. Least you could've done was to come and sit and watch for her soul. . . ."

Sweat so hot started itching under Mariah's arms, and her mouth was on fire. "I ain't had nothing to do with sending her up the road. Went on her own. Besides that, I ain't the onliest one that wasn't watching over to the house. I ain't the onliest one. Where was your pappy at, Jacob?"

"What you mean, 'where was *your* pappy at?' Where you think he was at? He was right there. Right there where he's supposed to be!"

"Whole time, Jacob?"

"What you mean the whole time?"

Pot of greens were just a-bubbling on the stove. And Mariah couldn't unfix her eyes from it.

"Ain't none of us been there the whole time, woman. You know we had to get out and get us a ride up the road to see about putting Aunt Cora Lou away. . . ."

"How come you all didn't go by Miss Bannie's and pick up that Cadillac hearse or whatever it is they call it? After all, it does belong to your pap. . . ."

"You know good and well why we ain't done such a thing, Rah. Papa give her the car to settle last month's payment."

"Title ain't never been changed to it. . . ."

"Leave me alone, woman. . . ." And Jacob's voice started in cracking, but he caught himself and got up from that table and went out to the shed kitchen to put on his sou'wester and things.

"You should have seen Aunt Cora Lou, Rah. State troopers said it ain't never been no accident like that on these roads. Said she looked worse than people killed in a

war. Jimmy Jamison and them hadn't even started to piec-
ing her head together when we got there. Brains was all
spilled out. . . ."

Next thing Mariah knew, Jacob was gone. Went out that
door making some kind of sounds like a dog with the dis-
temper. Must be choking with the cold and the bad way he
must be feeling.

"Jacob! Jacob!" And her voice rose to a scream. "Come
back here, fool! Jacob!" she cried on the doorsteps in the
dull blackness of the new morning. "Jacob, you ain't had
no breakfast. You ain't had no supper . . . Jacob!

"Jacob!" Mariah called until there was nothing left in
her eyesights but his lantern light bibbling and bobbling
way down the Deep Gut road. "Jacob, I wants to tell you
something 'bout Miss Bannie!"

Well, it was a calm day coming up. And he did have to
make haste to get on the water when the weather allowed.
She could smell a little snow in the air, but it was a long
ways off.

Messenger's coldness wrapped itself around her shoulders. Tried to make her say one more time, *He ain't nothing but a fool. Don't even know his own wife good.* But
instead she said, "Lord, take a-hold of my hand."

She trudged on back in the house. "Lord, which way
shall I go? I ain't nothing but a sinner."

And the Lord guided her to lay herself down. Helped
her to get herself up every now and then to put some wood
on the fire so the children wouldn't have a cold kitchen to
get their clothes on in.

And he helped her to pray, "Saviour, don't let the night
I just lived through be so. Don't let it be so."

It is so, Mariah, something said to her.

She pleaded, "Lord!"

And the Lord told her, if you will just only humble yourself and stop asking for so much, you'll not be judged guilty
in the end.

Her hands were right cold and her feet too, but she
made a-many a trip to the stove, putting in wood easy so
she wouldn't wake up the children too far ahead of time.
Wasn't any need for them to get up before six o'clock or so.

Quaking all the while, "Lord, I knows I'm guilty of sin.
But I did help Miss Bannie for to get home by herself didn't
I? I ain't never asked Aunt Cora Lou for to go up the

road. Onliest thing I wants to ask you for is to spare my
child. And I thanks you for the kicking I feels. Just spare
my child, Lord, just spare it. And let it be Jacob's. Only
other thing I want to ask you for, and that is to let me get
myself out of this house soon as morning comes and get
a-hold of some money. Got to get my children out of this
place."

And the Lord must have taken charge of her for when
she did get up all wobbly-kneed in the morning and went
out on the doorsteps to face the day and the Lord, it was
a good working day ahead of her.

Buzzards and wild loons made their first trip down the
Neck about a quarter to seven. Stayed down the Neck long
enough for Mariah to get the children straightened out for
the day. Told Rabbit and Skeeter to go over to Miss Bannie's house right after school and bring back a quart of
milk—"and talk to her nice, because the last I heard,
somebody told me in the field, yesterday, she ain't feeling
so well. And don't forget to say thank you."

Told the young'uns she wasn't feeling so well herself
about the legs, but the rest of her felt all right. And she
gave them two cents apiece for the red coal oil for the
Halloween Jamboree.

Buzzards stayed down the Neck so long, she figured they
must be feeding on dead fish cast up by the heavy seas. And
she thanked her Lord again that she'd helped Miss Bannie
get on home. Hadn't left her on the beach.

Soon as she started the long trek to Mr. Larmer's potato
field, a buzzard came sailing up the Neck, flapping in her
face.

"You got your gut full now, so go on your way." She
walked from under his shadow. Baby steadily nudging her.
She lifted her head a bit and smiled, and thanked the Lord
again for the working day.

Sound of a truck engine made Mariah turn, and she
saw Mr. Nelson's oyster house truck chugging down the
road. Just a-picking up women to shuck. Truck slowed up
when it got to Mariah, but she waved the driver on. "They'll
never fill me up with the cold or the pneumonia either in
them oyster houses. No more, Lord, no more." She said
to the unborn young'un, "We be gone from here before
long."

A couple of women on the truck waved to Mariah with one hand and held their coattails down with the other as the truck sped off. Most didn't bother. She waved back and plowed on her solitary way.

Truck stopped and picked up Jacob's mother standing down by the church. "Poor thing. She acts like I'm some kind of dirt, but I can't help feeling sorry for her. She ain't got no business having to go off and hustle in that cold wet mess of oysters on this day. Was gonna stop by and pay her my respects."

You can't pass by the house without stopping and saying something at least to the little children. Thought brought such a tightness to Mariah's neck. And her legs got so stiff and heavy to lift she almost ground the cardboard she'd stuck in her shoes for soles to pulp as she turned and walked up to the big house.

Didn't see how she could hold up under the crying and wailing this morning—nor talk, even for a few minutes, with the few old people she knew would be in the house with nothing to do but sit around and stare after death, and ask her questions.

But she had to hold herself up, even though those two shining-eyed black girls were a pain to see when she got there. And those three old people around the fire started in tugging on her about first one thing after the other!

"Where was you last night?" Mostly that, they asked. Especially the newsbody, old tight-faced Vanis, squatting by the fire with her legs all filled up with the water. Her tongue was a regular whip. "All the next of kin was here but you, Mariah. God don't like ugly!"

"Leave her alone!" Aunt Saro Jane told them two or three times. Little squinchy eyes shining just as confident. "She ain't got but one burden to be shouldered with right now and that is the new young'un Jacob plugged her up with. Ain't I speaking right for you, Mariah? Ain't I speaking right for you, Mariah? Ain't I speaking the truth? Lord, Lord!" And the little woman stomped all feeble and sassy about the kitchen.

"I ain't never criticized her, Saro," Uncle Isaiah said. "All I asked her was where she been. Looks like to me she could've dropped over here and sat with Jacob a few minutes. . . ."

"Shit, shit, shit! These menfolks ain't never gonna learn

no sense. Woman's about to have a baby." Aunt Saro Jane just turned her back to the others. "You all making me cuss this late in life. I ain't gonna be here many more days. . . ." And the little shriveled woman started in rocking and moaning. "Ain't we all here together?"

"Saro, you been saying that you was about to pass away ever since you was seventy, and you been a witness for the Lord for nigh onto twenty years since then," Uncle Isaiah grumbled.

But on and on Aunt Saro Jane went. "Child's supposed to be taken up more with life than she is with death. Green winter's coming in here now. I can smell it. Gonna be a fat graveyard come spring. Children is getting fooled by those cold days. Time of death's setting in. Why you all criticize a child for staying home and tending her baby? After all, children's got to go on even after we gone."

And Mariah said, "Don't worry about it, Aunt Saro Jane." But that didn't stop the old lady's droning, "I'll be down to the fields later on today, Mariah. I'm gonna get me a row right beside you. . . ."

But Mariah kept her eyes glued to those two little balls of shock sitting on the woodbox, just a-crying, and looking at her in an accusing way.

Started to break down and cry, too, but she held herself up right well. Wanted to tell those children so bad, "I ain't the one responsible for your mamma being dead. She went on her own to Calvertown." But instead she pulled Lil Bits from off that woodbox and hugged her up all close. Reached for Mamie too, but the littlest one just pressed herself closer to the woodbox. Said, "Cousin Mariah, why you send my mamma up the road?"

"I ain't sent her! Honey, I ain't sent her. God sent her. Little baby, I ain't sent her. It was God and this lonesome, no-good place what did it."

"Don't talk like that, gal, 'bout your own home," Aunt Saro Jane said.

She could hardly talk anymore, and she let go of Lil Bits. Felt like her eyes were dropping out of her head. But she said, "Honies, I ain't sent her. God sent her! Little baby, I ain't made up her mind for her. It . . . it . . . it was this new baby kicking in my gut what sent her." And Mariah started in crying. Raised her voice at the old people around the fire. "It was this young'un that I have to take care of that sent her. You all looking at me like you trying to blame me for everything!"

"I ain't trying to blame you for nothing," Aunt Saro Jane answered. "I knows what you going through." But Uncle Isaiah and them just turned their heads down.

Vanis said, "And a whore shall rip out her breasts in the streets of Jerusalem." And commenced to mumbling some kind of prayer.

"Children, I ain't no whore, I ain't." She turned to the little children all slunk up by the woodbox again. "I ain't sent your mamma." Didn't care if she did cry.

"Children, I wants you all to come over to my house soon as ever you see me coming up the road, because Cousin Mariah gonna bring baby pine cones and some sweet shrubs and holly berries from the swamp when she comes up . . . same as she always does when she has a few spare minutes on her hands. And don't call me Cousin no more. Call me Mamma. I promise the good Jesus this minute, I'll be a mamma to you."

And the children stared all trouble-faced at Mariah.

"I done told you that I was bringing you the baby pine cones. Now didn't I say that, Lil Bits? You all can have a good time making up things with those cones. You seen that centerpiece I made for my table? You all can make something just like that! Besides, I'm gonna get you all some new dresses soon as times comes a little easier. . . ."

Children followed her to the door and a piece-ways down the road. Mamie was the only one that broke down and called her "Mamma." Said to her, "Mamma, how come you sent my mamma up the road for to get killed?"

"You all go on back to the house. Go on back."

Time of death is a hard thing to take. Choking and blinded from the tears, Mariah fled from the children, hollering, "Go on back. I done told you what I had in mind for to do."

Irena caught up with her. "Sis, it ain't your fault. I was upstairs listening to all that old talk in the kitchen. Don't worry yourself about it. You better slack up, before you have a miscarriage."

And she slacked up a bit for the warmth of Irena. Young gal was just as head forward as she could be. "It ain't your fault. Fault's with this place." And with Irena all hugged up to her she made it on down that road.

When Mariah caught her first glimpse of the potato fields, she thanked her Lord that she had the strength left in her legs to kneel and grovel on down those rows. Thanked him that she was young. Wasn't twenty-three out! Asked him for the strength to drag full five-eight baskets down the rows. But mostly, she thanked her Jesus over and over again for the chance to work. She didn't pay any mind to Irena's talking all chipper in the row next to hers every few minutes—trying to cheer and be cheered, Mariah guessed.

Mariah just started the day in singing to herself:

> Lord, I hear of showers of blessings
> Thou dost scatter full and free
> Showers of blessings, so refreshing,
> Let one drop, Lord, fall on me.

On her knees, in the potato patch, she thanked her good Lord for the gray cold earth that kept pulling the warmth out of her hands, and for the heart in her chest just a-steadily pumping blood all through her, especially down to her hands, and into the ground. Ground pulling and giving back and getting all chinked under her fingernails and her skin and leaving her hands cold and rough and looking like the ground, but steadily going. She ran out of five-eight baskets before she knew it. Went up to the field shanty and got some more.

"I hope my die you are a picking woman." Irena kept trying to say something cheerful, instead of mourning, when Mariah sprinkled those empty baskets all up and down the row so they'd be situated right when she got to them.

"I didn't come out here for to play around, girl. Calvertown hospital's got to have some money to bring this child into the world. Course you, Irena, you going off from this dirt to Philadelphia pretty soon and you ain't gonna never know what it's like to bring a child into this place. Your mamma's gonna see to it that the money comes from somewhere for to help you make something of yourself in those cities. Better ask God for to bless your mamma. Hard as times is, too."

"I'm already something. You talk the same way Papa and them talk sometimes about how I ain't nothing, you ain't nothing, this one ain't from shit, and all that. And I'm sick and tired of hearing it. Hear Poppy tell it, you ain't nothing but some kind of murderer for sending Aunt Cora Lou up the road yesterday, and I ain't nothing but a slut for wanting to go off to the cities. But tell me who's worse than him. Coming in bossing everybody around like they dogs. In and out all night, but each time he come in he set in barking at people. Got so mad with me this morning, Rah, he started in foaming at the mouth when I asked him why he was out so much last night. . . ."

Irena talked herself into such a forward sprint she left Mariah way behind, clinging to a basket.

And try as she would, Mariah couldn't catch up with anybody else that day.

She ate a mess of oyster fritter sandwiches with the other women when they came in to the woods clearing for dinner. Choking was such a mess in her chest she didn't hardly have two words to say to anybody. Didn't half know most of them anyway. They came from on Back-of-the-Creek. Jerry Larmer could easily haul them over to Tangierneck for work because they didn't have anything over in their place but some kind of barren earth.

Tiredness numbed Mariah's legs right smart when she got back to her row. She said to the Lord, "It must be those cold oyster fritters I ate for lunch that's giving me such a shortness of the breath. People from the cities is probably right. I ought not to eat those cold greasy things when I'm carrying this young'un." Oysters weren't too fresh, anyhow. Been two or three days since Jacob brought them from the water. But molasses sandwiches she never did have much of a taste for so she never carried them for her dinner. Didn't have much of a choice but to eat them oysters.

If she could only belch and lift some of that heaviness from her chest. Heaviness in her neck, too.

Maybe it was Aunt Cora Lou that brought such a sad tired over her. And those poor little children! And maybe it was even Miss Bannie. The night and the running washed all over her.

She started in talking to herself out loud. "You dwelling on it too much, Mariah. You got to get on down this row. Day be done before you know it."

If she could only just go to sleep. Uneasiness itched her. Felt like something was pulling her down to sleep.

Hear tell, women in the cities take a nap after they eat when they're in a family way. If the field was a bed she'd lay right down in it. Didn't feel like lifting a thing.

Her gaze just lolled all sleepy-feeling over the swamp. Spruce trees were dark and warm to the eyes. Pine smelled so sweet. Wished she could go off into some kind of a warm, deep sleep. . . . Potato basket was just too much to push. Didn't care if she moved it another inch further. "Honey, you ain't got to kick me that much," she muttered to the child.

Jacob was right about these fields. They wouldn't see her tomorrow unless she felt a whole lot better. . . . Ought to get this basket up to the field shanty right now. Ought to cash in her tokens and go on home. Get a good dose of baking soda and get rid of that lump in her chest. Lay down a minute or two before those children piled in for their supper. Walk real slow so she could gather the shrubs she promised the children.

"Lord, I don't feel so good!" And the Lord helped her to get to her feet and start in shuffling her basket up to the shanty.

She'd no more than got up to the shanty when she spied Skeeter, running across the field. Streaking down on her like greased lightning. Hollered something! Irena running to catch him. Other folks coming behind Irena. Whole field of women moving in on her! Felt as if her stocking was slipping down. Legs going to pieces under her. Had to pull her stocking up. She tried to bend down. Thick pain walloped the bottom of her belly.

"Mamma, Mamma!" Boy must've seen a student-doctor —kind that steals children to experiment on—or a ghost. She had to hold her hand out to keep him from hitting her smack in the gut. Tears flew down his twisted face.

"Miss Bannie's dead, Mamma!" Child shook all over. "Tried to wake her up and get our milk. . . . I know she's dead, Mamma, 'cause she's cold and her legs is drawed up like Mary's. . . ."

The whole world turned dark, smothering green. Everybody's head swam together in one green, light green, dark green, sinking to black, stormy, swamp mess. World pressed down on her chest. She reached out her hands to cut her way through it. Noisy chattering was nothing but waves roaring, echoing. There was water all over her. Running over her feet. *But I ain't at the Gut!* If she could only separate things. Deep Gut water ran cold and angry, getting hotter as it ran up her legs. Hot pain banged away. Her jaws unhinged themselves. Her bottom was cracking. She clawed for light and saw Aunt Saro Jane's face. Big, warm lips moving right over Mariah's face. *When you get to the field, Aunt Saro?*

"Lift her up, Tillie! We got to carry her home. Lydy, brace her back." Aunt Saro Jane took charge.

"It's your time, Miss Mariah?" A little girlish voice floated in the water that kept creeping over Mariah's face. Big booming sounds bossed her eardrums.

"Gal, why you asking such foolish questions? Can't you see her water done broke?"

That was Ruth talking. Big muscular woman from up the road. Mariah opened her eyes to see Skeeter's little torn-up face. Aunt Saro Jane was begging and praising the Lord all at the same time. Hefty arms lifted her up, cradled her head.

Sickening pain thudded in her thighs. She reached for Skeeter. Tongue felt like it was stuck. "Everything's all right, baby. Mamma's just going to New York."

Skeeter backed away from her hand. Sounded so funny to hear that little boy crying, and away he went bawling and she couldn't get down to grab him! "Great God Almighty, Mamma's gonna leave us right here in Tangierneck. Got to tell Daddy!"

But it wasn't funny. "Somebody go catch my boy! I done told him 'bout New York. How come he ain't learned?" Her arms felt as if they were being wrenched from their sockets. "Somebody go get my boy and tell him I ain't going to that city, New York."

Ruth pinned her arms back in place. Talk swirled over her head.

"I never did think much of telling children that New York business. Some silly way to be fooling young'uns about having a baby."

"What else you going to tell them? They fresh as dishwater now."

Talk went away from her, talk came back. "My baby, my baby!" she tried to tell somebody.

"How close is the pains, Sister Rah?"

"Tell me a dry birth's a hard birth. Child's water broke too soon."

"Hush your mouth," Aunt Saro Jane said. "Don't you know when to say a thing and when not to?"

"I was just asking."

Mariah cracked her eyes to see Lydy, squirrel-faced and scared.

"Don't talk no more. You go get Lettie, gal."

Their talk became a fuzzy ringing in Mariah's ears.

"My baby's gonna be born in Calvertown hospital." Mariah thought she said it out loud, but nobody answered her. They just kept carrying her, a mile a minute. Joggling and heaving, and steadily going.

Crystal clear bell sounds went a-ding, a-ding, ding. Head shriveled up with the noise.

"Irena went to call up Dr. Grene and Bertha Ann to come from the oyster house."

Death rings sweet bells when it's coming after you. Pain hit her hard. *You left Bannie by the water too long! You ain't stayed to watch after her when you did get her home.* She gasped to scream. Pain snapped the scream half in two. She gnawed on her tongue.

"One of you all go git her mamma."

Mariah could make out Ruth's voice better'n anybody else's.

"I s'pect Lydy'll stop by her mamma's and let her know. Child needs love in a time like this."

Couldn't be anybody else but Aunt Saro Jane talking. She tried to see Aunt Saro Jane. Nothing in her eyes but the sky. "Don't want no Lettie Cartwright 'round me. . . ." If she could only get a-loose from them! But the arms tightened under her.

"It ain't likely Dr. Grene'll get here in time."

"Child's sick as a dog."

Gray-headed woman loomed over her. "Hold on to yourself, honey. Hold on."

Somebody way off was whispering. "I seen women go out of their minds in a time like this."

Jesus . . . Jesus, ain't that you? White angel was swooping down, almost brushing her face. *Ain't no Jesus. It ain't got no face! Death ain't got no face!*

"Lean her head on the side!"

"Child's choking on her tongue!"

"Look at her eyes, walled back in her head. Praise God! Have mercy, Jesus!"

"Stop gnawing on your tongue, Mariah. Stop it, gal. Let go your tongue, you hear me?" And that was her own mother's voice, panting from the running she did to catch up with the women toting Mariah home.

Mamma Effie's cold hand was wiping her forehead. Strokes were all mixed in with the smothering angel's wings swooping over her face. Almost fanning her breath away. She gasped for air, but it kept getting fanned away. Whispered, "Git Jacob. Got something . . . I . . . I . . . want to tell him. . . . Mamma, where's Gezee?"

"Took him over to Vyella's house. She's home early today. Rabbit went there, too. . . . Don't know where Skeeter's at. Hush! You ain't got nothing for to worry about."

"Ain't it snowing?"

"Yeah, it's snowing, honey. We soon have you home where it's warm. Hush, hush."

"Where's Jacob at?"

Eyes. A whole crowd of eyes looked down at her like she didn't say anything. Women just kept chattering. "We got to get her home in a hurry, Sisters. . . . Carry her easy. . . . We almost there. . . . What's she mumbling?"

Mariah closed her eyes. They were heavy under a blanket of wet snow. "Don't want no Lettie. . . ."

And the women carried her on home, saying, "Hush, honey, hush. . . . Everything's gonna be all right."

Bertha Ann wasn't long getting herself a ride from the oyster house so she could be by Mariah's side. She stood all stern-faced near Mariah's bed. Taking over Mamma Effie's place. Eyes were all sunk back in her head but just a-flashing. Head a-bobbing while she gave out orders to the other women hovering around and talking in low tones. "Is the washbasin sterilized? You all know you have to boil it a long time. . . . You all ain't got enough heat in this house. Lydy, s'pect you better go out and bring in a turn of wood. . . . How long she been like this. . . . Is either one of you thought to pray?"

Through the nauseous pain fog, Mariah heard Aunt Saro Jane saying, "We all been praying, Bertha. Now, it

ain't no need of you coming in here taking on so. Child's in
the Lord's hands. He'll bring her through."

Heard Mamma Bertha racing around the kitchen,
searching for the Bible. Asking about when Mariah got this
pain and that kind of bleeding. And then a long silence,
broken into with whispering. And then Mamma Bertha
saying, "Dead, when she get dead."

*Folks must be talking about Miss Bannie. I ain't dead, is
I, Lord?* Baby was just a-busting her bottom parts wide
open. She clawed on the pretty quilt her Mamma Effie
burdened her down with. But there was nobody in the
room except that white angel, full of heat now. Smothering
her! Felt like the thing was saying to her, *Streets of
heaven are paved with gold. You be eating milk and honey
all day.*

"Don't like no honey!" And she hit at that thing and hit
at it. But it wouldn't go away.

She could see Jacob's mamma hustling into the room.
"Ain't no point in us dwelling on Bannie now, Sisters.
Lord'll take care of her soul." And ordering—that's always the way Mamma Bertha Ann was. Ordering everybody but Pop Percy. She just carried on, telling anybody
who wanted to go or home and fix their supper for their
menfolks and children to go, for the snow was getting
heavy outside. And after all, it was her son's baby that was
getting born—that was her reason for being there. She
didn't need everybody all crowded around. Bad enough
that Vyella brought Rabbit and Gezee on home. Children
wouldn't be doing nothing but trying to sneak around gaping their eyes at their mamma's private parts. Boys would
grow up with such nasty ways, seeing all of that. . . .

"Children, you all get outside and play, or set in that
kitchen quiet," she snapped. And to the women, "Lord
don't will but for three people to stay in this room now.
That's Effie and me and Lettie. . . ."

"Child don't want no Lettie," Mariah's mamma stam-
mered, twisting herself past Bertha Ann and the rigid-
faced midwife, Lettie, and easing the quilt back from
Mariah's legs. Just a-steadily stammering as she went on.
"You don't want no Lettie do you, honey?" Talking all
wild-tongued, but Mariah understood her. "You ain't got
to have no Lettie less'n, less'n . . . Gal, who you looking
at so evil? Rah, ain't no need for you to be looking at me

like that. I did the best I could by you. Don't be acting
like no bitch, Rah, Rah! God!"

"Effie, you worse for the child than I'd be, talking to her
like that." Tall woman moved up to the bed. Hands moving all quick, and nervous. "Listen, Mariah, I ain't killed
Mary. Was the will of God. Hear me . . . the will of a
just and merciful God. Bertha Ann, keep this rag over her
head. . . . I don't even think she hears me. How long ago
since Irena called for that Dr. Grene?"

But Mariah did hear her. Saw her in that yawning hole
of pain in back of her head. She was bony as a witch and
she was flying all around the bed. Room was in a regular
commotion. Mamma Effie was talking in tongues, and
Bertha Ann praying loud enough to beat the band. Mariah's eyes flew wide when Lettie touched her. She said,
"No, Miss Lettie. No! No!"

White angel raised a gauze thin bat wing, and all she
could see of the angel was a smile. Its whole head was a
smile. White head kept getting mixed in with Lettie's stern
black head. White angel's lips were the color of the setting
sun. She was on fire all over. And the angel spoke in
tongues of flame that licked every inch of Mariah's body
until she moaned, "Water!"

*God said you're too tired to go on, Mariah. God said to
bring you home.*

"Death. Get away from me." Her hands clawed on the
flaming crackling mess all underneath her. Had to get up.
Baby hurting her so bad! *Jesus!*

"Hold her down, Bertha. Hold her down!"

Hands were on her belly. Wet rag on her head.

"Baby's head almost all the way down!" Must be
Mamma Effie screeching.

Bertha Ann's eyes wallowed in the sea rising over Mariah's ears. If she could only hold on to her mamma's
voice! That's what she was reaching out trying to hold on
to. Her hands didn't feel real to her.

"Effie, shut up and pray to God!" Bertha Ann talking.

Clapping in the kitchen made such a funny noise. Wasn't
nobody but Vyella talking, playing with her children.

"Come on, clap, Gezee. Your mamma's all right. Make
a happy sound unto the Lord. Rabbit, don't you be trying
to get into that room no more. Lord's in charge of your

mamma. Come on, clap. Pudding tan, pudding tan, where you been?—Round the world and back again."

"How come the Lord letting her hurt like that then? 'Cause she ain't nothing but a whore? Aunt Vyella, ain't my mamma nothing but a whore? Grandmamma Bertha said that. . . ."

Rabbit's voice . . . Rabbit. . . .

"Vyella, if you can't control those children's tongues out there, I don't know what kind of success you gonna make in the pulpit." Bertha Ann stormed away from the bed. Met Vyella coming head on into the room.

Vyella sounded like she was crying. "Mamma, ain't a worse thing nobody can tell a child than that its mamma's a whore. Ain't a worse thing. Rabbit said you the one told him. . . . I don't have charge of his tongue. . . ."

"I ain't told him no such a thing. Gonna lick his ass . . . Oh my God, take charge of my tongue. Oh my God. Give me the strength. We got the child's mother to look after."

"Well, I'm here to tell you Mariah ain't no whore," Vyella said. "You all better ask for the grace of God and do a good job by her in there. She ain't no worser than nobody in that room. She ain't never found her way back to the Church on account of you all."

Aunt Saro Jane said, "Amen."

"Vy, now Vy, don't lose control of yourself. You got the children for to take care of. . . . Go on back in the kitchen." Bertha Ann waved her on away.

A blackness came over Mariah's eyesight, but it didn't stick long. Heard first a door slamming and then Skeeter crying from the bottom of his stomach. Skeeter always cried like that. She tried to tell somebody, "Bring me my boy," but there wasn't anybody close except Lettie Cartwright, messing with her and saying things like, "I'll pray with you, Sister. Knows I don't know as much as those doctors, but I does know something!"

"You all bring Skeeter on in here." Mariah found something in herself to call out. And Skeeter, he flung himself all slobbering onto the pillow. Just a-kissing her and chasing away that cold angel.

"Where you been to so long, Skeeter? You ain't even had your coat fastened up. Boy, you wet."

"I couldn't find Daddy, Mamma. I skinned up the pole

by the ferry. But I couldn't see the boats. Goblins done filled the air up with snow. And I hollered for him, Mamma . . . Mamma, and he didn't even hear me. And I told him we was on our way to New York, and he didn't even hear me!"

"Somebody take the wet clothes off my boy. Wipe that snot off his nose. Set him by the fire. Bake the cold out of him. . . ."

But Skeeter wouldn't let go of her when they tried to unloosen him. "I turned to the east and I turned to the west, all the way up the road, and I crossed myself."

"Leave him alone. Leave my boy alone," she said to whomsoever it was trying to pull him off of her. He was so scared she forgot her own hurt.

"All the way home. Goblins was all around me. But they scatted away every time I crossed myself." His little breath was all hot on her neck. And he was sniffling so. *My Lordy, Jesus. My Lordy.* Why's the boy in such a tremble? Baby felt like it made it all the way down to her hole, just a-socking her in it. But she had to keep a-hold of Skeeter.

"And then I run into the posse on the way up the road where you go into Grandmamma's. And they grabbed a-hold of me and asked me if I wasn't the last one to see Miss Bannie. And did I give her the poison what killed her. And I said I ain't never give nobody no poison. Said to me over and over again if I wasn't the last one over to her house. Asked me who beat her up first, before I give her the poison. I said, first or last what difference does it make. She was already good and dead when I got there. She wasn't no good nohow. Done stole our land, didn't she? Posse man said to me, 'Git on home, you little nigger. You ain't nothing but a liar.' One of them tried to take my pants off me, Mamma. But I wiggled a-loose. Other one just hit on me all across my behind. Chased me piece-ways up the path, telling me to run a little faster. Run a little faster, nigger. That's all he kept saying. . . . Mamma, when we going to New York?"

Skeeter started coughing so. "We ought to get out of here and go. Leave Daddy right here if he don't hear nobody when they calling him. . . . Mamma, I ain't give no Miss Bannie the poison when I went there for the milk. She was already dead."

And Skeeter sank on her chest and cried. Sank all the

way into her chest it felt like. And she wouldn't let go of him. Wouldn't let go of the pain busting her thighs apart either.

Somebody said, "Take him away. It ain't fitting for the boy to be in here."

"They asked me what did I know about Dr. Grene. . . . What was he doing down here over to Miss Bannie, when he's supposed to be looking after my nigger mother. Said Jerry Larmer heard Aunt Irena calling up on the phone for him to come down and tend to you. . . ."

And it didn't matter to Mariah if she did hurt. No more, Lord, no more. She kept trying to tell whoever was pulling Skeeter away, "Rub Skeeter's behind down with the vaseline. Tell him I'll be able to talk with him more, now and in a few minutes. Tell him to pray to Jesus. . . . Tell him he ain't done it. Tell him I'm the one did it. Hadn't no business provoking anger. . . . Hadn't no business leaving her there with them pills by herself."

But she just lay all rigid.

White angel's fingers jammed down her throat, messed with her tongue. And she kept trying to tell Miss Bannie, "Lean easy on me. Take a-hold of my hand." She tried to spit her tongue out. It was too heavy. And it was as though it was heavy and swollen just like Miss Bannie's.

"Where you all taking Skeeter?" Words sank all back in her throat.

"Effie, keep that rag cold. Dip it in the water! Keep her head down!"

And Mariah felt, if she could only get her head up off that pillow, she could make somebody hear her words! She'd tell her mamma, take that wash rag off my head so she could see how to hit and hit and hit and knock away that filmy thing hovering in her sights.

"Bear down, Mariah. Let the little child out," Lettie said.

"I got to wait. . . . Got to get to the hospital."

"Even if you'd a-got there, strumpet, I mean baby, Jesus, God, it ain't no guarantee they'd a-took you in. Colored ward ain't that big. Sure wouldn't take you in the white." That was Mamma Effie crying.

"Let go my arms. You all hurting my legs. Mamma, your breath smells so bad. You ought to learn tooth brushing. Get out of my face. . . ."

Pain after pain came and she felt like she was drawing up in double knots. A violent shudder drew her up in half. And the face that wasn't even a face loomed over her belly, smiling. Sounded like the thing was singing. *Come to Jesus. Come to Jesus, ju-ust now.*

"Ain't going to no Jesus. Ain't going. Going to the hospital."

"Lettie, is your scissors ready?"

"No, no! Lettie ain't killing neither 'nother child of mine." Mariah blinked for the light. Saw Miss Lettie stepping back from the bed. Just a-rearing back. Looked to Mariah like Miss Lettie was running. "Murderer, get your ignorance out of my sight! That's right, run!"

"Come back here, Lettie. God knows what you is done and what you ain't," Mamma Bertha cried. "He's your judge, not Mariah."

"God! God! Call on Jesus, Mariah! He'll see you through," Vyella said. And Mariah tried to remember when Vyella came back into the room. "Let us pray, Sisters."

Vyella had a face like a young angel's. Kind that you walk through the fields with when it's spring. And the buttercups are all out. And the dogwood is perfuming up the world. Just light, light.

Mamma Bertha Ann started in praying, "God, only you know when the last germ's burned off of a navel bandage. If it was Lettie's fault that the last one got laid over in Cleveland's Field, guide her hands not to touch Mariah this time. . . ."

"Strumpet, open your legs!" Mamma Effie busted in on the prayer. "I'll beat your ass if you don't. . . ." Just a-crying and patting on Mariah's feet, she went on and on.

"Now Effie, that ain't no way for to be talking now. We in the midst of prayer. . . ."

"Mariah ain't no praying. . . . Got such an evilness in her. Only thing she ever felt was in her thing."

"Get her away from me! Leave go my legs!" Mariah lifted her head a little bit. Eyes seemed to be getting so clear. Cried, "Jesus!" when she looked down on herself. Skin of her belly was all knotted up in little pounding humps. She let go. Said, "Je-e-e-sus."

Thing slid out of her.

Mamma Bertha Ann grabbed it and lifted it head down,

up in the air. Called on Miss Lettie, "Where's your scissors at?"

And Lettie cut the cord. Just that quick.

"I sterilized the scissors good, Sisters. I ain't been no careless this time. . . ." String-beany woman trembled by the bed.

"Blessed be to God, it's a girl." Mamma Effie started right in wailing. Rocking herself from side to side. "Ain't making a sound. Say something! Say something!" And she started in spanking on the little wet thing until it commenced to make little air-grabbing sounds. Then it let out a holler to beat the band. She snatched it from Mamma Bertha Ann.

"Don't be hitting on her no more, Mamma. That's the last hit you ever gonna lay on her behind. She be gone from this Neck before you ever get a chance to break her back with the beatings!" Mariah, straining, shoved herself from under the covers. Got on her feet, blood running all over the floor. Shoved out her hands to push back whomsoever even acted like they was gonna touch her. "Give me my baby. Done spoke to God!"

Women in the room set up a regular commotion—reaching and wailing and yelling: "Oh my God, catch her. . . ." "Leave her alone. . . ." "God works in mysterious ways. . . ." "I don't believe he works that mysterious. . . ."

Vyella came through the clearest, saying, "Give her her baby, Mrs. Effie. God's with her."

Room got quiet.

And with nobody supporting her trembling body, Mariah took her only living girl child out of her mamma's hands. Handed it over to Vyella for the washing. Then she took the rag bandage Miss Lettie was fixing to burn away from that quivering woman. With tears streaming down her face she made it across the room to that little tin stove, saying, "I'm burning this bandage my ownself. Promise the Lord if anybody takes my daughter's life, it's gonna have to be me. . . . And I'm gonna see to it, Sisters. . . . Raise my hand to God. . . . This young'un's gonna live. Kill me if you want to. Kill me for all I'm guilty of, but ain't a neither one of you gonna hurt my children no more."

And she laid the muslin strip on the reddest part of the stove. Held it there until it turned black and her fingers started in hurting. Then she took it and waved it in the air for to cool it off. Tested its temperature against her cheek.

Mamma Bertha Ann called for prayer. "Come to Jesus. Let all who have sinned and are heavy laden come to Je-e-e-sus."

In the middle of the prayer, Mariah stumbled through a tangled pathway of reaching arms and wailing "Jes-us," and Miss Lettie grabbing a-hold of her. "Child, you ain't even brought the afterbirth yet! Give me that bandage and lay yourself down."

"No, I ain't giving you this bandage, Miss Lettie. I'm going to make it through, Jesus!" And she laid that bandage over the little girl child's navel her ownself. Hands were just a-shaking, but she laid it there right. Said to the quivering ball, "Ain't no germs on this one, honey. You gonna live. Ain't gonna end up in no Cleveland's Field."

Looked like the little thing puckered its lips up for her. Made Mariah so happy. She started in smiling and grunting and smiling and grunting . . . and rejoicing even over the clot of blood slithering down her legs.

"You is a pretty little thing, young'un. Onliest thing, I don't think you been washed off too good. Vyella . . . Vy, bring me that basin of water. You all ain't got all the baking soda off this young'un. She looks right white!"

Looked to Mariah like Vyella wanted to cry for her face screwed up so, before she blurted out, "We done washed everything off of her we could, Sister. Color she is . . . color she is. . . . What I'm trying to say is, color is a will of God. You can't go by no features when you first look at a new child. . . ."

The room went black for Mariah. She woke to find herself all tucked in the bed, and a new warm thing snuggling by her titties. Couldn't open her eyes though for the talk. All in the kitchen. All around her bed. Careful kind of whispering was going on . . . some she could get a-hold of.

"It ain't got no hair, just like white folks' babies."

"It don't favor Jacob. . . ."

"Now you all hush, now. It don't favor a thing, yet. . . ."

"God bless its soul though. . . ."

"Got a rattling in its chest already. Thing's done took a cold."

"Gonna be a green winter. . . . Bad sign, Lord, Lord, Lord."

"Maybe it'll be for the best if the Lord does see fit to take it. . . ."

Mariah just hugged the new little thing. Closed her eyes to the chatter and the ghosts traveling up from Cleveland's Field.

9

In a twilight, white with snow, Jacob plowed—felt like he was plunging—on in home. Couldn't seem to miss the snowdrifts—kind that make your knees buckle under you —though he knew the road like he knew the palm of his hand.

Pop Percy, wheezing and coming along behind him, said a time or two, "Boy, slack up!"

"I ain't got no time for to be slacking up, Pop! Ain't you heard Zeke and them say that Skeeter was down to the Gut this afternoon? Mariah sent for me."

"Done heard it all, Jacob. Done heard, too, that Bannie passed away from here. Funniest thing how death comes in groups. Now we got your Aunt Cora Lou to put away Sunday, and on top of that, Bannie's gone."

"We ain't got nothing to do with no Bannie! Good she's gone, ain't it, Pop? Now maybe we can talk some sense into those bank people about this land." Jacob couldn't keep the bitterness out of his voice. Couldn't help from noticing the way his father flinched.

"Ain't no sense to be talked into them, Jacob. Don't go so fast, boy! I'm trying to tell you something. Onliest thing I can do is fight them with my bare fists. . . ."

But Jacob sped on up that path to home. Didn't want to remember the way his papa had been trying to make up with him all day.

"I'm glad you getting out of here, boy. Gonna be one time in the land . . ." Pop Percy kept after Jacob all the way up the path. Just a-wheezing and a-panting. Every now and then, Jacob would try to give the old man a lift.

Arguing with him most of the time. "Papa, I got to get on in home!" Knew his papa had the heart trouble, but Jacob couldn't see where in and where out he had it that bad. For the old man just kept a-stopping him on the road.

Carrying on mostly over the way those white boys ran Cora Lou down and the way Bannie went away from here on the very day afterwards. But not even mentioning the way they were told Mariah had to bring that new baby into the world. And how some were saying she done went clean out of her mind!

When they got up to the house Jacob said to him, "Papa, I'm going in. Is you coming?"

"There's too many people in your house right now, Jacob. Mostly what's gonna be there is women just a-talking about death and all those dreams they had. Dreams of fat hog meat boiling and a naked man meaning death of a woman, and nose dripping a few drops of blood and then stopping clean . . . and that meaning death, too. That's all that's gonna be in there. I ain't in no frame of mind for to listen to it. Boy, these women can't see into no future."

So Jacob left his father hesitating on the doorsteps and grumbling about the women and the dreams.

Shivered in the shed kitchen for a minute or two. Tried to take his time getting off his coat and things. But he couldn't take too much time! Wanted to see Mariah and that new young'un. Dreams the women talked about could really mean death of a girl child—a woman even!

Heard Vyella and Aunt Saro Jane and he didn't know who all, just a-chattering in the real kitchen. "That must be Jacob coming in," "Warm these greens up again, girl. Ain't nothing Jacob likes better than greens."

Heard them all. But mostly what he wanted to hear was Mariah say, "I'm all right, Jacob, and the baby is, too." So he swept on through that kitchen filled with noise and tongue-wagging and thick smells of Welfare raisin pies and turnips and stewed muskrats and all kinds of donations from the kitchens of the Neck—into the room where Mariah lay, eyes closed to the world.

"Is you all right, Rah? Is you all right, hon? Heard tell you had a right smart hard time, hon. Oh my, Rah!"

Wasn't nothing but the good Lord keeping him standing on his feet. Ought to go down on his knees. Oh my God! Woman looked so bad. Didn't know whether to touch her or not.

She opened her eyes and smiled a little bit. Looked like the smile hurt her. "I'm all right, Jacob. How you, hon?"

"I'm all right, hon. I'm all right. Just wants you to know

I'm glad to see you. That's all. Just wants you to know, Rah, the boat made six dollars today. And Papa and Uncle Johnathon told me not even to split it up with them 'cause your time came. Said they'd get a-hold of the money themselves for to put Aunt Cora Lou . . . Rah, I . . ." But he got a-hold of himself. "Let me see the young'un. What you got her bundled up there so tight for?"

And he took Mariah's hand. Ought to kiss it, but he thought to himself that ain't nothing but some foolish kind of airs I feels like putting on. "Rah, let me see the baby."

But Mariah wouldn't let go of the little bundle, so Jacob just took it away from her and unwrapped its head.

"Rah!"

"What's the matter with you, Jacob?" Mariah moaned, not even opening her eyes.

"Well, she ain't got no hair, that's a sure thing." And Jacob's hands trembled on the white-looking skin. "And she sure is what you'd call a pretty young'un." *Like in them magazines. White-looking baby!* He couldn't move his eyes from the strange-looking skin. "A kish-a-kish or a mish-i-mish," he spoke to the child. "Now which one is it you singing?" His voice was a stranger to him. "Bard Tom Upshur was gonna be your name if you'd been a boy. What I'm gonna call you now?"

"Child was born with a cold, Jacob." Mariah's voice sounded strange and far away.

"Why you crying, Rah?"

"Got the headache," she murmured.

"Hon. . . ." But the word felt right strange on his tongue. Couldn't to save his life ever get over the way that new thing looked. He just stood by the bed like a confounded robot. His head thumped. Children were making such a racket in the kitchen. And on top of that, his eyes felt like they were nothing but burning white-hot patches. Tried to tell himself to calm down. Heart thundered: Mariah ain't betrayed me. This young'un's mine! White's in the family! That's how come she come out looking like this. Tried to hold on to the young'un and call it hon, but he shoved it on back into Mariah's arms. Shouted worse than a confounded woman at the noise coming from the kitchen and the pounding in his head. "Cut out that racket! Now Rabbit, I wants you to stop that racket! Don't you know your mamma's sick with the headache?"

Well what did he holler like that for? House went so quiet. God have mercy! So quiet for a minute that the only thing he could hear was his heart saying thoughts which he felt ashamed for even thinking. *It ain't mine is it, Mariah? Tell me the truth, Mariah.* Noise started rising up again.

And just that minute Vyella came bouncing her soothing-syrup self into the room. Just a-flying from one task to the other. First to the sideboard, hunting after aspirins. "Jacob, where's you-all's aspirin tablets?" And then to the bed, grabbing a-hold of the baby. "Come to Aunt Vyella, you little tweet t'ing you. Now ain't she some pretty young'un, Jacob?" Vyella cast him some kind of sly fetching glance. "She looks just like you for the world."

And Jacob flew out of that room. Grabbed himself a switch from the woodbox. He went for Rabbit. "Shut up. Cut out the racket!"

But that scalawag Rabbit had to keep right on talking. "Daddy, is we gonna call it Bard Tom like you said? It ain't no boy. . . ."

"Shut up, boy, else I'm gonna . . ."

"She don't even look like us. . . ." Skeeter had to get his two cents in.

"I'll tear up both of you-all's behinds if you don't be quiet."

"Daddy, is we going to the hall tonight?"

"Daddy, what we gonna call her?"

That's the way the children kept talking. Heat from the kitchen stove burned a steady roar. Jacob sat down. Held his head so close to the fire it felt like his very brains were melting. He tried to sniff back the pain running down his nostrils, but a stinging seized his eyelids. Had to snap them hard to keep from crying. Clamped his mouth shut, too. Wasn't gonna talk to nobody. Not to Sandy Fitzhugh trudging into his house all barefooted and slopping up the floor and running his mouth about the meeting at the hall tonight, and the new baby. "Jacob, now I'm telling you one thing, that's a pretty young'un. We ought to name the school after her."

Not to Ol Jefferson and his waddle-behinded, owl-eyed schoolteacher wife, both husband and wife stinking like each other, bringing the house a quick dose of "God's beautiful blessings" and another Welfare raisin pie. And prayers for the Lord's sympathetic understanding for the time of death in the family. Acting like they were trying to get out of his house in a hurry, but lingering at the door. Ol, all slope-shouldered, repeating after his wife, "We got to go to the meeting. Build up the community. . . ." Wished they would hurry up!

Not to his papa, who'd finally made up his mind to come in, sitting there wringing his hands by the fire. Talking about going across the Virginia line tomorrow. "We got to get a-hold of some money. . . . You right to leave this land, boy. . . . We ain't doing nothing here but going down. . . . Got to put your Aunt Cora Lou away decent. . . ." Just a-jumping from one thought to the other. And any fool could tell his mind wasn't on a thing he said.

No! Jacob wasn't gonna say a word to nobody, no more than "How you?" and a few things like that to the people passing in and out of his house bringing food and the Lord's blessings and reminders that it was Halloween—the night for the Dead Souls to come up cavorting—and sending his children into a fit to go out. And sending him into a double fit about letting Vyella or somebody look after Mariah so he could go out to the Hall for a few minutes and help them deal with that white man from the Sears Roebuck catalog.

"I ain't gonna leave no Mariah," he finally said to somebody. Maybe it was the whole roomful of them, he was burning that hot.

"You ain't got no reason for not going out a few minutes now, Jacob. We women can take care of the situation. Now you's a man. Who else we got to look to but our menfolks for to do something about something?" Aunt Saro Jane kept after him. "Mariah ain't that bad off. Her mind just a little bit strained. We knows what to do. . . ."

"It ain't the matter of that," Jacob tried to tell her something. But you can't talk sense to some old people. She just kept right on rattling away. "It's just a matter of . . ." And he said no more. For what was the use? Couldn't get a word in edgewise anyway, especially when you talking with somebody as old as Aunt Saro Jane.

But for Jacob, it was a matter of getting next to Mariah with nobody else in the house. Had to ask her that question searing his brains.

But Tangierneck wouldn't let up on him, especially the women. They just came in a steady stream. Taking over his house, his children, and finally just swamping that citified-looking Doctor Grene—kind of white-looking colored man that colored women got excited over anyway—who swaggered into his house to attend to Mariah.

Jacob never saw anything like the way those women waylaid that man with a whole lot of questions about this ache and that ache, and how much would he charge if somebody came up to his office, but mostly about how did Miss Bannie die. And did he see her for real. And what did the posse say to him. Most of them even tried to follow him into the room where Mariah lay. All except blabbermouth Tillie Ried. She never did like any kind of white-looking anything, so she just put on her coat and left, throwing some kind of insinuation back at him. "Well, Jacob, how do you like *your* new baby?"

Looking over Mariah didn't take *that* doctor that long to do, but it felt to Jacob like it was taking him a year. And he could hear that doctor poking in Mariah's belly. "Does it hurt here, Mrs. Upshur? Did that hurt?"

Touch her one more time and I'm lief to go in there and . . . But Jacob couldn't think of a thing he'd do except to ask her—ask him!

But a question like that won't make no kind of sense, fool. After all, white's in the family and you can't pay no attention to Rabbit and them's foolishness—nor neither to Tillie Ried's.

But Jacob wouldn't let go of that question. It followed the swagger of the harrow-browed, white-looking man around the kitchen when he did come out of the room. It curled around Jacob's, "How much do I owe you?" Lumped in his throat over the name Bardetta Tometta for the birth certificate. Almost made him jump up and . . . But to save his life he couldn't see what he would do if he did jump up. Maybe he ought to push him out of the door. Stop him from examining Pop Percy's heart and telling the old man to take it easy. Calling him "Father" like it meant something to him in that deceitful way most citified people had of acting when they had to deal with the country people.

And maybe, maybe Jacob ought to throw those prescriptions that the worried-looking-fool doctor stuck in his hands back into the leather-smelling man's face.

But Jacob did neither, for after all, what kind of fool

was he? He didn't have proof one of nothing. And Mariah was his Mariah. *Oh my babe!* He just listened to that doctor telling him about what Mariah needed to get herself built up again into some kind of condition, and what the young'un needed, too, for she'd caught some kind of a cold already.

"Skeeter, don't that baby look the same color as Dr. Grene?" Rabbit would have to get in something to say just when that doctor went out the door.

"Get your coat, Rabbit! Get on yours, too, Skeeter! Gezee, you just about sleepy enough to go on up to bed. . . ."

"Is Jacob taking them children out, Vyella?" Mariah's voice sounded like some little Silent Night, Holy Night thing to Jacob. But she wasn't gonna stop him! No matter how pitiful she sounded.

"It's all right, hon. He's bundling them up plenty good from the cold, and I'm staying with you. Menfolks ought to go to the hall. Ain't many of them willing to go that far for the school. . . ." Vyella answered, standing all gap-legged and wise-eyed in the doorway.

"I did want that doctor to look over Skeeter before he went. Child keeps a cold in his chest. . . ."

The way Mariah talked almost kept Jacob from shoving Skeeter and Rabbit out of the door. After all, he thought, as they sunk their feet in white blanket commencing on the doorsteps, I don't have to be right. Fact is, God, I ain't really altogether right. I got my faults. And Mariah did sound so pitiful. But he said, "Come on, boys."

Boys ran ahead of him, flinging a lot of snow up in the air. And just carousing fit to beat the band. All down the path to the hall they went, throwing that white stuff every which-a-way. A whole lot of it flew into Jacob's face. And for a split second, visions of that white-looking, oh my babe, girl child, oh Mariah, son-of-a-bitch Mariah, just worked through him like a dose of salts. And he hollered at the boys, "Shit, shit, shit! Cut it out! Don't want that white shit in my face."

He'd no sooner got those words out when the gas pains socked him all under his heart. And Jacob almost went down on his knees to ask the Lord to cleanse his mouth. Cleanse his mind of those evil thoughts about the white-ness, the blinding white-ness! For after all, he was probably wrong. Mariah was a good little woman. Life just hurt her too hard. Only thing for him to do was take care of her. And he was gonna take care of his new girl child, too.

Said to the Lord, "It was just my nerves giving me them notions."

And he made up his mind that when tomorrow came, he was gonna take some asafetida for his nerves.

10

When Jacob slammed that door, it seemed to Mariah that the very mattress on the bed split open underneath her, like a gate to Hell. And she almost went down into the fiery furnace.

She moaned, "Jacob . . . Jacob." And turning to Vyella, hustling in and out of the room, she said, "What is I done to him, Vy? Lordy, what is I done?"

"What you mean, what is you done, honey? Don't be acting so silly! You ain't done nothing but give him a pretty little girl child, and he better get up off his lazy behind and do something about taking care of it."

"Yes, I is too done something!"

But Vyella didn't even pay Mariah any mind. No more than to wipe off some of the sweat pouring down her forehead and say to her, "Go to sleep, gal. You's a woman. Woman supposed to have babies and Man supposed to take care of them."

And just as quick as you please, Vyella was gone out of that room and into the kitchen, playing Skin-the-Rabbit with Gezee to get him on upstairs to bed, and chasing people out of the house, and leaving Mariah to the ghosts just a-coming from Cleveland's Field.

Ghost of Little Mary wailing over the river flowing from Mariah's forehead:

> Carry me away from Tangierneck
> Daddy, Daddy, Daddy,
> Don't want no buzzard picking at my neck,
> Paddy pick, paddy pick, paddy.

The woman shrank. Closed her eyes and cowered from the vision, but still she heard the cry. Wailed so loud, her heart started doing a whole lot of beating. Heart almost choked her. *Should've gone long ago. Saved my children. Saved myself. . . .* She fumbled to close her ears. *Pills Dr. Grene gave me must've paralyzed my hands!*

And the wailing came right on. Came over her stricken-voiced squeak to her papa and her mamma coming back by to see after her. "Why you come by so late? I was just fixing to go to sleep?" *You all go away. Get out of my sight! Don't want you to have nothing to do with my children!*

And it was as though her mamma heard her secret thoughts for she took a seat on the bench by the stove. But her papa came right on up to the bed with his lips all pushed out and booming big in his consternation when he took a look at the child. "Well, what in the name of God has the Master sent us here?"

Mariah just cringed. *Voice so much bigger than him. He ain't that big. Just my size when I stand up to him!* But Mariah couldn't move a leg, an arm, a finger, nothing! Just listen to the wailing and her papa's voice tying her very brains up in whirligigy ropes—swirling and whirling, knotting up ropes and strings that were neck-reining her—a wild mare filly—back into the night of the sure-sign-of-death's-dreams. Got to get out! *You can't run your way through the brambles and bushes of life, gal. See my scars.* Her eyelids flew wide. Saw the naked man! Saw her papa stripping down clean naked to show her his scars. Dream of a naked man means death of a female! *See my scars.* Voice of her dream kept pushing its way over the sound of her father's voice funneling through to her just then.

"Look a-here, Vyella . . . Effie! This thing don't look a bit like me. . . . Pretty little old thing though. Must take after Jacob's side of the family. Else her mamma's done took too much baking soda . . . Mariah . . . Mariah, is you listening to me, gal? What's wrong with her eyes, Vyella? What that doctor give to her?"

Smile strained to work into Mariah's lips. Quivered and died. Tongue, like a slimy pod of okra, dribbled, "Born with a cold, Papa. That's how come she's that color." *Let me run. Let me run.*

"Well, she had a right smart hard time, Mr. Harmon. And the doctor give her some heavy pills. . . ." Vyella's hand was so cool—so soft, stroking Mariah's face down.

Wiping off her lips and stopping her words. "Said she had some kind of shock."

Mariah wanted to tell her papa so bad. Get away from my baby. Don't want your paws on her. Get gone. Didn't even want you to see her—especially you. Get gone! Couldn't stop the cringing though and the spit that kept filling up her mouth. Eyelids commenced to feel right heavy. But she had to keep them cracked. Fit in her mind just what she was looking at. So many visions floating in her brain! Eyes was even seeing them. Her papa was going! Putting on his undershirt. Covering up the scars! *Gonna let me run, Papa? Gonna let me run?* Couldn't get past him though.

"Mariah? Gal? Gal? . . . Guess your mamma's trying to fall asleep, young'un. Sleep's the best thing for her." Her papa's voice was getting so soft. Then it was loud, loud, 'til it turned into a steady boom. And there was the wailing coming, too. And the chill Messenger. *Je-e-sus.*

"Guess I better leave you alone, you little ol' t'ing you. Now you is a mess! Poorly already. 'Course that Dr. Grene'll bring you out. Clear up the rattling in your chest. It ain't a better or smarter doctor ever hit this peninsula . . . and he's a black man! White-looking, but he's black. People's going around saying he's passing for colored so as to get the colored people's business. But he's black. I'd swear by that from the way they tell me he argued with the cops down to Bannie's this afternoon. He'll tend . . ."

"Baby can't understand nothing you saying, Mr. Harmon." Vyella sounded so tired. Even kinda far away. But Mariah fought to hold on. "Why don't you come over here and sit by the fire for a spell with me and Mrs. Effie? Tell us what happened down there to Bannie's. . . ."

"Well, you know I wasn't there, Vy. But I did hear down to the store how the sheriff wanted to put the woman's death to some kind of mishandling. But that doctor proved them out to be wrong! Proved right there that it was a blue pill that killed her. . . ."

"Blue pill! Oh my Lord. Wonder why that poor soul took that? Them things is the poisonest things out!" Vyella whispered.

And Mariah moaned. Shrank from the chill Messenger's tap on her shoulders. Mumbled, "Bardetta, I ain't done it. I ain't done it! I ain't meant to do it. . . ."

"What kind of fool talk is that Mariah's talking?" Her Mamma Effie got up from the bench.

"I ain't heard her say nothing, Effie. You ain't heard her say nothing either. Just your mind going out of control. Sit down and leave that girl rest. What you messing with that quilt for? It's already fixed good enough!" Papa ordered. Mamma, creeping up to the bed, slunk back from it.

Vyella cut in on the infernal racket. *Understanding Vyella. Sweet thing!* Getting them out of the house with a "Now I *know* something about nursing. We better stop talking about these things in front of Mariah. She's trying to go to sleep! And we working against the doctor, just a-chittering and chattering."

And just a-chittering and chattering they went out of the room. But stayed in the house! *Please Jesus, tell Mamma and Papa to go on away. Don't want to hear him no more. No more, Lord. Shut him up. Jesus, I gots to talk with Vyella. Ask her to explain. . . .*

". . . Now Vyella, you aspiring to preach the Gospels, right? Well I'm here to tell you something about those Scriptures. . . ."

Ain't Papa never gonna get through talking? Jesus!

"In the history of mankind, this is still the reign of the first horseman, but he's about to give way to the second. The first one's white and he's a man of conquering. Never does care who he steps on to conquer. . . . Glad I ain't got but a few drops of that white blood in me. . . . The second one's red, the servant of the bullying white. Red as blood he is, and that means he's war. Next thing's gonna happen to us, Vyella, is war! It's gonna be bloody and it's gonna be war, and numbers of wars.

"But the third one's black, and he shall come after the plague of wars have ravished the earth. He's gonna come with the scales of the Universal God in his hands. Weighing the damages of the white and the red and living on in wisdom, ruling the earth until the coming of the pale horseman—the last messenger of God. Pale horseman's death, Vyella!

"But before the coming of the pale horseman, Ethiopia shall stretch forth her wings and take control! Black Ethiopia! That's what the third horseman stands for, according to the Book of Revelations: the black nations overcoming all. Bringing the ways of Godliness, which is love and peace to the nations of the world. Bringing these things to the white peoples who's even now running all the nations of the world. You got to learn your Bible, Vyella, 'fore you can take to the pulpit. It's a pity this young'un Mariah's got looks so much like 'em. . . . Ethiopia means Africa, and Africa shall reign again. . . ."

Mariah thought she heard the woodbox turn over. Such a brain-dulling thud resounded through the house. Jerked her back to groping to piece everything together that was going on around her. Door to her room was flung wide open. Saw Vyella just as plain as day dressed in the blue uniform she wore when she worked out in service. Standing with her hands on her hips in front of Mamma and Papa. She was just a-shaking her head.

"Now Mr. Harmon, for all you know, Mariah done heard you say something about the child that just ain't right. Furthermore, I wants to know from you what color shall God be. You interpret that for me 'fore you tell *me* I can't take to the pulpit."

"God ain't to be seen for that would require the breaking of the Seventh Seal. But he shall come as the fifth and last—a great spirit unseeable to the unclean heart. And a woman is a mighty unclean person unless they learn how to respect their menfolks. Menfolks just have to put up with them. . . . Women supposed to take to the keeping of the house and not to the keeping of business outside the house! Supposed to obey their man!"

"You ought to stop trying to interpret these Scriptures to me, Mr. Harmon." Vyella just laughed—so loud. Then she stopped laughing, like all of a sudden, to listen to Mariah's papa.

"Yeah, yeah, Vyella, we got to wait yet awhile before the coming of the third horseman. For our time has not yet come. We got to accumulate enough money for to go into business our ownselves. Build up something for the coming of the black nations of the world."

You ain't gonna be no part of the black nation, young'un. You ain't fitting to be a part of it. Me neither. Me neither. You ain't the right color. And I done sinned. Jesus, take me home!

So Mariah's heart pounded through the speech her papa acted like he was never gonna get through making, and through the never-ending messing with her that her mamma sneaked back into the room to do—tucking that quilt tighter and tighter, and droning, "You like the quilt, Rah? Least it is something for people to see when they come in to look at you. Have to be careful how people see you. You have to look decent. People around home is so quick to give you a bad name and say you ain't nothing 'cause your things don't look nice. . . ."

Quilt of my deathbed. That's what Mamma Effie's tucking in tight! All around me, Jesus, Jesus. Make Mamma get away!

But Mamma Effie didn't get away. Said, "Is you asleep, Rah? Want me to change your bed pad? Hear me talking to you?"

"Effie, ain't I done told you to shut up once?" Her papa came busting in the room.

But Mamma Effie didn't get away. Said, "Is you asleep, Rah? Want me to change your bed pad? Hear me talking to you? I'll stay out of the swamps tomorrow and go out to Tillie Ried's patch of ground and get you some good collard greens to build up your strength. . . ."

"Effie, ain't I done told you to shut up once? Now I mean it when I say it. Shut up!"

If her papa hadn't said it, Mariah guessed she surely would have. And for some reason or the other the urge to do it overcame her. Overcame the wailing coming up from Cleveland's Field. And the scars on her papa's back. And the shit, shit, shit! Said, "Hush up, Papa! All Mamma Effie's life you ain't never spoke a decent word to her. You ain't speaking no kind words to Vyella, now. Just a-strutting about my kitchen floor telling her she ain't got no sense. And you, Mamma, you ain't never spoke a decent word to me, neither. You didn't do nothing before except to tell me that I'm a whore and a slut and something to be hid away. I don't want you to be spreading no pretty quilt over me no more. You just wants to hide me from the people. Well, you ain't gonna do it. Tell 'em to take me now and crucify me. . . ."

Her papa said, "Jesus!" and backed away from that bed. And Mammie Effie let go of the quilt and ran to Vyella, crying, "Tell me what in the name of God is the matter with her, Vy? I ain't done nothing to her that I knows of." And Vyella said, "It ain't nothing *wrong* with Mariah. It's only that she had a hard birth. I think you all ought to go on to the hall and let Mariah rest."

And Mariah had some sickening feeling that she ought to stop talking. Heard Gezee whining upstairs, and the little thing in the bed beside her just a-wheezing, but she couldn't stop running her mouth. "Slut, slut, that's all I ever was in you-all's eyes. Just a no-good nothing that had to get turned into something worthwhile. Well, I ain't turned into nothing worthwhile. I ain't nothing but a whore and a fornicator and a disrespecter of my parents and a murd . . ."

"Oh my good God Jesus, don't say them things about yourself, Mariah." Vyella came tearing over to her. Sat on that bed beside her and talked to her same as if she was a mother. Stayed with her and talked and talked to her after her mamma and papa left. Said time and again, "You ain't done no disrespecting of Mr. Harmon and Mrs. Effie. You ain't done no lusting . . . no more'n nobody else, I don't expect. And you ain't done no envying and sloughing off of things."

"But I is done 'em. I is done 'em. Wants to see Jacob! Wants to tell him how I done murdered even besides."

"Murdered who?"

"Well, nothing . . . I don't exactly mean it that way." And Mariah buried her head in the pillow. Getting away from Vyella. "I ain't meant nothing, Vy. Ain't. . . ."

"Call on Jesus. You ain't got to tell nobody nothing but Jesus. Tell him all about whatever you think you done. He'll forgive. Lead you back to the Church. Give you a sign for your deliverance. . . . We needs you in the Church, hon. Needs you to help build up this place. . . ."

And Mariah called on Jesus. And her Jesus slung her down into a forest of briars and thorns and coiled serpents springing around the wilderness of her soul. And there was Pop Percy in that wilderness, too. *He's the one done it, Lord. He's the one done it!*

And the Lord answered her back! Look at your own hands, Mariah! Ain't they colored with blood?

And behold she perceived the accusing finger of God pointing to her hands. And she moaned in the fire blazing in the wilderness. Tried to run through it. Made it through it when she said, "It's me, it's me, me, oh Lord, standing in the need of prayer. Standing in the need of your merciful

. . ." And Jesus let her through the fire!

But she stumbled in the quicksands leading down to the path to Hell. Jesus holding out his hand for me! Can't get a-hold of it! Ain't deserving to touch him.

And she crawled, got up and stumbled. Fell down in the funk and the stink and nest of serpents writhing and twisting in the chilly mud, coiling and striking her. Needles all through her. Needles. Needles, hot as fire. Snake poison traveling through her veins. Up to her heart. Heart stopped. Started pumping again. Hard-hitting pumps. Ought to spew out her heart. Mouth tasted like fresh blood.

"Jesus?" But Jesus backed away. Tried to grab a-hold of the hem of his garment. Just the hem! If I could only touch the hem . . . sweet perfume of Jesus! Pure air of heaven. Floated down to her. "Je-e-e-sus!"

"Sis? Rah? What ails you? Want another pill?"

Couldn't see no Vyella. Heard her though.

"My feet done slipped in the miry clay. I'm inside the gates of Hell! Oh my Jesus, show me a sign!"

"What you say there, Sis? Needs a sign?"

"How you come to God, Vyella? You such a clean and Godly woman. Needs a sign for my deliverance."

Pure air of heaven. That's what Vyella's head is in. Floating over my bed! Sunshiny-faced Vyella.

"Where's your Bible at, hon?"

Cool clouds of heaven right here in this room. But I'm hot. Burning up in the flames. Eternal flames of God's wrath.

". . . and I opened up the Bible in the days of my blindness. Seems like to me, Mariah, that a voice come to me like a clap of thunder, saying, 'Read!' Never will forget that day! I was over to Mamma Bertha's. In the big room, and it was dark. Was just getting on my feet from having little Ned. Brightest light I ever seen flooded over the Good Book! Angels of the good Lord commenced to singing as I turned those pages. Then the voice come back to me, saying, 'Read!' And my eyes fell in this very spot here, Mariah. It's the book of Isaiah, fifty-nine and sixty. 'Cry aloud, spare not, lift up thy voice like a trumpet, and show thy people their transgressions and the house of Jacob their sins.' "

Book seemed to waver in Vyella's hand. But her eyes were looking deep into Mariah's. Not even blinking. Just staring. Pulling her. No! Sinking her deep, deep into the chasm of Hell. Cold tombs. Moss and the creepers inside. Maggots eating away at her. Squirming through every inch of her. 'Specially in her nose.

"Can't breathe! Can't breathe! Vyella! Jacob! Jacob!"

And a darkness came down. Thick and closing her all up in herself.

When she woke to find herself out of the tombs of eternity, she was saying, "Let me go, Jacob! Let me go!" And she was staring at the anxious-faced man who was just a-gripping her shoulders.

"Rah, Rah, whatever on earth ails you? Mariah, come to yourself. Rah! I'm home now. What was you talking before about God calling you home, Rah? You just had a hard time, that's all. Let me build up this fire.

"If I make good tomorrow, I'm gonna go up to Calvertown after the funeral and get these prescriptions filled. Aunt Cora Lou's funeral's tomorrow late, Rah. 'Course you ain't supposed to be worried over that. Drugstore's opened up until nine o'clock. . . ."

"Jacob, yes I is supposed to be worried. I done wrong when I let her go up the road. On account of me . . ."

"You ain't!"

"Yes I is!"

"Now Rah, I wants you to lay on back down. Wants you to get some rest. I'm tired my ownself. Rah, Rah, I'm tired. We had such a time out to the hall tonight. I'm clean wore out. That's right, Rah, lay down."

And Mariah laid on down, but she couldn't keep still. "I'll be working 'fore you know it, Jacob. 'Spect I'll be out in the fields by the last of next week. Wants to make it up to you. . . . If the Lord'll only spare me. . . ."

"Spare you? Now you know he's gonna spare you, hon. And you ain't going out in no fields last of next week or first of the next or either bass-ackward way you want to put it till you get well. And what you talking about some blamed bastard making something up to me for . . . I . . ."

"Jacob, is you cussing?" Tenderest feeling came to her for the mad-faced-, tucked-in-faced-, beaten-down-faced-looking man. Pacing up and down the room, and plopping down on the bed before he even took his coat off. Wanted to kiss him. Wanted to kill him. Wanted to tell Jesus all about how she done sinned against him . . . him, Jacob!

"Jacob, I ain't meant to be no heathen. God been with me tonight. Told me to go over a few things with you."

"Whatever it is, hon, it can wait for tomorrow."

"Can't wait for no tomorrow, Jacob."

"Oh yeah it can, Rah. What you squeezing this young'un so tight for, Rah? Gonna smother it first and last. Come to your daddy, hon. Come on, Rah, let go the young'un. That's it. That's it. Now you lay right down here, you little fresh thing you. You ain't old enough to have no cold. What you doing barking like that? Let your mamma rest. I got a good fire going for you. Talked to God right smart about you on my way to the hall and he said to me, Jacob, take care of the young'un and put some color in her flesh. Needs something fitting to eat and then she'll get to looking as pretty as her mamma. Put some beef and greens on the table regular and she'll turn out all right. That's what he said to me about you, young'un. Said to me, she's yours, Jacob. Now you look after her. Even told me to give you a doll baby for Christmas."

"Said it to you like that, Jacob? God said it to you like that?"

"Spoke to me as plain as day, Rah. Said for me to go on and look after my family."

"Said it to you like that, Jacob . . . Jacob?" And the tears of relief rolled all down Mariah's face.

Even after Jacob put the lamp out and lay down beside her and the new young'un, tears wouldn't stop. Tried to hold them back. Managed pretty good after Jacob got to rubbing her head and getting his fingers all tangled up in those knots which she should've had the respect to run a straightening comb through so she'd look pretty for time of birth. Couldn't hardly hold them back though, when he was telling her all about how things took place at the meeting at the hall. And how that white man down here from the Sears Roebuck catalog people tried to keep everybody out to the hall all night to listen to him tell about all this white-man's education they was gonna give the children. He talked so long!

"I said to him . . . Rah, Rah, is you listening? Don't want you to cry no more, honey. Things is gonna be better. . . . I said to him, Mister, I appreciates all you got to say.

Appreciates what you trying to do for us. But the first thing I wants you to know is, do you realize that we got children out to the hall tonight? . . . Well, you know, Rah, Skeeter, he gets tired out so easy. . . . Said to that man, these children is got to go home and get put to bed. Said more'n that to him, Rah. Said to him, I for one gonna be responsible for raising the five hundred extra dollars that's needed to put up a decent school here, but I have to go home right now. Got a new baby. Got a new young'un. And she's a pretty sight!

"And Aunt Saro Jane, she was out there, too. Jumped up and said, 'Time of birth in the land, Mister, and a long time of death coming up. Now, how we gonna get fed if we have to raise all that money and buy land for the school, too?' Well, you know Aunt Saro Jane, she's always harping on death. Said she saw many a green winter coming up."

Any way you look at it, night after birth ain't the easiest thing to get through. You got to be getting up whether the man's done fell asleep or not. Got to tend to your new baby. Try to get it to suck. Give it a little sterilized water in a teaspoon first and kiss it on the mouth.

Little old wet mouth. "Knows your jaws ain't locked, honey. Ain't gonna be no locked either! Thank you blessed Jesus! Your daddy's gonna get a-hold of some money by Christmas. Said he was gonna get you a doll baby. Now ain't that something for him to say when you ain't big enough to even know where my titties is yet! Hope your color deepens a little bit by Christmas. Lord, Lord, Jesus. Ought to wake your daddy up. Tell him what I done to him."

You ain't done nothing to him, Mariah.

Must be the Lord trying to comfort her. Felt so chilly though! Wasn't no Lord talking. Wasn't nothing but the chill Messenger. Hovering over the chaise lounge where she laid that Bardetta Tometta. Heading up a column of ghosts! Ghosts coming up from Cleveland Field. Little Mary right behind the Messenger, crying:

> Carry me way from Tangierneck
> Daddy, Daddy, Daddy. . . .

Wished she could get a-hold of little Mary. No! Oh my Lordy, send back the ghosts! Send back Death!

And the woman hobbled all about that kitchen. Added a few sticks of wood to the embers in the kitchen stove. Had to do it quiet so she wouldn't wake nobody up.

Embers from the fire pushed away the ghosts. Carried her through the night and the testing out of that little Bardetta Tometta's jaws over and over again.

"Now ain't that something for your daddy to name you! Wonder what in the name of God Rabbit and them thinks of that?"

Must've been about two o'clock when she heard Gezee coughing up a storm. Said to her Jesus, "Help me to see my young'uns through this night!" And she tried to make it up the stairs to give Gezee something to quiet the coughing. Legs wouldn't go along with her. And the Lord said, "Lay on down, Mariah." And there wasn't nothing for her to do but obey the Lord, and wait. Wait!

What you waiting for, Mariah? You ought to start running. Run!

Looked like sleep was never gonna come. Time of running was never gonna come! Breathing got to be such a heavy job to do. *Got to keep breathing. Got to take my children on up to Philadelphia. Oyster houses pays more than the fields. That's what I got to do. Get me a job over to Mr. Nelson's oyster house. Save me up some money. Right after Christmas the people starts making good money. . . .*

Hour from four to five just hangs. Can't see no sun, but it's straining to get to you. And Jacob, trying to make like he's asleep. Would've been done got up on an ordinary day when there was no birth.

Tell Jacob. Tell Jacob.

Ain't gonna tell him nothing! Ought to get his ass on out of this house and go to work. . . . Please Lord. Please Jesus, excuse me. Help me through the days coming up.

"Jacob! Jacob!"

"What you want, Rah?"

"Ain't you going to work?"

"Going if you feel all right."

"I'm fine, Jacob! Gonna be a clear day, today, Jacob.

Snow's stopped and the wind's holding still. Wished I was able to get up and make you some breakfast. And get out of this place and pick me some potatoes."

"What time your mamma say she's coming over here?"

"She won't be here till late. Vyella be over here, though, last thing she told me. Jacob, Jacob, hope my die she talks the word of God better'n anybody I ever heard. God's gonna prosper her."

"Uh-hum. I 'spect so, Rah."

"Wished I was that good, Lord, Lord, Jacob. But I ain't though."

"You good enough to birth God's children!"

"That's right, that's what I was gonna tell you, Jacob. If God give us his children, we supposed to take care of them. We ain't supposed to be slacking and stinting along the way. And crying after death. This here's God's child."

"God's child, Rah? Well now, I know that much, but she's mine, too. Got her to take care of. Honey, why you come here so sickly? Got to get you straightened out by Christmas. . . . Gonna give you . . ."

He ain't gonna give you nothing. He ain't able. He ain't your daddy! Don't want him to. Please, Jesus, let him be. Maybe she'll change features by Christmas.

And Jacob's hands glowed as fine as sunlight striking new red bricks when he touched that young'un in the tenderest kind of way just before he left the house.

And Mariah said to herself, "Lord, Jesus, I got to run!" Lord didn't answer her. But Death tapped her on the shoulder. Told her to get herself some blue pills just like the ones she didn't stop Miss Bannie from taking. And Mariah promised the Messenger she would. Get 'em and save them up for herself to take after she got the children out of Tangierneck. And she was gonna do that in a hurry. . . . May as well leave them on some hospital doorstep. Other people did it.

11

"Rabbit, Skeeter," Mariah hollered from the woodpile first Saturday morning right after she got up from the sickbed where it looked like the whole world had ganged up to keep her after she had that Bardetta Tometta. Kept her so long in that bed and that house—that house with that baby that it looked like no amount of teas and medicines was ever gonna bring out—till she just about lost track of the days and the weeks passing by. And here it is almost Christmas!

"Rabbit 'n Skeeter, if you all don't get your behinds to me when I call, I'm lief to take this ax and chop off both your heads 'stead of chopping this wood. . . . Stop breaking them nasty icicles off that house and sucking them. You all gonna die of the diptheria of the throat first and last!

"Get your tails down that road and go tell Pop Clem not to forget about me when he hauls the women up to Calvertown today. Wants you all to bring in this turn of wood soon as you get back. And watch after Gezee and the baby while I'm gone. Give her the medicine.

"Rabbit, what you got your hands behind your back for? You holding onto a icicle? And what your pockets so wet for? You hiding them things in your pockets, too? Put your hands on this chopping block. And I bet you gonna mind me after that. 'Cause you ain't gonna have no hands left to mis-mind me with. . . ."

"He ain't got no icicles, Mamma!" Skeeter, with that piece of flannel coming all untied she had wrapped around his nothing-of-a-head to keep out the cold, jumped in front of Rabbit.

"Skeeter, hush up your mouth. He's probably saving some for you in his pockets. I sewed up the holes in his pockets last night, but I know yours ain't got no bottoms in them 'cause I ain't got to mending yours yet! Just look at him all wet! Poor little thing. Well, now. Well, now!"

And Mariah took herself a good look at those boys, trying to bully her about those icicles. Said to them, "If you all don't get your asses down that road and get my word to Pop Clem you ain't gonna get nothing in your stockings for Christmas but ashes! We ain't got no kinda money that'll pay Santa Claus to bring you nothing like you wants nohow. I was gonna try to bargain with him a little bit today. Don't think I'm gonna go neither step now, 'cause you all ain't been nothing but bad all year. Ain't going nowhere, you hear me?"

Rabbit let go of the icicle he was holding behind his back and tried to throw it in a quick curvy way so it would land out of her sight, but it landed right by her feet.

Mariah got such a hunch to laugh. Quick as she got it, she got another one to cry. Rabbit was just a-shivering and shaking so, and Skeeter's face was all screwed up worse than Chicken Little's when the sky was falling down. Her boys wasn't nothing but some kind of little no way. And she did think maybe Santa Claus ought to do something special for them though they had been right considerable bad. But good a whole lot of times, too! Jesus, Jesus, ain't nothing fitting enough I can do for them. I ain't even fitting for them! Such a sickness in my soul!

"Mamma, I ain't knowed icicles was bad for you," Skeeter squeaked.

"Me neither, Mamma." Rabbit like to have shook his own head off.

Well she ought to stomp him, she thought, same time as she snapped, "Horace!"

And Rabbit jumped from behind Skeeter at the sound of his real name and started in turning his pockets inside out. Icicles that wasn't already melted were stuck to the lining of his pockets. That scamp was busy pulling them off and Skeeter was just a-helping him.

She threw down that ax and said, "Many times as I done told you all about the icicles carrying germs, you mean to tell me you all got the nerve to stand up here and make up a story?

"Skeeter . . . now I mean William . . . and Rabbit, if you all don't get out of my sight this minute, Santa Claus gonna bring you pure nothing! I was just now standing here thinking how busy he must be. He'll be done set aside all his nice things for the other children before I even get up to Calvertown. . . ."

Well gee-whiz-a-me-Christmas, those scalawags went running! She didn't even get a chance to tell them how they had to be extra careful about feeding the fire in the stoves. And how they mustn't cut their hands on the tin when they opened up those two cans of baked beans she was leaving out for their dinner, 'cause they might catch the poison. . . .

Mention of Santa Claus must have put all that pepper under their feet, leaving behind only the sounds of themselves as they went shilly-shallying off before they broke into that run down the hill.

Skeeter saying, "Shit, man, you ain't had to throw away all them icicles. You know Mamma ain't gonna chop off nobody's hands. She's too weak to even chop up that wood. . . ."

And Rabbit saying, "You better stop that cussing boy! Santa Claus can hear every word you say."

And Skeeter getting back at Rabbit, "You cusses all the time, bugger. Ain't no need of stopping now just 'cause you wants Santa Claus to bring you a train. . . ."

And Rabbit kicking up some sand, saying, "Yes, Santa Claus is gonna bring me a train, 'cause I stopped cussing last week. And I said my prayers. And he's gonna bring me that train so I can take Mamma out of this place and she won't even have to talk to that death man no more!"

"She ain't talking to no death man, Rabbit. She's just crazy. Grandmamma Effie done told you she ain't nothing but crazy!"

"You the one crazy, boy. I believes Mamma. . . ."

I believes Mamma. I believes Mamma. Hear what Rabbit said, Mariah. . . . He knows when I'm hovering about.

And Mariah heard that chilly old voice same time as she heard Rabbit's and Skeeter's growing dimmer down that road.

Gonna be long gone, Lordy, long gone soon.

And she grabbed that ax up from off that ground and commenced to chopping another chunk of pine. Hardly made a dent in it. She was right surprised her arms was so feeble after the sickness. But she swung it and swung it till she split up that piece of wood so the fires could burn it easy and keep the children warm. Had to keep them up the best she could till she got them to Levi or some of them very important people Vyella knowed up in the cities. Vyella was always talking 'bout the decentest kind of people she'd meet when she went off in the summer to make speeches. . . . Wished she was as good as Vyella. Wished the Lord would show her a sign for her deliverance from sin. Stop the death thoughts always closing in on her. Gonna get that Bible off the mantelpiece this minute and open it to whatever page the Lord would see fit to guide her hands to do so!

Got that Good Book down. Hands just a-trembling. Felt so cold. Something told her to go and read it while she was standing over the baby laying on the chaise lounge wheezing and reaching out with her pale little hands. Went to the chaise lounge but got a feeling she ought to put a piece of wood on the fire for she was shaking so bad. Threw the wood in the stove and went on back. Opened the Book and stood awhile over that sniffling thing—looking from the Book to the poor little girl child—but mostly at the Book. Gasped, "Ain't no sign I can read for my deliverance like Vyella did!"

She fell to her knees. Cried, "Baby, baby." Then, "Jesus, I can't read all these big words. You knows I can't read! Show me some other way. Ain't never had no schooling for to speak of. . . ."

Stroking the damp forehead of the baby she knew she was making no kind of sense to, she got herself quieted down. Said, "Gonna see to it *you* gets some learning, though. Gonna leave you in charge of somebody with some kinda sense.

"Gonna pay Santa Claus for to bring you one of them teeth-cutting doll babies from that five-and-ten-cent store up there to Calvertown. And get Rabbit a train. Mustn't forget that. Neither Gezee's wind-up clown. And Skeeter . . . Skeeter got to have a overcoat, 'cause he stays so chilly in that second-hand one I done patched up for him . . . except for the pockets. And shoes. Well, every single one of you all got to have shoes. Oh little baby!"

She placed the Bible back on the mantelpiece and picked up Gezee from the corner near the stove where he always liked to lay down on his stomach and talk to the pictures in some of the old magazines she had around. Stood him on a chair and said, "Hold still, boy, while I get a piece of paper for to draw your feet patterns on. Got to give Santa Claus the right size shoe to bring you."

Gezee's eyes lit up—all excited. Old thing managed to hold still except for giggling from the tickle of the pencil going around his feet. Rabbit and Skeeter acted the same when they did get back. Giggling and jumping fit to beat the band. Rabbit ran his mouth though.

"Mamma, Pop Clem's on his way. . . . What Santa Claus gonna bring you and Daddy? I knows what Daddy wants. He wants some handkerchiefs. And he likes beef. . . ."

For you, Mariah, death. Wages of sin are death. Don't forget the blue pills. Messenger's voice filled the room. She shook. Got up from drawing the feet patterns. She was through, anyhow. And she leaned for a minute on the mantelpiece. Said, "Rabbit, don't you hear nothing? I hears a voice." Stared right scared-eyed at Skeeter. "Skeeter . . . Skeeter?"

"I ain't heard nothing, Mamma."

"Me neither."

Her big boys moved over to the window. Started tracing Santa Clauses and angels on the frosty panes. So quiet you couldn't hear nothing in the room except for the hard breathing of the baby, and Gezee messing with the magazines, and *Don't forget the blue pills, Mariah. They waiting for you at the drugstore. Soon as you gets your children out of Tangierneck, you know what to do with them!*

She went out of the house a-calling back to Rabbit and Skeeter to go into the swamp when Uncle Isaiah stopped by to sit with the little ones, and get a cedar tree so they could fix it up pretty for Christmas. But the Messenger's voice followed her. *You know what to do with the pills, Mariah.*

Well, it didn't take no time for Pop Clem to get up that road. He called out to each woman heaving herself up on that cart after he left Mariah's yard, the same thing he'd said to Mariah, "We got two stops to make today: Calvertown and Triville. Going to Calvertown first and anybody that ain't on the cart for to leave by two o'clock is just gonna have to walk them ten miles back to Tangierneck. Some people wants to buy in Calvertown and some wants to get whatever is coming to them from the Welfare in Triville."

"That's right!" Tillie Ried said each and every time. Said to Mariah after they got up the road a piece, "Too bad you ain't signed up for the Welfare, honey, 'cause a few of us is, and we gonna get a little something off of them people for our children's Christmas this day. . . ."

"Course, some people's children is too good for their mothers to go and get slips for the shoe store to give them Welfare shoes. Some people's children is getting trained up white and highclass. Some of them even look that way. . . ." Ann Long put in.

"How's Bardetta, Mariah?" Jane Jones from on Back-of-the-Creek did look so miserable. She knew people was just insinuating about Mariah. She was just over to Tangierneck for a spell to visit with some of her renting people relatives.

And Mariah looked at her, heart busting with thanks and pity, for Jane Jones couldn't help it if she was born a albino.

"If all you-all don't enter into the spirit of Christmas, I'm gonna haul you straight back home this minute." Pop Clem stopped those horses and turned around looking from Tillie to Lydy to Ann Long to Mariah to Aunt Saro Jane and all who else was on that cart.

"Get on up this road, Clem," Aunt Saro Jane said, "else I'm gonna tell the Lord that *you* ain't got so much of a Christmas spirit. And he'll punish you sure 'nough. Done told you how I prayed with the Lord about my gums hurting me so. And he told me to see the colored dentist up there to Calvertown. Now what kind of Christmas spirit *you* got? You ain't taking me no back home!"

After that, the horses made a steady trot. Past the great marshy fields filled with bullgrass, giving off a strong scent of air cleaned by the winds blowing over the many waters surrounding and running all through the land—past the short stretches of stunted pine trying to grow up in the sandy earth. Pop Clem only slowed them down when they crossed the Haimawalkin Road to say to the women who were making more noise than a little, talking about what in all they were getting their children for Christmas, "Bannie's death ain't setting so easy with her old cousin Haim Crawford. Believe he ain't nothing but one of them

Ku Kluxers nohow. . . . Always wants to blame some of the colored for their own sins. . . ."

Wasn't a soul on that cart who didn't agree with Pop Clem. Most just expressed themselves like they was ladies, but Tillie said "Fuck 'em!" Sent the whole cart into titters.

"Bet Jacob and his daddy catching a hard time now running up to this Calvertown Bank to pay off the land that shit-ass done stole from us, eh, Mariah? Who in all got charge of the land anyhow now, Mariah?"

"That's Jacob and his papa's business!" Mariah snapped before she even knew that her right mind would have told her not to do such a thing.

"Business!" Tillie whooped. "Ain't never been able to figure out how people can do business when they ain't got nothing left for to sell."

Whole cart just roared with laughter. Even the horses seemed to step a little livelier after that. Seemed to Mariah they must be laughing, too. They must be laughing, too! Only one or two head that wasn't laughing. Mainly her and Aunt Saro Jane who was just a-holding her head and looking grim.

Mariah said to her, "You feeling poorly, hon? Teeth hurting you?"

Aunt Saro Jane peered at her through her one good eye. "I'm just praying over something. Praying over what I think we got before us, and asking the Lord to spare us."

Wasn't nothing for nobody to do but split up and get their own shopping done in a hurry when they did land in Calvertown where the stores was so high you could pile two Tangierneck houses on top of each other to equal them.

"Time's so short," Lydy said as she took off to get something for her children.

"Yeah, time is short," Mariah said back to Lydy. And she took off to the five-and-ten-cent store to look over things for her own children.

Got Rabbit his train first. Only cost her forty-nine cents. Rabbit was good-hearted enough to make believe it had a motor in it. Ones with motors in them cost a heap sight more. Got Bardetta her teeth-cutting doll baby, and that was only ten cents. Gezee's wind-up clown was the most expensive thing of all. Didn't think it was gonna cost her more than a dollar, but it cost her one dollar and twenty-nine cents.

And the pencils and notebook paper for her two biggest boys cost her thirty cents. Candy and two oranges apiece must have cost her at least fifty cents. Skeeter's coat cost her four dollars and ninety-eight cents. Blue pills that she told the druggist was only to clean her children's sores cost her forty cents. Hands shook so bad when the druggist handed her the pills. He said, "Gal, what's the matter with you?"

"Nothing," Mariah said, and walked on.

Christmas tree decorations was the most expensive things a person could buy! Cost her almost a dollar even.

When her legs were clean give out, she went in the back way of one of those restaurants where colored wasn't even allowed, and got herself a hot dog for a nickel to eat on the horsecart from some nice colored people working in the kitchen. All the other women did the same. Bumped into Lydy and Ann right there. And Tillie, too. Tillie just cutting up like she didn't have no manners. "They's only charging a nickel for these same hot doggies if you walk in the front. 'Course you got to be white to do that. Plus that, they even allows white people to eat a hot doggie and go to the toilet for the same nickel. Now who else is got to pee 'sides me? I ought to piss all over these people's backyard. But I'm too well raised for that. . . ."

"Well I got my time," Lydy muttered, "and I wouldn't pee in back of no white people's restaurant nohow. They's likely to lynch me."

"They doing it anyhow," Ann said. "Plus that they pissing anywhere *they* wants to, whenever they wants to."

"I thinks we best better go," Mariah said.

And the women walked with their Christmas treats for the children all up and down the streets of Calvertown. Those that had tickets for to get Welfare shoes stopped off and got them. Mariah didn't have no Welfare tickets for to get any shoes for nobody. Plus that she'd just about clean run out of the ten dollars she did have in the first place. Only thing left for her to do was to stand outside of Mr. Blum's Shoe Store and watch the big clock he had situated over the top of the front framing. Besides, somebody had to keep track of the time so they wouldn't forget Aunt Saro Jane who came up to see the colored dentist. Couldn't leave her, even if Pop Clem did give orders about what time they had to leave.

Well, they fussed and fumed but mostly agreed as they went past the Calvertown Boulevard crossing and past Cypress Street where they didn't even want colored people in the first place. Cypress Street. Now that was some place to look at! Stores so pretty with all their lights lit up in greens and reds and yellows. And imitation Christmas trees. And what all they didn't have in them stores! Except colored people with just as much spending change as those poor white heifers who dug potatoes right along beside them and who was allowed to go in and try on clothes and pick out this and that, and then tell the store people, "I'll give you fifty cents down and fifty cents next week." And the store people was always agreeing with most of them heifers. Some who didn't even have the decency to wash themselves up in the morning before they so much as come to a potato patch—let alone a store.

When they got to the dark of the colored section, the women really did start talking pretty bad about them stores. Talked loud and sighed. Talked quiet and sighed. Didn't lay off of them stores until they made it to the colored dentist's office.

Aunt Saro Jane got up from a bench. Spit blood in a piece of rag she had brought along with her. "It's time you-all young'uns showed up to take me home. I got a considerable headache. Need me some camus root tea and a little piece of clove to tuck up inside my jaw. . . ."

Dr. Barton come out of his office just then and said to her, "Ma'am, I gave you tissues. You've got no business using that filthy rag. . . ."

"It's my rag, ain't it, so how can it be filthy? *I* washed it. Come on, children, let's go!"

It wasn't so surprising that Pop Clem was on that cart waiting for to take all those who wanted to make it down the road to Triville and those who just plain wanted to make it on home.

But it was mighty surprising to Mariah when *she* got off that cart when it stopped in Triville. Took the feet patterns she drew of her four living children up to a girlish-looking white woman tippity-tapping every word she said about her children, her husband, herself, on a machine called a typewriter. Said to that woman, "I came before you because my children needs some shoes."

"What they wearing now?"

"Best I could get for them, but they clean wore out."

"Where'd you get 'em before? What did you say your name was?"

"Mariah Upshur is my name. I got the shoes before from the second-hand store back of the drugstore in Calvertown."

"How come you didn't get 'em there today? I hear tell you all was up there in Calvertown spending money free as a black mammy's milk flows."

"Ran out of money. Had to get my William a new overcoat." Her voice felt like rising, but it couldn't quite make it. Said to the lady, "Miss . . . Miss . . ."

"Mrs. Cramston is my name, Mariah!"

"Now what I'm trying to tell you is that Santa Claus done promised my children shoes. . . ."

Well, that Mrs. Cramston reared back in her chair. Bucked her hard brown eyes at Mariah. Said, "Welfare don't give out free clothes to nothing but the poor. . . ."

Mariah said nothing, nothing, nothing! Until that bitch screamed at her, "You're a liar! You do have some shoes for Christmas. I can tell by the way you're twitching same as if you wants to break down and pee. . . ."

Mariah said, "I couldn't buy no shoes! Didn't have that much money."

Woman said, "Prove it to me."

"How am I gonna prove it?"

Woman said, "We'll be down to help you to prove it. Can't trust most of you niggers worth a damn. But *we'll* be down!"

Mariah said, "When?" Straps on her pocketbook cut deep into her hands. She was clutching them so tight.

Woman smirked. "Some time *after* Santa Claus comes." And looking away from Mariah, she hollered, "Next . . . next!"

"But my children needs shoes now. Now, Mrs. Cramston!"

Mariah's feet seemed like they couldn't lift her weight as she made it back to the cart. Wished she could take her pocketbook and lam that woman in the face! Wished she could take one of her blue pills and drop it in her drinking

water. Poison the living shit out of her. Wished . . .
Stared at the poor-assed land lining the road all the way
back to Tangierneck, and the women babbling about their
Christmas plans. But most of all staring at the Messenger
who nobody on the cart seemed to see but her. Who nobody heard but her, saying, *Cheat 'em, Mariah, when they
come down to make you prove it. Hide all your things in
the cornhouse. Get your children some shoes before you
join my kingdom.* . . .

12

Days of Christmas and the night of watching for the New Year of Nineteen Hundred and Thirty weren't any time coming and getting gone. And after they left, such a quietness set in. Felt to Mariah that the quietness set as hard as the gray barnacle crusts that formed on the elbows and the kneecaps and the anklebones when the weather's cold made the oyster shell mud, and the potato field dirt, and the unsettled sands of Tangierneck, and of this earth's time—yes, Lord—cake up in the creases of the skin.

Hurtingest thing in the world was to scrape those barnacles off. Best thing a person could do was to leave them on—just give them a little light washing over until spring came and the rising of the sap loosened up the skin and the things wanting to grow in the ground.

Harder still for Mariah was to scrape off the crusts of the sores covering her soul so the light of God could bring a little sunshine in—wither the scabs of the sores—let the pus drain out.

Just a little taste of sunshine, Jesus! Please, Jesus, before I take myself away. She did sometimes pray. Wasn't even hardly any kind of praying she was doing, for any two times a person does so much sinning they ain't fitting for to open up their mouth to the Lord. She just thought the prayers way back in her head and hoped the Lord would hear her.

But sometimes when she just couldn't stand to attend to that sickly bundle of white-looking flesh and she was home all by herself, she'd break down and open up her mouth: "Take me, Jesus. Take me right now. Wash me whiter than snow. Clean me up! I stinks so bad from the sin. Soul ain't clean. Jesus! Take this young'un, too, Don't leave her to suffer down here in Tangierneck. . . ."

But Jesus didn't take the young'un, nor Mariah either.

Had to stay right here on earth, gulping down food into a throat choking with sin. Taking care of Rabbit and Skeeter and Gezee, and this flesh of her sin, Bardetta Tometta, with hands stained by the sin! Sleeping with Jacob, but just turning herself away from him most of the time because she was so corrupted with the sins. Hiding her few cans of food under the cornhouse when the Welfare people sent her a letter that they was coming, and even hiding her cinnamon and nutmeg, 'cause folks told her if they saw you had that kinda spice they wouldn't give you a thing. Taking the papers over to Vyella, after the Welfare people made the inspection, to sign Jacob's name so he wouldn't know nothing about it. Pleading to her Jesus, "My children need shoes . . . milk . . . had to cheat! Oh Merciful Saviour, I'm so corrupted with the sins. Show me a sign for my deliverance. Else let me pass over now. Blessed Lord, please move the gates of time."

But the gates wouldn't move. Only the signs of her final judgment shifted as those folks of Tangierneck who would stoop so low as to drop in on her came to the house and went. Came and talked signs. Looked down with consternation at the "child of God." Came and lingered in the heat from the little tin stove. Talking quiet—and mostly talking death. Green winter did set in.

"Death's coming to the land"—"Grim reaper's gonna take a-many come spring"—"Wall Street where they send out the money from is done crashed"—"God loves a cheerful giver, hates a sinner"—"Person stands a better chance of pulling through if they give to God's works on this earth" —"He'll forgive. He'll save. He'll snatch you out of the claws of death."

And Mariah gave whenever she could scrape up a penny or two from the Mason canning jar stuffed with a piece of an old newspaper so the children wouldn't know what was in it and steal those two or three dollars she did manage to keep in there—that is, when she wasn't borrowing from the jar herself.

Now that Rabbit, he was the pure devil himself about stealing a nickel or a dime off of her every now and then, no matter where she hid her change, so he could get some Mary Jane candy up to Jerry Larmer's store, and sometimes a ten-cent can of potted tongue so he'd have something to eat for his lunch besides molasses sandwiches.

Ought to wear his behind out with a sassafras switch. Ought to kill him, Jesus. Ought to . . . ought to hide her Mason canning jar with all the change she had in it . . . and all the blue pills stuffed in the bottom of it now under her mattress.

But she couldn't do a thing to that God-damned Rabbit except sometimes to holler at him, "Rabbit, I'll maul your brains out if you don't quit putting your head in my business." And sometimes, "Rabbit, bring me your head so I can bust it wide open and stick some sense into it! Ain't right for you to be stealing off of me! It ain't right!"

But Rabbit, he'd just run on away when she spoke to him like that. Either over to one of his grandmamma's houses, or sometimes, just sometimes, clean to China she did expect, for he wouldn't come home till late. Then he'd come home mad and trying to hurt her, she did expect. He'd wait till his daddy came on in home from Deep Gut. Then he'd just go sidling all up to his daddy and running his mouth steadily so she couldn't get a word in edgewise.

Remember one such a night. Caught Rabbit saying, "Daddy, I found a nickel in a jar with some newspapers stuffed in it. Mamma said it was hers and I should never ought to take things belonging to somebody else . . . and that's why she gonna get you to beat me when you come home. . . . Money she's been saving up so as to get us children out of Tangierneck. On account of I'm gonna die and Skeeter gonna die and all us children gonna die if she don't get our behinds out of here. And Bardetta before any of us 'cause she's so sickly and white-looking."

"Shut your mouth, boy! Why you can't stop making up things on your mamma?" Jacob didn't even sound mad at Rabbit. He just stared at Mariah all puzzle-faced where she was sitting on the chaise lounge nursing the baby. . . . Seemed his mind was more on that sickly affliction in her arms than on that boy.

And Mariah thought, *Go on and ask me, Jacob! Go on. If you don't, I swamp it! I swear. Oh my Jesus! If I see Jacob act like he's gonna open his mouth up one more time like he's gonna ask me, I'm gonna tell him: Yeah, Jacob, yeah, I'm a whore! She ain't yours. Ought to rip out my breast on the streets of Jerusalem.*

But Jacob didn't ask her nothing. Just said, "Mariah, I wants you to whip this boy next time you catch him story-telling. . . . Trouble is you ain't hardly ever getting these boys out to Sunday School or nothing like that no more."

"Whip him your damned self if you think he's lying, Jacob."

Rabbit, he just climbed up on his daddy's lap. Turning his face away from her same as his daddy was doing. Leaving her to listen to nothing but the condemnation which she could hear coming from Jacob's heart. And at the sound of her own crying for a way—a sign for her deliverance.

And Mariah listened for a sign in the swamps of the land when she did get strong enough so she could go foraging with the other women for fern to make funeral wreaths out of and tote those heavy bags. And in the kitchens of the land, too—kitchens smelling of stewed muskrats and oysters, and turnips and wintercrease, where the women congregated for the wreath making. Where the prickly fern—greenest of any year since many could remember—bulged in the grass sacks and brought squeals of pain from the little children accidentally tumbling against them, and grim mouths to the women as they wound the scratchy sprigs around and around the rings of maple switches and spoke of dreams of death.

Those who dreamed of hog meat—white hog meat boiling in a big iron pot for the making of lard to shorten the bread and fry the meat—were a-plenty. Any time anybody saw a thing like that in their dreams, it couldn't mean a thing but death.

"Time of hunger coming to the land"—"Hunger stalking the nation already"—That's how some women talked. "Poor hungry people is getting hauled down to Mantipico County by the busloads. They's just looking for something to eat"—"We ain't hardly got enough to eat our ownselves" —"Green winter done set in"—"I dreamed last night that I saw so and so up in the city of Philadelphia just having hisself a big time. Child must be having a lot of trouble. Saw him eating up a whole banquet by hisself. That means he's feeding death."

So the women talked as they made the crowns of this earth's final glory. Just a-piling up funeral wreaths to get shipped up to the cities of Baltimore and Philadelphia for Pop Harmon's business. Sometimes he'd be able to collect the money for to pay them and then again, sometimes he couldn't. Sign of death in itself! But decorations for the services of death kept getting made, and dream signs kept getting talked about.

Mariah couldn't even keep count of the nakedness dreams! Stopped stopping off in anybody's kitchens. Couldn't stand to hear no more about it. And neither for Mamma Bertha to be telling her about how death was coming. It was all around her all the time anyhow. Neither for any of them women to be messing over that Bardetta whom she had to lug right along with her most of the time. Saying things like, "Where's your hair at, you little old thing, you?" "You so pale-looking and coughing all the time. Your mamma ought to make you some raspberry leaf tea." "Camus root tea." "Ought to spank her little old hiny, laying up here looking just like white folks' babies." "When you gonna change colors, gal?" That's how they talked.

And the chilly Messenger kept hovering all around Mariah. Clinging to her shoulders. Throwing his shadow over that little old thing. *Jesus!* Sent his cold all the way down to her fingertips so bad sometimes she couldn't even shift one finger behind the other.

Got up on her feet in a great big hurry one day when a bunch of them were making wreaths in Mamma Bertha's kitchen. Bundled up that Bardetta and started in marching. Dragging Gezee along. And he was crying, "Mamma, I ain't done nothing bad. How come you pulling me so hard?"

"Shut up, boy! You best come on up this road before I lam your brains out."

And Mamma Bertha, she chased after Mariah up that road. "Where you going to, gal?"

"I done made me enough wreaths for today. Didn't even realize the hour was so late. Got to get home and cook up some turnips for the family." So Mariah answered her.

Got to keep marching, Jesus. Got to keep moving. Got to get my children out of this Tangierneck.

Old woman kept right after her, just a-shaking her head. Used to be more firm before they put Aunt Cora Lou and Miss Bannie away, but now it seemed like Mamma Bertha Ann's mind was going bad on her.

Woman wouldn't stop trailing after her. Said to Mariah, "Now Mariah, I wants you to know that in a time of trouble we ought to cling together. . . . Trouble's coming to the land. Can't get Levi and them off my mind. Saw that little old Levi laying up the other night with all his clothes on and a strumpet laying up beside him just as naked as you please. Saw that thing just as plain in my dream. . . . I don't think he's so well off up there in that city. Think sometimes he's gonna die and Em and Thomas, too. . . ."

"Mamma Bertha," Mariah hollered when they set foot in her house, "wants you to stop talking like that around my children."

And Mamma Bertha, she reared back same as a mule when you try to get the thing to wade through a ditch of water, and headed for the door just a-moaning. But Mariah didn't pay her no mind. Wouldn't even look up at that wispy-haired, crazy-minded woman when she lingered in the doorway letting a whole lot of cold air in the house. Didn't pay her no mind at all until she turned and said, "Saw Jacob naked, too, Mariah. Saw a woman in a casket. . . ."

Mariah backed clean back to the table. Tongue was so stiff it could hardly move. "Jesus, show me a way."

It wasn't too many days or nights later when the Lord came to Mariah a few times and told her to go get herself a job shucking oysters for Mr. Nelson over to Triville 'cause she'd make better money that way. Make more there than she would out of her papa's wreath business.

"Lord, you is gonna help me get a few pennies saved up so I can get my children out of this Neck?" That's how Mariah prayed about three o'clock in the morning of the first day and started walking those seven or so miles to the Triville oyster house. Mr. Nelson didn't send any truck to pick up people anymore. All those who wanted to go had to make it by their feet. Bottoms of her shoes that she cut out of a pasteboard box got soaked clean through with the water in the paths and the routes before she'd even walked two miles. Feet commenced to feeling like chunks of ice before long, but she made it. With Tillie and Emma trucking right along beside her, and steadily chattering about how the community was falling to pieces and pointing out new No Trespass signs tacked on the trees all over the land. Talking about some strange rumor they'd heard that Bannie left a will giving back the land to Jacob's papa and all her other property to that Dr. Grene.

But Mariah wouldn't pay no mind to that kind of foolishness. She just went a-tramping on.

Didn't hardly have any bottoms left in her shoes when she got to the oyster house the first morning, but she took that bench that the goggle-eyed foreman by the name of Jimmy gave out to her and stood all day in that water draining off of the cement floor just a-shucking those oysters. Said "Lord" every time she'd try to force open a hard oyster and the knife would slip and jab her hand.

Cried "Lord" when she trucked those seven dark miles back to Tangierneck, for she didn't have no shoe bottoms left at all then, and the road hurt her feet. Gravel in some places and soggy sand in the others. And the Lord told her to stop off at Jerry Larmer's store and pick up another pasteboard box so she could fix up her shoes to get started out bright and early the next morning. And Mariah said back to the Lord, "I don't see how I can make it."

But the Lord told her to go back. He even helped her wake up Skeeter and ask him to stay home from that school and watch after the young'uns until she could make some permanent arrangements with Vyella, or her mamma, or somebody. Somebody!

And the Lord helped her to figure out that she could save up twenty-five or thirty cents a day if she could shuck ten gallons of oysters each and every day——same as the top shuckers did. She jabbed her hands so full of holes they commenced to look like kitchen strainers, but in a few weeks' time she was up to ten gallons a day! By groundhog day she had herself saved up five dollars. More than enough for one train fare to . . . Jesus, Jesus, where am I gonna take my children?

Even got to the place where she could give Vyella and them a dime or two each week for the different Church funds. Gave most to the school fund, for after all, even though she was solid determined to get her children out of Tangierneck she still would like to see a good school built for the poor little children they'd left behind. Wouldn't be right for her not to help build up a school for that Mamie and Lil Bits that Aunt Cora Lou left on Mamma Bertha's hands.

The Lord helped her button up her mouth when Jacob came in one night——must have been late in March——all sad-faced. Looked like he was gonna break down and cry any minute when he told her how he didn't go out on the rocks that day for the rocks weren't paying off anything anyhow. Wind was so high. He told her how he hitched himself a ride up to that Calvertown Bank instead and asked those people to show him the papers on the land. Wanted to know who in all had the right to tack up those No Trespass signs all over the land. Wanted to know! Heard tell Miss Bannie left some kind of will giving his papa back the land. But the bank man wouldn't tell him. Neither would he show him the papers.

"Told me, Mariah, I had to find the murderer of Bannie and the motive, before they would do anything."

"Murderer!" Mariah winced. A gloom settled all over the kitchen, and the voice of death set up a ringing in her ears that deafened her to anything just about except her lonely prayer: "Jesus, help me to speed up and get my children out of here."

And He let her put on some speed through the rest of that month of March. And through a little piece of April, too, when work at the oyster house was just about clean give out. But he halted her heart and her soul when she ran into her mamma on her way to set out strawberry plants for Jerry Larmer one day in the last part of April. Almost made her drop that poor little Bardetta Tometta laying all sleepy on her shoulder from the way Mariah had dosed her up with the paregoric so the thing would sleep most of the day in a crib Mariah had fixed up in a basket by the field shanty while she hustled up and down those strawberry rows.

Her mamma was just a-wagging her head. "Saw Rabbit down to Jerry Larmer's store just last afternoon. Child must have spent at least a half-dollar on candy and cakes. . . . Giving most of what he bought to Little Ned and the rest of the children. Children was just a-standing back from the store porch waiting for all them sweets.

"Now Mariah, I wants you to keep better control over your children. Rabbit ain't had no business with that kind of money. Don't know where he got it from to save my life. There's enough trouble coming to the land. God's gonna trouble the waters if you young folks don't quit this sinning. . . ."

"I don't know where he got it from either, Mamma!"

Mariah backed away from the old glinty-eyed woman. "But I'll 'tend to it soon as ever I gets in home this evening."

Bright sun of that April day must have went clean to her head. Wasn't hot, but her head was just a-spinning same as if she was gonna have a stroke. And her hands wouldn't obey her. Gave up even trying around three o'clock and grabbed that Bardetta and flew on home. Got there before school even let out. Went straight to where she hid her Mason canning jar. Almost flung the mattress off the bed. Legs on her turned to water. The jar was there!

Count your money, Mariah! She could hear the very joints in her arm crack as she reached for the jar—unscrewed the lid and shook the whole mess of coins and paper stuffing out of it. Started to unwrap the little wad of paper she had on the bottom of the jar. *But the jar's already emptied clean out, Mariah!*

Hands just went a-fumbling through those newspaper wads. And the blue pills was gone! Unwrapped those pieces of newspaper over and over. Then squeezed them together again, so much so until her palms was decorated with nothing but streaks of that old ink on those papers. But the blue pills was gone! And so was about seventy-five cents of her money. She hollered, "Rabbit!" But Rabbit wasn't nowhere in sight. Stood by the kitchen window and watched for him. For she was gonna get him sure as daylight comes. He had no business in her Mason canning jar. He had no business taking them blue pills away from her. Had no business!

Stood by that kitchen window until she saw Rabbit and Skeeter coming up the path from school. Went down the road a piece-ways to get him. Said to him, "Rabbit, where'd you get so much money for to spend down to the store yesterday?"

Well, Rabbit, he just looked at her like she was stone gone crazy.

Said to him again, "Rabbit, where you get so much money?"

Rabbit, he just looked at her. Scared to death. She told Skeeter to go and get running. Sent Rabbit out into the thicket to break off his own switch. For she was going to whip his ass good!

And when Rabbit came up to the house bringing that switch, and he looked so pitiful, Mariah grabbed it out of his hands and let loose. Well, she beat him up beside the house and all around it.

Saying all the time, "Rabbit, give me back the blue pills."

"I throwed them away, Mamma," he kept bawling. Rabbit talked back until he couldn't even speak anymore. Said to her just before he fell down on the ground, "Mamma, don't talk to that death man anymore."

Mariah said to him, "Rabbit, you ain't never heard me speak to no such a person."

"Yes, I did too, Mamma."

And Rabbit he limped on off somewhere by himself. Best thing he could have done! Came nightfall and Mariah did miss him.

Said to Skeeter sitting by the stove looking all sad, "Go and fetch Rabbit, and also get Gezee from over to Vyella's house. . . ."

Skeeter, he went out of that house like a fly trying to stay away from fly spray. Came back bringing Gezee, but he didn't bring no Rabbit.

Said to her, "Mamma, I can't find Rabbit."

And Mariah said, "Well, I'll go and look myself."

She found him by the cornhouse. He was as cold as ice. Scars and welts on him looked like something terrible. Tried to wake him up, but he wouldn't do nothing but fall over. Then she went and got Jacob out of the field where he was plowing. Said, "Jacob, help me to get up Rabbit from behind the cornhouse. I do fear that I done beat him to death."

"On what account?"

"Well, he don't mind me."

And Jacob said, "Come on, let's go and get him."

And together, they traipsed over the field and on up to the house. Picked up Rabbit from behind the cornhouse. Laid him in the bed. Rubbed Vaseline grease on his sores and his welts.

Mariah, she kept kissing on him at the same time she rubbed him. Saying, "Come on, Rabbit."

It wasn't too long before Rabbit came to. And he looked at Mariah. "Mamma, don't talk to no death man no more."

13

Aunt Saro Jane was just doing some ordinary talking when Mariah bumped into her in a field one day after Mariah had cured up Rabbit. She was mentioning about the dreams she'd had. And who in all wasn't well—wasn't expecting to pull through this or that ailment—and then, oh my Jesus, Mariah's feet got rooted in her tracks. Couldn't take her eyes off of that little old woman, just a-canting and chanting.

"I tell you, Mariah, there's a terrible time coming to the land. . . . Paddy Rollers is coming around. . . . Bannie's death ain't setting easy with 'em."

"How you know, Aunt Saro Jane?"

Aunt Saro Jane just walked on away. And it wasn't until Mariah and Lydy and the whole bunch of them that was setting out the plants got up under the trees at dinner time that day, and Mariah was trying to wake up that Bardetta so she could give the child her titty, that Aunt Saro Jane broke down and told them all.

"White people's getting mean here, children. Getting mean all over these counties. You look at how they killed that Audible Lee up there to Fruit Grove. You all know it ain't been many nights ago since they went up to that Calvertown jail and pulled him out of there. Wasn't nothing but a poor migrant worker accused of doing bad with a white woman he ain't never even touched. They beat and banged on him right there on the Court House lawn. Accused him of killing her on that farm where he worked. Was that mean cracker's son what owned the farm that did it. Poor Audible Lee had come trucking it all the way up here from Georgia I hear tell. What for? Just to work in those Fruit Grove farms. And what all he got out of it but lynched by them Paddy Rollers. For nothing.

"They coming this way. They coming this way." And

that woman commenced to quiver and shake. Eyes right gray from the cataracts coming down over them, scanned the trees of the thicket, and the sky—grew right big like she was seeing a vision, and then it seemed to Mariah, that they just settled on her. "Seen Bannie's brother in the store yestiddy morning. Haim Crawford and some road cops right along with him. . . ."

"Bannie's brother?" Tillie let loose with a whoop. "And that old cousin of hers, Haim Crawford?"

Lydy asked the same questions, but only in a different way. Her hands was so nervous she slipped and cut one of them with the butcher knife she was trying to punch open a can of Campbell's baked beans with, and Mariah said, "Jesus!" And, "I swamp it, I'll go to shore!"

Mamma Effie got up from the nest of pine needles she was resting herself on, dusting off her backside just as frisky all at the same time. Said, "Saro Jane, you ain't seen no such thing!"

"Said what I said because I saw what I saw. Saw them road cops. You know them 'Big Boys'? Ones with the helmets on. You know any two times you see them down here they looking for a colored *boy*. And right alongside of those two Big Boys was Bannie's brother Will. Acted like he didn't recognize my favor. I ain't seen him since he was kneehigh to a grasshopper. Child didn't even speak to me. Don't care if he is been away from around here for nigh onto thirty years, he knows he knows me! Many times as I changed his diapers and comforted him in the times of his little storms. That old ungrateful Will, now he's done growed up and got them canning houses strung up and down Dormerset County. . . . Walks like he's the boss of this Mantipico County, too. Heard from a few people that he belongs to the Paddy Rollers. . . ."

Mariah just took her titty away from that sleepy-eyed child and laid her on back down in the crate she had fixed up for her crib, gulped down a few of those baked beans Lydy opened up and a little piece of her own molasses sandwich, put the other sandwich and a half that she had left down for Lydy or Mamma Effie, or, or . . .

And Mariah couldn't even see who for or what she was throwing those scraps of food down to. Her eyes just kept filling up with a whole lot of water.

Best thing for her to do, she said to herself as she

gathered herself together and got on back to the fields, was to get a-hold of some money. "In a hurry, Lordy, Jesus. In a hurry!"

But Jesus didn't help her to get a-hold of any money in a hurry and he didn't show her any sign.

Through a whole bunch of days she kept on calling on Jesus. Mostly in the pounding of her heart. In the night-times, Jesus, in the nighttimes! That's when her heart would pound the most. And she'd get up and walk the floors of that little squeezy house. The house she had to get her children out of! Most of the times just looking over those children and seeing if they was all right. Especially that Bardetta Tometta! That sick wheezy thing. That sin of her flesh. And praying over her, "Jesus, Jesus, lift the night in my soul. . . . Jesus, send a nighttime of stars for my children . . . Jesus!"

Soon came to be a night when she heard hollering in her sleep and woke up and found out she heard it for real! "For real, Jacob, for real. I hear Tillie hollering!" She shook her husband awake.

Jacob took a long time getting on his shoes after he did finally wake up from the fearsome rousing Mariah was giving him.

Said to Mariah, "Something *is* astir in the land. . . ." And all the while he was just a-shaking his head and trying to get his pants on.

"Jacob," Mariah cried. "You should-a put your pants on first. You knows you can't get 'em on over your shoes!"

"Shit, shit, shit!" Jacob said as he took off his shoes and put his pants on. "We best get on over to Willie Ried's house and see what in the name of God . . ."

"Lamps is all lit up all across this land same as if it's a Sunday night, Jacob! Trouble's coming!" She flung on a dress and flew down the steps right behind Jacob. Calling back to Skeeter and them, "Get you-all's behinds back in bed, 'cause I hears you all stirring 'round in there. . . . Trouble's coming upon us!"

She'd no more than got the words out of her mouth when a roaring truck's headlights splashed every nook and cranny of that kitchen. Reached out for Jacob in that blinding quilt-work of lights.

"Light the kitchen lamp, woman!" Jacob moved toward

the door. Talking all big and full-throated. "Believe that's Haim Crawford's truck out there in the yard."

"It is Haim's, Jacob. Paddy Rollers is done come around!" Mariah said as she ran for the box of kitchen matches and lit the lamp. No sooner got that done when trouble pounded on the door. Trouble took over the world! *Oh my God.*

Two pale-eyed boys of the oysterhouse man, stinking with whiskey and standing a-straddle so you could see the rising in their pants, hung behind Haim Crawford. Sam, he was Mr. Nelson's littlest one, and Grover, the oldest. But they weren't anything but ordinary field-wiper-looking snakes, compared to the big, bully-headed rattler, Haim Crawford, heaving in the door and beckoning to the tall, keen-faced man puffing on a cigarette just outside the door.

"This here's Miss Bannie Dudley's brother, Mr. Will," Haim said. "Come on in, Will! Ain't no need for you to stay out there guarding the truck. That Willie Ried's too drunk to get loose. He's tied up good enough anyhow. Come on in, Will. These some of the best quality niggers we got in the county. Most truthful niggers we got. Ain't that right, Reverend Jacob? Now, now. Ain't no need for you all to be scared. We ain't come to hurt you. . . ."

"What you all doing with Willie Ried?" Jacob asked.

"Same thing we do to any nigger who won't talk. We asked him about Bannie. Drunk as he is, he ain't opened his mouth yet. All the way here from Calvertown we rid him with his head hanging off the tail gate so the cool air would wake him up a little. You want him back, Jacob?" Haim Crawford pushed Jacob, but Jacob wouldn't budge from the door.

The first time in Mariah's life she wished they had a lock for the door.

"Now Reverend Jacob, you know I let you cut sparrow-grass on my farm last month. Done you hungry niggers a favor. Don't give me no sass now. We ain't gonna keep you up long, Reverend Jacob. Gonna let you get back right quick to your little cunting hole here. . . . Can't keep niggers away from their trim at night else you can't get no work out of them the next day. Ain't that right, Reverend Jacob?"

"What you want, Mr. Haim? You know I ain't no reverend." Anger worked in Jacob's throat so bad it looked like to Mariah that his words came out in whispers. And he didn't move from holding the door halfway shut until Haim Crawford wrenched his hand a-loose and shoved him in a chair. "Sit down, boy!"

"You all ain't no Law!" Scream from Mariah got broke off by Grover Nelson's sweaty hand clamped across her mouth, and holding her and squeezing her all up tight.

"Hell we ain't the Law, nigger wench! Trouble with niggers in this county, they got too much say about who's the Law and who ain't. Voting Republican . . ."

"Turn that woman loose. She ain't going nowhere." Will Dudley's thin hands itched nervously on the bulge of his hip pocket.

Got a gun, Lordy, got a gun! Mariah sighed and shut her eyes. Couldn't stand the sound of that man snickering and sneering.

"Thought you said these niggers'ud talk without this rowdiness," Sam said.

"And they will, too. Won't you, Reverend Jacob? You all gonna talk if you want Willie Ried back." Haim Crawford's hands hung like daggers before Jacob's eyes. "We always been bragging about how we raised a pretty good crop of niggers down here. Raised you all up to be Christians. Let you all pray all winter over Miss Dudley's murder. . . ."

"Ain't been no murder. . . ."

"Don't talk back to me, boy!" Haim let loose at Jacob again. And Jacob almost went down on his knees. Said, "God!"

"God don't pay no mind to nigger prayers. They ain't got sense enough to do nothing but monkey jabber when they pray." Sam Nelson giggled to his brother.

"Let Haim do the talking, Sam. He'll work it out of them," Grover said.

"Gonna talk reason to you now, Reverend. I want you to tell us exactly how you all propositioned that nigger doctor up there to Calvertown to do away with Miss Dudley."

"Ain't propositioned nothing. . . ." Jacob just hung his bruised head.

Then Haim just clean let him have it. Hitting him all up the side of his head again. And Mariah, she tore loose from that Grover and tried to get to Jacob. Grover kicked her on her hind parts almost clean across the room. Her boys had done got up and run downstairs and was just a-holding on to her. She cried, "Told you all to stay upstairs!"

"Leave my daddy alone!"

"Daddy ain't done nothing!"

The wails of the children tore through the night air. And Mariah couldn't get a-loose from the Nelson boys who was wringing her arms out from the sockets. Nor from her children either, clinging to her skirt. Couldn't get to Jacob. . . .

"Why you wake these little baboons up, Haim?" Grover said. "Little mother fuckers. . . ."

"Gonna use that kind of talk around my children, let's go outside. . . ." Jacob tried to get up from the chair.

"Mother fucker your ownself," Rabbit cried, and his water ran all down his nightgown. "Leave my daddy alone! You all let go of my mamma!"

"Give that little monkey a piece of candy. . . . Shut him up!" Sam Nelson giggled.

"He can't shut up. See, his monkey lip all peeled back. . . ."

It was the giggling and the beating on Jacob's head and the wails of the children. That's all Mariah heard in the screaming cavern of her head. And out, out into the night she yelled. Screams tore her head off her shoulders.

"Take me, take me! I done it! Leave my children alone. Jacob! Jacob! God! Jacob!" Mariah fell down. Tried to get up from the floor to get a-hold of Jacob. And to go upstairs and get to that little Bardetta just a-crying.

"Hold that wench down. Shut her up. Why you letting that bitch make such a racket?" one of them said, and she couldn't see who. *Oh my God, Jesus!*

"I done it, I done it! My baby child's gotta live! All my children . . ."

Then it was a booming and a great thundering crack on her skull. And she felt like if she could only get a-hold of her head. It went sailing off from the cracks. "Jesus," she muttered. Kept trying to get to her Lord. Just to touch the hem of his garment. Just to touch it. . . ."

"Why you hit my wife, Will Dudley? Mariah, is they done hurt you? Mariah! Rah!" *Jacob must have got loose.*

"Never seen the likes of it. . . . Nigger wench trying to be a martyr."

Which one of them's letting go of me, Jesus? Got to get up from this floor.

"Fire!" The white men's faces swam in a sea of flame.

"Nigger hall's on fire!"

"Fire! Fire!"

"Come on, Haim, let's get out of here. The whole place is up. Leave the niggers! Come on, Haim!"

"Fire! Fire!"

And the woman closed her eyes.

"Mamma, it's Cousin Ol running this a-way. Mamma, here comes Grandpop and here comes Irena and here comes everybody. Mamma, Mamma, here comes the whole Tangierneck! Mamma, Grandpapa Harmon got his gun. He'll shoot 'em. . . ."

It was the slobber and the tears of Skeeter washing over her face that brought Mariah to. And the soft, wet kisses, the snotty kisses of Rabbit, petting her head with little pats and rubs, and Gezee tugging at her feet, but mostly it was Jacob, standing over her with his face swollen and bloated from the blows and lifting her up from the floor, saying, "You ain't had to say you did it, 'Rah, to save me. God'ud take care of those beasts if they hurt me, hon. . . . God'll take care of them for what they did to Willie Ried. Lucky thing we got him a-loose. They just dumped him in the yard. He better come on in the church. Give his heart to God, 'cause it wasn't nothing but the hand of God sent Tangierneck this way this night to scare Haim and them enough so they'd throw him out of the truck."

"Go on back home and watch the children, Mariah. G'on back home, hon," Jacob said as she stumbled out into the night with him to put out the fire.

"Got to fight the fire, Jacob. Got to fight the fire same as anybody else. School wouldn't be burning down except for me."

"You don't have to fight no fire neither, Mariah. Go on back home. Fire broke out as a warning to the people. Go on home, Mariah."

But Mariah plunged on with Jacob, on the heels of what it looked like to be the whole Tangierneck, running in the night to save the school. Running, running.

Jesus, Jesus. Hadn't been for me, they wouldn't have done it. Running behind the whole Tangierneck alarming the night with the cries of "Save the church!" "Get water from the ponds!" "Sprinkle it around the church." "School's gone!" "Ol, over this way! Need water over here!" "Soak the ground around the church with water!" "Children, save the church." "Church is all we got left."

And they kept running in and out of the ponds springing up from the marshy bottom of the land around the church and Cleveland's Field. Water-soaked night. Fire-enflamed soul. Running. Throwing water on hot ashes. Cooling them down until they gave up to death.

"G'on home, hon," Jacob said to her, when the fire was all put out. But Mariah followed him and the rest of the people on into the church.

> *Before this time another year, I may be gone*
> *In some lonesome graveyard, oh Lord, how long*

So the church sang, in that night of spring, turned into a night of watching for the return of the Paddy Rollers. Sang the song of the New Year's Service, led by Pop Percy with tears and snot dripping from his beard. And Mariah just kept shaking her head. Hurting so bad from the blows. Saviour, hurting so bad while she listened to the voices— mostly loud ones, calling for the community to go and do the same thing to them white people that was done to Willie Ried and Jacob and his family—and some praying forgiveness in the way of Christians. But some soft ones, too, like Jacob's: "Ain't no need for us to go carousing and getting ourselves killed. Best thing for us to do is form a committee to go over and see Mr. Nelson 'bout his sons. . . . He's mighty powerful. Might be able to do something 'bout Will Dudley and Haim, too. . . ."

Mariah rested her head on the bench in front of her till Jacob got through. Came on back to his seat. "G'on home, 'Rah. And take Papa with you. We younger men gonna stay out here the rest of the night. Ain't you heard what I just proposed to the church? Ain't you heard the church vote for the forming of the committee? Ain't you heard . . . ?"

And Mariah got up from off her behind bruised from the kicking one of them white dogs had give her. Got up and left alongside that tight-lipped Pop Percy.

Devil seemed to speak to her as she and Pop Percy trudged up that old beaten road. Just a-sneering, *Mariah,*

ain't you heard Mrs. Jefferson speaking to the Congrega-
tion, telling them the fire was a blessing of God. A warning
to you all. A sign that it's time Tangierneck pulled to-
gether and got the money up for a fitting school? Well, you
know good and well you all niggers ain't never had nothing
down here. Ain't never gonna get nothing, neither. Got no
courage. Got no backbone.

You had some nerve letting Vyella praise you for the
pureness of your heart the whole time you all fought the
fire. Now the whole Tangierneck'll be praising you the
same as her for taking the blame on yourself for Bannie's
murder to save your husband. Where was God when you
left Bannie with them blue pills? Where was all this pure-
ness in your heart?

Mariah commenced into wrestling with Satan on that
long road—road that stretched on forever. Went in to
her secret closet praying, "I'm in your service, Lord. Clean
my soul. Clean my mouth that I may speak your words."

Seemed like as she prayed, the stars of the night became
the eyes of God looking down on her in mercy. And his
will moved in her. She cried out to the tall silent shadow of
a man stumbling along beside her, "Why don't you tell it,
Pop Percy?"

"Tell what, Mariah?"

"I'll stand with you, Papa!"

"Stand with me where, Mariah?"

"In the court. . . ."

"What you talking about, fool? I ain't got no right to be
going to no court. No court but the court of God." The
man shot up tall as the night.

"You beat her up so she died from it! You killed her!
You done it! You done it!" Mariah was just a-shaking.

"Killed who? What you talking about, woman?"

"Miss Bannie. . . ."

"Ain't done no such a thing, slut. Speak truth! God's
gonna strike you down, Mariah."

"She told me, Papa, she told me *everything*. Papa, I
seen her. I seen her where you left her, crying . . . crying, Papa. Woman cried so to me. . . . Told me Albert
Grene's yours, too, Papa. I helped her for to get home."

"She ain't told you no such things. Whore! Abomination
before the Lord! Nerves giving out on you. Now that you
ruined my son's life by bringing a young'un in the world

that ain't even his, you gonna try to ruin mine. Don't think nobody knows what you is! Hadn't been for you trying to make him leave the land . . ."

And the old man's eyes were the fires of hell burning into her soul, in the bright night, in the starlit night.

"She ain't told you no such things. Hear me!" His frenzy wound around and around her. "When she told you such a lie?"

"Just before I left her. Took her home from the swamp road off Deep Gut. Put her in her bed. That's what I did, Papa."

"Say another word to me, you heifer-and-a-half. Out roaming the swamp on the night of your Aunt Cora Lou's wake. You witch! Conjuring up doom! I heard tell it was some blue pills what done it. And since you say you was the last one to see her, what does that say for you?"

The old man's walking-stick reached up to heaven, it looked like. But before he could bring it down on her, Mariah ducked. Commenced in running from the old man. From the sight of him. From the thought of him. And Mariah just started singing. For it helped her to make it on up that hill going in home. Sang:

> I'm trampling, trampling,
> Trying to make heaven my home

Devil came to her again soon as she crossed that doorsill and said:

Ain't no heaven gonna be your home, Mariah. See how you done upset your own father-in-law 'bout something that's probably all your fault. . . .

Mariah's heart started in running. And she drew a-many a deep breath to ease up the pain it seemed her heart was making. Drew a-many until Jacob came home, and she said, "So glad to see you."

And Jacob said, " 'Rah, your head's just a-bleeding."

"Didn't get a chance to heal up the cuts them people left on me from wringing and twisting me and beating and banging on me. . . ."

And Jacob said, " 'Rah, look at me. I ain't got over it yet, neither."

Mariah looked at him and saw the way his head was all swoll up. At the same time she heard that baby crying upstairs, and she said to him, "Jacob, give me a minute. I'll be right back downstairs. Got to get the young'un."

And Jacob, he just went to the pump and got them a fresh bucket of water for to wash their heads and arms and wherever the bleeding was left on them off.

By the time Jacob got back from the yard and the pumping of the water, Mariah was downstairs with the new young'un, kissing on it and hugging it and soothing it down to sleep.

Jacob said, " 'Rah, committee we was trying to form out to the church didn't turn out exactly like I was thinking it would. Ain't nobody going to see Mr. Nelson but me and Papa and I guess we could get Willie Ried if he was healed up enough. But he ain't gonna be able to go nowhere. . . ."

Mariah said, "Jacob, wasn't Tillie and Emma and them there, too?"

Jacob said, "Now you know, Mariah, they was there—talking louder than anybody and wanting to go. . . ."

"When you all call the meeting with Mr. Nelson for, Jacob?"

"Tomorrow, soon as we get off from work."

"Gonna be nothing but grass seeds growing up in the asparagus fields tomorrow. And the rocks have done give out of oysters. And we done just about finished setting out the strawberry plants. So I reckon me and Emma and Lydy'll be able to come right along with you. Tillie got to stay home to nurse Willie Ried. Your mamma's not too able to go ripping and running these days. . . . And Aunt Saro Jane's too old to make that trek. Don't care if we even get started before daylight in the morning. . . ."

"Shut up, 'Rah. Don't want no women along. Nurse that baby before she wakes up the whole creation crying.

"Papa's done took that hearse car out of Bannie's yard. That's one thing he ain't never give her title to. So we'll be riding in that tomorrow. See, Mariah, it's just a natural fact of life that men and women's business is different. . . ."

Didn't nobody have much to say on the trip to see Mr. Nelson the next day. Main topic was how Uncle Isaiah set fire to the schoolhouse to alarm the people that the Paddy Rollers was around.

Wasn't but a handful that was able to go noway: Jacob, his papa, Emma, and Mariah—lugging that Bardetta right along with her. And Jacob was mad with Mariah anyway for hauling herself and that young'un along. Plus going behind his back getting Emma.

But he put his mind to his job when they did get to that big fine house of Mr. Nelson's.

Hat in his hand, he spoke right out to that gentleman-fied-looking man who came out on the back porch to meet them.

"Mr. Nelson, your sons, Grover and Sam, along with Haim Crawford and Will Dudley, came night-riding down to Tangierneck last night. Beat me and my wife right considerable. . . ."

"Well, Jacob, my boy, I do feel right sorry 'bout that. . . ."

"Said they was beating us on account of we knew something or had something to do with Miss Bannie's murder."

"Ain't been no murder!" Jacob's father towered over his son and the short, stumpy white man—man with a voice as soft as silk and hands looking even more so.

Mr. Nelson started playing with his watch fob. And it was just a-glistening in the soft yellow light hanging from the porch ceiling. Started in pacing all up and down that floor. "You all knows what it is to raise children. They don't obey half of the time. . . . Personally, I don't think anybody killed Mrs. Dudley, but . . . well you see . . . a whole lot of white folks around here does think so, even though they ought to know better."

All of a sudden he stood still, looking from one to the other. Swatted a candlefly buzzing around his head. "Now, I don't think you all will have any more trouble out of my sons, or the Paddy Rollers either, that is, if you stop pressing some claim you all think you got on the land and stop bothering the people up to the bank about it. . . ."

All of a sudden it hit Mariah like a bolt of thunder that it was not Bannie's death why they got beat. It was the land . . . the land! She looked to Jacob—to his papa. Both of them looking like lightning just struck.

"Guess you all wondering how I knows so much about the land. Well, now, I owns it." And Mr. Nelson just settled himself in his porch swing. Crossed his legs, and looked out into the night. "Yeah, Jacob, you all ain't got nothing to worry about when you deal with me. Just keep up your payments. . . ."

Felt to Mariah that she wanted to cushion Jacob's head when he couldn't get his mouth open for the longest kind of time, and neither could nobody else.

"Now look a-here, Mr. Nelson . . ."

Didn't take Mr. Nelson two seconds to get up from that swing. Started pressing them to the door, saying as he did so, "Mighty glad you all come to talk things over with me. Yes, siree, mighty glad indeed."

When they got in the hearse car, Jacob had a time getting the motor to turn over.

Mariah, feeling his feelings and God knows what all, said right easy to him, "Jacob, I think . . ."

He jammed on the accelerator. Went on out of that Nelson yard. "Shut up, woman! I'm gonna get our land back!"

14

Days right after they saw Mr. Nelson were more than a notion to take for Mariah, for it looked like Bardetta and Jacob just hung together in one long nighttime and then a mighty long daytime and then—and then another long nighttime of dying.

Bardetta stayed choked up with the cough and the cold anyway. But Jacob got such a grayness in his face right after his brothers, Levi and Tom, brought the other one, Emerson, home to lay him in the ground—dead from the TB.

And the grayness sank deep in Jacob's eyes 'cause Thomas was too sick to go back with Levi. Yep, Levi just left him home so that his Mamma Bertha Ann could doctor up on him.

"Let me touch the hem of your garment, Jesus," Mariah prayed as she chased down the road to catch Levi before he left.

"Levi, hon, write your address down on this piece of paper for me. Might want to get a-hold of you sometime."

Jesus, got to get my children out of Tangierneck.

But death sneered at her, even while Levi, all sunken-cheeked, eyes burning, lifted his little hunched shoulders. "Sure, hon, sure. Be glad to hear from you."

And yes, her chilly companion gloated. *You ain't getting away from me, Mariah. You ain't getting away from me.*

"Don't put your mourning clothes away, Jacob." Mariah had the funniest feeling when she said that to Jacob the day Levi left. Didn't know why this thought came to her.

Jacob walked to the window. Stared out at the chinaberry tree. Craned his neck to the sky. "First night of the new moon, woman. Best time for sowing beans. Be out in the South field early in the morning. Gonna get our land back from Nelson," was all he had to say. Didn't say a word to her either when she said to him the next morning, "Jacob, I 'spects we better go, too, just like Levi." He just went on down his rows and dragged Mariah to help and watch after this and that.

Watch for a break in the days of death coming and going. Cry for a break: "For my children, good God! Let me save my young'uns!" And sometimes when she'd have to leave Bardetta home bad off sick, she'd further pray, "Got to stop going off every day to these fields. Got to stay home and look after my children. . . ."

She screamed and watched when she heard how Rabbit was running over to his Grandmamma Bertha's house just as soon as he got out of that school they were holding in the church each day, emptying that spittoon of Thomas' and then running around Tangierneck describing to people what the clots of mess Thomas coughed up looked like. Beat him for putting his germy hands on that Bardetta. Railed at the infant child, "You heading for Cleveland's Field. Rabbit ain't got no sense patting on you and trying to 'tend to you when I ain't home. Gonna bring the TB right to you first and last. He's always trying to save somebody. Tried to save me by throwing away them blue pills. Although Jesus God, I don't think he told me the truth." Knew the little black-eyed affliction couldn't understand what she was saying.

But Mariah cried and beat herself with the whip of her God's conscience. Especially after Rabbit told her how Thomas sent little Mamie over to her house for him to run and fetch Mamma Bertha from the fields. Rabbit stopped off to see Thomas first. Said Thomas said to him, "I don't want to die. Go get Mamma. I want to sing." Said Thomas cried to him when he could stop the coughing, all the while bleeding from the mouth.

Thomas wasn't but twenty-two, but he went on and died anyhow. And Rabbit, he cried right smart.

That's when Mariah took to running up from the fields every time she took a notion to watch over that child of her sin. Said to her sometimes, "Child, I hope you ain't caught that TB. I'm pulling for you, young'un. But don't seem like you gonna last. You heading for Cleveland's Field. . . ."

Hollered at Skeeter and Gezee, too, till she thought

their nerves was gonna give out on them. And forever and ever to Jacob, "Jacob, we got to go!"

"Where to and what for, woman?"

"Anyplace but here . . . Baltimore or Philadelphia . . . on account of the children. I can get me a job doing housework. Get something fitting for the children. . . ."

"Fool woman, don't you see? More people than a little is getting hauled down here from the cities. Don't you know it's harder times up there than it is down here? People's dropping dead up there from hunger."

"It ain't so, Jacob! It ain't."

"I'm staying right here, woman. Done told you I'm gonna pay off Mr. Nelson for the land. That's my final word!"

Smells of dogwood and lilac and fertilizer began to blanket the land as Mariah and Jacob tilled and sowed the few acres left to them. And the clear cool rains of the new year's spring promised them—with the help of their Saviour —a good crop of beans come fall.

Ol Jefferson would come by ever so often bringing a good catch of trout or shad or catfish for to sell. And sometimes he'd come by for pure "D" nothing. Then he'd sit around on the doorsteps talking about everything except his own business. Cutting up and carrying on, mostly. Seemed like to Mariah he almost made the grayness disappear from Jacob's face some evenings. 'Course her—it didn't matter about her looks no more.

She had just got done with her supper dishes one evening and chased the big boys out to run their suppers down when she spied Ol coming up the road—shoulders all drooping. "Fact is," she said to Jacob, "his walk don't even favor itself," as she dragged herself out to the yard to set fire to a pile of leaves and rags to raise a smoke to keep the mosquitoes away. She went on back in that house soon as Ol walked in and saw that neither did his face favor itself! Looked like he was in a state of teetotal puzzlement.

"Something ailing you, Ol?" Jacob's face was one great big frown.

Words came tumbling out of Ol. "They got your papa, Jacob. Took him away. . . ."

"What you talking about, Ol? Who got him?" Looked to

Mariah like Jacob was gonna wring the arms off of the chair he was trying to stay put in.

"See, Captain, your papa asked me for to take a ride with him up to Calvertown this morning. Said he had some business for to take care of 'bout the land. I swear, I didn't know all this business about your papa and Dr. Grene. Didn't know what your papa was planning to do. . . ."

"Ol, make some sense! What are you talking about?"

"I'm trying to tell you, Jacob. See, it wasn't till we got close up there to Calvertown that your papa told me how he found out from some white folks that Dr. Grene had been arrested on account of Miss Bannie's death. Said to me he was gonna prove Dr. Grene didn't do it. Couldn't have murdered his own mother. Kept saying over and over that they was trying to frame Dr. Grene . . . they stole a will . . . trying to take away the land that Dr. Grene had come into . . . and your papa, too! I don't know, Jacob. Seemed to me like he was raving some of the time. I couldn't always make him out." Ol turned to Mariah. "He even was talking something peculiar about you and Dr. Grene."

"Get on with it, Ol!" Jacob jumped up from that chair so hard it flew to the floor. Sound sent Gezee and Bardetta into a crying fit.

"Jacob, we parked by the courthouse, and your papa told me to wait. Last words he said was they wasn't gonna kill no son of his . . . was gonna tell the whole thing . . . Jacob, it all happened so fast. There wasn't nothing I could do. . . ."

Looked to Mariah like Ol was gonna collapse. Something told her to run . . . get away! But she couldn't move.

"Next thing I knowed, the sheriff and one of them deputies was dragging him out of the courthouse. They had done beat him. You could see the blood running out of his nose. And they put him in a pickup truck with some road cops. . . . And they drove off, Jacob. I come down here as fast as I could."

Mariah saw such a dawning of horror and terror and everything else in Jacob. And before she could help herself she started blabbing, "It's my fault, Jacob. I drove your papa to it. I'm filled with the curses. God is wreaking his vengeance on me for my sinfulness. I best be leaving, Jacob. And taking Bardetta. . . ."

"Mariah, ain't got time to listen to that now! Got to go find Papa. . . ." And Jacob went over and got his hunting rifle from behind the bureau.

"I'm telling you she ain't yours, Jacob. This baby ain't yours!"

Jacob stopped. "Whose is she, then?"

"Don't matter. She ain't yours. This shitting-assed land of death'll drive a person to anything."

Jacob just stood rooted in the middle of the kitchen looking from her to Ol to the baby like he had never seen them before. Then he moved to the door.

"Come on, Ol. Let's get some men together. Got to find Papa."

"Your papa's limousine is still up there in Calvertown, Captain. I walked home through the woods. Don't know how we gonna get around . . ."

"We got horsecarts and horses, and we got legs that'll do for walking and running. Come on, Ol!"

Mariah hollered, "Jacob, bring that gun right on back in here. You know you ain't even got no bullets to shoot with. Jacob, you ain't never even learned how to shoot a squirrel. . . . Jacob!"

Well, they searched and they searched. And Mariah searched, too, with the rising of the sun and a few more that came, in the swamps, in the ditches, in the marshes, and the rivers of the land. They searched in committees and a whole lot of times by the singles—taking turns. It was about the middle of May when the old man disappeared, but it was the end of June before Willie Ried brought the news down the road from Haimawalkin that he thought he'd found him or what looked like it was him.

Jacob did the driving in his papa's Cadillac limousine, which he went up to Calvertown weeks before and picked up. Stopped by and got his mamma and Ol Jefferson. Even took Mariah along. Jacob identified his father's shoes. Mamma Bertha, the clothes on the ground. And Mariah, the bones—especially the skull that remained—for the buzzards had picked off all the flesh. Skull seemed to have eyes peering into her soul, saying, "Whore and a heifer-and-a-half."

Well, they took the neck bones down from the Royal Oaks tree. Rest of the bones they separated from chains on the ground. And they carried them back to Tangierneck for a decent funeral. Then laid them to rest in Cleveland's Field.

All Ol Jefferson could say was, "Did him the same way they did Bard Tom. Same way they did his father."

"God!" Mariah stared at the child of her sores, when she went up the house to swallow a mouthful of food one day. "Hadn't been for you and the rest of the children, your grandpoppy would be here today." And she cried all up and down the scraggly rows of raspberries Jacob left for her and the boys to pick by themselves while he went off to the south field to tend the beans. But she didn't cry long.

Percy Upshur's bones hadn't been two weeks laying in the ground when Jacob come out to the raspberry patch and said, "Woman, put them baskets down. Don't touch another raspberry branch, else I'm lief to pick up a stick of wood and kill you. We getting out of this place. Wants you to get on up to that house and pack! Giving you one day's notice to pack! Be ready tomorrow twelve o'clock."

"Where we going, Jacob?" Mariah asked him as she set her baskets down and trudged out of that field. Scared to look up at him. Scared not to obey him. *I ain't nothing but a sinner, Lord. A whore and a heifer-and-a-half.* Scared the whole time she was packing up things and gathering the children together. But Jacob wouldn't answer her back, not the rest of that day nor all through the night.

Mouth just trembled when she asked again the next day, "Where we going, Jacob?" Standing in the yard. Feet wanted to grow roots in the hot dry sand.

Buzzards in the burning haze swooped low over the yard—seeking carrion from the roasting fields of July. Swooped low over the blue-streaked hearse car of Pop Percy's better days, loaded now with pots and pans, a couple of chairs and things . . . things . . . things! Mariah didn't know what all she'd put in and what all she'd left out. . . . "Jacob, where we going?"

"Place called Chance." Jacob's mouth was drawed up all tight when he said that to her, and he just kept cranking that machine while she was trying to get him to hear her.

"Where's that at, Jacob? If it's the same place I'm think-ing of, I hear tell colored's living like dogs up there. They living in shanties up there, ain't they, Jacob? Working in tomatoes up there?"

"It ain't *up* nowheres, woman! Get on in this thing and shut your mouth!" Sweat ran in a steady stream down Jacob's face. "It's right across here from St. Mary's."

"For what we going, Jacob? I-I-I mean for what . . . ?"

"For money. Gonna ask me for what about that, too?"

"Well . . . what I mean is, Jacob . . ."

"You don't mean nothing, ain't never meant nothing!"

And Mariah thought that Jacob would bust from the anger when he went on to say, "Any other questions you want the answers to, you better ask 'God's child,' bitch! Or maybe you'd rather ask that Dr. Grene."

As that hearse car chugged down the road leading out of Tangierneck, Mariah wasn't for sure whether she was running or marching. Seemed like the most she was doing was marching. Just a-stompity-stomp went her heart as she held herself down tight in that seat next to Jacob. Least move she made she heard a bone crack. For she was stiff. Lordy, Jesus, stiff. Had on a girdle. Onliest one she ever did own. One she had put away for a special occasion. One she had on for her wedding so she could look pretty and nice and trim. Thing cut right into her ribs now, and the folds of the skin on her belly. It hurt her considerably, but she had to keep it on so she'd be presentable to those peo-ple over there in that place called Chance. Had on that nice, soft brown hat, too. One Jacob used to say made her eyes conquer the land. "Yes, Lord," she said to herself, "I done fixed myself up decent so I can look nice before the public. A different kind of public from this evil and crazy mess down here. . . . And maybe, maybe . . . Jacob'll just look at me sometimes like I'm something be-sides a . . ."

You got better sense than to think that, Mariah. Old Messenger seemed to squeeze himself right down in the seat with her.

And she said to herself, "Gonna!" Didn't know what all she was gonna do. But she did make her mind up that she was gonna get herself some money saved up somehow.

Anyhow. And she was gonna make sure thereby that Rabbit was left with some people that would see to it he went away to college, for he was the smartest one in the whole family. And the lovingest one. Had such a tenderness for that Bardetta that it looked like sometimes he'd just give his own life up for her. Couldn't get over the way Rabbit acted toward that sickly child. Least time he heard her coughing in the night he'd just pop out of the bed same as if he was in charge of things and sometimes he'd be shoving that cough medicine down her throat before Mariah could even get to her. *But that's all over with now, Rabbit. That's all over with.*

Mariah bit her lip and stared straight ahead as Rabbit called out to her, "Mamma, Lil Yellow Heif's coughing up blood!"

"Give her this rag to spit it out in!" Mariah reached in her pocketbook where she kept most anything a person would need in a hurry and threw a rag back to Rabbit. "Stop calling that gal Lil Yellow Heif. Hear me when I'm talking to you, Rabbit! Child might be light-skinned but that ain't no excuse for you to be calling her Lil Yellow Heif. Her name's Bardetta. I'm sick of this Tangierneck way of putting animal names on to my children and you repeating after them. Rabbit, Rabbit, hear me, I'm talking to you, Rabbit! People's gonna stop calling you Rabbit, too. Your real name's Horace. And Skeeter," she hollered, "you listen to me, now. People's gonna stop calling you Skeeter. Your real name's William!"

And Gezee, well there wasn't no sense in speaking to him, for he was asleep anyhow. Worms picked on him so bad they tired the poor little fellow out before he even got in the hearse car and got himself all squeezed up in between the folded mattress she brought along for Jacob to rest his back on, nights.

Heard tell they didn't have nothing but straw for her to make into mattresses for the family in that place called Chance. Heard tell. Oh my Lordy, heard tell. . . .

And Mariah kept staring straight ahead and marching, marching! Eyes just a-marching past the Committee of her Judgment, sprinkled like vultures in the July fields of scrawny raspberry vines. Lydy and all of them was just a-gaping and a-looking.

Some had even come right out and said that the child

wasn't Jacob's, in front of her children, and that was the reason God was letting it be so sick. Moreover it was always gonna be weakly and grow up to be nothing but a yoke around Mariah's neck, if God suffered for it to live. Hard as times were after that Wall Street, where they sent out the money from, crashed, many was already forecasting another green winter. A-many a poor soul done dropped dead from the starvation in spring as it was, in the rising of the sap. Looked like a-many a more wasn't gonna take the strain of the falling.

But you ain't gonna be here, Mariah.

And she remembered how in the months just past, Rabbit come home bringing her those tales of Bardetta . . . of herself.

Nothing but a whore and a strumpet, that's how they been calling you.

Didn't want to hear it. Didn't want to hear how the very same people who were always grinning in her face when she went out to work was chinking Rabbit's head full of dirt, and making him get himself all beat up. *I ain't gonna cry, Jesus. I swamp it, I ain't.*

Jacob didn't even pay her an inch of mind when she said, "Jacob, can't you speed on up?"

And the woman winced from the thoughts just a-burning all through her of how she used to get after Rabbit about repeating after people's children. But the talk always did seem to get right next to him. And he'd take on so, fighting and carrying on with the children to defend her and his "Chink," as some would call Bardetta, against the backbiting. Sometimes she'd even beat him so bad! So bad, Lord.

Said to him one time, "Rabbit, what you trying to do? Get yourself turned into a circus clown? Ain't your lip enough of a scar for you to be carrying around? Your whole head ain't nothing but a bunch of scars!"

Rabbit just cried so pitiful after she said that thing to him. Talk about his lip hurt him worse than anything. He had a right to cry, for when Mamma won't take up for you, kiss on your sores and tell you I love you, you something —anything—who else will, Jesus?

Mariah reached in her pocketbook, cleared her throat of the dust flying in the windows, and said, "Rabbit, here's a piece of horehound candy for you to suck on . . . and divide it up with Skeeter and Gezee so it'll ease the coughing."

Wasn't gonna say a neither 'nother word to Rabbit. Nor to nobody. No matter how they came running out to the fields now to see what in all was going on to make Mariah and Jacob move like that. In such a hurry!

Committee of her Judgment ran out to the road and gazed by the dozens it looked like. And Mariah wished Jacob would speed up but he just chugged on up that road. Slow as you please. Looking at the earth. Earth of his and his papa's dreams.

"I ain't coming back home no more till I get a-hold of enough money to get my land back. . . . At least twenty acres. With that, a man can do something to start off again. Need at least fifty acres to take care of the family though. . . ." Jacob talked to Skeeter. Made it clear with his disdainful eyes that he wasn't speaking to her.

And he kept on just a-talking to Skeeter about how they were going off to a place where there was just common migrant workers from down South and not dignified people like those of the Upshur family from Tangierneck.

"Some of them don't even know what the inside of a church looks like from one end of the year to the next. Just carousing and living loose lives. But I want you to hold your head up, boy, because you have got something. One of the best attended churches in this county. Got land of your own, too, least we gonna get it back. We gonna get a regular preacher to attend this flock, too, instead of sharing one with these other places. Hold your head up, boy, because we ain't never been just ordinary hired workers. You got land. . . ."

Jacob talked on to Skeeter, and tried not to pay any mind to Vyella hailing them down and leaning in the car window. He never had a good word to say about her being a preacher lady, anyway.

Mariah felt right glad when Vyella pinched Jacob on the cheek with a "Jacob, what you doing hauling our Mariah off from us? Menfolks ain't doing nothing but talking about our school project. Why you taking one of our women that can *do* something?"

"Oh, I ain't done nothing, Vyella. Nothing compared to you and you know it. But I'll be sending a little something along to you as I makes it for the school. But hold up a minute, Vyella." And Mariah, she stepped out of that car, said, "I do so much appreciate the good thoughts you give to me. . . ."

Vyella, with her big blooming face—well it looked like her belly was blooming just as big in a way—went on traipsing away. But Mariah caught up with her. Heard Jacob just a-racing that motor, so she had to speak quick, "Vy, hon, if I sends you something extra every payday, will you save it up for me?"

Vyella stopped short and just looked right on through Mariah so it seemed. "Don't you want Jacob to know nothing 'bout it?" And she broke out in a giggle. Stomach was just a-bouncing. People said the reason her stomach was punching out was because she was again in a family way. Some even said that she'd done away with a few so as to pinch pennies and help her husband buy the franchise for the bus route to haul the high school children. Well, you can't pay any mind to what people say against a person— especially when they're doing good. Most couldn't stand the thought of Vyella getting her license to preach. *But that ain't nothing for you to be dwelling on, Mariah.* Messenger had even sneaked out in the field behind her. *Save up some money, Mariah. Little bit of money for to leave to your children.*

"Sure I'll do it. Hold on to every cent you ask me to. When you coming back?" Vyella asked. And she had such a grin on her face.

"Ain't never coming back no more," Mariah said. "Except for to collect my money for the children."

And the spit just started dripping out of Mariah's mouth. Vyella spun around so. Looked like her eyes were gonna pop out of her head at the sight of Mariah. "You ain't coming back, Sis? You ain't coming back?"

"No, I ain't never except for to get my money for my children. Vyella, oh Vyella! Hates to speak to you about these things. . . ."

"It ain't nothing, Sis. Best a person can do is the best they can do." Vyella's face filled up with the shadows. And the day did, too. Funniest thing how that day did change. And Mariah knew she was going forever. Going forever into nothing but shit, shit, shit.

She walked on back to that car. Climbed in alongside of Jacob and that Messenger and Bardetta and Gezee on the back seat alongside of Skeeter and Rabbit carousing and just a-cutting up and carrying on.

Couldn't wait to get to Chance. Said, "Jacob, speed up!" But Jacob, he slowed on down. Said to him again, "Jacob, speed up!" But that son-of-a-bitch slowed down still further. Wheels on the car was just a-grinding in the sand. Sand is a mess to get out of. And Jacob was making the job even messier. Stuck a piece of horehound candy in her own mouth. Said to herself, "Jesus, let me march." Tried to doze off. But all the time she had to keep setting up straight while Jacob pulled off the road when people hailed them down. Most of them wasn't saying anything except something like, "Where you all going?" and "Why you all going there?" But some of them was saying how they expected to be leaving soon, too: "Looks like we all gonna be squeezed out, sooner or later."

Mostly, though, it was "When you all coming home?"

That's what Mamma Bertha Ann asked as she sprinkled water from a milk bottle around the burning bush of Moses in the patch she called a flower garden that she strove to make grow each year in the sands of Tangierneck.

"Well, you all be home soon, I guess." Mamma Bertha Ann's eyes were wells of sorrow. "I had a dream last night. Levi come and stood by my bed just as plain as day. . . . Jacob, I'm telling you the truth. . . . I could have reached out and touched him, he was that real. He was some pretty sight to see. I said to him, Levi, did you come home for to sing? And when I reached out to hug him, he was gone, children. . . . Ain't no need for you all to be running. Death's gonna find you. Dream of Levi was a sign. . . ."

Fool woman don't know what she's talking about. Mind going bad on her. Toting around milk bottles lately. Empty bottles! Always grieving over her sons.

Mariah was so glad when she walked on away. Said to Jacob, "Speed on up!"

"What's the matter, woman? Don't want nobody to see what a disgrace you brought to me?"

Must have been the good Lord what put her want to sleep when the headache grabbed her in the back of the head. Pulled a Stanback powder out of her pocketbook and took it dry before she did so. Took it dry and threw her head back, dreaming of water to rinse out her mouth and throat.

"What kind of a place is this, Jacob, for to bring my children?" Mariah gasped when she saw the shanties in that place called Chance. Buzz flies rose in clouds, making halos around the heads of little children playing near the slop ditch running a few feet from the back of the long row of yellow shanties. The ditch was a regular river of scummy tomato waste from the factory, with King-Po-T-Rik molasses cans, and Phillips baked bean cans, and all kinds of cans with labels soaking off of them in it. Everything that she could think of that a person would throw away was in that ditch. It was a regular feast for the flies.

Flies swarmed in the little yellow two-piece-of-rooms shanties made *especially* for the *decent* colored people of Maryland, as Jacob explained to her.

"And moreover," Jacob went on to tell her as he backed the hearse car up to the door of the shanty they got assigned to so they could move their things in easy, "these are the 'deluxe' shanties for people who have some self-respect. It ain't like them things the other people got across the road. Them brown shacks across there is just made especially for them ignorant migrants from the South, because that's all they're used to. . . ."

And Mariah just kept straight on going, saying to herself, "Anything's good enough for me." Just a-hauling in furniture and things. Fighting the flies lingering all lazy on her face. And the whining and carrying-on of the children. That Gezee was never gonna stop getting the loose bowels from the worm medicine she gave him. And that Bardetta was never gonna stop wheezing. Skeeter and that Rabbit was never gonna stop running off to get into things they had no business in. Fool done took his shoes off and just went a-running. *Lordy, Jesus, help me.* Woman broke down and cried. Screamed for Skeeter and Rabbit to get their asses in that shanty and help her to get things straightened out, and get off her nerves. Begged the Lord for to give her the strength in her arms for to clean up those fucking dirty floors of their "deluxe." *Just bare boards, Lord. Just bare boards.* Begged Him for to help her out with the children when they kept crying about how they was so hungry and how she ought to fix them something to eat when she was down on her knees trying to clean up so they'd have a fitting place to eat in. And she didn't know what in all she was gonna give them to eat when she did get up from that floor. And she didn't know whatever she was gonna do to make Jacob "get off her back" in a way of speaking, for he was at her, too, to fix him something to eat so he could hurry up and go on to get to the factory, and talk his job over with the bossman.

She said to him, "Jacob, this place ain't clean enough for to eat in!"

"I ain't knowed it was this bad myself," Jacob gave her that much. Even helped her to get a-hold of some screen wires and put them up in the windows of their "deluxe" before he went off strutting to the factory. Just went off, head held up just as high and mad-looking as you please, and leaving her a whole lot of instructions about how she ought to soak mattresses she was stitching up with the straw they allowanced out to her, with coal oil, and lay them out in the sun after she got through sewing them, to kill the ticks. Same as if she didn't already know what to do! *But I'm guilty, Lord. I'm guilty. He ought to kick me in my ass. Just let me get a-hold of some money, for to move my children before you throw me down in the burning pits of hell.*

And Mariah prayed that thing over all the rest of the day and that night, too, when she did lay her weary bones down. And through the next day, too. And from there on out when she made her seven o'clock march to the factory where she got hired as a tomato skinner. That big, sprawling yellow tin and wood structure which was nothing but hot steam and tomatoes on the inside. And it was decorated off with a yard filled up with tomatoes, as big as from here to yonder. And all during the time when it was just a steady grind for to peel enough of those steaming tomatoes without cutting off a finger like some people did to make a living—all during the time when people would just be a-laughing and a-crying, but mostly bitter laughing about how people's faces in the cities were going to look when they got a-hold of a can of those tomatoes and saw a sliced-off finger in them, and about the children they left up to the shanties getting acid sores from eating a steady diet of tomatoes—all during that time Mariah prayed and almost fixed herself in a steady trance praying, "Let me get some money." Pennies and dimes and quarters and dollar bills just kept a-dancing in front of her eyes. Didn't worry about nothing except getting a dollar or two mailed off to Vyella every now and then and looking out for her children the best way she could.

Came a day when Jacob got off about seven o'clock in the evening from that foreman's job he had worked up to, and come up to the shanty. Mariah was just setting on the steps cooling herself off from the steamy heat in the factory, and the heat over the stove in the cooking shanty where all the forty-some-odd women in the "deluxes" had to share four stoves! Jacob came up to her. Thought he was gonna knock her off of the tomato box they had to use for a doorstep. Said to her, "Mariah, you ain't even picked up the mail from the commissary today." Plunked a letter from Vyella down right on top of her new dress which she had got all washed and ironed to put on and feel like a person in someday's summer shade.

"Ain't had no time, Jacob. Skinned tomatoes all day till after the place was closed."

"Bet you ain't got nothing ready for me to eat, either."

"Is so got something! Potatoes and fatback on the table! And some tomatoes I stewed down."

"Bet you ain't even noticed Rabbit lately. He's filled up with the cold. Keeps a cough."

"I stays up all night sometimes, Jacob, rubbing his chest down and giving him the cough medicine. You ain't got no right to open up your mouth to me in that kind of a way. You ain't doing nothing but snoring the whole time."

Well, Jacob, he just stomped on into that shanty. And Mariah walked herself out into the field where some old white farmer grew corn. Opened up that letter. Eyes just a-straining to see by the lightning bugs and whatever little light there was left in the summer day. Letter read:

Dear Rah,
Sorry to bring you all bad news. Levi's gone. We bringing his body home today. Funeral's on Thursday, 3 o'clock. Died of the TB. Rest of the family is doing fine. Hope you all can get home. Saved up a little for you. Got my preacher's license now. I guess I'll have to preach the funeral 'cause we ain't got no regular preacher yet. It must have been Levi's time to go.

We are all so hurt. Thought it be best if you broke the news to Jacob.

Love,
Sis Vyella

P.S. Don't take it too hard.

Her breath commenced to coming so hard. Thought she was going blind! What's gonna happen to my children, Jesus? Jesus! Hope you took Levi's soul on up to heaven. Jesus, Jesus, got to go and tell Jacob. And through them yellow and green cornstalks Mariah walked until she could stop herself from the crying, and it was too dark to walk anyway, anymore. Got to get back to that shanty. Said to Jacob, all tired out, laying on the bed, "Jacob, Levi's gone. Funeral's tomorrow."

Well, Jacob, he sat bolt upright. "What you say?"

Mariah started right in crying again. Rabbit run to her. All he was doing was getting skinnier by the minute. Grabbed him up in her arms. Just a-crying. "Your Uncle Levi's gone. Funeral's tomorrow." But Rabbit, he just hugged her till he almost squoze the breath out of her neck, "Don't cry, Mamma. Don't cry no more. Where's the place called Funeral? We'll go find Uncle Levi."

Skeeter, he jumped right in on what Rabbit was saying to her. "Funeral's home in Tangierneck, boy. Where else it gonna be? You don't even know how to talk right, yet, asking Mamma where's that place called Funeral."

And Gezee wasn't doing nothing but bawling because Skeeter and Rabbit was a-tugging on her. And Bardetta wasn't never gonna stop that wheezing and grunting and gasping for that Goddamned life that wasn't even nothing but death nohow. Death in that Goddamned yellow shanty. Death in the muggy-assed summer heat oozing into the very skin clinging to their crumbling bones! And in the crying of children in the long row of shanties fighting off the mosquitoes swarming up from the funky-smelling ditch in the smothering air. *Death, Mariah, death.* Felt a chill coming over her. Turned around and said, "Jacob." But she was looking at an empty bed. Saw Jacob sitting on it just a minute before. Put down Rabbit. Said to all of the children at once, "Where's your daddy at?" Voice barely came through.

"He went outdoors, Mamma," Skeeter piped up.

"Outdoors? Outdoors?"

Mariah, she went running like some kind of a dumb-founded fool—out, out into the night. Found Jacob in the gloom, just a-messing with that hearse car.

All he said to her was, "Rah, I s'pect you ought to go and get the children together. Car's fit to go." Then when she was walking off, he said furthermore, "Rah, we gonna need some extra money for to help pay off Jimmy Jamison for the funeral." She could feel his eyes crawling all over her. Spun around like she was struck. "I ain't got no money, Jacob."

"You been making more than you been allowing, woman."

How Jacob know that? Well, he wasn't gonna get neither extra cent from her. Never could stop his ass from asking her about her money, and she told him so. Even had got to the place where he worried her about her chewing-gum money. Family short of money, let 'em bury Levi in a pine box!

That's the kind of thoughts Mariah still kept thinking when she loaded those children into that hearse car. Bardetta just a-coughing. Skeeter just a-wheezing and Rabbit and Gezee acting like they were gonna choke their brains out, dozing all fitful-like and laying up all over her—all down that dark road to Tangierneck. Brains started standing still on those thoughts when Jacob pulled off the road a couple of miles back from the bridge going across the Nighaskin River. Wasn't even any bridge left. Good the state troopers was right there telling the cars to hold back. "Hurricane done washed away the bridge."

Rain was just coming down. Funny how Mariah never noticed it before. All down that road to Tangierneck. Never noticed how hard the rain was coming down. Only thing she noticed was the children leaning on her. And the tiredness of death. And missing Levi.

"Jacob, it ain't no bridge for us to cross over on," Mariah cried out when they got stalled in the dark waters rising up from the overflowing Nighaskin.

"I can see just as good as you can," he snapped.

Funniest thought came to her! Wished she had drowned Bannie in them very waters. Wished she could get Rabbit off her chest. Stop him from hugging on her. Wished she could just go on and die. But then there was the funeral of Levi to attend to. And she really wished it was all over with and die die die! But then there was Rabbit laying heavy on her chest. And there was the state troopers trying to fix up that bridge. And she thought she even spotted Willie Ried and Tillie a-way up the road helping out for to build up that bridge. Thought the night would never pass. Nor the swirling of the waters all around the car, nor Jacob's backing back—and then backing back still further. Backing back until she hollered, "Jacob! Drive through the mother-fucking water! Get this funeral over with. Bridge is done been fixed up. Can't you see by the lantern lights. They done fixed the bridge! Jacob, we ain't gonna have nothing —not even a pot to piss in nor a window to throw it out of if we soon don't get back to Chance. Tomatoes is still coming in there." *Got to move! Mariah! Got to move!* Old death man still kept talking to her.

Jacob, he cut in on her, "Rah, we getting back to Tangierneck for to bury Levi. Rah, I don't think you got no feelings at all, sitting like that crying."

Didn't realize she was crying again her ownself. Said to Jacob, "You take this car forward. Stop backing back! I ain't no crying!"

And Jacob, he said right disgusted even after them people had built the bridge back up over the Nighaskin River, "Rah, cut out that sniveling."

But she couldn't help herself. Didn't even have a fitting dress for the mourning. Had to borrow something halfway decent to put on her back from Lydy. Had to see Mamma Bertha Ann toting them milk bottles around again. See all them blackgarbed mourners crowding into that same old going-down church. On a gray dark day. Filled with the smell of marsh and water and death. Couldn't help herself. Ducked in the darkness of the veil of her tears, and her mind just a-swirling around. Trying to march herself away—out of that dank death-smelling church where the long heavy wails rose clear to heaven and the gloom bore down to crush the stomach, the head, the whole person— clean through the floor boards down to eternal eating-up death. March away from the wails of the church singing:

> When we re-e-each that blessed homeland
> God shall wipe away all tears.

Almost said out loud: *If I ever get out of here. Place ain't never gonna see me no more. Ain't gonna be staring at no more shriveled-up gray-faced bodies laying up in coffins with their faces all painted up and bodies perfumed.*

Mind kept marching her away from the sight of that pine box with poor little hunched-up Levi closed up in it. Fixed up as decent as the family could make him. *Ain't gonna be no more singing in Tangierneck.*

Didn't hardly take no notice of the dirty-colored yellow Vyella's face was turning to, nor the way her belly was swoll up considerable—jaws all sunk in. Nor how she tried hard to cheer the people when she took over the rostrum just a-preaching:

". . . and I take my sermon from the Book of Ecclesiastes, Chapter Three made up of twenty-two verses.

> To every thing there is a season, and a time to every purpose under heaven;

> A time to be born, and a time to die; a time to plant and a time to pluck up that which is planted;

Mariah said to herself, "Vyella, stop that crying. Go on. Go on with the sermon." Hugged herself up to Jacob sitting right along beside her. But Jacob was as cold as ice. Wished Vyella would stop. Stop, stop, stop! Thought she'd take her fingers and plug up her ears. But she couldn't do nothing but every now and then say, "Levi, you ain't gone is you?" And try to take her eyes off of that pine box, and catch up with Vyella's words when she got herself together and was keeping on going through that chapter:

> A time to weep, and a time to laugh, a time to mourn, and a time to dance;

Listened to the Church rocking, crying, "Yes, Jesus," and "Oh Lord, he's gone."

> A time to get, and a time to lose; a time to keep and a time to cast away;

Listened to Mama Bertha Ann just a-moaning, "Levi,

you gone, too?"

I have seen the travail, which God hath given to the
sons of men. . . .

Turned her head when Lydy fainted clean away and peo-
ple jumped up from their pews to fan her.
What you gonna do, Mariah? What you gonna do?
Said to that Messenger just a-hovering around the peo-
ple, *I ain't gonna do nothing. Let 'em all die. Levi, what
I'm gonna do 'bout my children, now?*
Heard Vyella saying:

He hath made every thing beautiful in his time. . . .

Heard Mamma Bertha Ann jump up just a-hollering,
"Levi ain't no beautiful in that box. Open up that box, you
all. I want you to see him. See what the world done done
to him. Open up that box, I wants to hear him sing!"
And when they wouldn't open up that casket, Mamma
Bertha Ann tried to open it up herself. Looked like to
Mariah the whole Church went to pull her back from that
thing and fan her and get her sitting back down in her seat
again. Woman looked so bad. Chest was heaving like she
was strangling.
Vyella, well she come down from the pulpit, got to
Mamma Bertha Ann, and said to the women patting and
fanning on her, "Take her out of this church so she can get
some air."
But the women wouldn't do it. Took out quite a few
though who was fainting.
But Mariah, she said to herself, "I ain't gonna do no
fainting." And she sat and listened to Vyella—that strong
Vyella—going on with the sermon when she did climb
back up into the pulpit.
"Levi was so good—he was my brother." Child couldn't
even hardly go on. Kept on reading that chapter.

And go unto one place; all are of the dust, and all
turn to dust again. . . .

Tears did start leaking down Vyella's face, but she blew
her nose and threw her arms up to heaven. "Jesus, help me

to go on. He was my brother. He was my brother! Gave his voice to you. Know his soul's in heaven now!"

Church said, "Amen. Go on. Go on. Go on."

And she did go on until the last of the hundreds had filed past the coffin to view poor, poor Levi for the final time in their earthly lives. Some just plain weeping, some with faces turned to stone, like Jacob's, children staring all worried-faced 'cause a whole lot of them had never seen death before—whole lot of them crying 'cause they was scared, some like Mamma Bertha Ann, falling over the casket and others picking them up and fanning them from the fainting and the fits—but Mariah, she didn't do nothing but march straight past. Then she hugged up to Vyella— *Oh God, I wish you had made me like this woman*—all the way to Cleveland's Field, where they laid Levi in his final resting place: that dark hole in the water-soaked shifting sands.

And it was, "Oh, my God," when the people saw how the great tall oaks had been ripped clean up from the ground by the hurricane winds of an angry God. Roots of the trees were filled with the bones of the dead, and pieces of clothes, and broken boards of many a coffin.

And the air was rent with cries of the living glaring at the rotted bones and rags of their kin and friends just a-swinging in the winds circling about the land, and pulling the bones and rags—some crumbling and dry, some still squirming with the worms eating away at them—from those once mighty roots, and putting them back in the gaping holes.

When Mariah found little Mary's bones and pieces of that pink dress they'd put her away in, Jacob liked to have wrenched Mariah's arms off for her to stop her from collecting the little old bones for to keep with her. "Gonna take them back to Chance with me. Jacob, oh Jacob! Seem like I can hear her crying now. . . ."

"Jacob's right, Sis." Vyella was the only one that could get her calmed down. Lead her away from the sight of Jacob putting those little remains back in that lonesome hole.

"Take your mind off of these terrible things, hon. Child's in heaven. God's will. Never got a chance to be corrupted with the sins of the flesh like some of us . . . like me. . . . Let Jacob put them bones back. They be resting there nice when you all get home. I'll say prayers for her regular. If God will forgive my sins he'll answer and protect."

Looked like Vyella was trying to tell her something. Eyes looked so scared. They welled up with the tears, and she blew her nose again. Choked up, "I'm saving every cent you send me, Sis. Gonna have a nice piece of your change saved up for you when you get back home . . . when you get back home." And just as quick she walked on off. Head hung down, but traipsing mighty fast over those sodden sands of Cleveland's Field. *Be back to get my money, Vyella. But ain't coming back for to stay.*

Left Mariah standing in that wind smelling of the waters and decaying bodies to watch Jacob building up a new mound over little Mary. Watch him fall on his knees saying what all she didn't know to his God. Didn't take him but a minute. Then he come up to her. "Bones is all put back. Let's get out of here and get on back to Chance. Had to help out with Levi's funeral with just about every cent I had. Looks like the only thing we got left right now is Cleveland's Field. But that ain't gonna last forever."

And Mariah whispered to that Messenger, "Get away from me!" And she clutched on one of Mary's little bones which nobody didn't even know she had. "You ain't getting no more of my children, now." Flung her head back and marched out of that burying ground, thinking, How many miles to Chance!

Many a long dreary mile to Chance, and all Mariah could notice was how sickly those children was looking. Just as worn out and tired as they could be. Didn't want them to see no more death! Felt like pure D shit. . . . And she guessed she was. Guessed she was.

Pure D shit marched on when they got back into the shanty where Jacob kept messing with her about saving up money and what all she wasn't sharing with him. But she knew good and well she was gonna leave her children something. Said to Jacob one day, "Get the hell off my nerves 'bout this money part. Ain't nothing you can find decent to say to your wife. Hard as I works for to help out with these children."

Jacob's face was one great big sneer. "Decent, woman? You ought to laugh at yourself, Mariah. You ain't even clean enough for to touch no more."

Her whole self caved in to a whisper, remembering the long time barrenness of her loins. "Ain't nobody been begging you, Jacob." Wished she had them blue pills right then and there. *Rabbit, what you do with them?*

"You ain't even decent enough to tend to the children right. . . ."

Well, she didn't have to stay in that shanty and listen to no more of Jacob's lip. Went out and found all four of the children playing barefoot right near that ditch. Rabbit, the ringleader, leading Bardetta by the hand, who was just learning to walk. Gal just a-coughing. And Rabbit, too. Didn't know which one of them to start in on first. Snatched Bardetta from Rabbit's hands. Skeeter ran, and Gezee just sat his behind down in that mud and cried.

"I'm gonna kill all of you! I swamp it. You all boys go and break me off your switches." Went crazy and started spanking Bardetta. Child hollered so, and went into a fit of coughing. Couldn't even talk yet, let alone walk good, but Mariah spanked her until she just got down to a whimper. "Cough all that mess out of your lungs, gal. You're dying, dying! And you too, Rabbit."

Rabbit couldn't move. "Mamma, she's too little!"

Come to Mariah what she was doing and she started in crying. "Done told you a million times, Rabbit, if you fall in this ditch you'll drown in the slops from the factory. Walk barefoot out here, you'll get the hookworm in your feet. . . ." Didn't know what to say no more. No more, Lord. No more. "Come on, you all. Get up in the yard and play."

Guess Jacob was right. She just wasn't fitting for to raise 'em. Lot of women in the shanty row looked at her as much as to say the same thing. Felt like their eyes were chasing her clean out of Chance. And she was mighty glad when the last of the tomatoes was over and the most of them was packing up and leaving. Glad all their old talk to her children was over with about how their mother ought not to talk to them "that way." *Anybody turn my children against me is gonna have to meet up with me first. Ain't gonna be no more setbacks for my children.* Realized that even when Jacob was the last to get off from his foreman's job in the can labeling section. Then he had the nerve to come up to the shanty and say to her, "Rah, get the things all packed up." Well, any fool could see they was all packed up for to go back to Tangierneck. For to go back to the land of graves. *But I ain't gonna stay, Lord. Ain't made out worth nothing in Chance. But I can get on at Mr. Nelson's. . . .*

Jacob, he sat down on one of them straw beds, counting out his money. "Rah, we ain't got enough for to pay off the land that we actually needs—needs at least twenty acres, for to get a good head start."

Couldn't help but notice how Jacob's face was just about all caved in. And notice, too, how he spoke to her, like she wasn't thinking 'bout nothing but him and his land. Couldn't help notice.

Jacob, well he went on to say, "We ain't going straight back home. We going from here to Kyle's Island. I can get me a job on one of the dredging boats and you can be shucking oysters. They pay off a lot better in hard times such as we having now than messing up your whole day on them rocks in Tangierneck. . . . A man can make pretty good money over there. . . ."

"But Jacob, what's gonna happen to these children's education? You know Horace and William is in school. . . ."

"Woman, they got school over in Kyle's Island. . . ."

"But Jacob, what I also wants to say to you is, what's gonna happen 'bout Gezee and Bardetta? They ain't old enough for no school."

Jacob clenched his teeth so you could even see his jawbones knocking each and another out . . . turned his face so she couldn't see which one was gonna come disjointed first. Could see him thinking it over when he went out that door, saying, "Plenty old women on Kyle's Island for to take care of children that ain't of the age to go to school. Mariah, you 'bout the dumbest woman I ever saw. . . ."

Wasn't gonna think no more about Jacob. Said to that man of hers, she guessed, all hunched up over that steering wheel when they were on the way out of Chance, "Stop this car soon as you get to a store so I can buy some meat and bread for to make these children some sandwiches."

Jacob said, "Well, you know it's not a-many a store 'long this road that'll wait on colored."

"Children's hungry, Jacob. Hear me when I tell you. Stop this car!"

Jacob, he didn't say a neither 'nother word except, "I

ain't going into no place that act like they don't want me when I walk in."

"Rabbit's acting mighty poorly to me, Jacob. Much more so lately than he did so before."

"He was poorly before, woman. Be on Kyle's Island soon."

Seemed like to Mariah they was crossing over the rivers of many waters. All kinds of wooden bridges and everything to cross over on. Mentioned it to Jacob, but he just said, kinda proud, "Reckon you don't know what these waters is like. We be over them pretty soon. Be on Kyle's Island before daybreak in the morning. Wants you to fix up the shanty we gonna have to be living in with a little bit of that extra money you ain't been telling me nothing about. Think we ought to have some pretty yellow curtains like them you fixed up in that home place. . . ."

"Didn't know you even liked them before in my life, Jacob."

"You knowed I must have liked 'em!"

And he didn't never say another neither word to her like that.

Even after they got into that sagging gray shanty in the place called Kyle's Island, it didn't seem like he had anything worthwhile to say to her. And she nursed those children through cold after cold. First it would be that Rabbit, and the next night 'specially that Bardetta, and, well, it wasn't too many nights before or after or in between till it was Gezee and Skeeter. Skeeter had the loneliest way of looking that anybody ever saw. Always did have that way of looking since the day he was born.

Wasn't on Kyle's Island long, shucking them oysters till the water in her oyster buckets turned bloody from the stabs in her hands. Wasn't in that cold damp place long before Mrs. Amy, a real fat old woman with the smell of fresh earth and water all about her, come into the factory seeking out Mariah. Said to her, "Rah, 'spect you better come up to the place and see after Rabbit. He keep crying for you. Ain't breathing so good. . . . I been keeping a good fire for the children. But your Rabbit, I really do think he got the TB bad, or the worms. Worm crawled right out of his behind this morning. Think he choking on the rest. Seems he's burning up with the fever. You know I keeps the children decent. You got any medicine for to give him?"

It wasn't nothing for Mariah to do but drop that oyster knife right in the bucket. Run 'cross that gangplank from the oyster shucking factory, past the few white people's shanties that was propped up nearby, past the whole mother-fucking world.

"Rabbit, Rabbit. Whatever ails you? Mamma's here."

Noticed a worm crawling out of Rabbit's nose. But she hollered at Skeeter standing right by the bed that Mrs. Amy had laid out for Rabbit—nice and clean—"Go get your daddy!"

"Can't get him, Mamma. You know he out in the Sound. He's on one of them big old dredging boats—way out in the Sound. Ain't . . ."

"Go holler for your daddy. Get some of them fancy canoe people to get out in the Sound to get your daddy. Else maybe you'll find a skiff or two. . . . Understand me, tell 'em to tell your daddy, Rabbit's mighty sick. He's burning up sick. Got to get a doctor to him. Get out of here before I set fire to your behind, boy!"

Skeeter, he went flying out that door.

Didn't look like Rabbit was ever gonna come to, nor neither was Gezee nor *Miss* Bardetta sitting on the floor by the fire gonna stop their crying. *Shitting-assed children —crying-assed children. Jacob, get on here!*

"Rabbit, open up your eyes! Mamma's here."

"Here's a cool wet rag, Mariah, for to wipe him down." Mrs. Amy's trembling hand reached out to her.

"Mamma. Mamma, I can't breathe. Mamma, rub my chest down with some Vicks. . . . Mamma, don't go to sleep. . . . Mamma, my chest hurts. . . . My stomach hurts."

She took Rabbit up in her arms, just a-hugging on him and wiping him off. Kept it up until sometime in the evening dusk when her heart stopped moving. Heart stopped moving and she couldn't hardly breathe herself. "Rabbit, your daddy soon be here with the doctor. Him and Skeeter went for to get him. . . . Rabbit, I ain't got no medicine for to give you. Rabbit? Rabbit?"

And she let out with a moan.

Wasn't *her* heart that wasn't moving, it was Rabbit's. She ripped open his nightgown. Commenced to do an easy massaging all around his little heart. But she couldn't get not a beat nor a sound. Commenced in screaming.

Mrs. Amy, who'd been wandering around that shanty fixing up some oysters for all to eat, run over to her. "What in the name of God?"

"My baby's dead!"

"Oh, he ain't no dead, hon." Mrs. Amy's face turned to ashes. "Give him to me."

"Keep your paws off of him! My boy's dead!"

And she wouldn't let go of Rabbit. Not even when Jacob and Skeeter got back from Marvella with the doctor. Onliest thing she would do was just unloose him a little bit so that the doctor could put that cold stethoscope on his chest. Didn't do him no good. All that doctor did was to pronounce him dead of the round worms and the pneumonia probably. Thought maybe the worms was the thing that choked off his last little breath. . . . And all else that doctor did was to give them other children some medicine for to kill them worms.

No, she wasn't never gonna let go of no Rabbit. Never was gonna stop rocking him, and kissing on him. Not even when Jacob came over to her. "Give me my boy, Mariah. Let me hold him. Let me hold him."

Not even when Jacob got down on his knees so he could lean on her lap, crying and kissing on Rabbit his ownself. Not even when they went back to their own shanty for to make preparations for the trip home to Cleveland's Field. Not even when she found a jar of that blue pill solution stuck way back under the children's bunk when she went to gather Rabbit's things together. All she did was to turn to Skeeter. "Where'd this mess come from?"

"Rabbit saved up some pills from home. Said it was good for the sores if he mixed them in water. Told that boy it wasn't good for no sores, because *you* would be washing us down with it. . . . It did our sores good, didn't it, Mamma? See, I'm almost healed up. Said yesterday, it was even good for the worms to make 'em get out of you. He tasted some of it to prove it. See how the worms is coming out of him now. . . ."

"Skeeter, Skeeter, oh Skeeter. Don't ever touch nothing like that unless I tell you."

"I ain't never gonna do nothing like that, Mamma. Told

that boy not to do it, because that's what them people said killed Miss Bannie. . . . Mamma, can I hold Rabbit?"

"Let her hold him, Skeeter. She the one what killed him. Leaving poison like that around." Jacob got up from the table where he was waiting for her to get ready to go. "I'm going to be going now in a few minutes."

"I ain't done it! I ain't! Jacob? Jacob?"

Wasn't no point in keeping on calling his name. Wasn't no point in talking to him or Skeeter, or Bardetta, or Gezee. Even as they traveled across the rivers of many waters for to get home and lay Rabbit in Cleveland's Field, wasn't no point in talking to them. Onliest one to speak to was Rabbit. All wrapped up, dead, in her arms. Kept looking at his lips all drawed back and parched from the fever.

"Bad enough for the Lord for to have give you a harelip, but why'd he have to let your lips peel back so from the fever and the worms which you never would even tell me you had so bad. *Why'd you have to do it, Lord?* Rabbit, why didn't you tell me you was hurting so? Lord, Lord, Lord. Rabbit, why didn't you tell me you had the worms so bad? I should have knowed you wasn't doing nothing but feeding death when you started in gulping down so much food. I was giving everybody else worm medicine but you, Rabbit, don't go away. Don't go away. I loves you so. I do loves you, Rabbit. Rabbit, don't go. . . ."

"Boy's gone, Mariah. Ain't you got no sense? Cover up his face." Jacob couldn't even hardly see how to drive for the tears blocking up his eyes. But he saw the waters of his land, and the pine trees that couldn't even grow up to nothing but stubs getting a little bit taller after a-many and many forest fire. "Takes a-many and a-many a year for pines to grow up that tall. In one day and time we had them so pretty. So pretty. . . ."

"Jacob, take me straight to Cleveland's Field. Gonna put away Rabbit the way he ought to be put. By myself, Lord, by myself."

Jacob drove on through many a dark mile, and over many a dark hillside, and across many a dark bridge. Going thirty miles an hour in the most tolerant of places, toward Cleveland's Field—toward Tangierneck. Going thirty miles an hour until he had to slack up to cross those bridges that still hadn't got fixed up good and strong. Going thirty miles an hour, except when the tides came in so high so as to make them bridges creak and sway. Only thing steady was that ferryboat that Uncle Isaiah had got the job of pulling across Deep Gut since the schoolhouse burnt down.

Uncle Isaiah's face broke out in such a smile when he saw them coming. He was just a-tugging on them ropes.

"Whyn't you all honk the horn?" And he strutted up so proud to the car. "Good thing I was right out here. 'Cause you know if I'd a-been in the house I wouldn't a-see'd you coming. Hey there, Skeeter . . . hey there, Gezee . . . there's that little old Bardetta fast asleep. . . . Where's Rabbit at?"

"Mariah's got him in her arms." Jocob didn't even seem to hardly open his mouth.

"He's dead, Uncle Isaiah. Boy's done gone. We just brought him home for to bury him on home ground."

"Let me see his face," Uncle Isaiah said as he reached out his hands to uncover Rabbit's head.

Mariah butted right in on him. Said, "Keep your hands off of him. Ain't nobody gonna touch Rabbit no more but me."

Uncle Isaiah just said, "Glad you brought him home. . . . Glad you brought him home. Let me pull you 'cross the water. . . . Glad you brought him home to the land . . . he always knowed it was his land. Remember how that rascal used to run all over the place. . . . Let me put my hands on him one more time before we put him in the ground. . . . Ain't got a decent grave for to bury him in right now, but we'll get one fixed up in the morning. Glad you brought him home. . . ."

Mariah died in herself. "Yep, we done brought him home." She hugged that old Rabbit while Uncle Isaiah pulled the ferryboat across the river.

"Furthermore, Uncle Isaiah, we gonna put him in one grave and that's where he gonna stay. Little bones ain't gonna never be caught up in no tree roots. Bury him deep."

"That's where he's gonna stay," Mariah kept saying all through the funeral while she stared at that poor little thing's face—especially his lips. Said it even in Cleveland's Field when they lowered him in the ground right beside little Mary. Helped build up a great big mound over his body her ownself and make a marker out of nothing but plain old wood. Fell on that grave, crying, "Rabbit, Rabbit, I was gonna take you out of Tangierneck." Went to looking in her pocketbook just to make sure she still had that bone of Little Mary's. "And I would've took you away, too. Cleveland's Field ain't gonna get another one of my children."

Jacob pulled her up off those grave mounds. But she went running, straight behind Vyella, hearing Jacob hollering to her, "Come back, Mariah."

Caught up with Vyella and that poor thing was going mighty slow. Said, "Hon, I needs my money what you been saving up for me."

Vyella just put her arms around Mariah's shoulders and said, "Come on to the house, hon. I'll give it to you."

Got to Vyella's house and took notice of how much worse Vyella was looking. Didn't take notice too long. Just got her money off of Vyella. Didn't even take time to count it. Said to Jacob soon as she could locate him standing over Rabbit's grave and praying, "Let's get out of this place. Told you before it nothing but a place of standing still and death!"

And she took a-hold of his hand. "Come on, Jacob."

In the green grass of Hillards where they went to after the oyster season gave out on Kyle's Island, and where there was dew in the grass turning those strawberries they went to pick into bright red jewels, she'd cry to herself. Cried sometimes when she was chasing Skeeter and them running around barefooted out of them strawberry fields so they wouldn't get worms in their feet. And cried sometimes when she used to get a notion in her head that she'd like to have something more than some pieces of scrap material hung up in that big old plantation house where the inside walls had been knocked out so that the only thing the colored field workers could do was piece together all kinds of whatever scrap material they could get their hands on for to make some separate sleeping conditions for their families. Cried when she used to beg so quiet at night, "Jacob, Jacob, let's get us another Rabbit," and Jacob wouldn't even turn over in the bed for to kiss her. Well, after a certain time she just made up her mind time was giving out. Wasn't gonna talk to no Jacob no more. Didn't care if she felt lost in her groin or not without him. Didn't care nothing.

Didn't care nothing except but to get through the picking of the last of the strawberries and keep saving up money for to get her remaining children some place in the cities where they'd be treated decent. Didn't care nothing *else* but to get a-hold of enough money to help leave Jacob so he could get back that land he was always talking about. And a little bit more for to get Rabbit and little Mary some fitting tombstones. And a little bit more for to send Vyella for the school.

But that old death man just kept talking to her. *Mariah, I got you.*

Well, it wasn't no point in talking to her like that, because in the green grass of Hillards there was still dew and spring and there was a little bit of money to be made no matter how much people was dying from that old Wall Street collapse.

Gonna get her money. Gonna keep on walking. Gonna keep on marching. Said to her Jesus one day when the strawberries was giving out, "Help me to stay on my feet."

15

"I ain't come back for to stay," Mariah said to Aunt Saro Jane as she marched to the church alongside of her on the biggest funeral line ever seen in Tangierneck. Cars was lined up clean back to Jerry Larmer's store. People from Nighaskin and Royal Oaks and Back-of-the-Creek and some from the County of Countess Ann come. Some even from as far away as Baltimore and Philadelphia.

Grounds of Tangierneck roads and churchyard just seemed to shake as the people filed past the lilies and the daffodils in the sweet spring ditches gurgling along the paths and up to the gray clapboard church. Oaks that were left standing by the hurricane that swept the county in the fall moaned in the new spring breeze like voices lost in an eternity with their bushy heads high up. High up, yes, Jesus, in God's sky. Oaks that fell, especially in Cleveland's Field, where the digging for new graves that went on forever weakened the earth, just laid silent and gaping on the earth, as did the skulls and the pieces of clothing and the hip bones and the knucklebones and all kinds of bones belonging to a human body that was still caught up in their roots 'cause nobody could identify them. Marshy bullgrass had quieted down a bit with the coming of spring and the thawing of the freed water through the land.

Thank God nothing ain't touched Rabbit's grave, letting his little mound lay just as plump and in place.

Season was so pretty it was almost enough to make a person not hear the coming of another green winter and the singing:

> Carry me away from Tangierneck,
> Daddy, Daddy, Daddy,
> Don't want no buzzard picking at my neck,
> Paddy pick, Paddy pick, Paddy!

Almost quiet enough to make a person hear Aunt Saro Jane chanting along beside her: "Gal, now you know we need you home! Ain't Vyella got that letter to you? Me and Tillie was with her when she breathed her last. Well, anyhow, just before she breathed her last, and she said she was writing you a letter. Wanted you to carry on in her footsteps. Rah, Rah, what did she say to you? Told you her little Ned was Jacob's, ain't she, Rah? Ain't she, Rah?"

Don't answer her back, Mariah. Go on. Go on. You ain't even answered Jacob's question about what was in that letter. . . . Gonna answer them all when you get in that church. Gonna tear out your breasts on the streets of Jerusalem. Gonna rip them from the sockets in the church of Tangierneck.

"You ain't gonna do her memory no harm, is you, Rah?" Aunt Saro Jane droned on.

"Hush up, Aunt Saro. Can't you see Rah's taking it hard? Vyella's the only one treated her like she was anything," Tillie said. "Go on, Rah, and cry your heart out. Tangierneck ain't never treated you right hardly except for Vyella and a few others of us. Leave her alone, Aunt Saro Jane. If you had any respect for the dead you'd be crying your own self instead of steady looking up and down this line to catch you a boyfriend. . . ."

"That ain't no way to talk to me. I got some respect for the dead and the season, too. I ain't eat a piece of meat since Lent set in. Ain't eat nothing all day yesterday till Jesus rose. Must've been around four o'clock when he rose because I just kept looking at the place where the sun ought to be. Didn't show itself until way after four o'clock. Looking through the rain, yes, Lord. But then I figured if the Lord wanted us to make any money on a Good Friday, he'd a-brought some sunshine to us in the morning. Reasoned out, too, Tillie, that if the Lord wanted me to go scrounging around in these fields looking for a boyfriend on the day of His death, he'd a-sent the sunshine. . . . Sun's shiny now but I see Rah crying, marching back here with us instead of up front with her husband and the next of kin. . . ."

"Hush your mouth, Aunt Saro," Tillie stormed.

"You ain't gonna do her no harm, is you, Rah?" Aunt

Saro Jane rubbed Mariah's back. "Else I ain't gonna call on you for to speak. Last thing Vyella told me was to let you have the last words over her body. . . ."

"Oh, I'm gonna make me a fine speech," Mariah said and marched on, for there was no need of talking to Aunt Saro Jane and them. *They gonna be surprised what I say.* Best thing for her to dwell on was how to get that little girl of hers that she was tugging by the hand out of Tangierneck and her remaining boys, too. Said in her heart to the child: Wasn't no longer than yesterday when I beat you to make you as good as Vyella. Beat you, Bardetta, in that place called Hillards for squatting down to do your do-do in front of boys. A girl that's going to live and make anything out of herself can't be showing off her sin-hole in front of boys, because boys don't treat no wife right when they grow up and marry them, if the girls show off their sin-hole too soon.

Boys is the first choice of God. You can be as chaste as you want to in your heart, but they'll treat you as indifferent as anything if they see your thing ahead of time. See how your daddy treats me. He don't say good morning and he don't say good night. And I'm working, Bard. Don't you see me working?

Wasn't no longer than yesterday when I beat your legs good for running out in that strawberry patch and playing with those white children and feeling their hair. I caught you, I caught you. That's what I said to you. I'll beat your ass clean off if I catch you feeling them white children's hair again. I'm gonna rub yours down in sulphur and tar tonight. So it'll be just as good as theirs. Maybe it will grow. Gonna grow up so you can look decent before the people and do something good in life. Hold your head up high!

Wasn't no longer than yesterday when I beat you, gal, for talking so fresh to me when I caught you saying a bad word. Repeating the same words after me. Told you never mind what you hear me say because my sins weigh so heavy on me. Sins I ain't never told to nobody. . . . Want you to grow up to be somebody. Not a nobody like me. *You ain't gonna be here long, Mariah.* Messenger walked right beside her.

Beat you, gal, but I did beat Rabbit the worst for taking

up for you. Beat him so bad, I s'pect I'm the one that killed him. Made him run away from me more. . . .

Line marched on, and nobody paid any attention to Mariah when she did slip and say a few of her thoughts out loud. And then just cry.

Aunt Saro Jane said, "Let the gal cry. Vyella thought so high of her and likewise her of Vyella. Let the child cry. Vyella is done hurt her feelings. . . ."

A march to a big funeral in Tangierneck is a long and important march. Line stretched all the way back clean from here to yonder, where the important white people with their nice cars all parked tagged on to the end of the line and the Tangierneck children, second and third cousins to the dead, come on in behind them. Line wound itself over the piece of road made up of gravel and tar that the county started putting down. And then into the shade. April trees, leaning over the ditches and the brooks running in from Deep Gut, are the best shade trees in the world. Make you want to stop and rest yourself a bit. Get yourself together.

"Get yourself together." Aunt Saro Jane wiped Mariah's tears as they got near the church. "You ain't gonna do us no harm, is you hon?

"Get yourself together, Mariah. The only thing I faults you for is that you didn't come by Vyella's and forgive her before she went on through the gates of heaven. But Jesus, bless his sweet soul, he'll hear you now and tell Vyella all about how you forgave her, if you will. And I know her soul is in heaven with Jesus because I had the vision. . . ."

Aunt Saro Jane couldn't stop herself from talking in spite of Tillie's sassy way of talking back to her, but she did finally start in crying like everybody else on that line.

Line wound on and it moaned. Line hesitated just a little piece down the road from the church, so the people could get a good view of Jimmy Jamison's Funeral Home workers handing that mauve-colored casket over to the pall-bearers. Jacob was one of them, being a next of kin.

Line cried sorrow. Line wailed on this Easter Saturday, looking at the new six-foot-deep hole in Cleveland's Field. Line cried, "Jesus, spare me," or "take me" depending on the condition of the one that spoke.

Line chattered about how if it hadn't been for Vyella all these important white people wouldn't be down here today. All the big shots that's gonna give us the rest of the money to build this school—build this Neck up to something—give us jobs to pay off the land. For you have to depend on white people.

Tillie was talking the loudest of all about how Vyella did away with a few of her big-shot white men's babies just so she could keep on living in Tangierneck and giving money to the school and being "somebody." That's why she died of cancer.

Aunt Saro Jane agreed. Went over with Tillie every abortion Vyella ever had. Went over them in detail. "But I know how they feel, Lord, Lord. I know how they feel because I been that way myself. . . ."

Line seemed to slow up almost to a halt beside the ditch filled with spring lilies, flowing on the edge of Cleveland's Field just before you get to the church, so much so Mariah felt she could reach out to Rabbit: Wasn't no longer than yesterday that I said to you in that Chance, Rabbit, keep your bare feet off the ground.

Wasn't no longer than yesterday, Rabbit, when I beat the living shit out of you. Beat you because you stole my blue pills when you had no business with your hands on them. Found you behind the house dumb from the chills. Wasn't no longer than yesterday when I nursed you and brought you through till this winter's passing when the Lord saw fit to take you away with the worms and the pneumonia on that Kyle's Island. And I kept on saying, I ain't gonna let you be in a Tangierneck condition no more. And neither was I gonna do it to myself. Promised you I wasn't gonna talk to no death man no more.

"Was just trying to keep up your little spirits, Rabbit, Rabbit!" She called out so loud as they passed on by Cleveland's Field. Squeezed Bardetta so hard, the little thing started crying.

"Let me hold her for you, Mamma." Skeeter reached up to her. And Mariah just let the baby fall into Skeeter's arms. Old big-eyed boy was getting to be so mannish now. Had some feelings to him. Much like his daddy had in one day and time.

Gezee, well he just hung on to her dress tail, crying, "Mamma, I wants to go home . . . find Rabbit. . . ."

Aunt Saro Jane grabbed a-hold of Gezee. Said to him, "Come on with me. Your mamma's done broke down."

Done broke down. Done broke down. Mariah's brains got fixed on the thought when she took her seat in the church. Couldn't take her eyes off that casket holding Vyella's last remains. *Gonna get her, Lord. Gonna tell 'em all about her. When you cast me down in the burning depths of hell, gonna meet up with her and get her good and told off. . . .*"

Got lost in the madness tugging at her brain. Took herself a notion to just jump right on up and bust in on that Reverend Jenkins who was praising Vyella so high for getting him called to the parts where a minister was sorely needed. Praised her until he couldn't carry on no more, and Aunt Saro Jane took over.

Then Aunt Saro Jane almost lost her voice from the long eulogy she delivered over the corpse. She ranted and railed until the sun commenced to sink in the West, and the great red ball seemed like it was fire burning in the church windows. Ranted and railed about how good Vyella was, and how she ought to be a model for the young people in the community, especially the young women.

"Wasn't nothing but pureness to her. . . ." That's the kind of thing that old woman spit out to the dicky white people lining the back of the church. "Hadn't been for her, wouldn't none of you all be down here today. Hopes you-all see what a bad condition you-all left Tangierneck in . . . we ain't got no school—nothing but some boards. You-all can see that with your own eyes. You-all got the money. Some of us even worked for you to help you get that money. Some of us worked for your mamma and papa. Even been slaves for you for to help you get that money."

Then turning back to her own, she stretched out her arms, "Pray God, children. Pray to Jesus!" Church said, "Amen." Church cried. And the nurse that came along with Jimmy Jamison's Funeral Home people was running all over the place, fanning the fainting. When Aunt Saro Jane's voice started giving out, Miss Naomi was right up front, taking over.

Nothing but pureness to her! You know better than that, Mariah. Her constant companion nudged her in the heart, and Mariah just put her head down on the back of the pew in front of her. Roaring in her ears made such a blurring of the sounds.

"Come forward, Sister Mariah." Mariah jumped at the sound of her name. "Say a few words over Sister Vyella."

But Mariah couldn't move.

"God giveth and He taketh away . . . all, all for the eternal light and life. . . ." It was Miss Naomi calling. Whole Church was just a-swaying and rocking.

Calling out to her—reaching out to her.

"Help her. Somebody walk with her. . . ."

"Hush crying now, honey. . . ."

"Come forward. God works in mysterious ways his wonders to perform. . . ."

"Help her, help her dear Lord. . . ."

"Lord and Master, Jesus. Sweet little Lamb of God, Jesus," Aunt Saro Jane squeaked in the closing-in air, heavy with the perfume of funeral flowers, and the packed crowd breathing, sobbing. Sight of them dimmed with the lights of this earth's last service for the dead.

Seemed like something grabbed a-hold of Mariah, pulled her up that aisle.

"Tell the people how you gonna take over for Sister Vyella." Aunt Saro Jane was just a-calling to her, "Come forward."

Love is a funny thing. It just sneaks up on you all kinds of ways. Wraps itself around your shoulders sometimes. Just like it was doing now to Mariah as she looked into Aunt Saro Jane's face. Sometimes it won't do a thing but mash you down in the church grounds. But love *is* a funny thing. Makes you say things you don't even have a mind to say.

Wraps itself all around your shoulders even in an hour of death. "Jesus!" This lone hour of death. Wraps you so tight you can't even die on your own if you want to.

"Don't be saying nothing bad in front of these white people else I'll whip your behind parts if it's the last thing I do on this earth," Mamma Effie whispered as she walked beside Mariah. Mamma Effie jogged her in the back. "Don't bring no more scandal to the family. You ain't too old for me to handle. I'll make mincemeat out of you on this church aisle."

Committee of her Judgment ranged around her. Arms dragged her head down into the folds of mother-warm titties. Arms let her go, and she trembled in her leg sockets.

They pushed her forward. Pushed her forward and the whole Church was singing:

> In that far off sweet forever
> Just beyond the golden river

Church got her clean up front. Wanted to turn around and go back. Church was just a-looking at her. And she couldn't go back.

I want to tell them, Jesus. And Mariah took a swift look in her pocketbook for that letter she got from Vyella. Wanted to call that Mrs. Jefferson up there by the casket for to read it to the Church for her. *Acts like you ain't never been to a funeral before*, Messenger said to her.

Woman spun around. Caught herself staring right into the faces of Vyella's Little Ned and Poonky while Big Ned was trying to pull them away from that casket because all they could ask was things like, "Daddy, why they got Mamma in that box?" They was even patting on that box and picking off the flowers, until Big Ned could get them back to their seats. "Mamma said Aunt Mariah would help us for a long time, 'cause she was going to go home to Jesus and she wouldn't be back so soon, and she done prayed it over."

Mariah just said, "Sure I'm gonna do it. You all go on out in the churchyard and play with Skeeter and Gezee. I'll be getting home soon for to fix you some supper. . . ."

All Mariah had to say when the children left that church with the flowers they took off their mother's casket was, "I ain't got nothing for to say." Fumbling, she put that letter back in her pocketbook.

"Help her, Jesus!"

"Vyella . . . Vyella asked in a letter what she wrote before she crossed over, for to help Big Ned out with Little Ned. . . ." She started in choking, but she swallowed hard and kept on going. ". . . and continue on with the building of the school what we all been saving up for. . . ."

Gaze got fixed on Jacob and then Big Ned. Got fixed and wouldn't move. Tongue was a thickness in her mouth. "Knows we ain't got but so much, but Jacob and me'll share it. . . . Done lost Rabbit. Oh, my Rabbit!" And she squeezed her pocketbook all up in her breasts. Wiped the tears washing down her face. Sped to the pew where Big

Ned sat with his shoulders just a-shaking. "I means it, Ned. I means it. Come on over to the house for supper, and we can make some arrangements."

Didn't even feel like sitting through the rest of the service. Something come to her and she said to herself, And just to think I was gonna rip out my breasts on the streets of Jerusalem. Ain't gonna be staring after death no more. Ain't even following this hearse car to Cleveland's Field.

Got the funniest feeling, when they opened up that casket for people to see that poor shrunken Vyella. Cheeks used to be so fat. But now they was all puffed up from the cotton Jimmy Jamison had stuffed them with. Stood the longest kind of time over that casket. *Vyella, you the mother of one of Jacob's children, Little Ned, which you got the nerve for to ask me to keep, in your letter.*

But the perfume of the flowers of death is a still thing, and I got to keep marching. So many flowers cut off from their roots! Going dead now in some old kind of sweetish fix of decay.

Thought that devilish letter was gonna burn a hole clean through her pocketbook. Said to Jacob when he was trying to hug her up outside the church, "I got to get on home. Children be waiting for to eat, and I got to scrounge up something for them."

Jacob, well he just said, "Oh Mariah, God's gonna bless you," while he went off and got in line going to Cleveland's Field. But she stepped lively over those shifting sands to that little old slavery-time whitewashed house, hugging up Bardetta all the way, so as to get some food fixed up for their children. Guessed Vyella's was hers, too, now, plus Aunt Cora Lou's Lil Bits and Mamie, plus her own—her own.

Guessed when those seven little children got through with the strawberries she'd sugared down for them and the helping of them through their Easter Sunday recitations, she'd be able to forget, and keep on marching.

But she wasn't able to forget. Even when she walked around the graves of the dearly beloved just gone, after Easter Sunday service was over with. Wasn't able to forget the petals of the flowers still on the church floor from Vyella's funeral. And the children. *My God, the children.*

Said to Jacob late on Easter Monday morning when she went out of that house to help him clear the ground he was hoeing so as to plant new seed, "What's the matter with you, Jacob, looking all sad?" Couldn't even hardly stomach the sight of him. But she did say back to him when he said to her, "Rah, ain't I done told you I didn't have quite enough money for to get back twenty acres of the land! That's all we got to get for to get another head start. Done asked you for to give the money you been hiding from me. Seven children is a lot to look out for. And only three of them is mine."

She said to him, "Jacob, *four* of them seven children up there to the house is yours. That's Skeeter and Gezee and Bardetta. . . ." Thought she was gonna pass out when she got up from the row where she was pulling up grass. "And you know good and well, Jacob, whose the other one is. Little Ned's yours, Jacob! Vyella done wrote to me all about it before she passed. Poonky ain't yours, but you know Little Ned is. Mamie and Lil Bits belonged to your Aunt Cora Lou. You know your mamma ain't in no kind of shape for to look out for Mamie and Lil Bits."

Well, she took off from that field with Jacob tailing a pieceways right after her, calling, "Where you going, woman?"

She hollered back to him, "Going up to the house for to make some bread and peel some potatoes for the children's dinner. You welcome to some of it, too, Mr. Jacob, when you get your ass up from the field. Plus you be welcome to the money for to help you get back the land. 'Cause I'll be leaving it on the table when I go for a walk over to your mamma's house."

He just hollered right back, "You know Vyella was nothing but my adopted sister. Why would I have anything to do with her?"

"Oh shit!" Mariah said to herself, and she just kept on walking. Went straight into that house, peeled some potatoes, mixed up the flour and the lard and the water with a little bit of yeast powder thrown in it for the bread. Listened to all those seven children crawling on the floor or running in and out of the house with a "Mamma," or a "Cousin" or an "Aunt Mariah, when can we have a Easter egg hunt? Strawberries? Piece of hot bread? New school?" But especially to the sound of that Bardetta just a-wheezing and banging on the floor with a tin can and crying. Needed her diaper changed. Jacob needed her money. Said to Skeeter while she was throwing on some old sweater, "When your daddy comes up from the field, tell him I left what he asked for on the mantelpiece."

"Where you going, Mamma?" Skeeter's old big clapper was just loud enough to set all the children, except that Bardetta, toddling behind her down that road.

"Where are you going Mamma?" and "Where are you going, Cousin Mariah . . . Aunt Mariah . . . Aunt Rah . . . I ain't had nothing for to eat. My stomach hurts."

"Skeeter!" She turned around once. "Get these young'uns on back up to that house. You all acts like you don't even want me to go out for a walk. Tell 'em to eat the bread what I made up this morning. Some of it's left over. You all don't need no hot bread every two times I turn around. . . ."

Wasn't gonna turn around even for to look at them. Some skinny, some constipated from the foods what she couldn't even put in their diets what the 4-H Club was telling people they ought to have. Told Skeeter yesterday morning when he come crying to her that a turd was on its way out but every time he tried to push it out it hurt so bad. Told Skeeter, "Stick your finger up your hiny hole and pull it out." Told Lil Bits and Mamie when they was asking her to keep her promise about bringing them some sweet shrubs and pine cones from out of the swamp, for to go in the swamp and get 'em their ownselves. Told 'em. Told 'em. Told 'em all what to do!

Gone, Lordy. Gone.

Didn't even greet nobody on the road to the Gut. Didn't have no more time.

First thing she noticed was how nice it was to feel the water in the grass near the Gut. Shoes just a-making swishy-swishy sounds from the cool water soaking into them. Lord, Lord, Lord. Just to get to the Gut. Be no more hearing nothing. No more hearing:

> Carry me away from Tangierneck,
> Daddy, Daddy, Daddy,
> Don't want no buzzard picking at my neck,
> Paddy pick, paddy pick, paddy.

No more listening for the sounds of a regular song spar-

Acknowledgments

So many friends, for so long a time, kept the light alive in my oftentimes darkened inner eyes during the writing of this book, that it is with considerable hesitation that I give specific mention to any one of them lest I am inadvertently neglectful.

Perhaps it would be better if I simply repeated the dedication in my first book, *Give Me a Child,* which was co-authored by Lucy Smith, and let it go at that. For the feeling which guided the creative eye is still the same:

> To all who love: to humanity entire,
> To the borning of a child called Freedom
> And
> A very special dedication
> To those who labored with me,
> Giving whatever was necessary
> To make this book possible.

But since "the play is the thing," and the play doesn't come easily for any of us—least of all working women, mothers, wives—I am deeply moved to mention a few of the strong women in my life without whose production assistance and/or moral courage this book could not have been achieved: my seemingly invincible mother and grandmothers, and aunts, and sisters, and cousins—real and those adopted when those of my flesh were not always within seeing and hearing distance; Lucy Smith, whose relaxed confidence in the future of humankind helped me sustain what was sometimes seemingly an interminable effort, Marion Boyars, that stalwart of British Commonwealth publishing, whose ears were always open to my sounds, and to so many others whose personal interest and commitment to life helped me to keep working, working.

row! Nothing but the sound of water. Going on, going on. Going on out to the ocean. Powerful and mighty, tugging sounds.

Just wade on in, Mariah. River of Jordan is chilly and cold.

Didn't notice how cold the water was till her feet hit the first of the rocks. Rocks underneath the water. Old oyster rocks. Colder when it rose clean up to her knees. And she couldn't swim. Wanted to go on her knees. Looked up to the heavens. Said to her Lord and Master, "Let my children live, Lord. Let 'em have a pretty day."

Then the tears started coming down again. Flowed down with every step. Flowed and got mixed all up in the waters of the Gut. "Let my children live!"

Grabbed herself handfuls of water. Felt its iciness slipping through her fingers. Felt it soaking through her clothes clean up to her waist. Didn't know how cold death was before. "Lordy, I didn't know."

Caught herself saying that thing on the road back home. Caught herself saying it when she bumped into Jacob plowing on down that road toward her. And he was doing a new style of running. Faster than fast.

But she wouldn't pay him no mind when he grabbed a-hold of her. "Mariah, is you crazy! What was you trying to do, drown your fool self? Knows you can't swim, fool woman!"

Gritted her teeth. *Kiss my ass, Jacob.*

Didn't say nothing to him on the road back home. No more than, "Jacob, I forgot to put the dough to bake in the oven so you and the children could have some nice hot bread for your dinner."